ANALYZING THE PRESCOTTS

A NOVEL BY

DAWN RENO LANGLEY

Black Rose Writing | Texas

ISBN: 978-1-68513-349-8
Library of Congress Control Number: 2023942569
PUBLISHED BY BLACK ROSE WRITING
www.blackrosewriting.com

Printed in the United States of America
Suggested Retail Price (SRP) $22.95

Analyzing the Prescotts is printed in Minion Pro

*As a planet-friendly publisher, Black Rose Writing does its best to eliminate unnecessary waste to reduce paper usage and energy costs, while never compromising the reading experience. As a result, the final word count vs. page count may not meet common expectations.

Dedicated to

Drs. Shelley Armitage, Kezia Carpenter, John Fraire, Elden Golden, Glenn Kendall, Mina Kerr, Bryan Partridge, Ginger Rodriguez, Mary Wilby, and In Memoriam to Drs. Jacquelyn Taylor and Karsten Piep.

With great respect for Union Institute and University's Cohort 2 and with powerful memories of the journey.

Praise for
Analyzing the Prescotts

"*Analyzing the Prescotts* is the heart-wrenching tale of a family in crisis and the therapist who makes the tough decision to save herself."
–Marcia King-Gamble, national bestselling author of 45+ books and 8 novellas, including *Shattered Images*

"Langley's *Analyzing the Prescotts* is a delicately nuanced story of a therapist counseling a family in trauma, who finds her own professional objectivity gradually shifting into obsession."
–Nancy Christie, author of *Reinventing Rita*

"Dawn Reno Langley's *Analyzing the Prescotts* takes us from a therapist's couch into the lives of a family beset by an identity crisis. This engaging novel is by turns humorous and heartbreaking. Building on the recent suicide of one of the therapist's patients, Langley adroitly addresses the myriad issues of a spouse and children coming to terms with a father's disclosure of his covert identity as a woman. A rich, rewarding, page-turning, winner of a novel."
–Tony Whedon, author of *Drunk in the Woods*, and award-winning memoirist, essayist, literary critic, and poet

"Dawn Reno Langley's *Analyzing the Prescotts* is a sensitively told and emotional story of a traumatized family in the hands of a broken therapist. Langley elegantly delivers the harrowing plot and transfixes the reader with contemporary themes and engaging characters who stay with you long after the pages are closed. A riveting read!"
–Andrea Hurst, literary agent and author of *The Guestbook*

"In a time when transgendered bodies are under attack and suicide is escalating, Dawn Reno Langley delivers an intergenerational, evocative story that grabs the heartstrings and won't let go. *Analyzing the Prescotts* is a pivotal read for anyone who loves a transgendered person and is essential ethical canon for anyone who chooses to hate or attack the LGBTQIA + community."
–Melissa Seligman (She/Her/Hers), Author: *The Day After He Left for Iraq*, Co- founder: herwarhervoice.com

ANALYZING THE PRESCOTTS

Different though the sexes are, they inter-mix. In every human being, a vacillation from one sex to the other takes place, and often it is only the clothes that keep the male or female likeness, while underneath the sex is the very opposite of what it is above.
—Virginia Woolf

~ Book One ~

Gray Prescott

Though in Venice you may sit in courtyards of stone, and your heels may click up marble stairs, you cannot move without riding upon or crossing the waters that someday will carry you in dissolution to the sea.
—Mark Helprin

Cotton Barnes sucked in a deep breath and pulled open the Mental Health Alliance's heavy steel door to greet a visibly distraught woman wearing a heavy black parka, though the weather had turned unseasonably warm. Three months, two weeks, and six days ago, at 10:30 AM, Cotton opened the same door to her client, Brighton Ogelle, a bright and loving 15-year-old with a penchant for gray cats. Brighton died by suicide at 1:30.

Cotton has not worked since.

The client at the door: Gray Prescott (*age 35, white female, married, three kids,* Cotton noted) left an urgent message the day before that pulled at a piece of Cotton's soul. Something in the woman's voice cried, "please help me," and it was a siren call Cotton couldn't ignore. Throughout her 15-year career in psychotherapy, her commitment to the field was a selfish one. She wanted to help people in crisis, she derived a deep sense of emotional power when a client moved forward—psychologically healthy, and she savored the challenge of saving a person about to fall apart. Even if it meant facing a watershed moment of her own, Cotton couldn't turn down this new client.

"Please see us. My children...." Mrs. Prescott rushed over descriptions of each of them. Three kids. Father left home. A garbled reason. "Please, can you see me this week? As soon as possible? Please?"

Cotton heard the break in the voice. A physical break. Could there be a psychological one as well? She booked Gray Prescott immediately. It was time to go back to work, anyway. After three months, most of her client list had moved on to other therapists, but that was fine. A new beginning meant a new set of challenges, and that's what she needed. No memories.

Cotton mentally noted: *Mrs. Prescott is slight, attractive in a mourning-bird type of way. Her dull brown sweater's slightly ragged sleeves pulled down to her knuckles, one button missing, another dangling by a thread.* That inattention to her appearance, the way she avoided Cotton's eyes, and the slight smell of last night's wine, all summed up as depression, but *it's too early for a diagnosis.*

"Tell me a bit about yourself, Mrs. Prescott." Cotton settled into her wing chair, punched the pillow a couple of times so it would fit that low curve in her back, give her a bit of support because she knew she'd slump otherwise, and fumbled for her notepad. She squirmed again, punched the pillow one more time, and realized Mrs. Prescott was waiting for Cotton to stop fidgeting before talking. *For god's sake, this isn't your first rodeo, Cotton. Settle down.*

"I'm the chief financial officer for Enquiring Minds, my bookstore chain," Mrs. Prescott said. "We have four stores. I have three kids, married to... well, I'm not sure...."

Fingernails bitten to the quick, bleeding cuticles. Fragments of persimmon-colored nail polish. She's not usually this ill kept. Anxiety.

"Why don't you tell me the reason you're here, then?" Cotton loved this part of meeting someone new, "Sherlocking the patient," searching for clues that nervous habits revealed, the eye tics that appeared when someone was lying, the constant nail-biting that exposed a neurosis, the way a voice strangulated when the client held back grief. She made it a habit to tick off the traits on a laundry list in her mind and created a narrative, challenging herself to discover whether her first meeting diagnosis matched the one she'd come to later in the client's sessions.

"That is what happened," Mrs. Prescott murmured. "I don't know how much I'm going to be able to tell you." She shuddered, wringing her hands, then spreading her fingers like a fan, hovering over her stomach as if it was sore to touch. "I can't...talk. Can you just... can you read what I've written?" Pushing her curly, ginger-brown hair behind her ears, she thrust some typewritten pages at Cotton a little too roughly, as if afraid they wouldn't be accepted.

And she was right. Cotton waved the papers away.

"Let's try to talk. It's easier for me to help if you and I have a conversation. You can tell me what you want, and I'll probably have some questions. It's easier if we can work that way, especially since you're sitting here with me right now. So how about we start with introductions, Mrs. Prescott? I'll tell you about me, then you can tell me about you, okay?" Cotton nodded toward the iPod recorder and asked for verbal permission to tape the session. "I'm Cotton Barnes—no need to call me Doctor. You can call me Cotton. And no, my mother never intended for my name to be a Southern pun." She laughed, feeling somewhat nervous, though she'd used this joke to break the ice since she'd first started seeing clients over ten years ago. "The Barnes part comes from my husband."

Insert smile here, she thought each time she repeated that phrase for a new patient. She learned in Dr. Pipovic's class on Professional Behavior to: "Give them a warm greeting. Let them discover it's a safe place. Show that you're human. Demonstrate that you respect them. Yet, keep that professional distance. It's a delicate balance."

Cotton waited for the response, spun the pen she held in her hand, then stopped, gripping it too tightly in her fist. Gray chuckled a little, as most people did. Hers was a self-effacing laugh that appeared both nervous and guarded. Cotton never figured out whether her clients laughed out of Southern politeness or because her name was ironic, but it didn't matter. Gray's face lightened when she smiled, reflecting perfect teeth and some insight into what she might be like when calm and happy. Still, her dirt brown eyes remained blank as a slate. Emotionless. As if she weren't truly connecting with anything, as if she couldn't figure out how, and didn't really care. That kind of look both challenged and terrified Cotton.

She swallowed hard and forced a smile. "Though I live here in Raleigh, I think you can tell by my accent I'm not Southern. Barnes is my married name. My mother was a hippie and thought the name Cotton was a great Southern name since it represents something white and soft. She didn't miss the irony that I was born in Boston but grew up in Vermont. Didn't move here until after I was in college. Married." *Why am I telling her all of this?*

"I'm sure you get a lot of comments..." Gray's voice trailed off and her eyes went to the furthest corner of the room.

Small talk. That's good. Depression doesn't appear deep-seated, but something is going on. What is it?

Studying Gray's face, Cotton wondered whether she had experienced any depersonalization issues. The woman's eyes flitted back and forth, a sign she wasn't connected, but without further questioning, Cotton knew she couldn't diagnose so early in treatment. *Yet, how long do you wait? When can you decide how to help someone?*

For the next few moments, they talked about the area where Gray and her family lived, only streets away from Cotton's mid-century farmhouse, sharing what they both loved about life along the Neuse River in North Raleigh. They shared favorite hiking paths, sunsets over the river, the quiet of early mornings, and the value of raising kids in the country. Cotton mentally timed their chat, reining in the conversation at about the three-minute mark. They'd broken the ice. Time to get to the meat of the meeting.

"Well, this isn't about me." Shifting in her recliner, Cotton folded her hands in her lap, ready to move the conversation forward. "It's about you. Are there any other questions you have before we talk about what brings you here today?"

Gray stared down at the Oriental rug as if her thoughts were wound in and around its jewel-toned fibers. Cotton mentally counted the seconds, waiting for Gray's story to begin. Cotton loved narrative therapy, because clients repeated the stories they told themselves about their lives, why they find themselves in problematic situations, and ultimately, how they became who they are. Questions always arose, like what happened the moment before the accident, or how did the marriage crumble into half-spoken sentences? Where was the crack-addicted son or daughter? How many times did the mother have to apologize?

Humans weave stories to explain our lives. Those narratives were the reasons Cotton remained in the profession. No moment in her office was the same; no client bored her. Each story and person were unique. Each day as a psychologist, distinct from all the others. Each moment, impactful. And she knew the weight of every moment because it only took one to alter the trajectory of someone's life story.

One moment.

Cotton shook her head, even though she knew she couldn't erase the past with a shake. She couldn't change that one moment. She did not have that power. But she *could* remind herself to move on, to heal herself by helping others find their own recovery method.

"Everyone has memories, y'know?" She bent forward a bit, trying to peer into Gray's eyes, to determine if there was a flicker of understanding. Connection. "The interesting... um, aspect of those memories is that they're shaped and reshaped, depending on where we are in our lives and what our experiences are up to this point. I'm well experienced working with families and using this therapy—narrative storytelling is fascinating to me, because each member of that family tells the same story about the same moment in a different fashion. Know what I mean?"

Gray stared straight ahead.

Challenged, Cotton pushed her black cardigan sleeves up to her elbows and pursed her lips. People always tell her she looks like the actor Meg Ryan when she makes that face. *It's not the face,* Thomas told her early in their relationship. *It's the loose T-shirts, big coats, flat Oxfords, and your marvelously funny hair. That's the Meg Ryan connection, but then you purse your lips and it's all there. You're her. Or she's you...* Why do we always have to be someone else to be recognized?

"I help people reconstruct their stories." She *inserts-a-smile-here.* "We put them together like a jigsaw puzzle, trying to fit the pieces in the places that make sense, so that the whole picture is revealed, and when those pieces begin to create a shape, we see exactly how each of those moments impacted those people's lives and contributed to the whole. Then we can recognize that we are not the problem that we're struggling with. The problem is the problem. The person does not make the problem; the problem exists on its own and the person has control over the problem, not vice versa. So that's the reason that many of us feel powerless over our everyday lives. Like we don't have control over what happens to us. But we do. Only we do. You follow me so far?"

Gray's eyes flickered, her forehead creased, and she was gone from the conversation for a long moment. Then she caught Cotton scrutinizing her, and she jerked her shoulders a bit as if she'd come back to herself. Making eye contact, Gray smiled, a weak lift of her lips. A genuine effort. "My youngest, Marcus, makes up some whoppers. He's the storyteller of the family, even though my husband--" Her eyes widened, and her mouth fell open the smallest bit, as if she surprised herself with the easy way that information slipped from her mouth. She pulled back, tucked in her chin.

"Okay, tell me more about your kids." Cotton sat back, her head tilted a bit, expectant.

When she was in grad school, she used to practice this look in the mirror. She called it her "thoughtful therapist" look. It's become second nature through the years, a mask she slides on and off whenever necessary. Now, the look comes naturally. She *is* thinking. She *is* a therapist. She *does* care. And right now, she suspected Gray Prescott's kids weren't the problem. Maybe the husband was.

Staring out the window, Gray bit her lower lip, dug her fingernails into the palms of her hands. "Well... I have three children, ranging in age from 15 to 11. I've been married to the same guy, their father, Hayden, for the past sixteen years. And I'm here because... well, I gave you what I wrote. If you read it, you'll understand what happened." She gestured to the typewritten pages she'd placed on the desk moments after coming into the office. Cotton had been ignoring them. The elephant in the room.

"I'd rather hear you tell your story aloud, but I understand. Most patients are afraid to voice their deepest fears. I know that. We all hide from the truth in a myriad of ways." Cotton rose from her chair and retrieved the pages from her desk. "If you prefer this,"—waved the pages in the air — "I'll work with it this time, but I'll ask that you promise to work together in conversations after that, okay?" Cotton felt a bubble come up in her chest. *I'm the therapist, and this is my office, my rules.* But she couldn't be that abrupt. She cleared her throat.

Writing instead of speaking was nothing new. Lots of clients wanted to share their journals, but until trust was established, Gray needed to talk. The patient needed to talk. They had to voice the reason for being there. First steps first.

"Yes, I'll read it," Cotton said, "but before I do, can you share why you're writing about it rather than talking directly to me?"

Gray silently stared at the wall for what felt like a long time. "I don't know, I guess because I can't talk out loud about it. I don't want to... I don't know... say it, I guess. Besides, you're the therapist, so I figured you'd read what I wrote, then tell me how to take care of it ...."

"Well, I can't tell you how to take care of your life, Gray. That's something you'll decide yourself. But I can be here to talk to you. And to listen."

With a slight nod, Gray pointed to the sheaf of papers again. "Can you please read what I wrote?" The question was more a plea than a request.

Cotton paused, a long thought, then tapped the pages she still held in her hands. "I have an idea." She leaned in, making a point of narrowing the distance between them. "How about you read this to me? That way, if we need to talk about anything more specific, or if I have questions ..."

A look of genuine fear passed over Gray's face. She started to speak, then she censored herself, averted her gaze, and stared out the window for a moment. Her breathing slowed, and she released a long, tired sigh. When she met Cotton's eyes again, she reached out a hand for the pages.

"To your comfort level," Cotton said. "I'm here for you. We'll never make this a scary place. You decide when and if you're ready to stop. Okay?"

Gray shuffled the handwritten pages, tapped them on the table, took another deep inhale, and began.

"Nothing ever tasted like the chardonnay I sipped in Piazza San Marco in Venice on that hot day in June," Gray's voice caught on the first couple of words, then strengthened. She shifted her shoulders and settled into her chair to read her own story in the quiet afternoon gloaming of Cotton's office. "It danced across my tongue, vapors of apples and lemons. It tasted like those caramel-colored sunflower fields we'd woven through on Tuscany's back roads, of the precious moment of Venice, inhaling the magic of dusty pink palaces and seeing myself reflected in shimmering Murano glass. It tasted like freedom. Clarity."

Gray paused for a long moment, her profile bowed and thoughtful. Exhaled.

Cotton reached for her pen and flipped up the page on her yellow legal pad. She wrote on the page underneath: *Did she dream about being a writer? Jealous of husband's success?* Let the page drop. Some notes were meant to be private, not seen by other eyes.

"Only three hours later, I cherished that last memory of Venice, replaying it in my mind as the plane touched down at Raleigh-Durham Airport." Her shoulders slumped, and the light in her eyes extinguished as if the power had been turned off.

"I texted Hayden. I was looking forward to seeing him at the gate," Gray gripped so tightly that it started to rip around the edges, the rents in the paper mimicking the little tears in her voice. "I'd missed him, of course, and I expected him to be beside me when I turned to share a sight or comment, and I'd felt empty when he wasn't. I imagined him looking at the guidebooks, ready to suggest the best restaurant for dinner." She stopped and looked up at the ceiling, and said, "I always thought of him as regal, because he's tall and thin like King Charles, tends to stoop over like Charles does. His long eyelashes and those big, deep blue eyes drew me to him when I first met him, and at that moment, I considered myself lucky that they still did. I was so happy when the kids inherited their father's eyes, though the kids' eyes sparkle while Hayden's often reflect pain and sadness, even when he laughs. He has that look my mother used to call the poet's-sad-hangdog-face."

Gray glanced at Cotton, as if wondering to continue. Cotton nodded, waved her hand encouragingly.

"Anyway, I tried dialing Hayden's cell number from the plane. Still, no answer," Gray spoke quickly, as if she was tired of the buildup and wanted to deliver the one-two punch. "Maybe he was in a dead zone. Maybe I was. Traditionally, we had a deal that whenever someone came into the airport, they'd call to say the plane had arrived and was taxiing down the runway. If we left the house right then, we'd be just in time to pick up the person at Arrivals. I left another voice mail, then I sent a text." Gray tapped her fingers as if typing.

"Janis leaned on the seat in front of me, her voice impatient as all teenagers in their rush to be done with adolescence. 'When do we get off this damn plane? I want to go home,' she said. Janis is my oldest at fifteen, has her father's eyes, but she inherited my full and frizzy hair, and she hates being a ginger."

"At the luggage carousel, my 11-year-old, Marcus, leaned against the conveyor and whined, 'I thought Dad was coming to pick us up.'" Gray's head popped up, and she added, "He's my fifth-grader who can't sit still. This was his first trip out of the country, his first without some sort of physical activity, and the first time he'd traveled without his dad.

He called Hayden religiously every night, almost as though he wanted to be sure his father was okay without us." She said the last sentence as if she had something distasteful in her mouth.

"After about my tenth call and twentieth text to my husband, I realized he wasn't going to answer and told my sister, Lee (who'd been with us the whole trip), that we'd need a ride home, and when we got all the suitcases and kids snugly into the car, she asked me, 'Do you think something happened to him?' She raised her eyebrows, a look that meant she had a feeling there was something more going on. She's four years older than me and sometimes has ESP. I hoped she wasn't right.

"When we got to the house, Cherylynn yawned and pointed out, 'There aren't any lights on.' She's twelve, and the one who usually makes everyone smile, the easiest of the three kids. She loves playing sports—any kind of ball game—and stays out with the neighborhood kids until all hours. I discovered her missing one night around 10 PM when she was six years old, and when we looked out my bedroom window, there was Cherylynn, shooting hoops in the driveway."

Gray coughed and reached for her water bottle, took a big swig without glancing in Cotton's direction. Then she picked up the pages again.

"I'd been irritated on the plane, worried on the car ride home, but when I climbed the stairs to the master bedroom, I fought back anger. *No excuse is good enough for this*, I thought. Simply none. Still, I thought. *Where the hell is he? This is unforgivable.*" Gray gulped, the sound like the plop a fish makes when out of the water momentarily.

"In our dark and empty bedroom, the scent of his aftershave barely lingered in the air. I closed the door behind me." Gray's voice rose a note or two higher than it had been. "I stripped the rest of my clothes off, intending to go straight to the shower to wash away the stench of a day's worth of travel, when I saw the envelope in the middle of the bed. Hayden's scrawl. My name."

Now she looked up and spoke directly to Cotton. "I didn't want to pick up that envelope, but I did, and my hands shook so hard that I couldn't even read it. I kept thinking: *Don't do this to me, Hayden. Don't be one of those guys who abandons his wife, his children.*

"I kinda thought it was odd that the envelope was sealed. Hayden never sealed an entire envelope in his life. He just licked the corner, a slight dab of moisture, and pressed down hard. In my mind's eye, I can see him doing it now, with this look of distaste on his face. I always asked him why he licked the flap if he didn't like it." She shook her head.

"Inside was this single piece of yellow-lined paper, the kind Hayden uses when he writes the first draft of his novels." She pointed her chin in Cotton's direction, acknowledging Cotton's use of the same type of yellow-lined pad.

Gray cleared her throat and went back to reading.

"*Dear Gray,*

This is the fifth time I've tried to write this letter, and though I know you're wondering why I'd leave a letter rather than speak to you, perhaps you'll understand when you've finished reading this. First, I want to beg your forgiveness for not having the guts to come to the airport today. I should have. I know that. My kids are the last people on earth I want to disappoint, but I'm going to have to, and perhaps it's better that they start being mad at me, because I don't expect them—or you—to understand.

"My heart was pumping so hard I thought they'd find me face down on the Aubusson." Gray paused and turned to Cotton, tears hovering in the corners of her eyes. "In my mind, a simple word repeated itself over and over again: No. No. No. No." She picked up the pages again.

Second, what I'm about to say has nothing at all to do with you or with our marriage. It's all about me, as the kids say, and I take full responsibility for being unable to share this with anyone until now.

Third, you're probably thinking there's someone else. Stop thinking about that right now. There is no one else. I've always loved you. You'll always be my best friend, and I'll always think of you as my one and only love.

But... and this is where it gets hard... I cannot keep deceiving you. I must finally take control of my life and begin living it the way I've always believed I should.

This is tough to write to you, because you're the one I've always told everything. Except for one big thing. Since I was very small, maybe three or four years old, I knew that the person everyone else saw wasn't the one I felt I was inside. When Joey and Martin played baseball, I wanted to design dresses. Yes, you wouldn't guess that, because I did so well on the team. You wouldn't have known that I loved the feel of crepe de chine and the swish of a nice, heavy silk. I never told you, but you must have noticed that I enjoyed the heck out of dressing you. I'm sure you, of all people, can see how my creativity manifested in other ways—and you, of all people—must see what I've stifled through the years. How I went to all the football games, but I was thousands of miles away, lost in my head. You used to think it was because I am a writer. Partly, that's true. Building other worlds was much more fun than hiding in my own. I became adept at living my life in silence. Day after day, denying myself.

You probably won't understand this, Gray, but I've never felt like a boy or, worse, a man. Yes, I've played the role, but inside, in my heart of hearts, I was a totally different person. My life was a lie. I was a lie. In my brain, I'm a girl, but my body has betrayed me. I hate the parts of me that are male, always have, and even though I've dealt with them, I want to be rid of those parts that feel so damned foreign to me, like when your legs won't work after having them upside down for a while. That tingly feeling when you've been sitting too long and your leg goes to sleep, that dead feeling that stuns your muscles into submission. I hate that frozenness. I want to feel comfortable. I want to be rid of my male body.

Okay, I'm rambling. Let me make it as clear as I can: I need to find that person I "killed" long ago, the little girl that my parents denied and that I have shoved aside for so many years. So, I'm leaving, and I'm going to start transitioning toward the female me.

Again, I hope you will forgive me. I know I haven't explained myself well and that you deserve much more than this short—and possibly shocking—note, but I can't say more now. I will return when I can talk to the kids, but until then, I can't even begin to hope that they would understand what I need to do. I trust you will tell them whatever you need to. And I hope that you'll take advantage of our health insurance for therapy. I'll do my part to arrange appointments and coverage, if you think the kids and you will benefit from some help. I don't know how to help you with this, Gray. I don't even know how to help myself. I need to find out how, and I can't do that while I'm trying to be husband, father, male. I need to be the woman I am inside.

So, I took only a few of my clothes and my personal belongings. I will deposit enough money into the checking account to pay the household bills, you can be certain of that. I won't be far away, and if you need me, you can count on me. But, for now, I need my space and privacy.

We can talk when you're ready.

I'm sorry. I'm truly, deeply sorry.

All my love,
Hayden

Gray's face was wet with tears. "The letter fluttered to the floor," she said. "I dragged myself up off the bed, crossed the room and locked my bedroom door, then went into the bathroom and stood under the steaming hot water in the shower, fully clothed, for almost an hour."

For a long moment, Cotton sat with Gray in silence. The tears continued a steady flow down Gray Prescott's face and her shoulders quivered, even though she made no sound whatsoever.

"What are you feeling right now?" Cotton said quietly.

"Tired." Gray's hands released the pages, and she stared at them in her lap as if waiting for them to turn into puffs of smoke and disappear.

"I can imagine. It's been nearly two hours."

"Oh, I'm so sorry...it's supposed to be only fifty minutes for the first visit, right?"

"Don't worry about it. I haven't been taking clients for a while, so my calendar is light. No worries. You needed to talk, and I needed to hear your story. Now we need to figure out how to move forward."

They discussed appointments, plans for bringing in the kids, and after a few more questions to see whether Mrs. Prescott wasn't in any immediate danger (Cotton hypervigilant about watching for signs that a patient might be thinking of suicide), they completed the session.

As Gray shrugged into her sweater, her shoulder blades poked hills and valleys into the fabric of her dress. Cotton watched for a moment, noting the psychological pain in Gray's stiff posture, the sharp, and stalky way she moved. In the parking lot, Gray opened the Toyota Highlander's door and heaved herself into the car like an old woman.

A rumble in the distance, dark clouds on the horizon, a thunderstorm headed this way. Cotton pressed her finger to her temples and thought about getting home before the rain started.

~ Book Two ~

Cotton Barnes

People and the places where they reside are engaged in a continuing set of exchanges; they have determinate, mutual effects upon each other because they are part of a single, interactive system.
~ William S. Sax

The Indian summer air still hung heavy with unreleased moisture, storm clouds spitting an occasional lightning bolt, when Cotton returned home. She parked the BMW in the driveway, turned it off, and breathed. Simply breathed. The sound of a sprinkler—*psssst tuttuttut psssst tuttuttut*—and the call of a whippoorwill calmed her, and she relished the safe feeling of coming to the place where she didn't have to think, didn't have to analyze, didn't have to worry about people attempting suicide.

She shook her head like a wet dog, as if that would stop the constant replay of what she called Brighton moments. The moment Cotton felt like they'd had a breakthrough when Brighton kneeled in the middle of the floor, arms wrapped around her belly, chin to her chest, sobbing. She'd worked through the anger at her stepfather for the years of abuse, degradation, and neglect. She finally cried. The moments Brighton laughed, her bright blue eyes almost closed, her shoulders folding into her chest. The moment she'd told Cotton, she felt closer to her than her own mother.

Cotton took another deep breath and focused on her house. She sighed and heaved her legs out the car door, then walked through the breezeway that connected with the large kitchen in the back of the house. She saw Thomas through the doorway, pans on the stove in front of him, steaming. He sang along lustily with John Mayer, his gravelly voice typically out of tune. He loved to cook and loved to sing, but his food was better than his voice. She loved him for both. She seldom caught him unawares, so she stood there quietly for a moment, just watching him, and smiling. He had a cute habit of flipping back his fine brown hair, and he did it now as he banged with a wooden spoon on the counter, keeping time with the music. Though he usually wore glasses, he didn't wear them when he cooked, because they fogged up, and he squinted a little as he turned to chop some garlic to add to his creation.

Home.

For the past ten years, with each passing season, the house, and Thomas aged well. It felt like the house sunk into them, a good coupling, this old farmhouse, and the Barnes family—Cotton, Thomas, and Fred the dog. Around their acreage, subdivisions had sprung up, enticing thousands of others to join them here in North Raleigh, sharing the dense forest lands along the Neuse River, pushing herds of deer out of their natural habitats. Those subdivision house owners complained constantly about the deer eating their newly planted rose bushes and tulips, but Thomas and Cotton determined early on not to bring anything to this place that wasn't natural to it, and she reasoned that was part of what made it comforting to be here.

Quietly, she came up behind Thomas, arms encircling his waist, kissed him on the warm and wet curls of his hair against the back of his neck. He mumbled something about the sauce and how he must stir it.

"First day back. Was it the one client, or did you decide to take others?" He held the wooden spoon up above the pot for a moment, gave her a quick kiss, and smiled while their nine-year-old retriever, Fred, wiggled between them.

"Just saw one today, but I'm taking on the whole family," Cotton answered.

"How many in the family?"

"Five. Three kids and the parents."

"That might be enough for now, don't you think?"

She nodded and pulled away, using the excuse that she needed to go to the bathroom. They would talk in more detail about her plans over dinner as they watched their nightly food shows and caught up on the news of the day. Their routine. *When did that happen? When did we become that couple whose lives are predictable? Did it matter when it felt safe?*

She slid out into a pair of denim shorts and a worn-out Duke University t-shirt, swept her hair into a ponytail, washed her face with cold water, then headed back downstairs, the conversation with Gray Prescott replaying in her mind. Before she left the office, they'd scheduled the rest of the family members' first appointments for the upcoming two weeks, a feat that required Gray to share a multi-colored calendar: green for Gray, red for Hayden, blue for Janis, purple for Cherylynne, and orange for Marcus. An explosion of color on the page, and each day filled with soccer games, music lessons, teacher meetings, doctors' appointments, and dinners with friends. Not one hour was blank. Quite the opposite of Cotton's calendar, which was basically blank. She didn't show her own calendar to Gray and realized the reason was that she was too embarrassed that she had no other clients at the moment.

Thomas smiled at Cotton as she came back into the kitchen. "Hi, Baby. You ready to eat?"

She kissed him and sighed. He knew how to be a good husband, and she appreciated that.

At dinner, she told him she'd decided to work with the family, and Thomas listened, not warning her to be careful or raising questions about whether she was ready to handle new clients. Instead, he suggested she should keep track of their sessions in several formats, maybe intersecting their reports on a spreadsheet that he could set up for her.

"Sounds like a good journal article, and the clearer your research, the better," he said as he wound some spaghetti on his fork. Thomas understood her ambition and always urged her to push the borders of her practice. He also understood why it had taken months for Cotton to open her practice again. There was a time when she was ready to walk away, and though Thomas would have supported her, instead he simply took on the household bills without saying a word, letting her take her time to decide when to go back to work.

After they finished eating, they spent a little time on the back deck with a glass of wine, simply sitting, listening to the traffic in the distance, the sounds of the evening creatures settling in. But when the mosquitoes started coming out, they headed back into the house and cuddled a bit on the couch.

Cotton fell asleep in her husband's arms, stirring only slightly when he picked her up and carried her upstairs.

~ Book Three ~

Janis Prescott

If parents are the fixed stars in the child's universe, the vaguely understood, distant but constant celestial spheres, siblings are the dazzling, sometimes scorching comets whizzing nearby.
—Alison Gopnik

Janis Prescott materialized in the sitting area as silently as smoke. Alone.

For a moment, Cotton was taken aback, then she said, "You must be Janis," and the girl nodded but didn't speak. She seemed tall for a 15-year-old, probably 5'7", and resembled her mother, though her eyes were different: larger, sadder, a clear navy-blue color like the caldera in Santorini. On a trip to Greece with her grandmother when Cotton was six, she thought the caldera must be the opening to the bottom of the world. They had stood on a precipice, high above the apparently bottomless hollow that had once been filled with molten lava. Grandma said that the volcano erupted a couple of years before she was born, but Cotton-the-child swore her cheeks were hot and that the volcano was going to "spit again!" Staring down into that navy blue water was hypnotic, and she felt she would fall into it to be swallowed up and gone forever. Lost.

Someone would gaze into Janis Prescott's eyes someday and fall in love like Cotton had with that caldera. Janis's eyes were gorgeous, but they were also defiant, almost as though she dared Cotton to pose questions she would never answer. Slouched into the leather couch against the wall, Janis shifted and stared out the window at the trees shedding their pale yellow and deep burgundy leaves, her thin arms crossed over her flat chest as if to appear tough and silent. But Cotton knew better. Janis's defensiveness read as fear. Brighton used to do the same thing, and it had been weeks before she uncrossed those arms and began to talk about her life. Cotton suspected Janis might be an even tougher nut to crack. *Do I have the energy for this?*

As Cotton asked the usual opening questions, Janis answered, but she kept her lips thin and closed after each abrupt response. Cotton accepted Janis's curt answers with silent nods, mentally noting that Janis's answer to her reason for being here is "because my mother dropped me at the door and told me to go inside."

"Do I have your permission to tape our sessions, Janis?"

"I guess." She spat the words.

Cotton smiled again and tried to make eye contact, an effort to let the teenager understand she wasn't the enemy here. Adolescents could smell bullshit a mile away, so Cotton learned to keep it real and open from the very beginning. Most teens who crossed the office threshold were in the worst kind of pain, meaning their protective defenses were working overtime. Many she'd known constructed a protective barrier, a psychological wall, out of fear that the heartache they'd experienced might resurface. One glance at Janis told Cotton that this girl didn't construct her defense mechanisms overnight. At some point in her life, she'd become a master at avoidance. Not once had she looked in Cotton's direction.

Some of her fellow therapists absolutely hated dealing with teenagers, primarily because they were mercurial, sometimes belligerent, and often withheld the most important information. Or twisted it. Or lied. Or said hurtful things. Some colleagues simply considered adolescent psychology difficult. But Cotton loved the challenge when she first began practicing. Nothing was so rewarding as helping a person construct a healthy plan for embarking on the rest of their life. After Brighton's death, however, she wondered whether she had the skills to work with teenagers. She couldn't lose another one.

"Since we're recording, I need a verbal yes or a no, please." Cotton *inserts smile here.*

"Yes. I guess."

"Okay, thanks, Janis. Now, can we talk about how you feel about coming to our appointments?"

Silence.

Patient presents with adjustment disorder coupled with depression. It was a quick evaluation, though Cotton wasn't sure how deep-seated the adjustment disorder was right now. It would take a couple of sessions for a more accurate diagnosis.

Janis entwined her legs like wisteria vines, kept her arms straight down at her sides. She would not make eye contact or speak unless answering a question monosyllabically. Her internal motor appeared to have ground to a halt. A complete stop.

"Let me share a little about what I know about the situation. Then you can correct me if I'm wrong. Okay?"

"Mmmphfff," was Janis's profound reply.

"I take that as a 'yes,' so here's what I've learned." Cotton paused for a second, organizing her thoughts, then leaned forward, concentrating on keeping her shoulders open, her posture relaxed. Welcoming. Careful not to breach Janis's personal space. A delicate balance. This therapeutic alliance was tricky. Complicated. The slightest facial nuance and the initial interview would produce nothing. The goal was to create an agreement about the therapeutic format, sometimes by laying a groundwork for communication, which was difficult if the client didn't speak.

What are the facts? Stick with what's true, Cotton reminded herself. "This is what I know. You, your siblings, and your mom were in Italy, and when you returned home, your father was gone. He left a note saying he needs to live his life as he feels he is—as a female—and that he can only do that on his own. Am I right so far?"

Silence. Janis stared out the window, lips closed tight. She pulled the sleeves of her red hoodie down over her knuckles.

"You've nodded, so I'll take it I am correct. Now, your mother said she believes you and your siblings are having a hard time with this. Is that right?" Cotton assessed Janis over the edge of her rimless eyeglasses, noting *her eyes are glassy*, while keeping her own face passive.

"I guess."

"I'd love to hear your side of the story. Remember: Everything we say here is confidential. No matter what you say to me, I won't repeat it." Worried she'd pushed too much, Cotton sat back in her seat. *Did I just misstep?*

"Yeah, right." Janis followed her snarky comment with a snort.

"No, that's the truth. It's part of my oath as a therapist. Whatever is said in this room stays here unless you tell me you're going to kill someone or yourself. We can't let that happen." If Janis decided not to trust her, she could convince her mother to not make the next appointment. Logically, Cotton knew she had no control over the teen's decision, and that there were going to be times in her career that clients wouldn't connect with her, but she also knew she could help this family. *No more failures.* She counted to ten, determined not to speak until Janis did.

Janis studied her black-lacquered fingernails. "I believe you. Just don't want to talk."

In the quiet, the room settled around them. The faint sounds of bird calls and traffic filtered through the windows. The coffee pot on Cotton's desk emitted a soft burp and the rich scent of freshly brewed followed. She took a sip from the cup she hadn't quite finished. Janis stared at the ceiling. Cotton waited a moment. Two. Five. Sometimes the simple act of waiting opened the space for conversation, but at ten minutes, the hour was dwindling. *One more nudge.* "Would you rather tell me about yourself another way?"

"Mom wrote her story down, right? Is that what you're talking about? Another way of talking?"

It surprised Cotton that Gray had talked to her daughter about her own session. "Yes. That's another way, but just because it's one person's way doesn't mean it needs to be yours, as well."

Janis refolded her arms tightly to her chest.

Cotton knew that look of doubt. Few teenage girls wanted to emulate their mothers. They wanted to be different. Cotton remembered what it felt like to be Janis's age and unsure of everything in life. Everything required concentration. You knew where you were and what you were doing, but you constantly talked to yourself about what you were doing. Thinking. Thinking about thinking. Overthinking. Meta cognition. Teenagers use meta cognition in its maximum state.

Right now, even a novice therapist could see Janis turning the subject over in her head a couple of times, considering the options. Finally, she said, "UrPlace."

"UrPlace, huh? Isn't that old school?" Cotton laughed a little, though she didn't want to hurt Janis's feelings. "I'm surprised you're not on Snapchat or Facebook or Instagram or Twitter. Or whatever the newest social media is. I'm not up on all of them."

"That's exactly why. Everyone else is on there. Snapchat and Facebook and Instagram. Even Twitter. That's why I like UrPlace. No one's there but me, and maybe a couple hundred bloggers who suck so bad they don't get any traffic at all. It's nice and private. I got 27 friends, and that's enough. I don't need any more."

Janis probably didn't realize it, but during that short bit of dialog, her tone changed. Cotton heard every nuance of the spoken language. The slightest emphasis of a sharp consonant could tilt the scales from a sign of slight displeasure to an outright disapproval. Add that tonal inflection to a visual clue—like a facial twitch or the hike of an eyebrow—and the average person's deepest secrets were out on full display. She'd been proud of her abilities to read body language, but she'd doubted that skill after Brighton's death. Losing trust in herself left her unmoored. Who was she if her own understanding of her strengths and challenges was wrong? She'd taken the last three months to do for herself what she always told her clients to do: she gave herself permission to take a break.

Cotton felt confident now, refreshed, though tender, like the pink skin behind your ear. One thing was abundantly clear: Janis cherished her independence, choosing her own social media style. Cotton wondered whether she associated with the rebellious crowd at school. Maybe she even led it. And now that her father had declared an ongoing transition to a female identity, why wasn't Janis bouncing off the walls with support for him? Or frustration? Which was she feeling? Or was she feeling anything at all?

Cotton suspected Janis had been establishing her uniqueness long before her father left the family. Perhaps something else caused her to shut down.

"Okay, how do we go about doing this?" Cotton asked. "Do you need to friend me, like on Facebook? I'm not familiar with UrPlace."

"Just find me on UrPlace. My ID is JanisBabe. Friend me, and I'll friend you back." She offered access to a page that even her parents didn't have, yet her body language said she still considered this session a form of punishment and didn't trust Cotton. Pushing her shoulders back, Janis finally looked at Cotton, though it was a glance of absolute disdain. No fear whatsoever.

Cotton played it down, watching Janis closely and keeping questions to a minimum, and her voice low key and noncommittal, as if the answers were unimportant. Casual. She took her glasses off, removing anything that might represent a threat from Janis's perspective. If Cotton were to appear authoritarian, like a teacher or a doctor or someone who might betray Janis's confidence with her parents, Cotton would get nothing. Not one word. That meant failure.

For a moment, neither of them spoke. Janis squirmed and reached for the cell phone in her pocket. Cotton wasn't surprised. Screens had built a generation of people who were more comfortable with that type of discourse rather than face-to-face, yet social media offered people a chance to tell their stories to thousands of others they might never meet.

"We're building a generation of intimacy-phobes," Cotton told Thomas so often that he mouthed the line, mimicking her, whenever the subject came up at dinner parties.

Janis was quiet for a moment, fiddling with the phone, holding it straight up so that Cotton can't see the screen, though it's obvious....

"Are you texting?" Cotton asked. *Shit. That sounded as parental as "have you brushed your teeth yet?"*

"Yeah."

"It would be a lot easier to talk if you weren't. I always ask folks to put away their phones for our hour-long session. You don't mind, do you?"

"Sorry." Janis shoved her phone back into her pocket and twisted her mouth up. *What the fuck*, her grimaced face said.

"So, would it be easier for you if we communicated that way— UrPlace? You could tell me how you feel or what you want from our sessions on your blogs...."

"Why would I do that? I don't want anyone to know I'm here." Sitting up straight, Janis seemed alarmed, as if she suddenly realized that wasn't such a good idea after all.

"Can't you set it up so only certain people can see what you're saying?"

"I guess."

"Or use a code of some kind? Or don't say anything about our visits at all. Doesn't matter." Cotton scrambled to get Janis back on track, and from the way Janis leaned back onto the couch, she sensed it and retreated. "I just thought it would be easier."

Janis's feet dropped to the floor, her black motorcycle boots thumping hard enough to shake the vase of irises on the side table. "Maybe it'd be okay. But I don't want my mother to see it. You gotta promise you'll never show her. Or my dad either. Don't show him anything."

"How about if I just read it and we can talk about whatever portion you wish when you come in again?"

Another long silence.

"I'm not going to talk about my dad, if that's what you think."

Cotton glanced at the clock. Ten minutes left. "You can talk about whatever you want, Janis. We're here for *you*. No one else."

"Mom said you're doing this for the whole family."

"That's true, but the time we spend together—you and I—is just ours. Yours and mine. Like I said earlier, I will repeat nothing outside this room."

"How often do I have to come here?"

"I'll be honest with you, Janis. I'm not sure. Usually, my clients and I decide when therapy is over. I never can tell how long it will take. And usually, I work with my clients until we're done."

In the space between them, the clock ticked. Golden-brown leaves shimmered outside the window behind the couch.

"Is my father going to see you?" Janis's voice: small and timid.

"I believe so."

"Me, too. He's the one who needs this, not me. I'm fine. He's the one who left. He's the one who doesn't want to be a dad anymore. He wants to be my mom. Christ, I have enough issues with one mom, never mind two." She fiddled with her cell phone again, then glanced up at Cotton and put it away. "There's a couple of kids at school who are trans, and they all go to therapy." She nodded definitively, as if that fact proves her father needs the therapy more than she does. "The kids are mean to them. Not me, though. I don't say much. But I know they've gotten beaten up. A lot."

Cotton nodded, surprised that Janis knows more than one transgender kid considering the reputation of Goodman's, the rather conservative private school the Prescott kids attend. A few of her clients have kids who go to the same school, and they'd been bullied for not going to the right church, and that "right" church believed relationships were only between men and women. She didn't even want to imagine what LGBTQ+ kids went through.

"I suppose you can read my blog." Janis picked at her fingernails, flicking an infinitesimal piece of dirt from under her right thumbnail. "But don't say anything about my grammar."

"Okay. We can talk about the blog next time you come."

"Yeah, I guess so. We done now?"

"Yes, for today. Could you write down the directions for your blog before you go?"

Janis nodded and took the pen and paper Cotton handed her.

Cotton rose and placed her notes on the table, then reminded Janis they'd meet every week, but Janis was out the door and into the anteroom where Gray stood waiting like a meerkat, holding her pocketbook tightly with both hands. Gray watched Janis exit the front door without a word then raised her eyebrows at Cotton and mouthed, "What happened?" but instead of waiting for an answer, Gray caught up with Janis and put her arm over her daughter's shoulder as they walked to the car without a word.

Cotton opened her laptop before the Prescotts left the parking area. She logged into UrPlace, and within a couple of moments, she was engrossed in Janis's page.

Cotton entered the fake profile she'd created a few years ago after attending a seminar about social media addiction. She had often used it to see how her younger clients were doing, but she hadn't used it for a while. Logging in under this old profile rather than using the access password Janis provided would give her a different view of Janis's public profile. Unedited. Nothing hidden. She folded her legs up under her.

Janisbabe's Run-On Life

i'm 5,475 days old today. YAY! That means 5,475 days towards death. That Ol' freak Marilyn Manson sez "we're on a bullet & we're headed straight into god even he'd like to end it too we take a pill."

Cotton cut and pasted this section into a file labeled JP/blog. *Words can be twisted, and signs of trauma covered up. You know that, Cotton. Keep your eyes open.*

i'm not norml & don't wanna be, so don't ask! I'm totally addicted to UrPlace & to my friends who are soooo important 2 me. They know who they are & I know who they are & that's all that matters, right? I'm kinda crazy but that's me & I like it that way ^-^ don't have any animals but someday I want a black cat named Chloe. I love playing the guitar & hope I can study music at Julliard someday. I can't wait to get my driver's license next June. WOOHOO!

Cotton flipped through pics of Janis staring at the screen with her tongue out, eyes bulging like a Māori warrior. Some of Janis and five other kids standing in the Roman Forum like straight little soldiers, smiling for Mommy taking the picture. Janis with three other teens, laughing and hugging each other's necks, all dressed in black t-shirts and jeans, looped scarves around their necks, each wearing a hat that defined their personalities. One blonde girl in a cowboy hat; a younger boy (Eleven? Twelve? Might be Marcus, her younger brother) wore a white baseball cap with a royal blue D on the front; and another girl, shorter than the others and about the same age as Janis, wore a flat-brimmed black hat like the one the artist Georgia O'Keefe did, a white scarf around her skull underneath the hat. Cotton's kind of fashion icon.

There were other photos, dozens featuring the three kids, as well as several others. In her mind, Cotton named the ones she saw most frequently: *Cowgirl, Dukie, Georgia.* For the hell of it, she created a spreadsheet with columns for each of them, noting their characteristics, how many times they appear in Janis's photos, writing in the dates. Minutiae. A road map that might help her put the jigsaw pieces of Janis's life together.

The blonde girl must be Janis's sister, Cherylynn, and the kid in the baseball hat was Marcus. But Cotton did not recognize the other kids. Friends? Maybe a cousin or two that Gray had mentioned?

Cotton right-clicked on some of the gallery pics and saved them to a file on her desktop, then enlarged each pic, one at a time, analyzed body language, noting the way a child's brow arched, the lilt of another's head. Checked their hands to see if anyone subconsciously clenched a fist or flexed fingers. Checked the feet: were they pointing to or away from the others in the photo? She let loose a sigh of relief that the kids seemed realistically happy, even in the photos where she could tell an adult was directing the show.

She glanced at the clock, guiltily—an hour had passed—but she needed this research, she told herself, and scrolled to the next page: *Janisbabe's Interests.*

Fairly eclectic list. Everything from whales to Twilight movies, the Beatles, and Joan of Arc. Music choices ranged from Tal Wilkenfeld, the guitarist with the incredible blond curls that hung past his shoulders, to Jordan Rudess, an indy singer-songwriter. Cotton ran her finger down the side of her screen. The list ended with what Janis wanted to be when she grew up: a world-famous NASA astronaut. This child, this adolescent, actually navigated life with one foot mid-air, balanced in childhood, while the other foot was toe-testing the waters of adulthood. Cotton's finger paused on the screen, stopping the roll. Below her finger, a conversation. Words instead of emojis. A chat.

5.2: 10:04AM janisbabe: yo! Holla at me when you're on, friends! OMG it's been sooo long since I used UrPlace account and i'm having serious withdrawals

5.2: 10:05AM kikass: hey beeeeatch! Wasssup?

5.2 10:05 AM janisbabe: hey Kiki-too awful to talk about. There's been way 2 much drama going on at home like u wouldn't believe. Can't even believe it. YOU wouldn't believe it. Tooooo much drama!!!

5.2 10:06 AM: kikass: spill!!!

5.2 10:06 AM: janisbabe: told u we went to Italy, right?

5.2 10:07 AM: kikass: ya

5.2 10:07 AM: janisbabe: when we came back my dad was gone.

5.2 10:08 AM: kikass: no shit

5.2 10:08 AM: janisbabe: yes shit

.2 10:14 AM: kikass: wanna talk?

5.2 10:15 AM: janisbabe: no cell
5.2 10:16 AM: kikass: i'll come over
5.2 10:16 AM: janisbabe: can't—on lockdown
5.2 10:17 AM kikass: MoS-G2G
5.2 10:17 AM: janisbabe: tmw at school
5.2 10:18 AM: kikass: K

Just as I thought, Cotton scanned the rest of the conversations. *She lied. She's already talked to her friends.* Before this, comments had been fairly inane: "Nice!" on a pic from Italy. "I can't believe it" ad nauseam about a grade in "TrbL's Math Lab," but Janis had not shared even one word or a hint about what was happening at home. Now, though, she begged for some communication.

With a sigh, Cotton closed the laptop, sat back and mentally sorted through the data she'd already collected about the Prescotts through visits with Gray and Janis, the beginnings of their narratives, and how intertwined those versions were. Even though she hadn't met Marcus, Cherylynne, and Hayden, she'd heard about them from their mother/wife and sister/daughter. But the Prescott family puzzle wouldn't be complete without their stories. Cotton drummed her fingers and glanced at the clock. An hour before she'd call an end to her day.

Sliding into her big leather chair with a barely repressed sigh of relief, she kicked off her black ballet flats and pulled a needle-pointed hassock to the chair to support her legs. Tapping the Spotify screen, she chose her relaxation playlist, musing silently about how different her music was from Janis's.

Before the first song finished, Cotton's eyes drifted shut, and she concentrated on nothing but her breathing, all the while fighting images of fourteen-year-old Brighton Ogelle's Facebook entries, the calls for help Cotton hadn't seen, the depression hidden behind silly pictures with her friends.

I'll do better this time. I must.

~ Book Four ~

Cotton Barnes

Sometimes the things in our heads are far worse than anything they can put in books or on film.
— C.K. Webb

Halloween night. Cotton and Thomas loved the holiday, so each year they tried to create a costume guaranteed to top the previous years. This year, they dressed as the White Rabbit and the Red Queen from Alice in Wonderland. Cotton had worked for a month to craft the costumes, making both by hand, as she has since their first Halloween party. A few years ago, they celebrated their tenth Hallow-versary by attending their best friends, Deb and Danny's house party, dressed as a pair of anniversary cupcakes—complete with edible white chocolate mini-cupcakes they handed out to everyone. Cotton saw the masquerading as a healthy acting-out exercise (with the side benefit of hot sex at the end of the night). *What is it about masks?*

"I must really love you," Thomas's voice echoed from within the papier mâché rabbit's head. "This thing weighs a ton, and it's hot as hell in here."

"It's worth it. I think this is our best yet." Cotton adjusted his white waistcoat's tails and looped her arm through his. It was impossible to hold his hand since he wore big, white, furry mitten-paws.

The door opened and Deb, ghoulishly made up as one of the Walking Dead, squealed. "Oh, my god! Look at you two! Cotton, you're downright elegant! Where on earth did you get that gown? It's absolutely awesome. Turn around, turn around."

She inspected the frilly, blood-red gown, Cotton's sky-high tiara, the scepter she held in her hand, and the handmade silver heart-shaped bodice she had painstakingly sewed onto the front of the gown. She'd woven her unruly blonde curls through the tiara's frame, creating a bird's nest effect, but she had no idea whether she would be able to "unweave" it at the end of the night. And makeup proved to be more of a challenge than she thought. Perfectly bowed red lips aren't easy to draw when your own lips are nowhere near Kardashian fullness, and hand-drawing peaked eyebrows gave her a haughty-but-weird expression. The final touch was the sparkling red heels she had worn when they were Dorothy and Toto a few years ago. Bingo. The perfect Red Queen.

Thomas's costume, though unwieldy and heavy, was the unmistakable hit of the evening. Everyone felt the need to create an off-color joke or remark, so laughter followed him from room to room.

When midnight came and the fifty couples gathered in the huge backyard to crown the costume winners, everyone groaned good-naturedly when Thomas and Cotton won—their fifth year in a row.

Once the judging was over, Thomas took his head off and immediately downed an entire bottle of locally crafted beer, Danny at his side, urging him to chug. Thomas winked at Cotton as he slung a furry arm over Danny's shoulders and the two of them plodded away— the Undead and the Rabbit—to discuss the remaining ACC football games. Thomas, a die-hard Duke fan, loved to diss Danny, who graduated with honors in Chemistry from Chapel Hill.

Cotton floated over to the buffet table to find something to satisfy her gurgling stomach. Sometimes she forgot to eat, and this time, she hadn't eaten for 10 or 12 hours. It had almost become a personal game to see how long she could last before she noticed her own hunger. Probably not the healthiest game, she knew, but she told no one else, so it was her secret.

"It's all been pretty heavily grazed," Deb commented as they surveyed the table. She picked out a couple of chicken wings and some carrots, then poured some bleu cheese dressing on her plate. "Not the healthiest I've ever eaten, either. Oh well. Sit with me?" Deb tilted her head toward an empty table near the pool.

At the other end of the yard, the DJ ordered a group of dancers to bust a move, and three women who had come dressed as Beyonce and Destiny's Child happily obliged

"Haven't seen you in ages, girl." Deb picked up one of the chicken wings and began gnawing on it. "What y'all been up to?"

"Just work. Work, work, work."

"I'm glad you went back to the clinic, but you work too damn hard. Used to be we could get together for a game or some barbeque at least occasionally. Now I feel like we never see each other. I thought you were going to back off for a while. At least in the beginning."

Cotton grabbed one of the carrot sticks off Deb's plate. "It takes a lot of work and time to build a practice, you know. I've got to be back in there before I lose it totally. I had only been out on my own for 8 months, you know that. Just moved into that new office. Kinda lost that momentum after Brighton's death"

"Yeah, but you don't need to catch up on that lost time in a matter of months. Besides...."

"Yes, la di da. Doctor's orders. But going back into my own practice again also means I must pay all the bills. Translation: more hours."

Deb grabbed Cotton's arm and squeezed firmly. Nailing Cotton with her chestnut brown eyes, she said, "I didn't mean how's work. I meant how's Cotton? How are *you*?"

Those eyes. Deb could look deep into Cotton's soul. No way she could lie.

"I'm starting back slow. I'm working with just one family right now." *Just one family, but probably the most dysfunctional family I've ever met.*

"Sounds like you're doing it right." Deb nodded and took another bite. Cotton hated that she talked with her mouth full. "Well, I have no doubt that the space Daddy rented you will bring you the best of everything. He's got the Midas touch, that man."

Deb had that right. Everything Earl Penney touched flourished into an overnight sensation. When Deb and Cotton were little, he bought his first car dealership and now he had ten branches all over the state, plus he owned more office buildings than anyone in the Raleigh-Durham-Chapel Hill area. When Cotton decided to open her own office, everyone expected that she'd go straight to Mr. Earl for help, and she obliged. He looped his arm over her shoulders as he had throughout her life and told her, "Go choose the space you want, sweetie, and take it rent free for the first year. Get yourself on your feet, then we'll talk."

That gift of a free year made Cotton even more determined to pay him back as quickly as possible. Sometimes people made you feel special, and they dropped a bit of their soul on you. They blessed you with their belief in you.

"Go and help people," he told her. "Make me proud."

She was indebted to Earl Penney, the man she thought of as a second father, and every appointment with a client brought her closer to the promise she made to him.

When Cotton lost her parents, she thought she'd never have someone in her corner who believed in her as they would have, but she'd been lucky. Deb and her family gave Cotton a safe place to call home and a deep well of non-judgmental love. And there have been a few other steadfast friends she has counted on for both backbone support and pillow-soft understanding.

Yes, she'd been lucky. She glanced over at Deb now, whose pretty face was covered with jagged streaks of blood dripping down to her chin and deep black circles under her zombie eyes.

"You look like shit," Cotton told her. "You need a little meat on your bones." Within a heartbeat, they joined in a slightly drunk fit of wheezing and sneezing laughs out of their noses like ten-year-olds telling dirty jokes.

God, I'm lucky. I love this little chickadee.

~ Book Five ~

Hayden/Hailey Prescott

Analysis does not set out to make pathological reactions impossible, but to give the patient's ego freedom to decide one way or another.
  —Sigmund Freud

Hayden Prescott arrived precisely on time, shook Cotton's hand, exchanged a hello-how-are-you-nice-to-meet-you, and followed Cotton into her office. A bit surprised that Hayden still presented as a man, Cotton gave herself a mental slap. *Stop giving new clients faces and personalities before meeting them. You're never right.*

Tentatively settling into the overstuffed chair near the window, Hayden took the pillow from behind him, placing it flat on his lap, as if unsure where else to put it. Both of his wine-colored oxfords were on the floor. Flat and solid. Cotton sensed that the floor had crumbled on him many times in his life. He needed to stay steady. *She? They?*

It had taken a month to get the appointment scheduled, which meant Cotton had far more information and time with Gray and Janis, and though she tried not to create expectations, she admitted to herself that she was curious about this central character in the Prescott family.

"Okay, let's do intros first. How about who you are, your pronouns, your work?" Cotton made the pretense of settling into her chair. "Then, perhaps we'll talk?"

"Call me Hailey, please. Mr. Prescott is my dad. And I'm not Hayden anymore." Hailey shifted in the chair, crossing one ankle over the other. "I'm not used to Ms., or the female pronouns yet, but please just don't call me Hayden. He's dead. Okay, maybe you should just use 'she,' but I'd prefer you... kind of... well, don't tell my family yet."

Cotton nodded, glanced down at the intake form, and noted what Hailey said. "If you could give me a head's up when you tell your family, that would help me."

"No prob. You can use 'she' for now." Hailey's gaze followed the line of paintings hung on Cotton's walls, pausing a moment at each one, analyzing them as though someone would test her about the details later. Cotton suspected Hailey probably knew something about art since Gray called her husband 'artsy fartsy.'

There were other ways that Hailey appeared just as Gray described: an English professor at Duke, struggling speculative fiction novelist, haughty yet a bit befuddled. One leg haphazardly over the other, she wrapped her arms around her knees. Long, thin hands folded atop each other, she stared back at Cotton with curiosity. Hailey's ginger-brown hair was flecked with gray, and Cotton wondered whether that change was recent since Gray hadn't mentioned it. Seemingly uncomfortable with Cotton's scrutiny, Hailey coughed sharply, then pinched the pleat in her knife-sharp-pressed jeans and slid her fingers all the way down her leg. A wave of cologne floated across the room, a musky, pleasant aroma that smelled like patchouli.

"I'm sorry. I'm really nervous," Hailey said, hands shaking and a thin line of sweat providing a sheen to her wide forehead and high cheekbones.

Cotton took in a long, full breath, her own feet flat on the floor, and smiled. "How about before we begin, we take a full inhale together? Open our lungs and heart a little? It usually works to relax me a bit. Gets me into my own space and helps me settle in here. Might do the same for you." She'd learned in Dr. Frait's class on interviewing skills that patients mimic their therapists' breathing patterns, and she'd found it to be true, so she included at least a couple of deep breaths before launching into her session when a new client presented with recognizable anxiety.

Nodding, Hailey offered a thin-lipped smile, much like the one Cotton saw on Janis's face only a couple of days ago. Gray was right. Janis and her father shared the same deep blue eyes.

They breathed together for a few breaths, and Cotton felt her own heartbeat slow, so she opened her eyes to see Hailey, jaw slack, shoulders relaxed, a strand of wavy hair over her right brow. "Take one more deep breath," Cotton said, "and slowly open your eyes."

She waited until Hailey's eyes fluttered open. "So, can you tell me why you're here?"

"Well, because of my family and..." Shifting her glance down toward the floor, Hailey flicked a thread off her jeans. "Well, because I'm transgender and... I guess I need to help them understand that. I haven't done a very good job of helping them."

"How do you feel about that?"

Rolling her eyes, Hailey sighed as if she had expected the question, yet a distinct twinge of pain emerged in the lines along her forehead. "Guilty. And... I guess... responsible."

"Responsible?"

"For my family. For hurting them. I was trying to do just the opposite. I was trying to spare them, and now, well, here we are ...."

The words fell into the space between them, and Hailey raised her hands, fanned her fingers, as if by doing so she could wipe away the pain she'd caused, maybe even erase her own. The slope on Hailey's shoulders spoke of overwhelming sadness and the dark circles under her eyes said she hadn't slept well, that this entire experience was gut-wrenching. Yet there was something about the way her chin jutted forward that said she'd decided and wasn't backing down. That she'd waited far too long to make this happen.

"Even coming here today, I had to think about what I'd do if I saw them," she continued. "I haven't dressed like this, like a man, for a while, but it would disturb them—my family—if they saw me in the clothes I usually wear now, women's clothes, dresses, and skirts, so I didn't take a chance. They will not be here, will they? They won't see me when we have our appointments—when I see you individually?"

"No, they all have separate appointment times with me. I'd like to get the family together eventually, though. If that works for everyone."

"What have they told you already?" Hailey said, ignoring the suggestion about getting everyone together.

"I can't repeat what my clients tell me. Everyone who walks through my office door gets my solemn promise that everything they say will be held in confidence."

"What are my choices?"

"Choices?"

"Of how to tell my story."

"Well, there are a number of ways to build your own narrative." *What is it with this family and their need to tell their stories differently? We need to work on their communication skills.* "You can simply talk about whatever you want during our session. Or you can choose to let me drive the conversation."

"Verbally?"

"You can write letters. Or a diary. However, I'd prefer that you and I just talk. That's the most effective manner of therapy, but I'm flexible. I want you to do whatever makes you comfortable." Cotton's voice trailed off, and she sat back. She had learned patience, but she also knew how to drive the conversation so she could get to the heart of a patient's issues in the least amount of time. Usually, that worked, but this family wanted to drive the therapy car.

"How has my wi — how has Gray told her story?"

"I'm sorry...." Cotton held her palms up to the ceiling and smiled as if to say, *I already told you I will not share someone else's sessions with you.*

"I know. I know. I shouldn't have asked. It's just that... I never meant to hurt her or the kids. It sounds so trite, but it's true." Hailey coughed into her hand, then wiped her palm against her jeans. When she looked down, her eyelashes slid against her cheeks, longer and more luxurious than Gray's.

"Have you spoken to your family about your plans since you left?" Cotton asked the question though she'd already heard the answer from Gray and Janis. "How do they feel about your transition?"

"No. I haven't had the guts. I haven't been able to call. I just left the... Gray calls it the ghosting letter." She swallowed hard, like she'd been holding everything inside, and it took a herculean effort to do so. "You know... this is all I've wanted my whole life... and now... and now that I'm booking the pre-op visits... all I can think of is... well, how this is affecting everyone else. And that there will be no one there when I wake up after the operations."

Hailey pulled at her shirt collar, a salmon-colored button-down, crisply ironed. "This is my family. It's a cliché, but they're my universe. The one thing I don't want is to lose my family. That became crystal clear during those first couple of weeks when we didn't talk at all." Her chin dropped low to her chest. "I thought about this for a long time before I left that letter." Her long eyelashes now framed shiny eyes. "I thought it would be better to meet with each of the kids individually, talk to them for as long as each of them wanted. I dream about what I'd say to Janis. I think she'll get it. There's not one bone of judgment in that child's body. Marcus, now. Well, he and I are always in costume, so this is kind of a different one..."

"Costume?"

"We play WarCraft. We both have avatars. You know what that is, right?"

Cotton nodded and said, "Sort of," and Hailey laughed, a forced "ha ha."

"Ironic, huh? We can be whoever we want to be on the screen, yet in real life... I'm still not quite sure what I'll say to Cherylynn. Most people don't realize that her laughter is a coverup for her anxiety. Besides, of the kids, I never can tell how she's going to react. Janis has always been somber, a bit depressed, and Marcus is in another world.... Cherylynn, on the other hand... she's always seemed upbeat, then she crashes...." Hailey drifted away for another moment.

Cotton quietly waited, watching a myriad of emotions crisscross the slender panes of Hailey's face. The sharpness of her nose and the perfect vee of her lips softened when she raised her watery eyes and revealed the depth of her pain and confusion.

"I thought leaving would be easier for them, but no matter what I do, I'm hurting someone. I just can't live a lie anymore. I don't know what's worse. I really don't."

"What you're feeling is normal, Hailey. Everyone I have treated who has gone through gender transition has asked themselves, at one point or another, whether they're hurting someone else. I'm not here to determine whether you're a suitable candidate for a gender transition, but I can't help but wonder whether the psychiatrists you've seen have been privy to your concerns. Are you seeing a gender therapist?"

Hailey nodded.

"Okay, if you have questions about what you're going through, your therapist needs to know, and if the results of your discomfort with your physical gender have caused distinct trauma for you, tell your therapist or your doctor or me. But tell someone. Don't suffer. If you have questions about what you're doing, you can ask your specialists." She paused. *Have I said enough?*

Hailey didn't jump in to fill the silence, so Cotton continued. "Let's talk about what you mentioned about not coming out to your whole family yet. Do you think some of them don't know or understand? How do you feel about that?"

Hailey took a pale blue handkerchief from her shirt pocket and blew her nose loudly. "You must realize I don't want to hurt anyone. I still love Gray very much. I adore our kids. I just want to... no, I don't just *want...* I *need* to be the person I know I am. They've known the 'me' that everyone else told me I was. No one—not even Gray—knows the real me."

"Hailey, the one thing I've learned as a therapist is that many family members never truly recognize how much their transitioning family members care about what everyone thinks. And so many people are afraid to love and accept those loved ones who are changing. If that happens, everyone loses and I find that ironic, do you?"

The chair shifted under Hailey and creaked as if it needed a good oiling. "I've been in therapy before. I get how it works. I do want to help, really. Just don't know how I'm going to help Gray or the kids when I'm not even... not sure sometimes how to help myself. I really... really, really don't want to hurt them." Her voice squeaked a bit, as if she struggled to hold back a sob. "I know I'm repeating myself a lot. I'm sorry."

"Let's not think of being responsible for someone else right now. Let's just talk about you, okay?"

"Okay. I guess, but I want to make something clear. I didn't really leave my family. I tried to protect them. I made sure the house was in shape, I paid all the bills and still do, and I removed myself from their lives so they wouldn't have to explain what happened. I thought that was the best way to keep them safe. You know, with all that's been going on."

"All that's been going on?"

"You haven't heard. The violence in Raleigh? Those killings?"

Cotton remembered vaguely hearing something about a group of vigilantes targeting the LGBTQ+ community. She had purposefully ignored the news since Brighton's death, not feeling strong enough yet to deal with tough realities. Maybe she wasn't even strong enough to be back in the office, but here she was. She jotted a note on her pad to catch up with the news. Obviously, it would be important to the Prescotts.

"Oh yes, I know what you're talking about." *Why the hell am I lying?*

"I would never forgive myself if something happened to them because of me."

"Of course, of course." At that moment, Cotton knew it was going to take all the skill she had to work with his bruised family. Gray was on her schedule for three appointments a week, and Janis had already been in twice. Cherylynn and Marcus had appointments later this week, and Hailey should be seen at least two or three times a week as well. Not to mention appointments with the full family at least once or twice a week. At least a dozen appointments total per week.Good thing they were her only clients right now.

In a way, Cotton envied Hailey. She'd made a choice to be herself, entirely and completely. How many people have done that? Taken that step off the ledge and trusted that they could save themselves? How many of her clients longed to be their true and honest selves, yet never how to do so?

"I know, I know. I guess I'm still getting used to it. I mean, being 'out.'" Hailey created air quotes with her thin fingers. "Okay, I need to decide how to tell my side of the story, huh? How about if I show you my journal?"

Makes sense that the writer in the family is keeping a journal. Maybe I should charge a separate hourly rate for reading everyone's written stories. Strange that everyone in this family had an unspoken identity, a written self rather than a verbal one. *They must have awfully quiet mealtimes.*

She said, "It'll be fine, but let's continue our face-to-face appointments. They're the most effective."

Hailey nodded. "Do you want me to show you what I've written from the beginning, or is it okay to just show you the latest entries, the ones around the time I left?"

"Whatever makes you comfortable."

"I'll bring it tomorrow." Even though the session wasn't over, Hailey rose and shook Cotton's hand solemnly. "I'm going to talk to each of the kids before the next time you see me, I promise, and hopefully, by then, I can show them the real me."

Before 9AM the next morning, Hailey texted that she'd dropped the package at the office, and Cotton drove over right away to pick it up. The envelope was thick, and when Cotton rifled through the stack of papers, she noted the dates ranged from the 1980s until now. Hailey had given her journals she'd written from the time she was a teen. She groaned. No way in hell she'd get through almost 500 pages. Hailey's narrative weighed heavy in her hands, a metaphor for the way Hailey had released that old heavy life by delivering this tome to Cotton.

That realization reminded her of something she'd read while she was out of work, and she scanned her bookshelves until she found it. *True Selves* written by Mildred L. Brown and Chloe Ann Rounsley, the California writing partners, a sexologist, and a writer, she'd heard doing a keynote at a conference somewhere. She'd read the book on the plane on the way home, fascinated, and reread it only a month ago. Now she flipped quickly through the pages, until she found the quote she sought: "gender dysphoric children often feel as if they have a monstrous dark cloud hanging over them" and then, following her finger over the pages, she noted that "daydreaming is sometimes their only escape."

So, that's where Hailey found her identity and comfort in writing. On the page, she was who she was in her heart of hearts. She could enter a world of imagination, free to explore whatever realms she wished, in whatever shape she wanted to be. Her published work skirted the boundaries of science fiction, blending fantasy with urban fiction, and Cotton wondered whether Hailey brought that style into her personal journals, even though in reality, the world forced her to be someone she didn't recognize in her own mirror.

Cotton noted in her calendar that she needed to broach a discussion about this self-identity with each of the Prescotts. The imagined identity, the social identity, and the individual's true self. Perhaps she could connect the question to what the kids were going through as they made their own transition from boys/girls to men/women. Use it as a teaching moment. No more ignoring the elephant in the room with this family: every one of them struggled with identity issues. Why not use that commonality as a therapeutic tool?

Yes, why not?

~ Book Six ~

Cotton Barnes

Don't compromise yourself. You are all you've got.
　—Janis Joplin

Cotton kept her oar up for a moment as the canoe glided past a tangle of Southern pines and River Birches nestled in a pile of rocks. The uppermost rock moved and morphed into a large turtle that watched them intently before splashing into the water. Above the trees, a great blue heron soared like an ancient pterodactyl. Silently. Majestically. Cotton breathed deeply, inhaling the pungent pine and the clean smell of the river, then released it slowly. The early winter sun shone on her paddle as she dipped it into the chilly water, lifted it out again, watched the droplets cascade off like liquid diamonds.

She was thankful Thomas suggested they spend the weekend canoeing the Neuse River, following its two-million-year-old path from Falls Lake southward from where they lived in North Raleigh to the southern border of the city itself. They'd done the whole river, right down to the Pamlico Sound, during their first summer of dating. Thomas had loved being alone for two weeks, but Cotton was over it by the end of the first week. She'd never been a nature lover, but through the years, their trips in the canoe had grown on her.

She relished being in the fresh air on the river, watching the Great Blue Herons nesting along the shore, smelling an occasional end-of-the-season barbeque from somewhere beyond the tree line, feeling the burn in her upper arms from reaching her oar into the fast-moving waters to steer the canoe away from fallen trees and overgrown roots. She felt as if she'd taken a tranquilizer. What would happen if all psychiatric hospitals built their facilities where their patients would have access to lakes or rivers to soothe those with anxiety issues? It made sense to give patients what they need from Mother Nature, the great equalizer, rather than boxing them in rooms lined with silent cameras and alarms.

The canoe wended down the river for a few miles, passing an occasional stately home high on the river's banks and a line of barefoot boys with fishing poles on their shoulders, the sun glinting off the small fish they waved gleefully at Cotton and Thomas as if bragging about their catches.

Thomas suggested taking a break on a small sandy beach. He'd brought some white wine, cheese, and crackers, and they sat on the sand, sharing them silently for a few idyllic moments. The wine left a clean, cold finish on her tongue, giving her a little fuzzy pleasantness. She smiled at her husband and reached out to ruffle his dark hair. He winked back at her and leaned in for a kiss.

"Feels like it's been a long time since we've had time alone with no ringing phones or demanding laptops or needy employees or patients," he said after he'd given her a long deep kiss that tasted of Medoc and extra sharp cheddar.

Normally, she'd remind him she didn't have regular hours like he does at the laboratory where he works as a neuroscientist, but the sun burned bright in her eyes, and her mind was blissfully blank. She had no energy to argue.

Many nights the two of them could offer little more than a hello-how-was-your-day to each other, which is exactly why they have a standing agreement to fit low-tech dates into their life. They both needed the fresh air in their lungs, and in their marriage.

She was satisfied with their relationship. It was comfortable and safe, yet the passion between them remained very much alive. She had learned from many sessions with unhappily married couples that she and Thomas had it much better than most. They'd worked hard to maintain the relationship they have, even though they floated during their first couple of years of marriage, their love enough to keep them happy even when overloaded with dissertations and shitty part-time jobs that left them too tired to cook a decent meal but never too exhausted to make love. Now they reminded each other when they needed a nature break or more sex or some privacy. They knew how to communicate, and Cotton wouldn't want it any other way. She was happy with each other's rhythms, and it was a warm, uncomplicated relationship, made better when they found time to meet each other's needs.

"Perfect place for some river love," Thomas whispered in her ear. He nuzzled her neck, enticing forth that little moan she made whenever he kissed her in that spot. "No one around, just the two of us alone. Whaddya say?"

She answered with a soulful kiss of her own, but as soon as he began to lower her to the blanket, she realized she hadn't brought any protection. "Oh, Thomas. We can't ...."

"Why not?"

"I don't have anything with me." Cotton's gynecologist had suggested taking a break from the birth control pills she'd been taking after her last couple of particularly painful menstrual cycles and a nasty reaction to the antidepressants her psychiatrist had added after Cotton's depression about Brighton's death. Remembering to bring other protection (like prophylactics) was a challenge for Cotton, and it frustrated Thomas, but she wouldn't take a chance. In her gut, she'd always known she didn't want children, and it had become a sticking point with Thomas.

"Don't worry about it. What's the worst that can happen?" Thomas whispered as his fingers found her jeans' zipper.

"No, Thomas. No. We talked about this."

"Yes, we have. Many times." He turned and the Nike check mark on his jacket pocket was the only thing squarely in her sight. But she didn't need to see his face because she heard the chill in his voice.

"What do you mean?" She hated herself for pretending she didn't understand, but she didn't want to have the same argument. She was tired of defending herself.

"We talked a couple of months ago, right after that girl killed herself, and we talked in therapy—"

"Name!"

"Huh?"

"Her name was Brighton. Brighton Ogelle. Don't call her 'that girl.'"

"That wasn't my point. You'd asked what I meant, and I was trying to... oh, Christ, babe, you're shutting down again. I can see that thing you do with your jaw. Why does this happen every time?"

Cotton's first instinct was to deflect, to give herself time to reel in the warning flutters in her chest. Steer the conversation in another direction. It was self-preservation to detour what should be an open, honest, and safe conversation between two people who love each other very much. Unhealthy. She did this a lot lately, this mental duck-and-jab with Thomas. He would hold her accountable, but sometimes she'd like to have the freedom of working on her issues on her own timetable rather than his. She doesn't negotiate that timetable now. Instead, she clamped her mouth shut and hated herself for it.

He turned away. Her breath caught in her throat. No words. A soft rain began to fall, gradually becoming more persistent. Without another word, they packed up the canoe and headed back to the dock. She knew the drill. They'd find an Uber and get back to where they left the car, then drive down and pick up the canoe. The trip was entirely silent.

A couple of hours later, they wound up in separate parts of the house, because neither wanted to broach the subject they'd discussed *ad nauseam* with no resolution. It's the only thing they argue about. Thomas wanted children; Cotton did not. Never has. It's not that she doesn't like children. She loves them, loves them so much that she saw no sense in bringing a child into a world as scary as this. She'd told Thomas that many times.

"There's no superhero in creation who'd be strong enough to protect a child of mine," she liked to say. And after she lost Brighton, she thought it would be even easier for him to understand her logic, but he'd only become more adamant.

He doesn't understand.

Standing against the doorjamb to the porch as she watched the rain fall, Cotton struggled to stop thinking about what she might have said or could say now. Obsessive habit of hers. The only thing that stopped her mind from spinning was to change her thought channel, so she forced herself to focus, thinking about the river and what they'd seen before their first turn around the bend. How many Great Blue Herons? One by the Basin, two along the stretch between the big green estate and ....

Fuck it, I can't do this. We have to talk.

Cotton spun on her heel and returned to the living room, Fred trotting behind her heels as she called out Thomas's name. Silence. She glanced out the kitchen window to the driveway. The BMW was gone and so was her husband.

~ Book Seven ~

Marcus Prescott

Do not ask who I am and do not ask me to remain the same. More than one person, doubtless like me, writes in order to have no face.
— Michel Foucault

It was barely 4 PM when Gray Prescott stormed in, knocking one of the lobby chairs over. She righted it, with a loud, "Fuck! Goddamn it!"

The office door was ajar, so Cotton watched, eyebrows knitted. This was a completely different Gray from the silent, depressed woman who started therapy less than two months ago. Now she exhibited some manic tendencies, vacillating from almost non-responsive to this volcanic explosion of expletives.

Behind her, two pre-teens. *Marcus and Cherylynn.*

Cotton rose to greet them in the waiting room.

"I told you before we got here that there would be no games!" Gray shrieked. The blond girl with the wide-toothy grin, flicked her fingers 'hello' at Cotton. A younger boy, dark hair, and those fathomless blue eyes, wore a t-shirt decorated with a brontosaurus wearing a clown hat. He tucked his chin, dodging his mother's onslaught.

"Make sure you behave yourself." She pointed to the boy. "Sit over there, Marcus. Cherylynn, you stay in the lobby." Shooting both kids a last warning glance, her finger still pointed, Gray smiled tightly at Cotton. "Dr. Barnes, this is Marcus. He's eleven. Cherylynn, my youngest girl, is twelve, almost thirteen. They got out of school early to come to this appointment, so they're thinking that this is going to be fun. You can tell them otherwise. Tell them why they're here. They need to act like human beings, or else!"

Marcus arched his eyebrows and glanced at his mother, who fussed with his jacket, zipping it up and down. He shot his eyes to Cotton, then back to his mother, who barked more orders like a drill sergeant. Cotton nodded at him, winked, but he didn't respond. Cherylynn stood behind Gray, grinning delightedly at her brother as if enjoying that he's getting the tongue lashing and she's not.

Cotton checked her iPhone calendar. "Marcus has the 4 PM appointment."

"Yes, I know," Gray said, her attention finally taken from her son. "Cherylynn has homework to do so she can sit in the lobby and do it while her brother's in with you, then you can switch. He has homework, too. You both do what Dr. Barnes tells you. I'll be back by 6, okay?"

"I can't allow unaccompanied children in the lobby." Out of the corner of her eye, Cotton saw Cherylynn already establishing a place for herself on the lobby's tweedy couch, settling in, spreading out.

Gray stood right in front of Cotton, and for the first time, Cotton noticed the violet half-circles framing Gray's eyes, and they reminded her she and Gray were the same age.

"Oh Lord, I have a dentist's appointment. I've been waiting almost a month to get in." Gray's voice was full of panic. "Crap. They're going to do a cleaning, and I know it'll take only an hour, and I'll be back in plenty of time to pick them up. They'll be good, I promise." A slight pause. She waited a moment for Cotton to object, but quickly added, "If you say they can't... maybe I can get someone to bring Cheryl back, but I don't know who ...." She sputtered, pausing mid-sentence, standing like a stork, one leg up as if ready to take a step, her cell phone raised in the air like an antenna.

It's obvious she's anxious, but her stance was comical, and Cotton choked back a laugh. The woman was as endearing as she was confusing, but her kids seemed to find her irritating.

"I don't know what to do." Gray sighed and plopped down on the oak chair she'd knocked over earlier. Defeated. If a blue jay's feather dropped on her shoulder right now, she'd probably collapse.

"Go. We'll deal with it this once," Cotton said, though the rollercoaster driving through the pit of her stomach told her she was taking a big gamble. Sometimes rules had to be broken for the sake of keeping a client from breaking down. "Just this once," she repeated. Hopefully, some time alone may help ease Gray Prescott's stress.

After their mother left in a cloud of "don't forget to" and "you'd better behave," Cotton asked Cherylynn if she needed anything before bringing Marcus into her office.

As she closed the door, she watched him assess the space. Marcus was slim, almost to the point of being skinny. His elbows stuck out of his torn shirt like twin missiles ready to launch in both directions. His hair—a warm chestnut color and fine texture—flopped over his forehead, covering one eye. His father's eyes.

She did her usual introductory spiel, but he aimlessly wandered the room, touching everything, picking up the magazines next to her desk, pulling open her file drawers. ("That's private," she told him.) Finally, he settled down into the leather chair next to the couch, the furthest away from where she sat.

"Marcus, are you into soccer? Online games? I have a nephew your age. He loves something called AI-Evolution."

He nodded without looking at her or answering, his attention still scattered around the room.

"I see you're curious."

Sticking his hands under his legs, he rocked back and forth. "Yup."

"Do you mind if I ask you a few questions?"

"Sure. No prob."

"So, tell me about the game you're playing." Cotton nodded at what he held in his lap and smiled. Maybe she could institute some play therapy and make a whole session work. It would be a first for this family.

"It's just a Flame Game Boy. Nothin' much. The games I really like are online. Y'know, WarCraft, mostly. Sometimes, AI. Then there's Draco ..." He put his finger on his chin and looked up at the ceiling, cool and studied, as if he was aware he knew more than Cotton, this adult, this therapist, and he wasn't going to reveal any secrets. She wondered what he was thinking.

"I don't know too much about online games," she admitted. "Guess I have a lot to learn. So, you and your father play?"

"My dad and I have fun. Had fun." He sniffed and swiped at his nose, using the past tense verb as if he'd already accepted his father was gone. Then he unexpectedly let loose with some sobs. Loud, wet sobs. He gasped back the emotion, as if talking about his dad made it real. Pulling his T-shirt up, he wiped his nose with it.

"It's okay to cry, Marcus. Hey, don't worry. It's okay." She handed him the tissue box, and he took it, tucked it next to him, but continued to use his T-shirt sleeve instead. "Tell me about your dad." *What makes Marcus want to hide?* He hadn't met her eyes, burrowing into the chair as deeply as a mole.

"My dad... he... he taught me how to play WarCraft. Pretty cool game. Dad and I, we were in the same guild, so we played together all the time." He stopped and looked at her before reaching for the tissue box. He wiped his nose and tucked the used tissue into his pocket. "Sometimes we would go up into the attic, y'know? And he'd be on one computer, and I'd be on the other one. Mom used to get sooo upset 'cuz we'd be gone for hours. When we made our avatars, he... he told me that... he told me I could be anyone I wanted. That was dope. Sometimes we were monsters. Sometimes we were... oh, crap! I didn't want that to happen!" He thumped the red Nintendo unit in his hand, and it fell to the floor. He didn't make any moves to pick it up. "Crap!"

"What happened? Did you lose?"

"Yeah. Stupid game anyway." He kicked the Game Boy with the toe of his sneaker. His cheeks reddened, and his fists clenched.

"Well, let's talk more about the ones online. They sound pretty cool. Tell me more about the avatars you created. Did you just stick with one, or did you use several?"

He nudged the Game Boy one more time, then eyed Cotton as if not sure he still wanted to talk. She nodded and smiled, then waited for his answer.

"I like to switch around," he said finally. "Dad always used one, but I had this one that I made, he's a Blood Elf, and another time, I was real lucky because I was a Death Knight. He was really cool, could kill some of the other beings with his icy touch." He hissed, then snapped his fingers as if imitating the Death Knight. "I called him Higlar the Powerful! Man, he was *ugggggly*, and I got so many pieces of armor and everything that I was like... winning all the time."

"Sounds like you must've been proud of yourself."

"Dad told me that was pretty cool. But he used to say that being a Druid was the best. You could always be ahead of everyone else, y'know? Beat them up, then take off and change into something else so no one can find you. Sometimes I'd even change it to be a girl." He peered at her from beneath his hair, then flipped it back. "Mom says that's what Dad did. He changed into a girl. That must mean he's not my dad anymore. Is that true?"

"Your dad's still your dad." Cotton paused and let that sink in for a moment. Hailey had made it clear she wanted to remain "Dad, no matter what." Perhaps there'd been no chance for her to tell the kids that news yet. "I can tell you more about transgendered people, if you like, or you can ask your dad."

"Have you seen him?" Marcus's shoulders round down as if this isn't the first time he has had to deal with life.

"Yes, I have, but I can't tell you anything more about what he says to me, just like I won't be able to tell anyone else about what you and I talk about."

"So, you're under some kind of code of silence or something?"

"Something like that."

"Oh. Cool." He smiled and nodded, as if she'd passed some kind of test in his eyes.

"Tell me more about your avatar. Do you enter another world or something?" If he created a being that he wanted to emulate, maybe it would offer some insight about how he thought and felt about himself.

"Sorta. It's a lot of worlds. Lots and lots of people." Marcus's face lit up. Again, he pushed a strand of hair out of his eyes. "Wizards, magicians, monsters. Lots of quests. I've even gotten to one of the highest levels, but Dad's much better than me. He's really, really good at it. He likes imagining things. Guess that comes from being a writer, huh?" He lifted his chin a little, as if proud of his father being a writer. "My other avatar—I call him Nyphon—he's one of the best on raids, but Dad had this knight he used to use, and sometimes he got really into it, the game, I mean, and he could beat everybody and go from realm to realm like it was nothin'." He let out a deep evil laugh like one of his characters might use.

Cotton laughed along with him, encouraged that he had a sense of humor. "Do you play this game with anyone else?"

"Yeah! Millions of people play this game! All over the world! Sometimes we play with these guys from Japan. And sometimes some kids at school play. My friend Keelon plays all the time. He sits behind me in homeroom. There's a bunch of kids who play."

"Is your dad still playing? Do you see him online?"

"I look for him all the time, but he hasn't been there lately." Marcus's voice softened, the animation in his eyes fading.

"Do you miss him?"

"Is that a trick question?"

"No, of course not."

"Then why are you asking me? You gonna tell my mom?"

"Marcus, I already told you that anything you say in here I can't repeat to anyone else."

This time, he didn't respond. He lifted the red Game Boy and turned it on again. Cotton waited another moment. The Game Boy beeped and whistled. Obviously, Marcus had no intention of relinquishing it. She was losing him.

"Can you take a break from the game for a minute to tell me what you're feeling, Marcus?" In a lot of respects, play therapy or anything resembling it was the toughest on therapists. You had to be "on" and ready to shift gears at any point in the session, and as much as she struggled with that, she had treated a fair number of clients under the age 16. Brighton had loved playing Covet Fashion, and Cotton joined her occasionally. When they played, Cotton felt she could get through. *But it wasn't enough. Never enough.*

"Not feeling nothin'," Marcus answered.

"Do you want to talk some more about your dad?"

"No... not really. But, yeah, I miss him. I miss him a lot." He sniffled.

"How does that feel? To miss your dad?"

"Crappy." He sniffed again and reached for another tissue. His eyelashes lifted, revealing a child rather than a boy on the verge of becoming a pre-teen.

"I'm sorry, Marcus. How does 'crappy' feel?"

"CRAPPY!" He kicked at the rug.

"Crappy sad? Crappy crazy? Crappy horrible?"

"Yeah, all of them."

"It's okay to cry, Marcus. And it's okay to tell me how you feel right now."

"I don't wanna cry."

"Sometimes crying is the only way we can kind of release the steam we build up inside. Kind of like when you open a bag of microwave popcorn, and all that hot stuff comes out. We need to do that every once in a while. Release all that steam."

"People around my house do that a lot."

"Release the steam?

"Yeah, Mom's always crying. Or yelling."

"Does that bother you?"

He started fooling with the game again. Cotton knew she was pushing a bit, but until she sensed he was pushing back, she determined to keep on pursuing him, getting him to open up. It appeared this inability to relate was a Prescott family trait, something he learned how to do to survive.

"Marcus?"

"Yeah?"

"Does it feel better to play the game than to talk to me?"

"Yeah, I don't really wanna talk anymore."

"Well, that's okay, because our time's up, anyway. I've got to see your sister, but I'd like you to come in again. If your mother agrees, we'll make an appointment."

"Can I talk about my dad?"

"Absolutely."

"Can I see him?"

"We can talk about that."

"Okay." He gathered his stuff and scuffed toward the door, his head down, the game making its pinging sounds.

"Thanks for telling me about the avatars and the games," Cotton called to him.

He turned and laughed, and there was a glimmer of the innocent young boy he should have the chance to be. "You're a noob!" he told her.

After her door closed, Cotton Googled the term Marcus used: *noob. Someone new to the game, specifically WarCraft,* the online definition reads.

Accurate. She was beginning to feel like she was new to the game of life, particularly as defined by the Prescotts.

~ Book Eight ~

Cherylynn Prescott

We cannot say that if a child is badly nourished, he will become a criminal. We must see what conclusion the child has drawn.
—Alfred Adler

"You look like your brother." Cotton said. "You have the same eyes." She gestured for Cherylynn to come in, then waited for her to settle. Without hesitation, Cherylynn walked to the rocker and immediately started moving it back and forth.

Outside, the streetlights flickered to life, and a dusky, winter-violet light softened the bare limbs of the gigantic oaks lining the neighborhood. Despite being in downtown Raleigh, the area was quiet, the side streets populated by turn-of-the-century cottages repurposed for use as medical centers, yoga studios, and an occasional coffee place. If she and Thomas ever wanted to leave the house on the river, she would happily move into one of the neighborhoods near her office. Especially at moments like these. It was Cotton's favorite time of day. She stirred in the honey into her afternoon cup of tea and settled into a comfortable spot to wait for Cherylynn.

Unlike Marcus, Cherylynn dressed immaculately, right down to the purple and pink shoelaces wound through her bright white Converse high-tops—shoelaces that matched the vibrantly colored t-shirt emblazoned with Taylor Swift's latest album cover. Though

Cherylynn's ginger-brown hair swung around her shoulders much longer than her brother's, it was the same curly-silky texture. It surprised Cotton that the children looked nothing like Janis, their older sibling, though they all shared the same startlingly blue eyes. Maybe it was Janis's tendency toward heavy black eyeliner, or it was the width of her nose or that she tightened her lips, making her mouth smaller.

Cherylynn smiled openly at Cotton, a light on her face that made her seem innocent and approachable. Friendly. "I know the drill already. Mom and Janis told me. Sure, you can video the appointments, and yes, I give you permission to do whatever else you need to. I know you won't say anything to anyone else, and what I say to you is a secret, so let's not waste any time!" Her words ended with an up-the-scale giggle that appeared more humorous than nervous. "You've seen my father already, right? Has he said anything about us? Does he care about what's going on at home? My mother says he's weirding out on us. I think he started a long time ago." She giggled again, as if she and Cotton were already girlfriends, and she was telling Cotton about the kid in homeroom she had a crush on.

"Yes, he's been here."

"Oh." She moved over to the couch and grabbed a pillow, hugging it into her chest, studying Cotton over the top of it. "Doesn't he have to see you every week, too?"

"That's up to him. People come to see me when they're ready. I can't make them."

"Why do people want to talk to you? They could come talk to me!" She popped up and went to the window, poking her fingers through the blinds and pulling them apart for a good look before coming back to her seat. All within a second or two. She grinned at Cotton.

"They come to me because I've been specially trained to help them."

"So, you're a doctor?"

"Yes, I am." Cotton shifted in her chair and pretended to hunt for a blank piece of paper. *Why was this child so intimidating? Why did she make me nervous?* "So, it seems like you want to talk. That's good. As for your father, I won't be able to tell you about our conversations. I don't repeat anything. Ever."

"Sure. I bet you don't." Cherylynn swung her right leg over the arm of the chair and fiddled with her hair. "I'm sure you're going to tell my mother everything I say in here. You already talked to Janis, huh?" The giggle again. She wasn't being a smart-ass. She joked with Cotton as if they'd known each other forever. It was disarming. Yet, textbook middle child syndrome. She adapted to please people, but her self-confidence surprised Cotton.

"Yes, I did," Cotton replied.

"Everyone thinks they know how everyone else thinks in this family. No one knows what I'm thinking, though." She blinked her eyes several times, as if she had the superhuman capability to send her thoughts. Or at least, she was trying to do so. "Do you want to know?"

"Sure, I'd love to. Anything you want to share with me about yourself is important. I would like to understand how you feel."

"My mom took down all of Dad's pictures. I'm kinda hot about that." She laughed again, this time a one-note, nervous laugh, instead of the delight Cotton had heard earlier. "And Janis told me she didn't want to talk to you. She said she just gave you her UrPlace account." Cherylynn twisted a button at the top of her jeans. "What if I don't want to talk to you?" This time, she didn't punctuate the comment with a giggle. In an instant, she went from open and affable to completely shuttered. Here was the middle child Cotton expected to see.

"That's up to you, but it must be lonely with no one to understand. Might be easier to come here and have someone to talk to."

She snapped her gum. "Yeah, I guess it would... But I have some questions."

"Like what?"

"First of all, what's transgender anyway?"

"Good question, and I'm glad you're asking. People who are transgender feel like they were born into the wrong body. Like they are pretending to be something they're not. Usually, what they feel on the inside...is not the same as what everyone sees on the outside. Some people say it's like you're wearing a Halloween costume all the time. When transgender people finally take off the costume they've been wearing their whole life and start wearing the clothing and looking like the person they truly feel themselves to be, they become much happier. They feel normal."

Cherylynn screwed up her face. "That's just downright weird. I don't understand that at all. Why would you pretend to be someone you're not?"

"Another good question. Well, how about considering this? Think about how you see yourself. Do you think of yourself as better or worse than your friends? Do you compare yourself to them? Or to someone else?"

She shook her head hard enough to whip her hair across her face.

"That's a definite no, huh?" Cotton said. "Okay, let's think about it this way: do you think you're pretty smart?"

"Yeah, I think I'm okay. I mean, I get good grades and everything."

"Then your image of yourself, how you feel in here--" Cotton pointed to Cherylynn's heart space "--is pretty clear, right?"

"I guess so."

"Do you think everyone else sees you the same way you see yourself?"

Cherylynn paused, considered the question for a second, looking to the ceiling. "Uh-uh, no way. My mother's always telling me how beautiful I am, but I don't think so. And who cares anyway? And my father, I'm not sure ...." She stopped short, her breath stolen.

"Yes?"

"It's not important what he thinks."

"Why not?"

"If he thought I was important, he'd still be around." She pushed the pillow she'd been holding to her chest aside and leaned forward, elbows on her knees, chin in her hand. Sure of herself and of her standing in the family. Typical middle child.

Again, Cotton found herself wanting to correct Cherylynn, to tell her that Hailey preferred to addressed as she/her, but Hailey needed to make that announcement herself. *It needs to be soon.*

"Have you talked to your father?"

"Not really."

"It must be hard when you have all these questions."

"A little. But we text every once in a while."

That surprised Cotton a bit. Cherylynn was the only one in the family who had any contact with Hailey at all. "How do you feel about that? Just texting, I mean."

"It sucks. It's not the same as seeing him every day." She hugged the pillow more tightly, as if transferring her anger to that inanimate object. But no matter how hard she hugged that pillow, she kept a bright smile on her face. *Competing pieces of body language. Confusion.*

"But how does that *feel*? Can you tell me? How would you be feeling if you saw him every day?"

"I dunno ...."

"Okay, how about we pretend I'm your father? Tell your dad what you did today. Share something you would have said if... if your father... still lived with you."

Cherylynn laughed and shrugged, a suddenly shy expression on her face. Her eyes shifted to the side, and she scrunched up her mouth. In that moment, she appeared like an elf, mischievous and curious, with bright eyes and perked up ears. She cocked her head.

"You're looking at me like I'm crazy. It's okay. We're just role-playing. Acting. It's safe to do that here. You can tell me anything you want. Just pretend it's your father sitting here instead of me."

Another nervous laugh. "What do you want me to say?"

"Whatever you want to. Tell your father whatever you want him to know. Or ask him a question. Anything goes."

Silence. She chewed strands of hair, never taking her eyes off Cotton. Again, she popped up and poked her fingers through the shades at the window. Just as quickly, she came back to the chair and pointed a finger.

"Okay. The big question. The one everyone wants the answer to. Why did he leave us?"

"Ask him. Not me." Cotton pointed to the empty chair. "Pretend that's him."

"Okay, Daaaad." Cherylynn's voice went up an octave. She was humoring Cotton, poking fun at the process. "Why did you leave *us*?"

"Good question. Now, pretend you're him and answer it."

"How can I do that?" She looked askance at Cotton as if convinced she had lost her mind.

"You know him, right? He's been your dad your whole life. Imagine how he would answer your question. What would your father say if he was sitting right there?" It felt so wrong to use the masculine pronoun, but how else would Cotton be able to continue the conversation?

Cherylynn flipped the pillow up in the air. "This is crazy."

"Maybe, but what do you think the answer would be?"

"I'm not sure...."

"Well, let's try something else then. How would you *like* your father to answer that question?"

Pulling at the pink laces on her high tops, Cherylynn ducked her head and said, "I want him to say he's sorry and that he's coming back, that he didn't mean what he wrote to Mom, and that he'll be my dad. Always." Big sobs came from the bottom of her stomach. This child might not be the one to demand answers, but at least she was more vocal than her siblings.

"Go on...here, take a Kleenex."

"But I want to know... I want to know... whether he... whether he still loves me. Did I do something wrong?" She twined her fingers together tightly.

Cotton wanted to probe a little more, but it was too soon. Cherylynn was obviously fragile. She fidgeted, lifting her sneaker to her knee, and playing with the laces again. Then she cried again, and she leaned against the corner of the couch as if in need of support. "No one's around anymore. Mom's always... working. Dad's gone. Janis is with the high school kids." She parsed her words with a weariness

Cotton often saw in older patients. A look of resignation. It was obvious she thought a lot about her parents and that she felt frustrated, tired of dealing with the situation that she and her siblings found themselves in, but she couldn't do anything about it. Her face shifted as if a feeling of defeat crept over her. The adolescent anger that had flashed earlier dissipated, and she became that scared twelve-year-old girl in the middle of a traumatic situation that she simply doesn't understand, nor can she control it.

In a split second, Cotton saw Cherylynn's future as clearly as if looking through a pane of glass. Throughout the next couple of years, things would transform. Her father would slowly become a woman, and she and her siblings would mourn the loss of their old father, but they'd gain a new female family member, one they would learn to accept or understand as a replacement for Dad. They would explain the disappearance of their old dad to friends, schoolmates, teachers, and other relatives. They would intimately understand the meanings of words like transgender, gender dysphoria, hormone blockers, transition surgery. They would listen to arguments between their parents about many things, they'd renegotiate visiting rights, they'd see the family struggle to redefine their roles. They might even have to deal with never seeing their father again. Or all the above and more.

Already, Cherylynn saw a family divided by their father's need to follow his own life. On top of all the changes to her family identity, Cherylynn would navigate her own changes as she moved from adolescence into womanhood, and maybe she would have more in common with her father during that tender period in her life than at any other.

"Are you saying that you feel like he doesn't love you?" Cotton asked.

"If he did, he would've stayed, wouldn't he?"

"Leaving doesn't mean that the person doesn't love us, Cherylynn. Sometimes it just means that they don't know what else to do. Or maybe they just need to figure things out for themselves." Cotton paused and checked whether Cherylynn believed, but she couldn't tell because Cherylynn had tucked her head between her knees. "Do you want to see him?"

"I didn't think I did, but now maybe I've changed my mind." Her muffled voice sounded petulant. "But it doesn't matter. Mom won't let us see him, anyway. She thinks it's better if we stay away from him. Calls him weird."

"How do you feel about that?"

She punched the pillow. "I'm pissed. But maybe it's okay that we don't see him because I'm pissed at him, too. Parents suck!"

There's no child on earth who hasn't felt that way at one point or another. Still, the words chilled Cotton. "Sometimes they do. Sometimes we all suck!"

Cherylynn giggled delightedly with Cotton this time, then they both fell silent. For a moment, the only sound in the room was the slight rumble the laptop made.

"How are you feeling?" Cotton wanted to tell Cherylynn how well she worked in today's session, how proud she was of the deep questions Cherylynn's able to face, but for now, *keep it simple. There'd be plenty of time for more discussion later.*

"I'm all right, I guess," Cherylynn answered.

"Are you okay enough to leave? Our time's up."

"Not really, but if I have to ...." She hugged the pillow tighter, as if unwilling to let go of the comfort it had brought in the past hour.

"We can see each other again, Cherylynn."

"Okay. And you won't tell my mom what I said?"

"Promise."

"Can you talk to my dad and tell him we want him to come home?"

"Maybe you can do that yourself."

In the waiting room, Gray and Marcus sat on opposite chairs. Both rose when the office door opened and created a small flurry as the three of them left the office. Cotton walked them to the door and watched them go, feeling that the Prescotts were like opening Pandora's box.

More and more shadowy, emotional curses released with each family member's story. It would take all her powers as a therapist to bring this family to some kind of acceptance and understanding of themselves and how they related to one another. With a hand to her lower stomach, she wondered whether she was up to the challenge.

~ Book Nine ~

Cotton Barnes

"I believe in everything until it's disproved.

So, I believe in faeries, the myths, dragons.

It all exists, even if it's in your mind.

Who's to say that dreams and nightmares aren't as real as the here and now?"

— John Lennon

Cotton slid behind the wheel and sat for a moment before hitting the ignition. It was Saturday morning, and her list of errands had been long, but now she only had one left: to drop off the bags of used clothing and household goods at the Goodwill Box on Falls of Neuse Road. She'd met with her therapist, Dr. Carbinetti at 8 AM, and at 10, picked up a pair of glasses at the optometrist's office, swung over to Starbucks for a cup of hot mocha before continuing to CVS for Thomas's sinus prescription, and finally, to the dry cleaner to drop off the wool coat stained during last month's trip to the Outer Banks. Cotton hadn't found it funny that a seagull deposited its load on her new red coat, but Thomas insisted the look on her face was priceless. "Besides, it's good luck, too, isn't it? Bird poop on your head?"

Carbinetti had applauded her ability to get back to work slowly, one family at a time. He never asked about the Prescotts, even though other therapists might have pushed it, particularly since he'd once considered her a suicide risk. It took a concerted effort to convince him she would not make that choice. I'd call you first, she promised. That satisfied him. Today's session felt like a win, of sorts. Toward the end of the hour, they ran out of subjects, so Cotton promised she'd make up the time when she had more to discuss. When you don't talk about the most interesting part of your life, there's not much else to fill up the time. If she could have told him about the Prescotts, she'd still be there. If he had asked whether she was having flashbacks to that day, they'd still be talking. But she hadn't, and now it was a gorgeous day for opening the roof.

She checked her watch, satisfied that she still had time to swing by Deb's and finish the dregs of her Starbucks before heading home. She'd still arrive earlier than Thomas, who'd left with his golf clubs before she finished breakfast. Obviously, he needed some time with the guys, and that was fine with her. He wasn't the best at joining her for errands, watching the time as if he had an appointment with the president, and never saw the benefit in checking the sales tables at Barnes and Noble, so she'd rather go alone, anyway. Having a day apart had been one way they learned how to appreciate each other in their marriage. She relished an hour or two apart, even if it was simply doing errands.

She turned the radio up, blaring her Spotify 'Road Trip' playlist, and rolled the roof back so she could sing at the top of her lungs. Sometimes that was the only way to clear her mind of the thoughts that repeatedly rolled around in her brain, the fears that were unfounded and often confusing, and the worries that she'd forgotten to do something. All part and parcel of what she'd dealt with for years: anxiety, obsession, stress. She knew how to handle her neuroses, though she hated them with passion, and often complained to Dr. Carbinetti that singing loudly gave her an acceptable opportunity to scream away her frustrations. Sometimes, she even had fun doing so, especially after an intense therapy session like this morning's when Dr. C repeatedly asked her how it felt to be back at work, and she said it was great, though she felt frustrated. No idea why. She just didn't feel like it.

The traffic around the intersection where 540 met Falls of Neuse slowed for the lights, and the dove-haired woman in the next car glanced over cautiously when Cotton sang along with Katy Perry's "Peacock." When the light changed, Cotton adjusted her sunglasses and pressed the BMW's gas pedal a little too hard and the car launched forward, the tires squealing. She laughed for a moment afterward, then settled into the song again, thinking about what she needed to do at home before Thomas would be back and they'd start cooking dinner.

At the next light, she thrummed her fingers on the wheel and casually glanced left. The parking lot at Goodman's, the conservative high school the Prescott kids attended, overflowed with soccer mom SUVs, and in the middle of the field closest to the road, a soccer game was in full play. Cotton watched as girls burst out of a huddle and scrambled around the ball, passing it back and forth with fluttering kicks and head bumps. Something about the way the girl on the right pulled at her jersey and shifted back and forth made Cotton look more closely.

Cherylynn Prescott.

She spurted forward with strong legs, as if she'd been playing all her life, and as the team chased her down the field, protecting her, blocking for her, she launched her shot at the goal and raised both arms in the air when the ball shot flew past the goalie, bouncing into the back net. A resounding shout from the people on the field, and the team surrounded Cherylynn.

She's the star.

Behind her, a horn sounded. Cotton pulled the car into the school's parking lot, her palms a little sweaty. What would she do if the Prescotts were there in full force? What would she do if Cherylynn spotted her? She parked in a spot close enough to the field to see the game, but not close enough to be recognized. Turning the radio down, she caught sight of herself in the mirror, her curly blonde hair recognizable from the moon. Grabbing Thomas's Durham Bulls ball cap from the back seat, she shoved her hair inside, pushed her sunglasses snug on her face and sank into the driver's seat to watch *just for a few minutes.* As the teams regrouped, she scanned the audience, and it didn't take more than a few seconds to spot Gray sitting by herself in a lawn chair at the other end of the field. But she didn't see any other Prescotts.

For the next fifteen minutes, Cherylynn led the team back and forth on the field, and from the excited yells from the Goodman's side, points accumulated. Cotton knew next to nothing about sports, but she knew how much a kid's confidence could be boosted or shattered on a playing field. From the looks of what was happening, this was Cherylynn's domain. The other players sought her out regularly, asking her for advice on a play, and they followed her directions. Trusting her because of her obvious self-confidence.

Watching Cherylynn interact with others outside the office was worth three years of therapy appointments. People rarely describe what they do, how they interact, what they're like in different situations, particularly because they don't see themselves from the outside. When they're totally being themselves, it feels as though the door opens to the person's psyche. Vaguely illicit.

When the players left the field, Cherylynn followed her team, glancing briefly to wave in her mother's direction. Gray lifted a hand. Even at this distance, Cotton could tell that Gray wore the same stained hoodie she'd worn to the office yesterday, her hair piled haphazardly on her head. She did not speak to the other parents yelling for their kids. It wasn't a big surprise that Gray was doing the bare minimum. Cotton had recommended she see her general practitioner for the proper depression medication. She made a mental note to ask Gray whether she'd been able to get an appointment.

At least she's here.

~ Book Ten ~

Hailey and Gray Prescott

People not only gain understanding through reflection, they evaluate and alter their own thinking.
—Albert Bandura

Hailey bustled into the office, chattering as she shrugged off the black wool trench she wore over a blue-and-white striped shirtwaist dress like a 1950s homemaker, low black heels, and a wig almost the same color as her own hair, yet shoulder-length, curled and shiny. Pancake foundation covered her face, though in the light from the wide office windows, a five o'clock shadow defined her jaw. Cotton quickly calculated how long it would take for the beard to stop growing so vigorously. Another couple of months, at least, until Hailey's features would soften, her hair would lengthen but her facial hair would stop growing, and after another year, she might have progressed to estrogen therapy, developing some breast tissue. Cotton noted on her yellow pad to talk about Hailey's progress during their next individual session.

Hailey crossed one slim stockinged leg over the other, aligning her black heels carefully together. The shirtwaist rustled softly when she smoothed it with Pepto-pink painted fingernails, pressing the dress down over her thighs, ironing it with her hands to control the crinoline petticoat underneath. *So retro.* She seemed pleased with herself, smiling slightly as she glanced down at her own legs, then she casually reached for something out of the black purse she carried over her arm.

On the other side of the room, Gray, in jeans and the same food-stained Duke sweatshirt she'd worn during their last couple of meetings, her frizzy hair up in a clip, settled into the chair as far away from Hailey as she could get. She didn't make eye contact, say hello, or express any kind of interest in either Cotton or Hailey.

Cotton took a deep breath and *inserts smile*. "Thank you both for coming. Are you comfortable? Need anything? Water? Tea or coffee?"

Gray nodded. "I'm fine. Brought my own bottle." She lifted a bottle emblazoned with the Enquiring Mind logo and plunked it on the side table with more enthusiasm than necessary.

"Thanks, Dr. B, but I'm perfect." Hailey fluttered her fingers. "Just finished a big, iced tea a few moments ago. I believe I've had my liquids for the day. I'll tell you what: Bojangles iced tea is way too sugary for me! Why do they have to make it so sweet it curls your hair?" She chattered too much. Her voice, high-pitched and shaky.

Averting her head, Gray took a sudden interest in the small Chrystal Hardt landscape on the opposite wall. Cotton had chosen the painting specifically because of its pastel peacefulness. Gray stared as if it was the Mona Lisa.

All the while, Hailey continued idly chatting to no one in particular about the weather being cooler, how the football game this weekend is going to be packed since it's leading into the Super Bowl playoffs, and that she hopes the kids are good because she misses them. Her voice cracks a little.

Finally, the chatter stopped when Hailey realized no one else was talking. She and Gray shared sidelong glances but wouldn't look at each other directly in the eye.

"You look fucking ridiculous," Gray muttered, pulling the hoodie up over her head like one of her teenaged kids.

The comment dropped into the conversation like a chemical bomb. Cotton, taken off-guard, watched Hailey's eyes fill and her cheeks redden.

"Never let my kids see you like that." Gray's mouth twisted as if she'd tasted something venomous.

"Let's set some ground rules here," Cotton interjected before the conversation went further, knowing that if she didn't exert control, this first meeting could quickly become their last. "How about we start over? Let's save the emotional conversation for after we're all clear about how this will work. Okay?"

Both Hailey and Gray nodded like school children.

"Well, the way I usually start is by setting a couple of simple goals. That okay?"

Again, they nodded.

"The reason I asked you both here is that usually when a family goes through therapy, we bring the parents in together to talk," Cotton started, taking her time, and checking in with each of them. Nodding as she spoke. "Alone. No kids. This won't be easy. Sometimes we need to agree to disagree to help your family heal. I have known you now for about one month, and throughout this time, if there's one thing I know for sure is that you both love your kids." She paused and took a moment to nod at both. They were nodding back at her. *Good start.*

"As I see it, the work of psychoanalysis is to get to the deepest truth of your life story." *How much of this have I already said? They're still nodding. Keep going.* "When telling our life story, each of us imposes our own form on the story. We tell it the way we want to. What I'd like to do today is to briefly talk about your relationship with each other, but I'd also like to discuss your expectations for the children. Then, we can outline a plan for working together. Deal?"

Cotton sipped her tea, inhaling the deep, minty fragrance, then she put the cup down, smiled at both, and said, "Let's see what we can concentrate on moving forward, okay?"

"That's all I've ever wanted, just a conversation, a start," Hailey said. "I really would like to have some time with the kids to explain what's happening with me. Marc and I still play WarCraft, and I can see what he's doing when we're in the guild, but I haven't talked to him face-to-face. And I'd like to do the same with Janis and Cherylynn. Cherylynn and I have texted, but I would love to see her. Give her a hug. I want to come to her games again." Hailey slid her eyes away from Gray to

Cotton as if begging for the cavalry to ride in and save her. She was probably right to be nervous.

With a huff, Gray turned in her chair, her rigid back to Hailey. "I can't even think about that right now. If that's what we're here for, then I need to go home." Gray balled her hands into fists and stuffed them in the hoodie's kangaroo pocket.

"Let's backtrack for a minute here." Cotton knew that if she tapped into Gray's simmering anger right away, she'd lose both, and Gray looked about to explode. "It appears you two really haven't discussed your feelings about the marital split since the day you found the note, Gray, so maybe we should start there. I'm curious about how you felt when you wrote the note, Hailey, and how you felt when you got it, Gray. Maybe talking about that can get us to a point where we can at least understand each other's feelings about that moment. One moment at a time."

Silence. A crow cawed. Several cars passed by. The vintage alarm clock on Cotton's desk ticked into the hour. A small moth hovered between windowpanes in the window behind Gray. Cotton watched the moth, but in her peripheral vision, she saw Gray working through her decision, her mouth pursed, teeth tightly clamped. *What's going through her mind?* Wishing (as she often did) that a foolproof way existed to teach clients how to talk honestly without hurting each other. Even brilliant nuclear physicists sucked at communication.

"I'm trying my best to support my kids." Gray jutted her chin forward, her eyes dark. "They didn't buy into this. Their world has shaken ..." She stared hard at Hailey, eye to eye for the first time. "They're shaken to the core."

Hailey shifted in her seat, wiped her eyes. Unable to speak.

"You can talk all you want about your pronouns and your identity-this and gender-that, but you don't seem to see that it's all about you. What about the kids? *My* kids? What about them? Did you think about what they'd go through? What about *me*?"

"That's why I removed myself! I love my kids, and I have always loved my wife. You." Hailey stared at Gray, a half-smile lifting the corner of her mouth. As if to reassure, she reached out a hand, then as if immediately realizing that would not be the best idea, she pulled her fingers back into a fist and placed it back in her lap. "I've never stopped. You're the most incredible woman I've ever met."

Gray passed a dramatic hand over her forehead. "Kill me now."

Cotton ignored the comment, looking instead at Hailey. "Tell Gray that, Hailey. Talk to her directly. I'm sure there's lots you need to tell her."

Hailey hesitated, as if uninterested in getting shot down again. "I'm no good at talking. I do so much better when I write it out."

"No, you don't." Gray raked her fingers through her frazzled hair. "You just take the easy way out by putting stuff down on paper that you're too chicken to say to my face."

"Guess I deserved that."

Nodding and crossing her arms over her chest, Gray huffed once more. She looked just like Janis, impenetrable and miserable.

"Okay, let me try again." Hailey gripped the handle of her Michael Kors bucket bag and placed both feet in vertical alignment, perfectly even, flat on the floor. She tilted her nose down at the polished black leather pumps with their sturdy heels and spoke. "I'm not perfect, Gray, and I admit that the way I handled this was not right, but I really thought at the time that it was the best decision. Lord knows, living the way I have has forced me to push a lot of things aside and to try... to kind of... guess how people feel. I'm afraid all my strength is going inward right now. Concentrating on me. Going through tough changes."

Hailey released her hold on her pocketbook and wrung her hands as if she'd been clenching them so tightly, her fingers had gone numb, then pushed them down the sides of her dress. "I didn't do a good job with the person I thought I knew best: you. I always had this—what could I call it? Fantasy, I guess, that when I finally got the gumption to man up and say something, that you'd understand. But when the moment came, I just didn't have the guts. I didn't want any."

Exhaling, Hailey glanced guiltily at Cotton. "God, 'man up.' What an expression. I'm so sorry! But you get it, right?" She didn't wait for an answer, faced Gray again, this time positioning herself so that Gray had no choice but to look at her. "You've always been my best friend, Gray, the one I can count on knowing what's going through this dense meatloaf head of mine before I have the thought. Guess I was so caught up with worrying about myself that I didn't realize what I was going through was something you plain and simple wouldn't understand." She laughed. "Kind of ironic, huh?"

"How the hell can I understand that the guy I was married to isn't a guy at all, but a damn screwed up... screwed up half-and-half?" Gray shot her fists up toward the ceiling. "How could you possibly have expected me to understand *that*?" She paused, then her mouth dropped open. "He's shaking his head. You see that, Dr. Barnes? Like I'm the crazy one! He shakes his head!" She pointed to Hailey, laughed, a short and raspy wheeze, more scoff than giggle. "Did you think being married to me was going to fix it or something? Really? How fucking stupid can you get?" For a long burning moment, she focused a laser-beam stare on Hailey.

"Gray ...." Hailey warningly put up her hand.

"Don't give me the hand, damnit. You really thought being married would solve everything, didn't you? Give you a good screen to hide behind. A safe place where you'd have everything you needed. You thought you had it all worked out. Did you think about the kids, you dumb fuck? Did you think about what your choices would do to them?"

Hailey grimaced. "Actually, the thought did go through my mind. A lot. I thought that you and the kids would kind of keep what I felt at bay. I thought that maybe being a father was enough." She pulls a tissue from her purse and dabs at her eyes. "And soo many times I've felt that maybe time would just take care of... things. I don't know. Maybe what I felt was some kind of craziness on my part. And if I shared it with you or with anyone, the guys in the white suits would come for me. No offense, Dr. B."

"Maybe they should. I think you *need* to be put in the loony bin." Gray laughed again, only this time sadness and more than a little regret tinged the laughter. She blinked and looked away.

Cotton shifted her body in the chair purposefully to gain their attention. "Let's focus on talking about how we feel. Let's try to really listen to what the other person is saying, okay? How are you feeling right now, Gray? Can you describe the emotion?"

Gray started. "Which one? There's a ton of them. They're flying at me like machine gun pellets. I feel hurt, angry, betrayed, confused, abandoned. Want more?"

"Yes, I agree. Let's get them all out on the table. Talk about the hurt. Tell us when you feel that way."

"When he says he loved me." Her eyes glistened with unshed tears. "That hurts. How can you love someone and then turn around and leave? How can you love someone and never let them see who you really are?" Her questions punched holes in the office atmosphere. "Why even tell that person you love them? That fucking hurts even more. It's like they set me up from the beginning. It was all just one big lie. There-that's another emotion: betrayed." No longer able to hold back, she bent forward from the waist, sobbing hard.

Hailey reached a hand toward Gray, hovering above her back, the fingers shaking a little but not connecting with Gray's body. It's like there's an invisible force field around her. "It wasn't a lie that I love you, Gray. That's never been a lie." Hailey's hand lowered now, stroked Gray's back, moved through the force field.

"Don't touch me!" Gray slapped Hailey's hand away. "I made love to you. We had sex! Christ, Hayden! How could you do that if you thought you were the same gender I am? How could you? And what am I supposed to do now that you've dumped all this on me—on us? How am I supposed to move forward?" Glaring at Hailey for a moment, she squeezed her hands into fists again.

"Hayden's my dead name," whispered Hailey.

"I don't give a fuck whether it's dead or alive. What I care about is our kids... the kids don't understand a damn thing about all of this.

They're falling apart—*we* are falling apart. The Prescott family. But you're moving forward in your life, like *la-di-da*, going through this... this sex change, while the rest of us are trying to figure out whether we ever knew you!"

"I know," Hailey said. "I know. It's my fault."

Another uneasy silence falls in the room, but Cotton didn't allow it to last. She ran through her options. Pause the session and talk about boundaries? Ask Hailey to explain more to Gray? Request that they both listen to each other and parrot back what they'd heard? *So much for the plan to talk about family goals.* She reminded herself that sometimes it's okay to lose control of a session. What they're working through with very little coaching from her is far more important than setting goals, even though the conversation sizzled with frustration and anger.

"How does that make you feel, Hailey?"

Hailey's rapid eye movements, her body language, all screamed an anxiety level that was at an all-time high. *Time to dial things down or someone would have a heart attack.*

"Responsible. I feel like I need to take care of everything, of everyone. I'm just not sure about whether...."

"Not sure about what?"

"I'm not sure I've done the right thing."

"What could you have done otherwise, Hailey?"

"Probably just live with it, hide it, go out in secret. Just hide." She takes a deep breath, shakes her head as if at once negating the thought. "But I couldn't do that anymore. My whole life has been a lie. I just couldn't live like that. Not anymore. I want to be. I just want to be me." She pounded a fist against her chest, then tucked her hand back into her lap.

"What are you thinking? Don't you think that the kids are paying for this?" Gray spits her words. "Don't you realize the kids at school tease them? Or, even worse, ostracize them? Janis hasn't gone out of her room in days, and Marcus asked me what a Daddy-Mama was the other day. And if you don't think about the kids and about me, then what about you? Aren't you afraid of being beaten or made fun of? Killed, maybe? Everyone seems to have a gun these days, and you might as well wear a sandwich board. This," she waved at him with dismissive fingers, "is not something anyone understands. You're the neighborhood sicko now. No one's going to stand by you." Her lip curled up.

Cotton raised her hand, asked for no name calling.

"I have friends. There are some people who understand." Hailey protested weakly.

Gray laughed again, loudly, and forcibly. "People like you are not people at all! They're freaks, and they belong in a circus just like you!"

Cotton ducked her head and moaned, just loudly enough to warn Gray she'd gone over the line. The cruel insult clearly defined the level of Gray's pain. People strike out like animals when they're hurting.

Hailey jumped out of her chair, unsteady on her heels. "That's enough! I thought you might not understand, but I never thought you'd do this, Gray. No need to get nasty or to call names. Jesus! Maybe you don't think I'm the person you thought I was, but someday you'll realize that I did nothing purposefully to hurt you. Nothing. If anything, I've tried to keep it together for a long time just so we could avoid this. And this isn't what I deserve. This... this treatment. You can be angry all you want. Go ahead. Be angry, be hurt, be confused, but don't do this, Gray. Don't strike out at me like you hate me. This isn't the Gray I know."

"Like you're going to know me when you can't even define who you are!"

"I. Do. Know. Who. I. Am. I told you that, but you don't seem to want to listen, Gray." Hailey wobbled a little, held out a hand, then stabilized, drew her shoulders back. "What you're saying is that you never loved me for being who I am. The real me."

"Oh, gawd." Gray slapped a hand on her forehead. "You know what bothers me the most? You knew when you married me! You knew who you were, yet we had kids together! Did you think of them? How would this decision affect *their* lives? You obviously don't care about mine, but what about theirs?"

"I really... really didn't think ...."

"That's obvious!"

"No, I didn't think I would ever come out. You don't understand. I thought I was crazy. I knew this wasn't what everyone thinks of as normal. So, I didn't... I really didn't think I'd ever be able to do this—to be the person I am in here." Hailey patted her heart area. "I've always had to pretend to be what's on the outside. Really. Can you appreciate that, Gray? Can you imagine what it's like to pretend? Every day? I hate lying. You know that better than anyone." Hailey slid to the edge of her chair and reached toward Gray.

To Cotton's surprise, Gray didn't flinch, but she also didn't look Hailey in the eyes.

"Gray, I always loved you. I always will."

"Stop. Stop, stop, stop." Gray palmed both hands as though pushing away the very air that might have touched Hailey. "I never want to hear you say those words again."

"Okay, I get that, but I want to tell you that even while I struggled with my gender, I never questioned my relationship with you or my pride in our kids." Hailey dabbed at her eyes with a lace-trimmed hanky she'd pulled from her pocket. "Our kids, Gray. We made them. Both of us. Each of those kids have a mix of our DNA running through their bodies."

Gray was silenced.

So was Cotton.

Everyone stared at the walls, as if tapping into the strength they might still have within. Cotton should have jumped in, be the good therapist, but she wanted them to do this work on their own.

Finally, Gray looked at Hailey's hand and put her own atop it, but not in a friendly manner. She narrowed her eyes. "I'm not making any promises about the kids. I'll do what Cotton thinks is best for them. Not you."

Hailey moved her own hand, but Gray snatched hers away, as if warning she was not ready to go any further.

Their time was up. Cotton felt somewhat defeated because none of what she planned came to fruition, but she reminded herself that this difficult first stage of communication might lead them to a healthier arrangement with the kids. She made another appointment with them, then watched them leave: the tall and slender, conservatively dressed woman holding the door for the smaller woman, dressed in an outfit she'd wear to clean the garage.

Standing there, Cotton wondered whether some old habits would never end for Hailey.

~ Book Eleven ~

Cotton Barnes

The bedsheets rippled, a white tide of airborne cotton in the mid-morning light. It always felt a little sinful to make love with her husband before facing the day, especially if making love would make her day start late. That's what made it so good.

Cotton stretched her leg alongside Thomas's and pushed her back into him. His immediate response warmed her, and she reached for his head, pulling it to her shoulder.

"You want something, missy?" he whispered into her neck.

"Absolutely," she replied, guiding him between her legs.

His hair smelled of grass and whatever he'd used in the shower last night. He raised his head, his eyes so close to hers that she could see the viscous covering over his eyeball, but much better than that was the warm need that rose in his eyes whenever they made love. She called it his sexy scientist look, and it still turned her on after more than a decade.

She slid out of the long t-shirt that barely covered her and sighed when he pushed her hands up over her head and slid his mouth over one nipple, then the other. He moved his mouth in concert with his hips, bringing her quickly—too quickly—to orgasm. Then another, slower, and it was his turn to come.

They lay on the pillows facing each other afterward, another gift of afternoon sex, and talked about dinner and Fred's upcoming veterinarian's appointment and what to put in the garden this year.

Somewhere between broccoli and silver queen corn, Cotton's phone buzzed. Two times. Then three.

She and Thomas had agreed long ago that they would not deal with their phones during bedtime.

"But three buzzes, Thomas?"

"If the world is ending, it won't matter how many people call you. The only thing that matters is us right here, right now." He wrapped his arm around her shoulders and pulled her close. She relaxed into him, knowing he was right.

As soon as he got out of bed to take a shower, she checked her phone. Three messages from Hailey and one from Gray. *Uh-oh*.

She pulled the first one up, then heard Thomas cough. He stood at the bathroom door, a towel over his shoulder, and the steamy shower clouding up the mirror behind him. "Want to join me?"

She dropped her phone on the table and walked the few feet to her husband. "Don't get an invitation like this every day, do I?"

In the shower, her hands flat against the glass door as Thomas massaged her with soap, she wondered what was so important that the Prescotts had to leave three messages.

~ Book Twelve ~

Hailey Prescott

I thought how unpleasant it is to be locked out; and I thought how it is worse, perhaps, to be locked in.
—Virginia Woolf

A chilly day. Bitter, in fact. The Raleigh area expected snow tonight, but ever since the sun went down, black ice literally stopped traffic. Thomas called earlier, and he said he was going to stay with a friend close to the office. "Be safe," Cotton told him, secretly relishing that she would have the evening to herself, and she wouldn't have to make excuses for digging into Hailey's journal. Thomas had been making comments about bringing work home, and he was right. They'd agreed not to.

She turned on NPR and settled into the chair next to the fire, fighting the memory that had been haunting her all day. The last time Brighton came to the office, she'd asked, "Do you believe there are dogs in heaven?" Because Fred had been unusually quiet since Cotton came home earlier, the line popped into her mind. Since then, it repeated itself countless times, and even though Fred was sitting at her feet, brown eyes begging for a treat, she still found herself watching his stomach when he napped.

Maybe the journal will stop the cycle.

She hoped.

I can't see past these tears, Hailey wrote. *Good lord, I'm crying like I did when I was 12 and Skinny Jack and the kids from the Four Corners chased me down High Street determined to make me either lose my knapsack or my breath. They'd land on me, all of them connecting a punch or a kick or a scratch. I'd hold my breath and curl into a ball, counting backwards from a hundred until it was over.*

They knew as well as I did I was different. Kids are like little animals who migrate to the biggest and strongest of the pack. But I wasn't one of the boys.

How could I tell them I didn't feel as coordinated as they were? Nor did I care? How could I tell them I'd rather have been doing anything other than running bases or tossing that stinky leather football? How could I tell them I wanted to cook coq au vin or to make clothes like Alexander McQueen? I wanted to do what the other girls did.

The other girls ....

Cotton scanned the next couple of pages: fast forward to today. Hailey lamented not having the guts to talk to Gray face-to-face, worried that "taking the coward's way out" wasn't the right way—exactly as she'd said in the office.

A log crackled and fell. Fred lifted his head, grunted, then set his big brown head down, instantly falling back into the snore.

When I look around this bedroom now, I can't believe I'm walking away from the home I love, Hailey wrote. *Gray and I built this two-and-a-half story bungalow about three years ago. Our first proper home together. Before this, we lived in apartments that became larger and larger as each of the kids were born. Then we rented houses until, finally, I agreed with her it was time to get our own place. At first, we couldn't find one we both liked, so when this lot became available, we jumped on it and simply built a house that suited all our needs. Our dream home.*

I loved that time in our life. It was exciting to design our home together, to choose how to decorate it, to make it our own. One of the happiest moments in my life was when we found the Windsor hoop back chairs that were perfect around our dining room table. We collapsed into them simultaneously, trying to maintain our cool. Couldn't let the dealer see our excitement. We had a secret signal between us, Gray and I did, and it worked that day. We played a perfect good cop/bad cop routine and ended up with the four chairs for a fraction of what they were worth. Then we laughed all the way home like burglars who had gotten away with stealing the crown jewels.

That night, our first in our own home, she looked at me (her hair clipped up, a streak of dust on her cheek, a high school cheerleader, all teeth and ponytail), and she smiled. "We're home, honey." Her tired laughter was precious. I'd never seen her so happy. Remember thinking how much I loved being her partner and friend, but later that night when she wanted to christen the new bed by making love, I couldn't perform for her and blamed it on being tired. That excuse worked for a while, but, I had to get with the program again. I did everything but the physical fucking and thought that was enough. She seemed satisfied, at least for a while, until the day she asked me to go to the doctors to see why I couldn't get hard.

That's another story. I don't want to go there now.

The house.

The outside stairs creaked as Cotton turned the page, and she swore under her breath when Thomas arrived through the back door with a puff of chilly wind that made the fire whoosh. She stuffed the pages under her laptop. He dropped a kiss on her forehead, then chattered away about the cold spell coming their way, and headed upstairs, saying, "I couldn't stay at Mike's. I wanted to be home with you. You coming up?"

She didn't want to, but it was easier than telling him she wanted to work, because he'd start nagging her about keeping it at the office. As she crossed the room to turn off Alexa *because she records you and figures out algorithms and your privacy is gone,* she stopped for a moment to hear the last of an NPR piece on the latest LGBTQ hate crime in downtown Raleigh. A homeless person, beaten to within a moment of death, in front of the First Presbyterian. *A church!* Passersby filmed the brutality, but the cops didn't get there in time to catch the perpetrators. "When will it stop?" one woman asked. "Seems to me that this stuff all happens after the Congress fights about some bill or another. Leave the poor people alone, for god sakes. They ain't doing nothing to deserve this. Leave them alone!" Her angry voice echoed in the room.

"It would be a lot easier for all of us if they did," Cotton told NPR. "I'd rather have no clients than be witness to more of this bullshit... people gotta stop hurting each other."

Cotton pressed Alexa's off button. Tucking the journal and her laptop back in her briefcase, she nudged Fred with her toe, then both joined Thomas in the bedroom. He was still talking, leaving the bathroom door open as he brushed his teeth.

She counted the seconds—*thirty-two, exactly; just as every night*—until he started flossing. Fred snuggled against her hip in the bed as she turned the TV on, fumbling for a channel, and watching Thomas come out of the bathroom, his chest bare and still warmly damp from the shower. Either he'd pick up one of his scientific journals from the bedside table and climb into bed with it (*which meant no sex, because he'd fall asleep within fifteen minutes, glasses askew*) or he'd crawl over to her side, nuzzle her face for kisses that would eventually become what he affectionately called "our special movements." She didn't know which she wanted tonight, and she hated that he decided for them both every time.

He reached for *Scientific American.*

She rolled over and shut out her light, too tired to even take a shower.

~ Book Thirteen ~

Gray Prescott

The psychology of women hitherto actually represents a deposit of the desires and disappointments of men.
—Karen Horney

Cotton pulled back the drapes to look out her office window at the approaching rainstorm and with a shiver, pulled her cardigan closer around her throat. When she first started seeing the Prescotts, Raleigh's weather was sultry, an extended late Summer, golden days, shirtsleeve nights. Now the winter's frost chills the night air, and the daytime hours are unseasonably cool. A drastic temperature switch often sets people on edge. When their regular routines are off, and they don't know what to wear and how to plan their days, it sets off anyone who has even the slightest bit of anxious tendencies. Weather changes and phases of the moon. Every therapist has tales of what happens to clients during unusual natural phenomena. Every hospital worker in the ER knows the department was busiest when the moon was full on hot summer nights. Hospitalization for bar fight injuries always spiked during the full moon, while some women reported chest tightness and anxiety attacks during thunderstorms (and some domesticated animals reacted the same way—Fred always tried to crawl under the bed during windstorms, even though he could never fit more than his nose underneath the box spring), and people were more likely to attempt suicide during a long rainy period. The effect of weather on mood even had a name: Seasonal Affectiveness Disorder.

"Meteoropathy," Cotton said aloud as she pulled the curtains closed. "Meteoropathy, meteoropathy, meteoropathy." Tapped the back of each chair with the syllables. Sometimes repeating fun words aloud brought her back to the present. She needed that right now. She was one of those people who couldn't concentrate on rainy days. "Meteoropathy," she said again. "Weather-affected behavior."

If any clients were likely to experience meteoropathy, it would be the Prescotts. Any of them. It truly surprised her how each of them tended to withdraw from the world, yet they were hyperaware of what was happening around them. Except for Gray. Often, the woman seemed totally disconnected like a floating balloon bobbing around in the atmosphere, occasionally dropping below the cloud line only to disappear again without warning. Half the time she made no sense at all, half-sentences, odd idioms, mumblings, and that tendency to miscommunicate caused Cotton to grit her teeth sometimes. She couldn't be sure Gray could take care of her kids, but she also knew how damaging it would be if they were separated from the custodial parent. If she started any paperwork to put the Prescott kids into foster care, they might end up in court, and this family had enough to deal with. No, she'd watch Gray closely. *Two more appointments a week should help.*

Several times during the past couple of weeks, Gray dropped the children off—individually—to see Cotton, and they've also spoken on the phone. Cotton underlined the rules as clearly and kindly as she could. No more kids in the waiting room, and Gray listened. She'd take the waiting child with her during the other kid's therapy hour and run her errands. Technically, she was still doing what Cotton asked her not to: leaving a child alone at therapy with the therapist. Normally, Cotton asked a parent to be in the room, even if they weren't speaking during the session, but at the very least, in the waiting room. She followed the unspoken rule that a guardian be at least close by. When the kids knew their parents weren't around, it allowed them to talk to Cotton directly.

No parents monitoring a child's conversation meant no filters. It made her job easier.

In their often-rushed sessions, Cotton talked to Cherylynn about cheerleading tryouts ("Dad wants to be there, but I think Mom wouldn't like that.") and to Janis about the problems she was having in Science ("Has nothing to do with the shit at home. I just freaking hate science. Seriously. Why can't they give me another art class?"). Gray called every other day to see whether Cotton could referee one fight or another between the kids, and Cotton's answer was always the same: "Why do you want me to do that, Gray?" And Gray's silence was the same, as well.

Stalemate.

Having only one set of clients meant that Cotton's schedule was determined by their availability, though she never shared that information with them. This week, Marcus had the flu, and Hailey had a last-minute meeting, so they both cancelled. That opening in the schedule meant more time with Gray, Janis, and Cherylynn. The 'week of the women,' Cotton was calling it when she talked to Thomas at the dinner table. Though she never named them, Thomas understood she was working with a challenging family. That's all he needed to know. Anything else, and she'd be breaching that patient confidence.

Today was the sixth individual visit with Gray since their initial appointment. Sometimes, Gray came in with Hailey, sometimes with one of the other kids. She was the Prescott Cotton saw most often, and most of the time, she arrived late. Today was no different. She presented at five minutes past the appointment time, giving no excuse, dressed for her workday in a wrinkled pair of khakis, a white button-down, and a gray cardigan, a tired expression on her pale face, her dirty ginger hair still lank and lifeless. She appeared to have lost weight since yesterday. How was that possible? A muslin bag emblazoned "Shakespeare Institute" and full of books slid off one shoulder and a patchwork-quilted pocketbook rode the other. In her hands, she held her usual sheaf of papers that she immediately shoved at Cotton without a word. It's surprising that Hailey was the writer, yet Gray did the substantial part of her communicating through the written word, telling a story in much the same manner as a novelist: creating characters, scene, dialogue, conflict. She distanced herself from reality by writing her story as if it belonged to someone else.

Cotton was sure by their third meeting that Gray's disorders were multiple and complicated: first, depersonalization, noticeable when she detached herself from others; second, a major depression that was now being treated with Prozac; and third, possibly an eating disorder, as well as problems with alcohol. Even alcoholism. Cotton couldn't tell for sure, but she was worried since she had smelled liquor on Gray's breath every time they're close enough to get a whiff.

Some of Gray's symptoms were typical of those who were thinking about suicide, but Cotton would not report her since Gray had given no indication that she was considering taking her own life. *You can't accuse someone without direct evidence.*

Sitting now, Gray crossed her arms over her chest, shifting in a way that her bra strap showed, a dingy white. She should take a shower, wash her hair, curl it, put on some perfume, and find an attractive, clean piece of clothing to wear. It was a cliché Cotton thought, but studies have proven that the simple act of showering will lift a person's mood, even momentarily, and eventually, those moments add up. If Gray tried some aromatherapy, maybe she'd find it easier to get out of bed, work wouldn't seem so threatening, and she eventually might find a friend to have coffee with one afternoon. *Magic.* Maybe the friend might be interested in hearing about what's going on in Gray's life or share some laughs or tears. The actual connection with another human being might remind her what it's like to live her own life. The problem was that Gray didn't know what that meant. She had lived in a family with a working partner for the better part of her adult life, and she had expected to maintain that relationship forever. Lately, she had been building a mantra: "my life is over. Who the hell am I, anyway?"

Cotton took the pages from Gray and mentally switched into administrative mode, deciding she'd give Gray another week or so to exhibit some good coping skills before trying a different mode of therapy. Perhaps cognitive-behavioral therapy might assist Gray in developing some tools to help her look at her life more positively. If she sunk any deeper into the depression... *she won't. I'll make sure of it.*

Stop controlling, Cotton reminded herself, but it was frustrating when you know what would work for a client, but they simply won't try—for whatever the reason. And when she cared about her clients, she wanted them to get better. It was a personal goal to make them better.

Even though it often felt like managing a freight train with mismatched cars through a hairpin-turn mountain pass. *Scary as fuck.*

Folding her legs beneath her, Cotton didn't lift her gaze to Gray until she took a deep breath and centered herself. She smiled warmly, wishing she could wrap Gray in a hug and tell her *everything would be alright. No one's dead. No one has cancer. No one has murdered another individual. And your kids need you. You need to take care of them first. Put the oxygen mask on the kids before you put one on your own face.*

"Do you want to talk about this, Gray?" Cotton pointed to the pages sitting on the table beside her. Typed, double-spaced, like a novel would be. "It feels like we're having a one-way conversation—you, writing; me, reading—and it might feel better for you to have someone to talk to. It would be easier for me, too. I could see your facial expressions when you talk to me, ask questions, help you get through what's bothering you."

"What do you want me to say?" Gray deliberately sought the sunny spot on the couch, as a cat does, lifting her face to its warmth. Yearning.

"Whatever you want. Tell me how you feel."

"It's all on those pages." She pointed with her chin.

"I understand that, but it would be better if you tell me out loud how you're feeling. Sometimes when we relate our stories aloud, it helps us figure them out more quickly."

"What can you say about something like this?" Gray laughs thinly. "It's too freaking painful. Please. Just keep reading. I talk better on the page than I speak...you know, spoken words. Always have."

"No one's going to judge how you talk. I'm just saying it might be easier to do this out loud. That way if I have questions or want clarification, I can ask, like I said before."

"You can ask while you're reading, too."

Now it was Cotton's turn to sigh, but she held it back. "Gray, why is it you don't want to talk? Let's think about that for a moment, can we?"

"I am talking. But I remember all the details when I write it down, and if I talk...you know. I get, um...it's better if I write. I can think, you know, in more, you know, clearer. More detail. I remember better."

"I understand that," Cotton said, "but can you see how helpful it would be for me to see the expressions on your face when we talk about different topics? That's a big part of my work as a therapist, to see both the verbal and the physical cues to what's going on and how it affects you. That's what helps me to help you. I'm sure you understand that."

Gray's pocketbook clattered to the floor. After she picked it up, her face reddened. "What's the point? Is it going to change anything if I talk to you? Is Hayden or Hailey, whatever the fuck his—her—name is—going to suddenly realize he—she! Christ! —doesn't want to be a woman? Shit! How the fuck does someone get past this?" She shifted in the chair and a spring popped, startling both women. Gray picked up her bag and tucked it in tightly beside her, patting it to ensure it would stay, like a child.

"Do you think your partner has changed as a person now that she identifies as a woman?" Cotton paused to let Gray think about that. "After all, you had a family—a life together. People's personalities, their identities, are formed by many factors. Gray, you know that our upbringing, our culture, the surrounding society, all of that determines who we are."

"I do not know who that person was." Gray wouldn't make eye contact.

Cotton might as well be talking to the wall, yet she continued, unable to pursue another avenue until she exhausted this line of reasoning. One of the few things she disliked about herself. Her persistence was both a detriment and a complement to her therapeutic style.

"All of those factors and many more shape our identity," she said, "but, don't you think that person's character—whether they are likely to steal or to lie or to beat their children—don't you think that remains the same whether they're male or female, homosexual, bisexual? Transgender?"

Gray folded her arms across her chest once again. If she could turn her back against Cotton, she probably would. "I have no clue. No clue whatsoever."

"If you're angry, let's stay with that anger for a while," Cotton said, reading Gray's body language. "Let's navigate it and resolve it, if we can."

"I don't know what good that would do."

"Sometimes when we voice what we're angry about and how it makes us feel, we can work it out enough to understand it. Usually, when you understand what's at the core of your emotions, you can learn to accept the process of what brought you from there to here and how you can move forward."

Gray didn't unfold her arms, simply arched her eyebrows, silently saying, "Prove it."

"Okay, let's look at it this way. If you were to tell me the story of how you met... your husband... Hayden and what made you love him, what would that sound like?"

"When I first met him...." She inhaled and hiccupped. "When I first met Hayden, I thought he was brilliant. And respectful. And kind. I hadn't met anyone else like him before, and I was a bit in awe of him. But, obviously, I didn't really understand who he was. He was hiding so much." She shook her head as if that movement would rid her of the good memories she had of her husband. She wanted to deny them, or else she didn't trust the truth of her own memory. Remembering was the first step in coming to terms with a new reality.

Cotton sensed a crack in the walls Gray had built. "Tell me about that day, just that day, and get out of your head. Don't judge yourself or compare how you felt them to how you feel now. Tell me how that day made you feel. Connect with your emotions instead of what you think. Big difference. I want you to think about connecting with the emotion you feel in your heart, your gut, your loins. Tell me about that day. What was it like? Remember all the sensory details if you can. Pretend you are there right in the moment. See it. Feel it Tell me what the weather was like, what you were doing, what you were wearing, how you felt when you started talking to each other."

"All the details? Why? How is that going to help anything?"

"It might trigger something else that will help you understand. Or it might help me understand how you feel."

Gray screwed up her face and transformed into one of her kids. "Okay, okay. I was in college; it was a... a Wednesday, I think. I had a test the next period in my Biology class, so I was on the lawn studying. I don't know what I was wearing. A t-shirt and jeans, probably. That's what I wore all the way through college. My hair was longer then, and I hardly ever combed it." She absent-mindedly tucked her hair behind her ears, then her eyes shifted as if suddenly realizing she needed to wash her dirty hair.

"I remember it was one of those days when you could tell autumn was around the corner, but the temperature still felt like summer. The sun lit the corners of the leaves, outlining them in gold, and they shivered slightly with the afternoon breeze. It was one of those picture-perfect days, you know what I mean? The kind that become minted in your memory because the light is as perfect as if the scene were in a painting. It was mid-October. Don't remember the exact date, but the leaves were changing. Hayden says it was the 15th, but I'm not sure how he remembers that."

She paused, studied her fingers for a moment, then lifted her face and looked toward the window. There was a slight smile on her face as if she felt transported back in time. When that look filled a client's face, Cotton knew she was about to hear a story. She folded her fingers under her yellow-lined notepad.

"You look like you're having a happy memory," she said, her voice a bit too cheery.

"Mm-hmm. I've always thought he was wrong about the date. Thought it was closer to Halloween, because we went to a costume party for one of our first dates. Isn't that funny? Even then, he loved dressing up." Gray fell silent for a moment and stared at a spot on the wall as if considering whether to continue. "Anyway. I remember stressing about the test. My Brit Lit professor—we used to call him Dr. Pickles, because he made faces like he was sucking on a big ol' sour pickle when he lectured—he was a stickler for details, and when I took tests with him, I always felt all goober'd up." She laughed and glanced at Cotton for a precious, soft second, and her face transformed into the girl she was then.

It was clear Cotton had broken one of Gray's walls, but it was critical to keep her talking so she didn't shut down.

"I really messed up," Gray said softly. She slowly shook her head from side to side, side to side, then took a deep breath and pushed her thick hair away from her face and wrapped her hands around it, gathering it into a ponytail at the back of her neck, then letting it loose. She twisted the engagement ring on her finger as if she had only now realized she was still wearing it. "I was sure I was going to flunk that test, and I must have looked it. Right before I was ready to go back to the dorm and complain to my roommate, this guy sat down next to me and says, 'You look down in the mouth.'" She chuckled, shaking her head again and stealing another glance at Cotton, "What a pickup line, huh?"

"Describe him. Tell me what your first impression of him was."

"Hmmm... He was one of those guys you wouldn't look at twice if he passed you on the street, but when he was sitting there in front of me, I noticed his eyes right away. I had never seen someone with navy blue eyes before. So dark. They were almost black. He had this kind of look that pinned you down like you were a fly and he was the spider, bless his heart." She snorted emphatically. "Hmmm... bless his heart. Ha! Haven't said that about him for a long time."

"What do you mean when you said: 'his look pinned you down'?" Cotton kept her voice quiet and reassuring, pushing down her eagerness to keep Gray talking.

"Umm... I don't mean it negatively. He's just got those eyes that kind of... they drill right through you. For a girl like me to meet a guy like that, well, it was just exciting. I mean, here I am: a Math geek, hadn't had more than a couple of dates by that time, and those dreamy writer guys, they were the guys who I wanted to take me to the dance, know what I mean?"

Cotton nodded, encouraging Gray to continue. She was on a roll, and the memories were positive. She needed this next step in her grieving process. Throughout their appointments, Gray has grieved the death of her marriage, a relationship she thought she'd have until the end of her life. To Gray, Hailey's transition represented as much a death as if she had been killed in a car crash.

"And there he is, this guy who always got into intense, intellectual conversations with the English prof about characterization and point of view, and things like 'narrative exposition' and 'expressive plotting.' It horribly impressed me. Even though I majored in Math, I loved books, and his brain was something else, but then, those eyes. Good lord, he got me right away with those eyes. He could say anything he wanted to without even opening his mouth just by the way he looked at me." She fell quiet but a dreamy half-smile rested on her lips. "I loved those damn eyes." Another long sigh. "That day... our first date... they were... incredible. That's what makes it so hard. To think about how it was then, and how it is now. It's just too hard." Her tears flowed smoothly down her cheeks, but she made no sobbing sounds. It was the type of crying that happened when someone had already cried out most of the pain. Pure sadness. Gray was so used to the tears, she didn't bother wiping them off her face.

"It's okay, Gray, take your time. Just focus on that day."

"We talked about my class. I had the same prof for Bio that he had the semester before, so he told me what to expect. And he asked why I was studying alone, said that he had noticed me on campus the week before, and that he wondered who I was. He said that I looked smart like I was always concentrating on something." This time her laugh was forlorn. Empty. "We sat there for hours on the grass, just talking and laughing, until the sun went down. It was perfect. Like meeting someone I had known before. I always told him that. That we had known each other before. To be honest with you, I felt that day like I'd finally met someone I was completely comfortable with. That day, he became my best friend."

"How did you feel about that?"

Gray met Cotton's eyes. "How did I feel? God, I've never thought about it." She shifted in the chair and slid her hands under her knees, sitting on them and swinging her legs like a child. "Lucky. I felt incredibly lucky. And you know, Dr. Barnes, that feeling never went away. That's what hurts so much. It makes my chest feel like it's going to implode. Drives the stake through my heart." She pounded her chest with her open palm to make her point. "Damn it. I always felt so fucking incredibly lucky to have met Hayden Prescott. In all the years we've been together, I never told him that. Maybe I should have told him that. Maybe he wouldn't have left."

"You still can, but I wouldn't expect that to change Hailey's mind about who she is."

"What the hell good would it do? No, I can't say that anymore. Best friends don't screw each other like this. They don't lie to each other." She smacked her hand against the arm of the chair. It reverberated like the crack of a whip. The sound brought her back to the present. She checked her watch. "It's time, isn't it?"

"Sorry. Yes, it is," Cotton agreed with a glance at her own watch and a shiver of surprise that the session was almost over, "but if you want to say anything else, please feel free...."

"Will you still read what I've brought if I agree to talk like this?"

"Yes, I can read some of it. But, you had a genuine breakthrough today, and I'd like you to continue exploring. How about when you write your next letter to me, you try to stop using third person to refer to yourself? When you do that, you're putting distance between yourself and what happened. One of the best ways to heal is to recognize and accept what has happened in your life And considering what you just did, I think you have."

Though the session was over, Gray didn't appear emotionally ready to re-enter the world. It was always difficult to stop someone when they've made a breakthrough and to wrap things up, then give the client a summary of what they've done, as well as a goal for the next session.

Gray left in a little flurry, creating a breeze that lifted a pile of autumn leaves.

~ Book Fourteen ~

Cotton Barnes

In my early professional years, I was asking the question:
  How can I treat, or cure, or change this person?
  Now I would phrase the question in this way:
  How can I provide a relationship which this person may use for his own personal growth?
  —Carl Rogers

Cotton had far too much time on her hands, so she filled every moment and then some. She wrote and rewrote her notes from the past two sessions with Hailey, she outlined her therapeutic plan three times (four, if you count for proofreading), she cleaned her office twice, and she read Hailey's journal two-and-a-half times. Pored over it, underlined segments, highlighted words, and created a list of regularly used phrases. Copied it. Two copies: one for the file, one to take home.

She glanced at the clock, reminded herself it was past time to go home, but she couldn't leave the office until she finished the rest of the journal. She needed to read it completely a total of three times, just to close the loop. *Three. Magic number.*

She glimpsed herself in the mirror, hair crazily swept up into a half-assed bun, her sweater buttoned wrong, and realized she appeared manic. *Christ.* Her eyelids closed wearily, and she sat, forcing herself to do some yogic breathing, recognizing the thoughts flitting through her mind, acknowledging she needed her medication, her Clomipramine, but it made her feel so stupid. Slowed her down. She couldn't multitask like she used to. The medication helped her control her obsessive thoughts, but she really didn't want to think because thinking puts her back to that night. To Brighton.

There. You did it. You thought of her.

Cotton's eyes flipped open, she reached for Hailey's journal, and read it clear through to the end. No pauses. No room for thoughts about other patients. Clear through to the end. The journal was everything Cotton expected it to be. Hailey beat herself up for the way she told her family, and she shared bits and pieces of childhood memories. It was the way the story was told that fascinated Cotton. Sometimes white space was as interesting as the most intricate patterns.

Whatever that means.

Finally, she could no longer procrastinate. She headed home, but halfway down the 540 on ramp, Hailey's words crawled into her head like an ear worm, repeating themselves over and over again. *I always felt there was something left unsaid. I never knew what, but something was left undone. Not finished.*

Cotton found herself at a railroad crossing, grateful that the passing Amtrak train forced her to sit still. *Fourteen, fifteen, sixteen* sets of double doors. *Eleven-oh-six,* the number on the caboose. *Five* loud, long whistles. *Ten* seconds before the barrier lifted, and she could drive again.

It was 9:08. Thomas is home, but five more minutes won't make a difference.

351 North Walden Road. Hailey's condo.

The GPS said arrival would be 9:11. *Only three minutes away.* Cotton's heart beat a little faster. Only 15 hours and 11 minutes ago, Hailey sat on the couch and gave Cotton the journal.

9:11 "You have arrived. Your destination is on the right."

"I see it, Matilda." Cotton shut off the GPS and stared at the blue and gray building that had once been an insurance office building and was now repurposed into high-end, industrial-design apartments. Four floors, sixteen windows on this side. Must be four apartments per floor. Sixteen apartments. *Sixteen times sixteen is two hundred and fifty-six.*

Hailey said she was on the second floor, loved the light in the living room because she had extra windows that overlooked the Falls Lake dam. A corner apartment. Cotton pulled into the parking lot and stared at the lights in the second-floor corner window.

What the hell am I doing here? What if Hailey suddenly brings down her rubbish?

She comforted herself by reasoning that it was after 9, the lights were on, and chances were good that Hailey wasn't going anywhere tonight, so *it's okay to sit in the lot for a full nineteen minutes, making it a total even number: twenty minutes staring up at the window like a stalker.*

Twenty minutes probably legitimately made her a stalker. Her feet were ice cold, and there'd been no signs of movement from the apartment, so this was a waste of time. Hailey was probably writing. Or maybe she fell asleep on the couch.

Which is where I should be right now.

Cotton's phone buzzed. Another text from Thomas. She ignored it, but turned on the car, relishing the almost-instant heat through the vents. A minute later—a full sixty seconds—she felt guilty and texted Thomas back, telling him she had the phone shut off while Face Timing with her therapist, but she was heading home now.

Pad Thai in the fridge, he replied. *Going to bed to watch the game.*

She sat in the parking lot for a couple more moments, telling herself she was warming it up, but in truth, she wanted to see Hailey moving around in her own environment. She wanted to see what she hung on her walls, what she watched on TV, what she wore when she was alone, what she was writing.

At 9:45, Cotton knew it was time to go home. *What the hell are you doing sitting in a dark parking lot watching a client's house?*

The flash of blue lights and blip of a siren behind her took her off guard, a rush of adrenaline tingled in her back teeth. The cop passed her, following a speeder, but Cotton's heart beat as wildly as if the blue lights had been for her, like she was going to get arrested for sitting in a dark running car watching her client's apartment. She scared herself out of the parking lot and flew through stop signs until she fully stopped and shut the car off in her own driveway.

Her heartbeat didn't slow until she drew her naked body up against Thomas's back. He rolled over, wordlessly taking her into his arms, and they shared an unexpected hour of sex that surprised them both.

She was finally relaxed and beginning to fall asleep when Thomas whispered, "Where did that come from?" It was a rhetorical question, one that really didn't require an answer, but she said, "I missed you," when she didn't know.

~ Book Fifteen ~

Gray Prescott

Ever has it been that love knows not its own depth until the hour of separation.
—Kahlil Gibran

The warm, spicy aroma of Thomas's famous Southern Chicken Marsala tempted Cotton, but she postponed following the scent into the kitchen, and remained in the wing chair in front of the fireplace. Gray's latest journal pages lay in her lap, and other than the occasional kitchen noises and the constant thrum of chilly rain against the living room windows, she had no interruptions. In the fire's coziness, Cotton read Gray's words, realizing they provided the details she'd unable to offer during their therapy sessions.

Since her husband deserted her, Gray spent more hours huddled under the blankets on her king-size bed than she is ready to confess. Sometimes she can't force herself to get up at all, especially on the weekends when her kids are busy with friends and the house echoes with her solitary footsteps. She can't lay on the right side of the bed, his side. Can't even touch it. She'd done everything possible to cleanse the bed, short of buying a new one: bleached all the sheets several times and now has faded tie dye

sheets and pillowcases that match nothing else, changed the mattress pad, and burnt the old one. Still, it seemed tainted. Stained by the bald-faced lies he told her, especially the biggest lie of all: He wasn't a husband, wasn't even a man. When she could bear to think about their marriage, which wasn't very often, she can't define their relationship. She isn't sure about anything anymore.

"Do you want me to make some *naan* to go with this?" Thomas yelled from the kitchen.

"That's a good idea," Cotton called back and wondered if this simple conversation about dinner was typical of how Gray and Hailey communicated when they were married. They probably had unspoken routines like most married couples. One of them might have been helping the kids with homework while the other threw a pizza in the oven. What was it like then?

In her mind's eye, Cotton envisioned the three kids at the kitchen table: Janis, earbuds in the ears, texting someone on her cell. Marcus telling Hailey about the history test he aced the day before. Cherylynn, ruler in her hand, lining it up on the page of her literature book to help her read, a trick her mother taught her to keep focused.

Cotton kicked the knitted Irish throw off her legs and let the Prescotts go for a second. The fire had made her toes toasty and her eyes heavy. She leaned her head back, trying to get into Gray's world. She claimed a loss of identity and that was devastating, Cotton knew. Would she be able to see the signs if Thomas was gay or trans or cheating? Did she know him well enough to read the subtle changes? His occasional lack of arousal could be a red flag, but every married couple goes through peaks and valleys in their sex lives. She'd never thought about it before, but she'd like to think she could see the signs. She imagined Gray did, too, and in that respect, she understood Gray's frustration with herself. Cotton knew how to read body language like a cop, knew how to keep the lines of communication open, and was hyper-sensitive. It was one reason she made a good therapist. But what if she was a bookstore owner like Gray, up to her ears in staffing issues, fighting the giant megastores every day, managing three kids with their sports and school schedules, making sure everyone gets fed (though, it appeared Hailey did the cooking, while Gray was responsible for the shopping), and so tired by keeping it all together that all she really wanted at night was a good, long, warm hug.

It did not surprise Cotton that Hailey kept her secret as long as she did.

In the kitchen, Thomas hummed that funny little ear-worm thing he did that was partially "You are my Sunshine," but also, "We are the Champions," and sometimes sounded like "Silent Night."

Everyone would face the holidays soon, she realized. Thanksgiving was not such a big deal to her, but maybe to the Prescotts, it was. Holidays were triggers, so she made a mental note to check in with each of the family members, schedule time in the office, and somehow create a pact to keep in touch over the long weekend. Maybe even suggest a family activity so they'd spend the time together rather than drifting away from each other.

She and Thomas always went to her family's home for Thanksgiving since there are more people in her family than in his, but she'd rather cook at home, and after the cooking is done, take a hot toddy to the living room and cuddle on the sofa watching old Tom Hanks movies.

Something told her that Gray and Hailey might have done the same thing through the years. A tradition. The Prescott Thanksgiving tradition. Those positive memories were more difficult to forget. Broken hearts happen because things were good, not because they were horrible.

Cotton turned the page in Gray's journal. A list. She'd given Gray a task last week. *Write down all your unanswered questions,* she'd told Gray. And now, here they were. A couple of pages' worth and all written in third person. Distancing herself. Not owning it as "me, my, I," but saying, "no, this isn't my life, it's hers."

o   *Should she have been more loving?*

o *Should she have taken on a more passive role, not going after her career but letting him find his own place in the world?*

o *Should she have been kinder about his mediocre writing career?*

o *Should she have encouraged him to take over the finances instead of doing it herself?*

o *Did she satisfy him in bed?*

o *Was that even important?*

o *Had he found some satisfaction with someone else?*

o *Had he thought about being with men?*

o *Did he think she looked like a man herself?* (That thought makes her examine herself in the mirror late at night. She has even gone through each piece of clothing in her closet, tossing those that appeared too masculine. No more Ralph Lauren shirts and sweaters.)

o *Should she have married him at all?*

o *Would it have been different if she had said no when he first asked so many years ago?*

o *Was he really trying to hide from himself by marrying her?*

o *Had he thought she would change him?*

o *Did he believe the marriage would take away the feeling of being a woman?*

Gray's questions were normal. Anyone who had lived in one reality for years only to discover that reality turned upside down will question everything. Cotton jotted on her pad: *Work on the answers to these questions. It's okay if there aren't any.*

Sometimes when Cotton worked with families in situations they couldn't cope with, it usually wasn't the person at the center of the conflict who spun the family dynamic. Usually, it was everyone else. Sometimes in families where a trans person was in transition, that person had a better handle on what the future might be than the rest of the family did.

Cotton tapped her pen against the page and stared into the flames. Gray couldn't make good decisions right now, the kids were hanging on by their fingernails, and Hailey was carrying an immense amount of guilt. It was the perfect storm.

She hadn't even talked to Hayden since he left. Nor did she want to. She didn't even want to mention his name, and she wished more than anything that she could wipe him out of her mind completely. Forever. He had bought the coward's way out by leaving a note on the bed rather than facing her. She no longer respected him. But, worse still, she no longer trusted her own judgement. She'd lost her moorings.

Since starting therapy, she has read some books about transgender people, and they always talk about the "coming out" part. (It would surprise her therapist that Gray's doing 'research.' She's proud of herself for doing it, though it sometimes sickens her to realize her husband is one of those people. Yes, she refers to them as "those people," and she knows how politically incorrect that is. She doesn't care. She's fucking hurt.) Ironically, she felt that the coming out has not really happened, because only the family knows. And part of her fantasizes he might come to his senses and return home someday. She even believes she might find him in the kitchen one afternoon, and that when he turns to smile at her and ask her how her day was, she'll realize all of this was a horrible dream.

She thinks of how Hayden/Hailey will look if he gets surgery to transition from male to female. He's slight. Probably would look good in a pencil skirt and heels. He is feminine looking. Christ, she used to wear his jeans! She wonders if he'd let his hair grow and get it streaked, and that thought makes her mind spin. He'd look like his daughters if he let his hair grow. How would they feel about that? What kinds of conversations would she have to have with them about their father, then? It was tough enough trying to maintain a normal life, getting them breakfast in the morning, making their lunches, and seeing them off to school. It would be near impossible to answer questions they had if they saw him change his physical appearance like she already had. God, that was weird seeing him in a skirt and heels. Heels. She couldn't even walk in heels. How could her size 10.5-foot husband do so? Where did he get his shoes? Did he dress up before he left?

Yes, her kids would have enough tough questions. That was the hardest part about going through this: answering the kids' questions.

Only last night, Marcus crawled into bed with her and asked whether he could call his father. When Gray didn't answer right away, he scrunched up his face, pointed to her, and whispered, "You don't want me to see him because you don't like him anymore."

"No, that's not it," she said, but she wanted to scream that Marcus was right. She did *hate his father right now. Hayden had lied to her in the worst way possible, had ruined their lives, had become some sick weirdo that everyone would point to when he walked down the street.*

"Why then? Why can't I see Dad? He's still my dad, right?"

She didn't know how to answer that question. Was a man who wanted to be a woman still a father to the children he made? And what kind of man—what kind of person—didn't even bother contacting those children after disappearing from their lives to do something so insane?

Sometimes she thinks it would have been easier if he had died.

Thomas's fingers surprised Cotton, sliding down the sides of her head, settling at the base of her neck, massaging in gentle circles. "Time to put that down and come eat," he whispered in her ear, then gave it a nip.

Absentmindedly, she patted his hand. "I just have two more pages."

He laughed and dropped a kiss on her cheek, sending a chill down her back. Amazing that he could still do that. "Never fails. You always make me wait."

"I'll be right there," she promised.

Thomas grunted and shuffled back into the kitchen. The fridge door opened and closed. She heard the distinct pop of a wine cork, then the splash of the pour into two glasses. One would wait for her when she joined him in the kitchen for dinner. He'd give her another ten minutes before coming out again.

Cotton jotted down the questions she wanted to ask Gray: *how often do you stay in bed all day? Are there guns, tranquilizers, antidepressants, painkillers, narcotics of any kind in the house? How often do you think about being sad, confused, depressed?*

And Cotton asked questions of herself. She wondered if what was going on between Thomas and her resulted from the Prescotts' struggles. Maybe Thomas's need to have a baby was making her rethink her own identity, especially considering the family trauma she saw every day. And to be honest, she didn't want to have her identity determined by others' expectations.

This must be how Hailey feels: unable to be completely herself throughout her entire life. Now that she's started the transition, she's zealously guarding the process.

But are any of us truly 100% binary? All female or all male? Nothing in between? Why not a combination of all genders? If we defined intellectual strength as "male," then Cotton figured she could be called masculine, especially when she defended herself. But they would define other aspects of her personality as feminine: loving the touch of soft fabrics, wanting to hug her clients, dissolving into tears during sad movies. She's thought about it often, the many definitions of gender: lesbian, gay, bisexual, androgynous, transsexual, and even within the binary male/female construction. Every man isn't a he-man; every woman doesn't want to have kids. No human being is 100% one thing or another. The only thing we have in common, she knew, was that we're human.

It hurt her head to grapple with it all, yet she was on the outside looking in.

Fingers twisting around the pen, Cotton knew she needed to talk to Gray about scheduling more sessions, more time in the office where Cotton could observe whether Gray was responding to the ongoing narrative therapy. Next step, if she didn't show improvement or if Cotton decided the kids were at risk, would be to find a clinic for Gray.

Cotton didn't want to do that. Everyone else in the family would tilt sideways, and the Prescott train would career off the tracks.

"Cot-ton," Thomas singsonged from the kitchen. "You prommmm-isssed."

"Just a second." She entered another reminder on her cell: *Get Gray in asap*. There was enough room in her schedule for more sessions for all of them. The whole family. Cotton could be the mother hen, gathering the Prescott chicks around her, making sure they were all safe. Every single one.

She touched Thomas's tight forearm when she sat at the table. "Sorry, babe. Needed to finish what I was doing."

Snapping his napkin, Thomas smiled thinly. "I feel like I need to remind you we agreed we'd leave work at the office." He spooned some chicken onto her plate, then ladled the sauce over the top, and did the same for himself. Cotton's stomach growled. They both laughed as Cotton slid into her seat and into the comfortable half-listening daze she adopted when Thomas gave her his day's itinerary. She wasn't ignoring him or not listening. She was multitasking, listening to him, but also thinking about what else the Prescotts needed to help each of them find their own answers.

~ Book Sixteen ~

Marcus Prescott

Enter into child's play and you will find the place where their minds, hearts, and souls meet.
— Virginia Axline

Marcus and Cotton sat opposite each other on the floor of her office. Scattered in front of them were hundreds of Legos pieces, various shapes, sizes, and colors, to create a figure of Princess Leia from Star Wars. Cotton had the Legos project since grade school and she rationalized that bringing it into the office for clients would be a reason to keep it. Her office closet was full of toys, from the softest plush animals to complicated jigsaw puzzles and everything in between, literally a game or toy for every aged person she treated.

When she conducts play therapy, entire stories come tumbling out in unguarded moments. With Marcus, he concentrated on fitting Legos pieces into buildings and cars. Half the time, no talking at all. Just grunts. Occasionally, she slipped in a question about school ("I'm stuck on polynomials. I mean, really?"), or what he liked to eat ("Chipotle makes this great chili. Have you had it? Janis works there, so she can bring it home every night. Super cool."), or whether he ever watched the Star Wars movies (Silence for a moment, then "we binged with Dad....").

Cotton didn't rush to fill in the blanks when Marcus stopped talking and focused his attention on the pieces that would become Leia's arm.

In a moment, he turned to look at Cotton expectantly. A little surprised. "I miss him, y'know. I miss my dad."

"You still play online games with your father, right?"

"Yeah, not the same."

"Have you talked to your parents about how you feel?"

"No, just Janis."

Knowing Marcus had someone he could talk to made Cotton feel better. And though she wondered how Janis felt about becoming her siblings' caretaker, she realized the youngest Prescott was desperately seeking an adult to guide him. Cotton made a mental note to check with Janis about the role change.

She wanted to ask Marcus more about what he'd shared with his sister and try to get him to a place where she could help him put a plan in place for himself. Identify a place where he felt safe. Make sure he had emergency phone numbers. But he'd picked up Leia's other arm, back in the world of Legos, while telling Cotton about the other characters in the Star Wars series, which ones were favorites, which ones he'd never liked.

He hugged her waist impulsively as they walked to the door when the session was over, and she patted his shoulder, gave him a little shoulder squeeze, and opened the door to the empty waiting room.

Cotton bit her lip. Gray was supposed to be here at least a few minutes before the session was over because Cotton had a dentist appointment she'd been waiting for since before the pandemic. This was one day she didn't have time to wait for Gray, who was making a habit out of stretching the kids' appointments by fifteen minutes to half an hour. It wouldn't be a problem any other day, but today?

"Hey, Dr. B, thanks for not asking a lot of questions today," Marcus said in a whispery voice as if he expected his mother through the door at any moment, and maybe what he was saying was disloyal to her, so he didn't want to be caught. "Sometimes I need a break, y'know? Sometimes I don't want to talk."

"I understand, but know that I'm here," she said as she led him to a chair. "I'm always here if you want to talk." She flicked the blinds open on the waiting room window and checked the parking lot. No Prescott SUV anywhere, and the streetlights were on, illuminating all corners of the parking lot. *Where was Gray?*

Marcus perched on the edge of an armchair Cotton had picked up at a local estate sale last weekend. Its overstuffed winged back dwarfed him, looking like he was seven rather than eleven. The faint tinge under his dark eyes made Cotton wonder whether he was getting enough sleep or eating properly. If nutritional needs aren't being met, the brain and body don't work, especially with young kids.

"We might have to wait a few minutes for your mom," Cotton said. "You hungry?"

Marcus grinned. "Whatcha got?"

~ Book Seventeen ~

Janis Prescott

People know what they do; frequently they know why they do what they do; but what they don't know is what they do does.
　—Michel Foucault

The headache that nagged Cotton all morning wouldn't quit, and she knew it was her own damn fault. Downing the fifth shot of tequila at Deb's house the night before put her over the edge, but she didn't stop. Usually, Thomas made a comment that reminded her she really couldn't handle her liquor, but he didn't the night before. She pressed her fingers against her temples. "Not his fault," she whispered aloud. "This is all on you, Cotton Barnes."

She swallowed the rest of her bottled water and told herself she'd drink another bottleful before Janis Prescott arrived.

But Janis arrived ten minutes early. *What's up with this family? Are their clocks not working these days? They're either late or early. Never on time.* Cotton watched her walking to the office door from where she sat at the desk, reviewing her notes from their previous session. Was it an invasion of privacy to watch someone when they do not know they are being watched? An act of distant intimacy? It didn't matter. Cotton had Janis in her sights. Janis wore iPod headphones and held her cell phone in her right hand, texting with her thumbs. Then she fell out of sight, the door banged, and she slumped into a chair. From the telltale clicks, she did not stop texting (*why do people keep that sound on? It's so irritating.*) If Cotton opened the door right now, Janis probably wouldn't even raise her head.

It's 3:51 PM. Cotton had a few more moments before their appointment at 4. Feeling just a little belligerent, she closed her eyes and leaned back in the chair.

At 4 PM, Cotton beckoned Janis in and stood at the office door, holding it open. Janis neither spoke nor raised her gaze from her cell as she lifted her body out of the chair and shuffled her two different-colored Chuck Taylor corduroy sneakers (red and purple and both hand-decorated with stars and crescent moons) in Cotton's direction. Janis's red and blue t-shirt appeared decorated with the same artistic hand and under her ragged jean shorts, she wore a pair of purple tights. She'd twisted her hair Rastafarian style, trying to make dreads, but her hair was not full enough to hold together well, and the loose ropes fell to her chin, making her look comically disheveled. Cotton didn't even want to think about the appropriation aspect of a middle-class white girl sporting would-be dread locks. Everything about Janis screamed rebellion, but was it normal adolescence, or was it her reaction to her parents' separation?

Janis ignored Cotton completely, which seemed to have become standard with the Prescotts. Each member of the family retreated to their own domains to avoid conflict. However, the written narratives they shared spoke volumes about the ways the family avoided personal interaction. The Prescott house was truly the center of an emotional hurricane right now, and that stress affected the climate in the therapy session, forcing rapid emotional shifts depending on Cotton's interactions.

They lost their North Star, their bearings as a family, once Hailey left the fold. Every member of the family was reaching out for some stability, but they created their own dangerous roles in the family turmoil.

For a moment or two, Cotton waited patiently. Janis continued to text.

Janis's passively rebellious attitude screamed for attention, in a strangely silent way. By simply ignoring Cotton, she created an empty conversation hole, and by doing so, she relieved her parents of the responsibility to maintain control of the family nucleus. Without speaking, she created drama that forced them to focus on their parental responsibilities.

Cotton had been putting the pieces together. Each of the Prescotts held a different puzzle piece of the family's story. Gray told Cotton last week that she got regular calls from Rob Barber, the high school principal. Calls that started warm and friendly have turned more forceful in the past couple of weeks. "I realize you folks are going through some family trauma—don't know/don't want to know unless you think we need to... but Janis's grades have taken a nosedive. I must inform you she has to maintain a B average to hold her place here, but right now, she's got two D's. Thought you might like to know. You could help her out."

Gray translated the comments as a threat, and Cotton thought she might be right, though she didn't say that aloud. "Any other time, they'd send a letter," Gray said. "He is probably getting pressure from parents to get us out of the school."

Janis was really the caretaker in the family, the glue that kept them together. Each of the Prescotts mentioned her when they talked about what was happening at home. *Janis does the wash*, Hailey had said, and Janis helped Cherylynn with her homework, picked up Marcus when Gray worked late, changed the batteries in the fire alarms, scheduled the pool cleaning company every month, and checked on her mother every night before shutting out all the house lights and going to bed.

She needed to stay in school.

Marcus, too, was having problems at school, but it was because he was immersing himself in his games, ignoring everything around him. He was in terrible pain, having lost his role model, his dad.

Cherylynn, on the other hand, appeared to be the "dutiful child," as normal as one could expect, maybe outspoken, but carrying on with her life, playing hoops in the driveway and trying to stay connected with her father. In her own way, she, too, cared for the rest of the family. Her biggest rebellion was that she wanted to date a boy five years older than she. A minor rebellion but pushing the boundaries all the same.

Now Janis plopped a set of wrinkled papers in front of Cotton, who stifled a sigh.

"You're not going to read it, are you?" Janis asked, offended by Cotton's reaction. Her voice was edgy. There was a challenge in her words. "There's a letter from my dad there, and I copied the UrPlace pages special for you."

Cotton struggled to stifle another sigh. She was working from sunup until the moment her eyes closed. Exhausted, she has spent too many hours in the rabbit hole, researching what might help the Prescotts, reading their journals and watching their social media. It's sucking up valuable time. She's never satisfied with reading something once. She read once for the overall meaning, twice to underline and analyze certain phrases, and the third time, she created a table full of notes that she referred to several times afterward. Three, minimum.

It wasn't the Prescotts' fault that she was working so hard. They told her all they could, but they didn't have all the answers to their family interconnections. They couldn't make the connections, but neither could she. *Damn it.*

"I can read it after you're gone, but I'd much rather talk to you while you're here in the office. Gives me a chance to really catch up with you."

"Everything I want to say is on that page." Janis twisted a strand of her purple hair and snapped the gum she's chewing.

"Don't you want me to continue looking online? I didn't know you were going to print it out."

"If you want. I don't care." Janis lifted her phone and started texting.

"Janis, I feel ignored when you're texting while you're here with me." Cotton kept her tone calm and pleasant. She struggled to keep it that way, and she was sure Janis could hear that.

"What?" Opening her Prescott-blue eyes wide, Janis feigned ignorance.

"Let's start again," Cotton said, this time smiling. Warmly, she hoped. "What can I help you with today?"

"I'm just here because the parents want me to be." Janis kept her head down, the cell phone in her hand.

"Do both of your parents want you here?"

"Supposably."

"How do you know that?"

"Well, it's obvious, isn't it? Mom makes the appointments and brings me here. Same thing for my sibs."

"Do you realize that when you're in here, I'm working for you? I'm not your enemy. I took a vow to do no harm, which means no lying to anyone. Whether your parents want you here or not, this time is yours, and nothing you say is repeated anywhere outside this room."

"But I don't pay you."

She had a point. "No, your mother's insurance does. But when you're here in my office, it's you I'm working with."

"Okay. So, that means you'll read what I brought?"

Got to give it to her. She's tenacious.

"Is that what you want right now?"

"Yeah. That's why I came."

"Okay, I'll read it if you'll talk to me before our time is up." Cotton shifted her legs and adjusted her white blouse into the waistband of her brown suede slacks, buying herself a little time.

Janis considered this possibility. She leaned forward in her chair as if about to eat a fabulous dessert, anxiously awaiting that first, lusciously rich chocolate bite. Right now. "My father's letter first."

Cotton paused for a moment before picking up the letter.

My sweet Janis,

I'm sure you know by now that things will not be the same at the house, but I wanted to tell you my side of everything before you make assumptions. First, before I try to explain, let me say that one thing has not changed: my love for you. You will always be my eldest, my beautiful child, no matter what else changes in our lives. And, as I write this, I'm thinking of the moment I first saw your precious face, only seconds after you emerged from your mother's body, and how I felt so proud to be your parent. That feeling will be one I cherish until the day I die. Please don't ever forget that, sweetie. I love you and always will.

Second, whatever you need, whether it's talking to someone or to help with your homework (you know I can't do Math, but I'm good with English), I'll be there for you. All you need to do is say the word, and I'll drop whatever I'm doing to be available to you. I promise that.

And, finally, I need you to be part of my life. Without my children, I feel like nothing is important. So, please write to me, call me, come see me. It might not have seemed that way after I first left, but I need you, I need all of you kids in my life, and I'm sorry if I ever gave you the impression that I didn't.

Now, let me try to explain. Sweetie, you know I wouldn't do anything to hurt you, but I couldn't deny myself any longer, and I knew I could not "be me" if I were still at the house. I must embrace the female me who I've always felt I was deep inside. You probably don't understand it, but my body has always felt wrong for me. I need to change that. The only way I could do that was to be on my own. That probably sounds selfish to you, but I am hoping you will understand what it means to feel you've lived a lie throughout your whole life.

I could tell you about my childhood, about the friends I've lost because I wasn't the person they wanted me to be, and about all the years I'd look in the mirror expecting to see a woman and how disappointed I was each time I saw that man's face looking back at me, and about how I thought being with your mother was going to make everything right, but the truth of the matter is that I didn't want to admit what was going on, because it felt too strange.

It wasn't until the past couple of years that I knew I had to show the rest of the world the person I really want to see in the mirror every day. I also needed to give myself that option of being comfortable with myself, *and that means not hiding in a male body. If I couldn't be honest with myself, who could I be honest with? I have always tried to impress upon you kids is that you should be yourself, that there's nothing more important than knowing who you are, and that being you is the smartest, most likable, and best way to live. You understand, right? We've had this conversation many times. You know, it's really weird, because every time I've said that to you, I've realized that I shouldn't give you the advice that I don't take myself.*

Yes, everyone will look at me strangely, and you kids will probably have a tough time dealing with people who can't understand, but they aren't important to me. You are.

I need to see you in person to explain how I feel in more detail. I want you to see me as I really am, and I want you to know from my heart how important it is to me that you understand I truly haven't changed inside. I just look different outside. But in my head and my heart, I'm the same person I've always been. Now I look like I've always felt. If we could talk face-to-face, I'm sure you would see that.

I'll be at the Bojangles by Triangle Town Center on Saturday at 2 PM. Please meet me there. We can take a ride up to Falls River Dam and just sit and talk. You can ask me whatever you want, and if you're mad at me, so be it. You can yell at me to your heart's content, and no one will hear us but the birds. I just want to see you.

I love you. Dad

Cotton finished the letter with Janis's eyes on her. She balanced on the edge of the chair, stiff and expectant. Cotton folded the letter slowly, then handed it back to her.

"Well?" Janis's voice was a little high-pitched.

"I'd like to ask you: How do you feel about that? This letter... what your father says."

"If you read my blog on UrPlace, you'll find out."

"Why don't we just talk about it now? That's easier."

Janis picked up her cell phone and retreated again.

"I'd really like is for us to have an honest conversation about what's going on in your life." Cotton's mouth twisted, realizing she sounded like a parent. She made an error in judgement. *Shit.*

"Why do you care? You're getting the insurance payments whether or not I talk."

Cotton shivered a little. She hated it when patients got combative. "I care about what's happening with you."

"You don't even know me." Janis's words were a challenge rather than a statement.

"I care about you, because ..." Cotton stopped herself. She almost said *because you remind me of Brighton Ogelle.* She recovered quickly. "... I understand you're going through some tough times right now, and that you're not quite clear what's happening with your dad. If you let me, I can help you deal with this."

"Right. I'm sure you learned a lot about this in school. Maybe your father is a woman, too?"

Cotton's breath caught. "No, but I've helped many people through difficult situations. Other families with a member who's transitioning. Other kids your age." She paused. That was enough explanation. "Why don't we talk about the letter? Tell me how you felt when you saw it was from your dad."

Janis pulled her knees up to her chest, tucking her chin, a defensive posture. "Isn't it good enough for you if I write things down?" Her voice was a little muffled by her knees. "My English teacher always talks about how writers keep journals and how it's cathartic. So, I write and now you won't read it."

Most teens were great at explaining themselves by throwing back an adult's words, particularly when what they really wanted was comfort. That's the hardest thing to ask for. Cotton shifted her hips and tucked a leg underneath herself. It gave her just enough time to decide to bargain. "How about this? I'll read your blog today if we have a proper conversation next week."

"Okay, deal."

As Janis left, Cotton grabbed her tablet and quickly jotted a mini report for Janis's file: *proficient at manipulation and maneuvering, so she gets what she believes is the goal. The prize. What is that prize? And what's the price she'll pay?*

It was uncommon that more than one or two people in a family this size used this coping mechanism. But every one of these Prescotts demanded something they wanted from their therapy sessions, whether it was the length of the appointment or the type of communication they'd use, or which chair they'd sit on. Each wanted to be in control.

~ Book Eighteen ~

Cotton Barnes

Life doesn't make any sense without interdependence.
  We need each other, and the sooner we learn that the better for us all.
  —Erik Erikson

Shoppers mobbed the Triangle Town Center, the Christmas season in full swing, but Deb and Cotton wove their way through the crowds, arms entwined so they wouldn't lose each other, chatting like magpies, as they always did when they're together. It was a tradition for them, this afternoon of shopping for the special presents for family and close friends, a long lunch full of creamy food and bubbly prosecco, then they'd spend the rest of the day wrapping presents and laughing about the year Cotton had two dollars leftover from shopping and spent it on a box of Altoids because "the tin container is so pretty."

They'd been doing this since high school, when they helped each other choose ugly Christmas sweaters for their moms and English Leather soap-on-a-rope for their dads They okayed the first Christmas presents for each other's latest boyfriends, and during those years when special people weren't on their lists (for whatever reason), Cotton and Deb consoled each other as if they were blood sisters, though they looked nothing alike—Cotton, blonde, curly, and tall; Deb, dark, straight. They called themselves sisters of the heart. Cotton knew that any time she spent with Deb was always more valuable than a therapy session. They had gone to college four states away from each other. Deb attended Princeton and became a high-stakes lawyer, while Cotton went to Boston University, fell in love with New England, and honestly didn't think she'd ever return to Raleigh. Through it all, they still made it a point to keep up the tradition when they were home to visit family over the holidays, and now that they were both back to living only a couple of miles from each other again, they took advantage of it every chance they had.

"Ooh, look at this," Deb said, stopping in front of JJill and pointing toward a gray cashmere hip-length sweater. "Doesn't that look comfy?"

"For whom?"

"Me, silly!"

"We're shopping for other people, Deb. That's what Christmas is all about. Other people." Cotton squeezed Deb's arm and clucked her tongue. "It never fails. We always end up getting something for ourselves whenever we're shopping for others, but it's okay since neither of us shops for ourselves at any other time during the year."

"Speak for yourself, woman. I'm not leaving my money for anyone else to spend. So, back to Thomas." Deb ignored Cotton's attempt to change the subject and dramatically flipped back her frizzy jet-black hair and squinted her dark eyes.

"I feel sometimes like I'm looking in a mirror when you do that." Cotton snapped her fingers in the air, whipped her head like a runway model, strutted down the corridor past Zales Jewelers, then dissolved into laughter. Behind her, Deb skipped a bit to keep up.

"It's the baby thing again, isn't it? I knew it. Thomas is bugging you again, isn't he?"

Deb grabbed Cotton's arm and made her stop. "I get the feeling that if you don't agree about starting a family soon, I'm going to be talking to you about divorce. Now don't make me go there!"

"How the hell do you do that? I never even said anything about him." This was why they were friends. Deb called her on bullshit. "As for divorce, we're not about to do that. We've got too much going for us. We've been together too long."

Cotton can't figure out who she's trying to convince: Deb or herself. Deb's right that the baby conversation is taking over every moment of the time Thomas and Cotton share a room together, and both are losing patience with each other.

"Just last night Thomas said, 'Another birthday in a couple of months, right, babe?'" Cotton rolled her eyes. "I don't need to be reminded."

"You got that right." Deb fingered a red silk blouse. "He's cruisin' for a bruisin' if he keeps mentioning age."

"I heard a clip the other day about how much higher the markers are for Down syndrome babies when mothers are over 36."

"This is a big topic, sweetie. You need to sit down and talk about it with him."

"We have, and I'm not ready. I'm sure I don't want a child. Why should I bring a baby into this fucked up world? Besides, he's not the one who needs to carry the baby. I am. And I'm just not ready. I really don't even want to consider it."

"Why?" Deb stopped and placed her hands on her hips, staring at Cotton as if demanding that there's more to the story. And there was. "Give me a more specific reason."

"You know why. Do I have to have more reasons than I already said? I'm just not ready. And why are you pushing me, anyway? You sound like him."

"Dr. Barnes, you know me better than that." Deb had her hands on her hips and cocked her head, smirked. "Besides, would you take that answer from one of your patients?"

Deb had a point, but Cotton wasn't going to let Deb push her into a corner. She turned around and walked toward Dillard's. Deb's heels clacked as she jogged to keep up.

"What the hell. Cotton. Cotton! *Cotton Barnes! Stop!*"

Cotton slowly turned around. Only Deb could get this close, forcing Cotton to act like a child. Not her best behavior, but her worst. It was embarrassing.

"It's time for coffee," Deb announced. Their code that she was calling a truce. Whenever a disagreement went too far, they always stopped and had coffee (though sometime, coffee wasn't coffee but simply a metaphor). That's what best friends did. They knew when to quit.

They slid into the booth at Ruby Tuesday's, and a server named Michelina was at the table to take their order before they'd even shrugged off their jackets.

The first glass of wine went down quickly, then the second, and Deb pushed Cotton into what she called *the-spotlight-is-on-you-conversation*.

"You're hiding in your job, sweetie," Deb said after she drained her second chardonnay and motioned for the waiter to bring them both another. "You need to realize that what you have at home is just as valuable as those patients of yours. It seems like you're really obsessed with the family you're working with... and I'm worried about you."

"Clients. They're not patients. They're clients."

"Clients, patients, whatever. They're not as important as Thomas. Besides, you wait much longer, and your biological clock is going to stop ticking."

Cotton had heard that so many times (from Thomas, his family, her family, other friends) that it made her face burn, but it was the first time that Deb had said it, and for that reason only, she made Cotton stop and think. It felt like a betrayal. And it pissed her off.

"I don't have to have babies right now. Probably never. Besides, I don't *have* to get pregnant at all. We can always adopt, and we can do that anytime. If we want to. Or we can go without having children completely. What a concept! Why is it that everyone thinks that because you're female, you have this innate desire to be a mommy? I'm surprised I'm even having this conversation with you."

Deb raised one eyebrow and smirked. "Excuses. Excuses. Excuses. That's all I've heard from you. What you really need to do is ask yourself what's most important: your marriage or your clients."

"I thought you were on my side."

"I am. That's why I'm pushing you. You're going back into the same rabbit hole you were in last year, and I think there's a lot more here that you're not talking about. My biggest question is why you're so deep in your job that you're ignoring what's going on in your relationship."

"The only thing going on is that Thomas wants babies, and I don't. I thought we could work this out. I still do."

"Is that all that's going on? Are you sure there's nothing else?"

Michelina arrived with more drinks and the artichoke dip they'd ordered, and by the time she left, the conversation drifted back to Christmas presents.

But hours later, Deb's question still reverberated in Cotton's mind.

Is that all that was going on between Thomas and her? Or was there really something more?

She found herself comparing their relationship to the Prescotts, though she had been trying not to lately.

As the Prescott family struggled to understand their own identities, Cotton had rethought her own: therapist, wife, friend, dog mom, outdoors-woman. Why should that identity be determined by others' expectations? She had trouble enough without trying to satisfy everyone else, and she realized she wasn't alone.

She empathized with Hailey's feelings of being trapped by societal definitions of gender, but wondered why anyone needed to identify as either male or female. Why not a combination of all genders? Are any of us truly 100% all female or 100% all male? We might define some aspects of personality as male (her strength, for one. The way she became violent when she was angry. Crashing dishes to the floor, slamming doors. She wanted to control that tendency, but it was there, under the surface.), while other aspects were female (liking soft fabrics, wanting to hug her clients, dissolving into tears during sad movies). None of us were all one or all the other.

So many gray areas, not only in gender but also in relationships.

It hurt her head to think about it all. No matter how much education and experience she accumulated, she still found the human mind to be an incredible mystery.

She struggled to understand how some could withstand incredible pain and loss, while others shut it all off, every bit of reality, every moment going forward. Ending it, taking back control by taking the one thing that was intrinsically and completely one's own: one's life.

Even though she could put the pieces together, she never really understood. She spent a lot of intense hours in research, some brutal soul-baring, but there could never be a total cure for whatever ailed the human spirit. And that's what bothered her the most. If we, as human beings, couldn't take responsibility for each other, if we couldn't care for our fellow human beings, then this earth would truly self-destruct. It was just a matter of time.

But she believed people could save each other. She had to believe that. She had to.

~ Book Nineteen ~

Janis Prescott

Much learning does not teach understanding.
— Heraclitus

Janis stood silhouetted by the light coming through the office windows. Hooking her thumbs in her jeans' belt loops, she rocked back and forth in her old western boots, blinking back tears. "My life sucks, and I don't care who knows it." She rubbed her fists against her eye sockets, appearing younger than usual. Unsure of herself.

Cotton wanted to hug her, but she kept her hands folded on her lap instead. Janis needed to work this out for herself. Even a couple of words of encouragement or a simple "Why?" would probably shut her down. Better to just sit. Wait her out.

"I know there's millions of kids out there who've gone through a divorce with their parents, but I bet not many of them are going through what I am right now. It sucks! Dad's living who-knows-where, Mama is living mostly in her bedroom (which stinks like roadkill), and I'm more or less taking care of my sibs who are clueless about everything and just keep crying about how bad they want Dad to come home. I personally don't care if he ever comes back. He sucks too. Him and his lame-ass note. The crackhead didn't even have the guts to tell us in person."

"But you're talking to him. Why not ask him about that?"

Janis took a breath and plunked into her chair, stretching her legs out in front of her. She laced her fingers in front of her eyes. Traces of royal blue nail polish told the story of the self-mutilation Cotton had already noticed. Janis pulled on her hair regularly and chewed it. Obviously, she's chewing her nails and picking at her polish, as well.

"So, listen to this," Janis continued, "my Sissie, Cherylynn, tells me the other day that she thinks this boy likes her. Whathafuck! She's like barely 12, for chrissakes, and I'm almost four years older and I don't predict a relationship in my life for *years*. Whathafuck is up with that? Another reason life sucks. The worst part is that this kid Cher likes is older than I am! Mama would freaking flip out if she knew, and Cher made me promise not to say anything, but if I see this kid anywhere around my sister, I'm gonna make sure he gets the message that this ain't happenin'. No way. No how. This kid—his name is Joey Martin, and he lives about three streets away from us but in a different subdivision up near the Falls River Dam—thinks he's gonna take my little sister to the Halloween holiday carnival, and of course, Cherylynn thinks it's ok because Mama won't think anything about it since we go every year. I told her she can't go, but she says to me, 'You can't tell me what to do. You're not my mother.' Ha! I would've said the same thing to her if I was doing what she is, but it's not gonna work. I'm gonna make sure she doesn't go, even if I have to tie her to her bed."

"You aren't really thinking of that, are you?" Cotton smiled, all the while hoping Janis had no intention of doing so, that it was all bluff, but Janis wasn't paying attention. She was up from her chair again and playing with the blinds at the window.

"On top of all this shit, Marcus is in his room constantly. Gaming. And I mean 24/7/365. He doesn't play ball anymore, doesn't eat right, doesn't do his homework, just plays that stupid ass game he used to play with Dad all the time. His room is right next to mine, and I can hear those bombs exploding and the screams all night long. I bang on the wall, tell him to wear his headphones, but he doesn't listen. I even went in there one night and pulled the plug on the computer, but he had it back up and running like that." She snaps her fingers. "I don't know when he sleeps! He's playing the damn game all freakin' night long. I wouldn't mind if he didn't make any noise, but the howls and the screams and the groans sound like he's from some other planet. I can't stand it anymore! Doesn't anyone care about how I feel?" She threw her head back and hung out her tongue.

Cotton couldn't help but laugh. Sometimes Janis acted like she was 10, and at other times, she seems as old and wise as Methuselah. If she were the same age as Janis, Cotton felt they'd be friends.

Cotton regularly checked in on Janis's URSpace page, especially reading the conversations she has with her friends about music. They reveal insight into the creative process and a critical genius that Cotton admired. She'd never met a teenager like Janis: full of angst, yes, as most teens are, but able to hold forth on "the stellar colors of that Stevie Ray Vaughan riff" and go on for three paragraphs, comparing Vaughan to the classical guitarist, Julian Bream. She knew her shit.

This is the child I should have had, Cotton thought. She was the perfect age, and when Cotton saw the two of them reflected in the mirror on her office door, the resemblance between them surprised her. Janis could be Cotton's daughter. *If she was mine, I'd get her into music lessons.*

"Maybe I'm too far gone," Janis said, obviously not finished with her rant. "Maybe I'm too far away to come back. Maybe I don't even want to come back. Maybe I just want to fade away and hope that everything in my life—" she underlined the air with her finger — "will turn around and disappear, and I'll miraculously be someone new. Yeah, I know it's an impossible dream, but you can wish upon a star for anything your heart desires, even impossibilities. If serendipity ruled my life, maybe I wouldn't be sitting in a messy room in Raleigh all by myself wishing that time would go backwards. If only such dreams were real, maybe my life would be okay again."

"What would you do to change things?" Cotton asked.

"I don't fucking know." Janis clapped her hand over her mouth. "Sorry," she said from behind the hand.

Cotton flicked away the curse. "If you could do anything at all ..."

Janis shook her head. "Not much I can do, right?" She peeled away some blue polish on her middle finger. "I know one thing for sure. I'm running on my last nerve."

That's a saying Gray used regularly. Cotton wondered if Janis realized she was mimicking her mother.

"Yesterday one of the Lithuanian chicks in the lunchroom starts screeching about something didn't have zip to do with me, and I lost it with her, almost knocked her out. She had her girls around her—three of them—but they kinda backed off. People do that a lot around me. Then this other dickhead says something about my clothes, and then I *did* lose it. Knocked her books all over the place, and I didn't even get in trouble because no one said anything." She laughed, shooting Cotton a guilty look.

"I didn't go straight home that day." Janis yanked on the shade pulls, opening and closing the blinds. Once. Twice. Three times. "Couldn't handle that fucking god-awful stink from the bunch of us hibernating in a leaky house with no hot water, so no one's showered for the past 3 days. Instead, I went to Mr. Schulyer's record store. Y'know that place?"

Cotton shook her head no, but she was thinking about Janis's offhand comment about the shower and connecting it to what Gray had said only three days ago: she hadn't paid the gas bill, but she should have taken care of it by now. *If the kids are going without heat or electricity, I have to report it. I have to.*

"It's this little, tiny place, sort of closet size, in one of the old brick buildings downtown. Used to be a factory or something. He's got thousands and thousands of vinyls. Dad gave me his old record player two years ago, and I've been on the lookout ever since for new-to-me music. Today I got a collection by this group called 'The Creation.' Mr. Schulyer introduced me to them. Their guitar player—I think his name is Eddie something. Phillips, I think—crazy good with his instrument. Makes it squall. Most of the album is this two-beat country stuff, but the guitar... whoa."

The hour was up, though Janis wasn't quite finished and grumbled her way out the door to the waiting room where Gray instantly put down her *People* magazine, slung her pocketbook over her shoulder, and shepherded Janis into the car without more than a nod in Cotton's direction. Cotton suspected Gray was mad about their last meeting. Or embarrassed.

Cotton watched them from the window where Janis had stood only moments before and pulled her cell phone from her pocket, dialing PSNC Gas. She hit 'o' for customer service and when 'Edward' asks what he can do for her today, she says, "I want to pay my friend's gas bill, but I don't want her to know who paid it. You know, I want to sort of make an anonymous gift. Can you help me with that?"

~ Book Twenty ~

The Prescotts

Parents must not only have certain ways of guiding by prohibition and permission, they must also be able to represent to the child a deep, almost somatic conviction that there is meaning in what they are doing.
—Erik Erikson

At 2:13 PM on Thursday, Cotton was filling out her weekly progress report for her supervisor when Gray's number popped up on her cell. A phone call, not a text.

"It's Marcus. He's been rushed to the hospital. I don't know what's wrong. They didn't tell me; just said I should meet them at the hospital. Oh my god, my baby! Dr. Barnes, can you meet me there?" Gray hadn't paused for a breath, and she sounded like she was running, but she wasn't in shape to run.

Cotton didn't hesitate, asked a few pertinent questions like *where are the kids*, and *are you able to drive*, and Gray answered affirmatively to both. After a slight pause, Gray added, "And can you call Hayden... Hailey... and tell him? Her. Tell her. I don't have her phone number." Without waiting for an answer, she hung up, as if saying more would require a conversation she didn't want to have.

It was a step in the right direction for Gray to ask for Hailey (even though Gray doesn't seem able to curb the habit of using Hailey's dead name). No matter how Gray felt about her partner, she still reached out to the person with whom she had three children. But why would she call Cotton first when they rushed Marcus to the hospital? Why not call Hailey—Marcus's other parent—immediately instead of putting it off?

Cotton stopped, the phone still in her hand. Usually, calls like this mean there was a suicide attempt made, and they needed Cotton's services as therapist of record.

God, no. Not again.

Cotton pressed the cool cell phone against her forehead for a moment and closed her eyes. *Only takes a moment for a kidnapper to grab a child and disappear.* Something felt wrong, and she wouldn't get an answer unless she went to the hospital. *Only 55 seconds for a child to drown in a pool.* She yelled upstairs to Thomas that she had an emergency and needed to leave immediately. *Twenty-two veterans a day die by suicide.* He was in his office, and the TV was on, so she suspected he was watching the Duke game instead of concentrating on the project he brought home from work. She yelled again and heard a disgruntled, "Okay." *Suicide is the second highest cause of death for pre-teens.*

Throwing on her camelhair coat over her jeans, she checked her reflection as she passed the hall mirror and dug in her coat pocket for an elastic to gather up her dirty blond curls, grabbed her car keys and left through the front door instead of the garage. *Guns kill approximately 1700 teens each year.* A gasp of cold air made her button the coat as she sprinted down the driveway to her BMW, still parked at the odd angle where she left it, too tired to care after arriving home late from work the night before. *LGBTQ people whose families reject them are eight times more likely to commit suicide.*

She pulled the door handle and slid into the car, whispering, *fuckfuckfuckfuck.* Today was supposed to be her down time. She looked forward to spending a few hours on the couch with Thomas, to watch a movie, and maybe, to snooze. But she spent the whole day reading and doing some much-needed household chores, while Thomas worked elsewhere. As a result, they haven't spoken much. In fact, when she yelled up the stairs to him, that might have been the first time they'd spoken in almost three hours.

This separation between them had become the norm. Thomas had been gone two or three nights out of each of the last couple of weeks on brief business trips. When he was home, he was researching a new product his company was developing (she wasn't even sure what it was), so she'd taken advantage of the quiet time to do research of her own, widening her scope on the various treatments being used for families like the Prescotts.

The car warmed up, and Cotton sat for a moment, thinking of the form she'd been filling out when she got the phone call. She needed to check in with her therapist, her supervisor, but she'd been putting it off. Her supervisory plan was six months long, and she was barely two months in. *So much riding on this.*

Some of Cotton's colleagues disagreed with her that hospital visits and home visits should be part of the therapeutic practice, especially with families. She argued there was no more powerful tool for diagnosing a patient than to see him/her in a natural home setting. *Look at all that I'm finding out about the Prescotts.* People could hide a lot in a formal office visit, but at home, their true selves emerged, and when she made a home visit, visited family members in a crisis, she discovered more about a person in an hour than she did in ten or more office visits. As a result, she could pinpoint issues and speed up the therapy process, which was invaluable. That technique has helped her to grow as a therapist far more than any other. But she couldn't deny there were times, like today, that she'd rather be chilling on the couch watching a mindless movie than planning the next step in a family's healing process. And that would never be something she ever admitted aloud to anyone.

On the way to the hospital, she dialed Hailey's number and got her voice mail. "I got a call from Gray. Marcus has had some kind of accident. She said you should meet her at WakeMed." She left directions to the hospital (though Hailey had probably been there before with one of the three kids), then headed there herself.

Cotton checked in at the Emergency Department and slid her ID badge over her head, adjusting it on her neck as she did at least once a week when she made rounds as a substitute for her colleagues. She hated this part: visiting clients in the hospital. She often drifted off when she was at a patient's bedside, gazing into an unconscious face that might have been talking animatedly only a day ago about a fight with a mother over something silly, like picking up the kitchen. Overdoses. She always thought about what might have been for this person. What if? *If only*.

She shook her head and moved down the hall. She had admitting privileges here at Wake Med and the hallways were familiar: the acrid smell of cleaning bleach, the garish lighting, the buy-them-by-the-dozen paintings of lilies and roses on each hallway wall. She had memorized the emergency room procedures, could name most of the nurses and their hours and their kids, and she had visited the morgue all too often. That's why she hated this part. But she also knew which bathrooms were the cleanest and quietest at those times when she needed a moment to gather herself. And she always needed those moments. She thought at the beginning of her career that they would become fewer, and that the clients who disappeared would become less of a mystery. But she was not becoming more immune to the tendency to take on her clients' pain. She'd lost seven patients over the past ten years to suicide. Three of them were in the military, but the rest were kids. And the last one nearly killed her. All their lives ended in the emergency room.

The place hummed with patients, all the examining rooms full, and the lobby was standing room only. She wondered how many of them could have stayed home, taken a covid test, bought some over-the-counter medications.

Marcus was in the last room in the hallway. Three of the ER nurses gathered in a tight cluster at the door to the room. They nodded, acknowledged her, and returned to their quiet conversation.

Cotton paused in the doorway, unzipped her jacket, let her eyes adjust, took in all the monitors, noted the bottles of fluids and blood and the trailing wires and tubes leading to the tiny figure on the bed. Gray perched on the edge of the bed, her hands hovering right above the blanket as if she was attempting some kind of levitation act. She turned as Cotton came in, moving to the side, revealing Marcus in the bed behind her. Seeing him took Cotton's breath away.

His face was tiny against the pillows, and his dark head created a silhouette against the hospital white sheets. Both eyes were almost closed, caked with maroon chunks of blood, and swollen like little purple and red balloons. He was unrecognizable. Nothing to be seen of the serious little boy with the deep ocean blue eyes. In his place was a bruised and beaten 11-year-old who moaned like an arthritic 80-year-old when he shifted his legs.

Gray twisted the wad of Kleenex she held in her fingers. Nothing intelligible came from her lips except little bursts of "I can't believe this," which she repeated over and over, accenting the words differently each time, as if amazed in ways she couldn't even describe. "I *can't* believe this. I can't *believe* this. I can't believe *this*."

Cotton watched her closely, concerned about which triggers might deepen Gray's already clinical depression. After much thought and discussion with her colleagues, Cotton was convinced that Gray's depression is anaclitic, set into motion when her identity, as defined by her family relationships, was thrown into question because of Hailey's transition. *No big surprise there. Hold it together, Gray.* They'd been working on Gray's depression in therapy. Individually. Now, she needed to be part of the family team, to step in as a healthy mother. Cotton's job would be to keep Gray's head above water. The family relied on her, even though she was the weakest of the clan. Cotton would help (even though she knew she shouldn't).

Nurses and doctors bustled about, making it impossible for Cotton and Gray to talk. One nurse gave Cotton the sign to *please move the family out of the way for a moment*. When Cotton touched Gray on the shoulder to escort her out of the room, she was taken aback momentarily when Gray threw herself into Cotton's arms.

"He'll be okay. The doctors will take care of him. Let's let them do their jobs." Cotton ushered Gray into the hallway, found a seat, and promised her a cup of coffee. Gray's eyes were unfocused and watery, her hair uncombed. On her feet: one loafer and one ballet flat.

They sat in silence for a moment in the comfy club chairs in the waiting room.

"They beat him, Dr. Barnes! They punched and kicked my little boy!" Gray swiped at her reddened nose with a crumpled tissue and sniffed hard. "They beat him because of his father. God, they could've killed him. He's not that big, and he's sweet... damnit, he's a sweet boy. Quiet and smart. Damn it!" Her face changes from a pained white to livid red in the matter of a heartbeat. "I can't believe this! I just can't believe this. Hayden needs to see this. He needs to see what he's doing to us. Damn him! Damn *her*! Shit, damn Hailey."

"Slow down, Gray. Do you know who it was? Take a deep breath and tell me what happened."

"Okay, okay." She exhaled, her tongue curled and sticking out so that it made the tiniest whistle. Her hair was frizzier than usual, and she grabbed at its reddened curls, as though trying to flatten them against the sides of her head. It was a losing battle. She seemed tiny within a Duke sweatshirt that looked ten years old and four sizes too big. Taking a couple of deep breaths, as though getting ready to do a yoga stance, Gray said, "They called me at work. Said Marcus was being taken to the hospital, and when I got here, his teacher met me and told me there was a problem in the schoolyard while everyone was at recess. No one seems to know exactly what started it, but there were at least three other kids involved. All of them are older than Marcus. She found them all on top of Marcus and broke it up. Can you believe it? Bullies!"

She swiped at the air with a small, pale fist. "One of them is the frigging Anderson boy from down the street. He and Marc have never really got along. The other two, well, I don't know them, but the teacher seemed to feel they weren't that bad. Yeah, right, not that bad." She tosses her head back with a rueful laugh. "But they've beaten my son to a pulp."

With pink cheeks and feverish eyes, she punched her fist into her open palm, reacting as any mother would. Angry. Protective. She was a lioness at this moment, the strongest Cotton had ever seen her. In a weird way, Gray's depression might lift a bit if she focused on her children. Right now, she was alive. Ready to fight anyone who hurt her kids. Maybe even kill someone who would harm those she loved.

Cotton reached for Gray, placed her hand flat on Gray's upper arm and tried to make eye contact. "What set it off? Do you know?"

"Guess something was said by someone about some online game, then Marc stepped in, the other kids challenged him, then one of them called his dad a fag, and from what Mr. Niele told me—"

"Mr. Niele?"

"The teacher. From what he told me, the whole schoolyard got into it after that. One kid got a rock from somewhere, which is how...." She broke down crying, sloppy, and loud sobs that echoed down the oddly quiet hallway. Her shoulders quivered, and she sunk into her chair.

Cotton patted Gray's back and shushed her like a baby. Still, Gray's eyes didn't focus. Cotton did what everyone does when there's a trauma: she brought Gray a glass of water. As Gray dutifully sipped, Cotton urged her to breathe deeply, then to release the breath while counting to eight. Within two more sips, Gray's sobbing stopped.

She peered up a bit apologetically at Cotton and said, "I didn't know who else to call. My sister doesn't know what's been going on, and I don't think any of my friends would understand." She sighed and shook her head. "All of this has been horribly exhausting. I don't know how much more I can take." The pasty downturn of her lips and the red tinge around her eyes hinted at a debilitating fatigue. "I just can't figure out how the kids found out about Hayden, I mean Hailey, and I'm so fucking pissed that they did, but he needs to be here. He's their fucking father, for god sakes."

"Who's been minding the kids until you get home from work?" Cotton asked, thinking that a change of subject might work to focus Gray's scattered mind.

"Sometimes I let Janis watch them; sometimes I come home early; sometimes my sister will come over to the house for a little while, but I've tried to make sure she doesn't stay. And I've made the kids promise they won't say anything about their father to anyone who's there. If I can't find anyone, the woman across the street will watch Marcus and Cherylynn until I get home. Hayden used to be there all the time for them, but ...." She blew her nose loudly.

"Hailey," Cotton corrected quietly.

Gray slid her eyes to the side and didn't respond for a moment.

"I've already called her," Cotton said and studied Gray's reaction.

She furtively glanced down the hallway toward the room where Marcus lay, bloodied and broken. "Good," Gray responded, nodding curtly. "He needs to see what his kids are going through." A flash of anger arose in her red-rimmed eyes, but was just as quickly replaced by sorrow. "He needs to be here," she repeated quietly. "I need him... his help."

"*She* would help." Cotton placed a hard emphasis on the pronoun.

Gray grimaced. "I want him—her—to be the parent he—she used to be, but I don't know whether I really want support or help from Hailey or that I'd like to dump some of this anger on him. Her. Could be both." She laughed shortly. "The kids still need their father."

As if confused by her own tumultuous emotions, Gray flutters her fingers. "The kids really need him. Marcus cries out for him in his sleep, and Janis is withdrawing more and more every day. Cherylynn's asking me whether she should move in with her best friend, and I just...I just...don't know how to answer them anymore. And now this. Now, *this*!" She shifted to her feet and grabbed her pocketbook. "We need to be there with Marcus. I can't wait down here to find out what's going on."

She started wandering down the hallway, but Cotton rose, took her arm, and they meandered together. Gray's breathing slowed a little.

"Are the other kids still in school?" Cotton asked as they walked. She clung to Gray's arm, because she could feel Gray shivering.

"As far as I know. Shit, it's hard to tell what Janis is doing anymore. She usually gets out of school around 4, then she goes over to one of her friends' houses. But Cherylynn doesn't get out until about 6 today. She has cheerleading practice."

"Okay. And when was the last time you ate?"

Stopping mid-step, Gray squarely faced Cotton and pulled back her shoulders. "I'm not a negligent mother, you know." Her fingers dug into Cotton's forearm as her eyes silently begged Cotton for sympathy and understanding.

"I know that. We all do the best we can when we're placed in situations we don't understand. We try to act normally in abnormal circumstances, but that doesn't work. Ever."

"I don't want you to think it's my fault."

"This? How could a beating like this be your fault? This is schoolyard bullying at its ugly worst." Though Cotton could never say so to her clients, she would love to see rules put into place that would mandate immediate counseling for any child caught bullying another. Allowing the bully back into a group situation without counseling should be against the law. She had seen far too many children and adults destroyed by the verbal taunts and physical beatings that were a daily part of school life. In her heart of hearts, she saw bullying as the germ of all abuse, but it was an opinion she kept under her hat.

"Not this... I mean, the whole thing with Hayden and how he... well, how he doesn't want to be male anymore."

"Gray, it's probably not the right time to discuss this." Lightly, but firmly, Cotton touched Gray's hand and released her arm, "but let me give you something to think about. There are many reasons people transition to another gender, and some researchers believe it's a biological matter. Some say it's psychological. Whatever the reason, it's always a huge life decision that the transgender individual has thought about making—actually, has longed for—for most of their lives. No one can *make* someone else change their gender." Cotton stressed the words, fervently hoping Gray would understand. "It's not something that happens because the person is unhappy with their agreement or their lives. It's the very thing that makes a person unhappy: being forced to be a gender they don't feel they are. Feeling like they're not living in the right gender is something that's harbored deep inside and usually begins when they're very young. This is not something that happens overnight. Believe me, you are not at fault—and neither is anyone else."

Cotton squeezed her hand, and Gray stared directly into her eyes, as if wanting to believe everything.

"Perhaps when Marcus has healed and we are back on schedule for our visits, we can discuss this at more length," Cotton continued, "but I'm sure right now isn't the time. Right now, you need to be paying attention to your son."

At the door to Marcus's room, the physician in charge pulled Gray aside and updated her on her son's condition. Cotton overheard, "... fractured humerus, lacerations on his face... looks worse than what it really is... really needs to go home tonight..."

Gray nodded, thanked the doctor, then moved to her son's bedside, grabbing his hand and reaching for his cheek. Then she stopped, her hand mid-air hovering above his face like a hummingbird. She leaned over and whispered something to him that Cotton hoped might be, "Don't worry, everything will be all right, Mommy's here."

If she could see his eyes, Cotton was certain she'd be able to tell if there was any psychological trauma, but moving would mean alerting Gray to her concern. Does he feel safe, she wondered?

Gray and Cotton didn't speak directly to each other for over an hour after the doctor's visit. The time went by quickly as other physicians and nurses moved in and around the room, bandaging the cuts on Marcus's face, then splinting his arm. All the while, Gray interacted with her son in perhaps the first truly sympathetic manner that Cotton had observed since starting to treat the family. This event might snap—hopefully, would snap—Gray from the precipice of a deep depression. She finally seemed to realize that her family needed her, especially her youngest child. Perhaps Cotton wouldn't have to request that Gray visit someone to adjust her meds, as she had planned on doing, if Gray hadn't improved by their next session.

When it was clear that they were going to discharge Marcus and that Hailey either hadn't gotten the message or would not be arriving soon, Cotton told Gray she must leave.

"My husband's expecting me home," Cotton said.

Gray glanced up at Cotton. "Already? I was hoping you could at least stay until we were ready to go home. There's no one else...my sister's out of town ..."

"Marcus? Are you okay, son?" Hailey's voice came from behind them, and before Cotton could turn to say hello, she could tell by Gray's stunned expression that Hailey dressed as herself and that Gray still wasn't comfortable with it. And Marcus's face told Cotton he'd yet to see his father dressed as her true self.

~ Book Twenty-one ~

Cotton Barnes

We may define therapy as a search for value.
— Abraham Maslow

Snow. Ice. Freezing rain. Around lunchtime, a front moved in from the Northwest and coated the Raleigh-Durham area in a solid sheet of ice. The storm shut down the whole Triangle by attacking its soft spot: the area doesn't have the capability to salt and sand its roads and highways against an ice storm that came on so unexpectedly. Within an hour or two of its beginning, the storm's sheets of icy rain had painted everything in sight, then the temperature plummeted. Everything froze.

Schools dismissed kids before lunch. Major corporations sent home everyone except essential team members. Cotton canceled her afternoon appointments with the Prescotts, which was fine with her since the safest place for everyone was in front of their own television set watching the storm play out. Safe and warm.

But what no one had considered was that everyone would drive the untreated, icy roads home at the same time. Gridlock. What normally would be a pleasant twenty-minute drive home for Cotton ended up being a two-hour white-knuckle ride on Route 540, skirting Raleigh. Carolinians were not practiced drivers in ice and snow, but even someone who had driven in New England's legendary winters would struggle to maintain control on a solid sheet of ice. The worst part about today's storm was that cars had slithered off the highways and into embankments. The small army of sand and salt trucks couldn't do their jobs, even if they had plenty of warning—which they didn't.

When Cotton pulled into her own driveway, she spent a full five minutes sitting in the car, forehead resting against the steering wheel, trying to breathe deeply and to unclench her fingers from the wheel. She checked her watch: 4:05 PM.

Thomas and she had been texting all morning, but she hadn't heard from him since leaving the office, which was fine since she didn't want him texting while driving. Now that she was home, she felt tempted to pick up her cell and call him. He was obviously not home; the house is completely dark. But even if she called Thomas, she wouldn't be surprised if she couldn't get through. He had a bad habit of not charging his phone. She could only hope that he had a charger in his car with him today. If there was one day he shouldn't be without a cell phone, it was today.

When she finally decided she was ready to go in, the garage door wouldn't open. Frozen shut. She navigated the ice-covered walkway, punctuating each slow and cautious movement with enough expletives to melt an iceberg. Carefully, she pushed her feet along the ground for only an inch or two before falling against the house, but eventually, she made the front door.

It was freezing inside the house, and the cold did not cause the shiver that ran up her spine. It felt odd to walk into an empty, cold house. Thomas had a standard 9-to-5 day, so he was always home before she was. On the rare occasion when he traveled, she took herself out for dinner or met some friends for a glass of wine so that by the time she returned home, she was ready to fall into bed and watch a little late-night TV before her eyes closed. Whoever invented sleep-timers for TVs had her vote for a genius award.

Since they had a standing agreement that whoever got home first started dinner, she started a fire to take the chill off, then raided the refrigerator, taking out the ingredients for a bowl of comfort food: an easy fish chowder. Thomas would want something warm to eat when he got home.

She thought of him, wondering where he was, as she cut the onions, watching the stick of butter sizzle at the bottom of the stockpot, then blending the onions with some stock she had in the fridge, half a dozen red potatoes, a tablespoon of garlic, chunks of cod and flounder, and finally, a good dollop of heavy cream, kosher salt, and crushed black pepper. Comfort food.

She was on her second glass of Sauvignon Blanc, the fish chowder cooked and covered to stay warm, and it was well past 6 PM, but Thomas still wasn't home. She hadn't heard from him for hours.

The kitchen TV had been on while she was cooking, and the reporters said the accident toll leveled off since most people had arrived home. The major arteries in and out of Raleigh were looking less like parking lots and more like empty freeways. She didn't want to succumb to worry, but she was wondering whether her husband was one of the dozens stranded on the side of the road or, worse, involved in an accident.

The temperature dropped 20 degrees in less than an hour, causing schools and businesses to send students and workers home.

Her only solace was that she would have received a phone call if Thomas was in the hospital. Cold comfort, but it was all she could think of right now.

Thousands of motorists have left cars stranded alongside roads and in parking lots.

By 7 PM, she started calling Thomas's phone every ten minutes like a frantic fool. Each time, it went straight to voice mail. Logically, she knew after the third call that the phone was probably dead, but she still called, counting the rings—twenty-two—before the full mailbox message announcement.

Outside, the moonlight reflected on the snow like a thousand mirrors. Silvery ice coated every tree, and while the scene was Ice Queen beautiful, it was a horrible and dangerous beauty that had already killed three people on Raleigh's highways.

She threw on a ski jacket and Uggs, determined to at least walk out to the end of the driveway to see whether any salt or sand covered the road. She grabbed her hiking pole from where it had been gathering dust beside the front door and stepped out. One more step and she was flat on her backside, bouncing down the three stairs to the walkway. Fred watched her from the doorway, whining a little that she wasn't taking him out.

"Shit." Her hands scrambled on the ice. Nothing to grab. She grappled for anything, but slid again. Carefully, she maneuvered herself to her knees and crawled to the stairs, pulled herself up, and promptly fell right back down. Finally, Cotton baby crawled back into the house, the ice cold and crunchy against her palms, giving up on walking down the driveway. "There's no way Thomas can drive in this," she told Fred as she shimmied herself into the kitchen. The dog's tail wagged hesitantly.

Now, she was ready to call the State Police to ask whether the local hospitals had admitted matching her husband's description. Her chest tightened. *Twelve point six-seven miles to Thomas's office. Twenty-five-minute drive. Normally.*

Back in the house, she stood at the kitchen sink, a perfect view of the ice-covered driveway. Her silver BMW reflected the blue and white ice. She couldn't imagine what it was going to be like to get into the car tomorrow morning, especially since the weather report said the temps were going to dip even lower overnight.

Fred toddled into the kitchen. Nuzzled her hand as if wanting reassurance that she would stay home.

"What kind of watchdog are you, ol' boy?" She rubbed his ears, and he leaned his thick retriever body against her legs, as if he sensed she was upset. His muzzle was whitening, and she suspected he was going deaf, which explained why he didn't come to greet her the instant she got home anymore. "Where's your dad, buddy?" she asked him, as if he could answer.

Fred was ultimately only interested in relieving himself and took her to the front door for that purpose. Though he had better luck staying upright than she did, more than once his aging paws went in different directions, making it look like he was ready to try out for the

Olympic Ice-Skating team. He didn't need to be coaxed back into the house and went straight to the hearth in front of the fireplace, the only area that was warm.

The heat's off. Why do we still have electricity? It probably won't be long before they lost it, so she busied herself gathering all the candles in the house—*twenty in glass mugs, thirteen tapers, forty-two votives*—placing some in each room and lighting half of them. *Thirty-eight, because it's an even number.* If they lost electricity, she could light the rest later.

She struggled to control her imagination, telling herself that Thomas wouldn't answer his phone if driving in these conditions. Thomas was probably the last one to leave the office, making sure everyone was gone before he himself got behind the wheel. And she reminded herself that if he passed someone on the road who had slipped into a ditch, he would pull over and stay with the driver until help came. He was just that kind of guy.

Tonight, she wished he wasn't.

Tonight, she wished he was that guy who left the office first so he could get home to his own family.

Tonight, she wished she had driven up the driveway to see their house lights on and his face at the kitchen window.

When 9:30 came and headlights finally shone into the driveway, she'd had *three glasses of wine* and didn't think twice about flinging open the front door and *sliding down the three stairs*, flailing, half-running, slipping across the driveway to collide with her husband as he exited his car. Together they collapsed on the icy surface, laughing hysterically and trying to hold on to each other as if their lives depended on it.

"It's fucking freezing," he said, and they held hands and slid toward the porch like cross-country skiers, *pushing their legs forward three times* to reach the door.

Later, when they were between the warm flannel sheets of their king-sized bed, Fred snoring gently on his mat in front of the smaller fireplace in their room—that they never used—she reached for

Thomas, wrapping her legs and arms around him as if encasing him within her hold to keep him safe forever, and they made love the way they used to when they first got married and couldn't get enough of the taste of each other's skin. Completely, freely, with no thought of tomorrow because tonight was all that mattered.

And it was only when she was falling asleep that she realized she hadn't thought of *the Prescotts in seven hours, 18 minutes, and 42 seconds.*

~ Book Twenty-two ~

Marcus Prescott

Courage is fire, and bullying is smoke.
—Benjamin Disraeli

Gray and Cherylynn waited in the office lobby while Cotton talked to Marcus alone. His eye was still swollen shut and new black-and-blue bruises shaped like small countries rose on his face, arms, and legs. Still, he smiled as he settled into his seat. She fought the urge to hug him.

"Thanks for coming to see me in the hospital, Dr. B.." Marcus's voice was high-pitched and tender, a little boy's rather than an adolescent. He tugged at her heartstrings. *No child deserves to be beaten by bullies like this.* But even worse than the physical beating was that he'd carry with him his memory of that moment. The black and blues would go away, but the fear might never leave.

"Are you feeling better?"

He didn't answer. Outside, a cold rain pelted against the office windows. Vehicles made sloshing sounds as they navigated the puddles. All it took was a few clouds for this street to flood. In a short ten minutes, a rainstorm could cause a two-foot swell to build up and swallow the road. The thought of it made Cotton pull her sweater tighter around herself, and she kicked her shoes off so she could tuck her cold feet up under her hips. Enough with the bad weather for the entire season. *Mental note: bring wool socks to the office.*

Marc must be cold, too, she thought, because he kept his hoodie up over his head, sinking into it so far that it covered half his face. He stuffed his hands deep into the kangaroo pocket.

At 11, Marcus took life more seriously than most forty-year-olds. When the kids bullied him, he seemed to grasp the psychological underpinnings of his tormentors. ("They heard things from their parents, probably.") His hypersensitivity opened him up to depths of emotion that most never feel, and he was far too young to have experienced the various textures of despair, anguish, and grief that engulfed him.

A charcoal shadow of pain rimmed his round and solemn eyes. The depth of their emotion took her breath away. He rarely lifted his eyes from his games, so the visceral connection of his gaze now took Cotton off her game for a moment.

Mentally, she did a retake, wondering how long it had been since she'd looked at him full faced. Most of the time, she watched his profile as he played a game or held his Game Boy in his hands while talking to her. He ducked his head when they talked, almost as though painfully shy. Second, had she ever seen him in more agony? Even after the first weeks of living without Hailey, he hadn't lifted his head. That was painful to watch. Maybe the sea of sorrow in his eyes was the reason he hid in his games. By deflecting the family drama, he could deny any existed.

Cotton gripped the sides of her chair, once again fighting the urge to hug the youngest Prescott. Comfort him.

"You okay, Marc?" Cotton kept her voice low and didn't move though her nails dug into the chair frame.

"I'm okay, I guess." The way he gingerly shifted in the chair told Cotton otherwise. He was still hurting, probably tired of answering questions, and she sensed some embarrassment. "Janis's making me take aspirin every couple of hours so that I don't get sore," he added. "It kinda helps."

"Okay, tell me if they still give kids ice cream like they gave me when I was in the hospital when I was five. They think ice cream fixes ev-er-y-thing." She drawled the last word, pronouncing every syllable, and Marc's little laugh rewarded her.

"Nah, they didn't give me any ice cream, but they did come in all the time to check the ice bag they put on my head. Glad I don't have to do that anymore." Marcus's shoulders shivered a little with the memory.

"But you're home now, in your own room...."

"Yup, and Cheryl's being too nice to me. Scary nice."

Cotton nodded sagely, as if she agreed that, *yes, sisters being nice can be scary sometimes.* It might make him feel a little more comfortable if he had an ally. She needed him to trust her. *Tell me everything.*

"She's bringing me food and crap. I think Mom's making her."

"Really? Why do you think your mom's making Cherylynn bring you food?"

"Because every time Mom comes in the room, she cries. Probably doesn't want me to see anymore, so she sends everyone else. Janis is okay, I guess. She's nice, but Cheryl and I ... she's mean to me, but I give it right back to her. Not used to her being nice to me, is all." He shrugged as if it didn't matter and dug deeper into his pocket, brought out the Game Boy, shutting Cotton from his peripheral view. The ambient screen light casts a ring of blue onto his face, making him almost skeletal.

Cotton's fingers tapped against her lips as she watched him. *Nineteen, twenty, twenty-one... should I wait for him?* "You must get to play games a lot now, huh, Marc? Are you spending a lot of time in your room?"

"Yup, Mom doesn't say anything. She doesn't care, I guess." The game's sounds oddly coincided with the tapping of a sudden, sharp rain against the window.

"Since you're playing a lot at home, how about you take a break while you're here and we'll just talk, okay? That way, when you get home, it'll be much more fun. What do you say?"

He glanced up at Cotton for a second, then back down at the game. It was easier to immerse himself in something that took absolutely no interaction with people. He'd talked about what happened to him with every member of his family, with multiple officers from the Raleigh Police Department, with several teachers who'd visited him in the hospital. He was sick of talking about what happened. *Wrong thing to suggest.*

"How about you tell me about WarCraft?" she ventured. If he took the bait, she could learn more about him and slide in some questions about family dynamics, too.

"I already told you about it. You're a noob." He snorted a little and continued to focus on the game. Dismissive.

"I want to know about characters that you build. What happens if someone gets bored with a character? Can you delete it? Or do you have to keep all those characters?"

"They're avatars." His hoodie muffled his voice, and the Game Boy etched his profile in a Grinch-like green.

"How many do you have?"

"Dunno. Maybe about thirty. Maybe forty."

"That seems like a lot."

"Nah. Some guys have like a hundred." His fingers slowed for a moment, and he sidelong glanced at Cotton. He was adding up two-plus-two and coming up with suspicion. "Why do you want to know this stuff? You want to play or something?"

"Maybe. I'm curious about whether I could do it. Do girls play?"

"Sure. I have plenty of girl friends who play. Not girlfriends, y'know, just girls who play."

"How would I start if I wanted to play?"

His eyes lit up. For the next twenty minutes, he explained how to build an avatar, where the weapons came from, and talked about the other girls he knew who played, and how many times he'd won a battle. Not once did he mention his father, nor did Cotton ask. *He will, eventually. I'll get him to talk to me. Trust me completely.* Finally, she ran out of questions, and he reached for the Game Boy again.

"Tell me about what happened at school." Cotton addressed the elephant in the room, throwing caution to the wind, and hoping that slipping the suggestion in when he least suspected would cause an automatic response. She didn't want him to think.

Marcus stopped short of picking up the Game Boy and looked at her with terror in his normally placid, Prescott-blue eyes. "I don't really wanna ...."

"Nothing else can happen, Marc. We're here in the office. Maybe if you talk about it...." *Oh, fuck, this is exactly what I didn't want to happen.*

"No! I'm sick of talking about it. All Mom does is talk about it all the time. I'm tired of it." This time, he picked up the Game Boy and his brows knit together as he made a production out of playing one fast and furious game. His cheeks were flushed, and his breath came in short pants.

"Are you mad at your mother?" Cotton asked when he paused. He acted like he didn't hear her. "Marcus," she said, raising her voice a little, "are you mad at your mother or something else?"

He whipped his head back and forth, a very clear negative answer.

"Are you mad at the kids who beat you up?"

"Shit, yeah," he said. "Do you think I love them for it?"

She wasn't surprised by the venom in his voice. "How many of them were there?"

"I don't want to talk about them."

"Marcus, you know we're here to talk, not play on the Game Boy, right?"

"I told you I don't want to talk!"

"You don't want to talk about the beating?"

"I don't want to talk all!" He glared at her, cheeks flushed and his eyes full of unshed tears.

"What would you like to do?"

"Not talk. Nothing."

"Would you like to just sit there and wait out the rest of the session?"

He nodded. "I have a headache." His hands shook the Game Boy in wavelike tremors he seemed unable to control.

"Okay, we can do that." Cotton sat in the chair with her hands folded, silently watching him. Thirty-two minutes left in the session. It was a waste of valuable session time, but she had waited for clients before. Sometimes silence gave people time to think about what they wanted to say. Often, people couldn't let over thirty seconds go by before they need to fill it with conversation. She counted the seconds regularly.

But with Marcus, the seconds quickly became moments, then counting those moments became a challenge. This was a standoff. *Is he counting the minutes, too, or is he just playing that damn game?*

Ten minutes passed.

Fifteen.

Marcus hadn't lifted his head. Impressive.

She scratched her ear, coughed, and shifted in her seat. He lifted his eyes toward her, but she pretended not to notice.

"Are you really going to just sit and wait?" he asked.

Bingo. I win.

"Yup. Unless you want to talk."

"It's all Dad's fault." His head was down again. "That's what Mom says, anyway."

That comment didn't surprise Cotton. Parents often shared comments about their former partners with their kids. Sometimes without thinking about it. Sometimes because they wanted the kids to side with them. Sometimes to make the kids feel inferior. Always inappropriate, but more common than parents would admit.

"Do you believe that?"

"Not really."

"Whose fault do you think it is? Who or what caused those kids to beat you up?"

"Dunno. They're assholes." He cut his eyes at Cotton as if expecting her to tell him not to cuss.

"Not so nice, I agree."

"Can I still call him Dad?" The question came out of nowhere. He paused, and this time looked at her sincerely. Tears in the corners of his eyes.

"That's up to him and you, I think, don't you? That's not something I can decide."

"Chad Kimbrough says I can't. He says once someone decides to change, they're not the same person. I don't want Dad not to be my dad anymore."

"I think that's something you need to discuss with your dad."

"Mom's really pissed at him. She's not going to let me see him anymore. Forever." This time, the tears fell in earnest.

"Forever's an awful long time, Marc. Are you sure that's what she meant?"

"That's what she said. She said Dad's a sick person, and he doesn't have any right to have kids anymore. That's what she said." He sobbed, sucking in air, and swiping at his nose.

Cotton wanted to reassure him you couldn't take away anyone's right to have kids, but it wasn't her place to do so. Instead, she asked the toughest question: "Do you believe your mother?"

Marcus's eyes widened, and his sobbing turned into a hitched-up sigh. "Will you tell?"

"Never. I will never repeat anything you tell me unless you tell me you're going to kill someone. What happens in here is between the two of us."

He shook his head, slowly at first, then so fast that his hair flipped back and forth. *Like a younger version of Thomas.* He didn't believe his mother. No way. No how. And he didn't even want to speak the words.

"Sometimes people hide who they are." He glanced up at the ceiling, thinking. "But sooner or later, you can see it. Sort of like Grogar and Rothkine. He's so mean and angry, but when Rothkine is around, he relaxes and laughs, and you can kinda tell that's who he really is."

A knock at the door stopped her from asking another question. She heard Gray on the other side of the door saying something.

"That's all for today, Marcus." Cotton rose, and so did Marcus. For a second, he paused, then he wrapped his arms around her waist and hugged her. Hard. She hugged him back, fighting tears at the back of her eyelids.

As he joined Gray and Cherylynn, Cotton wondered whether she could help Marcus learn to protect himself when his world was falling apart around him. Someone needed to be there for that kid. For all the Prescott kids.

~ Book Twenty-three ~

Hailey Prescott

To say that gender is performative is a little different because for something to be performative means that it produces a series of effects. We act and walk and speak and talk in ways that consolidate an impression of being a man or being a woman.
—Judith Butler

"The more we tell a story about our past, the more we believe the re-telling rather than what actually happened. We have the power to shape those stories differently." Cotton leaned back and watched Hailey's reaction run the gamut from doubting to considering to almost agreeing.

They'd been talking for over fifteen minutes. More than a quarter of the way through the session. Hailey slumped against the overstuffed wingback, her hand dangling as she talked. Cotton, feeling warm and philosophical, was in her usual position, one leg tucked underneath her hip. The hum of the space heater between them was almost hypnotic. Comfortable. Two people having a casual conversation over tea mugs.

Cotton lifted her still-warm cup to her lips.

"You know, I think that's true," Hailey said slowly, gazing up at the ceiling. "I can reshape a narrative in fiction anytime, but I don't know what that means here...in therapy."

Cotton cocked her head for a moment, thinking about the whole family and how they argued over details when she had them all in her office for family sessions. *No, I had Rice Krispies for breakfast,* one of the kids would say, while someone else swore that the person ate the last of the Cheerios. An argument like that could go on for a full hour-long session and accomplish absolutely nothing.

"You want to tell me your version of the fight at the hospital?"

Hailey tucked her hair behind her ears. "Well, when you called, I was already dressed in a nice black wool pencil skirt and hip length white angora sweater with black tights and boots. I'd bought the outfit the day before. Thought it would be professional. I really didn't think it would be a problem being dressed that way. It wasn't like I had a pink feather boa wrapped around my neck. 'Fuck it,' I told myself, and I headed for the hospital. No hesitation. They hurt my son. I needed to go to the hospital."

Hailey's jaw was rigid, as if she'd thought of this often. "Gray is the first one I see. She's frozen in place, and it's obvious from the pain in her eyes that she instantly resents that I'm there. Know what I mean? She glares at me, recognizes me, running her eyes up and down my body. She curls her lip. I know that look. Disgust. She's so angry that I'm Hailey. Hates seeing me like this." She waved her long fingers like Vanna White, to show her dress and heels. Today's outfit was red and black, with a geometric design on the dress. Her shoes: the same low black heels she always wears. *Sexy on the top, sensible on the bottom.* Hailey was what most would call attractive, with a style that was feminine but business-like. She could have been an administrative assistant for the local real estate attorney.

"Shit, I thought when I saw her look from Marcus to me, then back again, that she was hoping she could stop my son from seeing me somehow. Marcus really didn't seem to recognize me, and I wondered if it was the medication they gave him or the fact that he can't see very clear with his eyelids swollen shut. Oh my God, Dr. B. My heart lurched. Nothing else mattered."

"I cannot imagine how that felt," Cotton said, though she can imagine it and she doesn't want to. When she saw Marcus in that bed, she gasped. Yes, she understood how Hailey felt.

Hailey nodded. "So, I ask Gray what happened, and she's moving her mouth, but she's not talking."

"Sounds like you caught her off guard."

"Whatever. Anyway, eventually she says 'Marcus got into a fight in the schoolyard. We won't know much more, as far as details go, until he's more talkative'."

Cotton put herself back into that moment in Marcus's hospital room and remembered seeing Hailey enter the room in her stylish outfit and Gray's shocked reaction, but she didn't remember saying anything. "You told me about the fight."

"Right, right. Now I remember. Then the nurse came in ..."

"And I asked, 'Excuse me, can I ask about my son?' I realized right then that I was getting a different reaction than I would have if I were here as Marc's dad. So, I asked point blank: 'Can you tell me about his injuries? I'm his ...' And I couldn't find the words, so I just said, 'other parent.'"

Cotton nodded.

"And when that nurse's eyes popped open wide that I hadn't done a great job covering my five o'clock shadow with foundation. I'm still learning." Hailey laughed at herself, a warm and almost forgiving sound.

Cotton shared in the laugh. She had learned to recognize and appreciate Hailey's dry, self-deprecating sense of humor. She'd spent almost fifteen minutes during their last session doing a hilarious monologue about watching YouTube makeup videos. She used a Julia Childs voice to talk about the various shades of foundation, making up over-the-top names for each (*sickly brown puppy brown, pale sky at dawn, cinnamon toastie, peachie queen*), bringing Cotton to the type of laugh that made her gasp for breath as she wiped rivers of tears from her cheeks.

"I almost died when she said I thought Mrs. Prescott was already here." Hailey glanced down to the side. "I knew then that I had to say, 'I'm his father,' but it wasn't until I saw Marcus staring at me, too, that I started shaking."

"That's when I left the room," Cotton remembered. "Right when the nurse told you Marcus had a broken humerus and some bumps and bruises, but it wouldn't take him anytime at all to get back to normal."

"I know. While you were gone, I asked Gray if Dr. Ralkizi was available, or whether she got the doctor on staff. And when she looked at me, my heart hurt for her. She's aged. Her face was splotchy, and her eyes, man, were they red. Doc, I am seriously worried about her. That t-shirt and jeans she wears look (and smell) as though she has worn them for a few days. That's just not Gray. Her shoulders are bony. She's as damaged as Marcus. Beaten. Broken. God, I hope I didn't do that." Sighing, Hailey's head sunk into her shoulders.

Cotton had thought the same thing about Gray that day, but she couldn't tell Hailey that. She also couldn't tell Hailey that she's in better shape than the rest of the Prescott family. She had support from other therapists, a team of doctors working on every aspect of her transition, and a new group of friends who understood. None of the other Prescotts had that much encouragement. Instead, they struggled with classes, budgets, bullies, false friends, lost weight, and a lack of sleep.

"She wouldn't even look at me after you left," Hailey continued, as she picked at a thread on the corner of the armchair. "Maybe that's just as well, though. There's hatred in her eyes when she looks at me, and that breaks my heart." She reached for her cup of tea, which had to be cold by now. She took a gulp, then wiped her mouth with the back of her hand and continued.

"You know, Dr. B, she motioned to me to come to one corner of the room, and I had this sense of...I don't know...my heart was beating really fast. I know that look in her eyes. She was ready to pounce. And she did. She whispered in my ear, 'It's your fault about this Hayden. You're the one who started him on WarCraft. If it wasn't for you and this ridiculous game and you. You....' She made a sweeping gesture that made a statement about the way I was dressed and how my hair was done. '... we wouldn't be in this damn mess.' Can you imagine? She's the best when it comes to slinging guilt around. Believe me. But if that wasn't bad enough, up pipes Marcus from his bed, 'It's not Dad's fault ....' He's always had incredible hearing. And Gray snapped right back at him: 'Well, whose is it then? Mine? Your sisters'?' She's never been good at keeping the kids out of our discussions. We might as well have had transparent walls in the house."

Cotton mentally noted that statement, jotting on her yellow pad to write it in her session notes later this evening.

"Maybe part of it *is* my fault," Hailey says. "I know it's too late to apologize, but I'd like to... and... I don't know... make it better?"

"It's never too late to apologize," Cotton said, "though I think the only thing you might apologize for is the fact that you left a note. Other than that, you don't have anything to be sorry for, correct?"

Hailey nodded, her face serious.

Cotton wondered whether an apology would truly repair any of the hurt the Prescotts felt, though she didn't doubt that all the Prescott kids would take an apology and a hug any time. "So, is that what you want to do?" she asked Hailey.

The only sound for a long moment was the gentle whirring of the space heater's fan.

"I don't want my kids hurt." Hailey's voice broke. She dug in her pocketbook and came up empty.

Cotton pointed to the box of Kleenex on the side table. "How about we table this discussion until we all can meet in my office and, instead, concentrate on Marc? He's more important right now."

"You're right." Hailey blew her nose. "We need to figure this out as a family."

~ Book Twenty-four ~

The Prescotts

The doctor should be opaque to his patients and, like a mirror, should show them nothing but what is shown to him.
—Sigmund Freud

It's the week before Christmas, the toughest season of the year for many people. Those under treatment are usually affected more intensely than people who are currently at a healthy place in their lives—and even the healthiest can feel a lull of some sort and a downturn after the big day. Expectations are high during the holidays that happiness will miraculously arrive as a perfectly managed family get-together, a perfectly arranged and accepted marriage proposal, or the perfectly kept surprise about the perfectly perfect gift. It's a season of soaring highs and crushing lows, the time when psychiatrists' appointment calendars are full, and suicide hot lines have endless calls waiting. Everyone is having money problems, the couples are all fighting, the kids are asking for impossible gifts, and those who already have issues with family acceptance are riding rollercoasters of emotion.

It wasn't Cotton's favorite time of year anyway and to be in family therapy during this holiday season presented enormous difficulties for everyone involved. Years of dealing with health crises, mini wars that seemed to pop up everywhere, crazy people committing racist crimes, and Mean Uncle Joe, who happens to have a rifle and wants to "teach the kids a lesson" by scaring them, but it discharges, and he's not sure how it happened. Normal issues multiplied during holiday time. Family issues that were ignored throughout the rest of the year came to the forefront. Holiday parties and traditional rum punches tested addictions to the limits, and when you mix unresolved family issues with alcohol, up comes disaster.

Cotton had been anxiously waiting for the Prescotts all afternoon. They were not late. She simply didn't have anyone to wait for other than them. She thought about them all the time, wondered how they were doing at ten o'clock at night when she was turning off the television and taking Fred out one last time, or when she brewed her morning coffee and watched the woodpecker arguing with the cardinals at the bird feeder, or when she drifted away when she was with Thomas, thinking about the Prescotts rather than what her husband was telling her. She was worried about them. Really worried about them.

Marcus was still recovering from the bullying, which Hailey had decided was her fault. Gray was a hot mess. Clinically depressed, Cotton was certain. Janis had developed several defense mechanisms and took on more responsibility than she could handle. And Cherylynn employed avoidance techniques that made it appear that nothing bothered her. She wasn't fooling anyone.

Cotton had her work cut out for her today, but it was a challenge she was excited to face. She couldn't let any of them slip through the cracks. It was a personal promise she made to them. Not verbally, but in her heart. She promised she'd make everything all right, and that she'd keep them safe. No one was going to hurt themselves or anyone else on her watch. She promised.

When Cotton entered the waiting room to gather them for their visit, Gray was in the far corner chair reading *The Art of Racing in the Rain*, Marcus slumped on the couch with his face backlit by the Game Boy he held in his hands, Janis stared sullenly into space, and Cherylynn texted from her place on the floor where she'd propped on her elbows on a pillow. Hailey stood by the door, studying one of Cotton's paintings as if attempting to memorize it. She did that often.

It seemed transparent walls surrounded each family member, keeping them in their own little silos. No one was close enough to another person to reach out and touch, and it didn't take a body language expert to interpret what was going on. The room was full, yet no one made eye contact with anyone else, and the air bristled with unspent anger.

It wouldn't be an easy session.

The office was smaller than the lobby, so the Prescotts had no choice but to sit near each other. Still, Cherylynn sat on the floor, Marcus played his Game Boy (his face was healing nicely), Gray busied herself putting her book away, and Janis folded her arms across her chest and stared angrily at Cotton as if she was to blame for everything that had ever gone wrong in the entire universe. (She needed a target, and Cotton was a safer one than her parents.) Out of all of them, Hailey seemed the most uncomfortable. She held her pocketbook tight against her belly as she perched on the edge of the straight-backed chair, feet primly planted against each other on the floor. She was the only one, besides Janis, who ventured a glance in Cotton's direction.

Cotton smiled brightly and clapped her hands together, immediately hating that she was acting like a nursery schoolteacher. "So, how were your finals?" She looked at each of the kids, forcing them to make eye contact. "Everyone happy to be on break?"

They all murmured at the same time, looking in different directions.

"Okay."

"Fine."

"Not doing anything."

Cotton couldn't tell who said what.

Hailey shifted her pocketbook. "Last time I had to worry about grades was so long ago, it feels like the Ice Age." She giggled.

Marcus glanced up from his Game Boy with arched eyebrows and stared at Hailey as if trying to figure out who she was and not quite believing why he recognized her. Janis's eyes flittered from one face to the other, her lips set in a straight line. Cherylynn stared at her mother, who was still busy fitting her novel into her handbag.

"It looks like your face is healing, Marcus. How are you feeling?" Cotton smiled at him encouragingly when he looked her way.

"Feel okay." He squirmed a little, uncomfortable that Cotton watched him so closely. "No probs."

"Do you want to talk a little about what happened that day?"

"Nooo... not really," he drawled, irritated. "You already asked me that question last week."

"Can you at least tell me what started it all?"

"We just got into it because of the game."

"What game?"

"The one online." He continued to concentrate on his Game Boy, his dark hair conveniently flopping over his eyes like a visor.

"WarCraft?"

He nodded without looking up.

"Do they play, too?"

He nodded again. Across the room, Janis snorted and bounced angrily on her chair. Cotton ignored her obvious need for attention. *We'll deal with that later.*

"Was the fight about the game?" Cotton continued to push.

"Sort of." He still played, purposefully ignoring her, and she wasn't surprised. They'd already been over this subject, but not with the whole family in the room.

"Marcus, when you play on the Game Boy while I'm talking to you, I feel like you really don't want to look at me or speak to me. Is that true?"

Gray and Hailey exchanged an unexpected glance. Both leaned forward as if ready to discipline their son. Hailey opened his mouth to speak, but Gray's hand flew up toward the heavens: a silent signal they'd probably employed so often throughout their marriage that it had become habit. *Hush,* Gray silently told the person who used to be her husband. *I'll manage this.*

"Naw, I like you, Dr. Barnes. It's just ...." Marcus's silky brown hair fell over his bruised eye. "It's just I don't want to talk about it."

"You can talk to her, Marc," Gray said. "Go ahead. Tell her what happened."

Marcus's shoulders squeezed up toward his ears, and he pulled back into the chair, lifting the Game Boy a little more and concentrating on the screen. This child did a much better job communicating during individual appointments. He appeared intimidated by the family members. Cotton noted during their last session that he'd made eye contact with her throughout the entire hour. With both his parents and his siblings here, he deflected rather than opening up. His own coping mechanism.

"How about if we talk about it the next time you're here on your own, Marcus? Would that be easier?"

A wave of relief washed across his face, and he nodded gratefully. Cotton smiled and turned to the others. "All right, let's talk about the Prescott family and what's going on with the rest of you. How's your week been?" No one jumped right in, but that was all right. She needed to control the questioning and the discussion, making sure everyone felt they'd had an equal amount of time and support during the session. Everyone. Not a simple task.

"Hailey, I wonder if you'd like to start. Do you want to share how everything is going with you?" In one of the first meetings with Gray and Hailey, Cotton had told them there might be a time when she'd rely on them to set the tone during a family session. It would help the children to trust Cotton if they saw that their parents already did. Even if they didn't trust each other.

Hailey cleared her throat and colored slightly. Her makeup was more natural now than it was the first time she arrived as Hailey. The hormonal treatments must have started long before she left the family house for them to have made such a difference in her appearance in only a couple of months. Usually, it takes at least five months for substantial changes to be noticeable. *Has it been that long? This is the third meeting with the whole family, but there've been at least four or more with each family member separately. Several months of therapy.*

"This isn't going to be easy." Hailey twisted the pocketbook strap between her fingers. "I wanted to tell you all before I left, but I wasn't sure whether I could explain it in a way you'll understand it."

She paused, screwing her mouth one way, then the other, as she struggled to find her next words. "Like Dr. Barnes says, we all have a story. A life story. We might, um, share scenes from that life, but we each see them... from... what's the term you use, Dr. B? Perspective? Like point of view in stories. We all have a point of view or a different perspective." She looked at Cotton.

Cotton nodded, but her eyes roamed the room, watching how riveted everyone was by Hailey. They wanted to know the complete story because her story is also part of theirs. Cotton glanced back at Hailey and smiled, encouraging her to continue. It was time.

"All my life... ever since I was about two years old... I have felt inside that I was a little girl. Now I feel like a woman, and I finally look female. But when I was younger, I always felt that dressing in boys' clothes and playing boys' games was... well, it was kind of foreign to me. I felt like I was being forced to do something I just didn't want to. Like I was lying."

Hailey coughed into her hand and glanced around the quiet room. Though only Janis and Marcus met her eyes, the air felt electrified, as though all the lights could run off the current generated by the tension between them.

"Lord knows, I tried to convince my mama and daddy that I was their little girl, not their little boy, but after a while, I realized no one believed me. When I was in second grade, the kids all made fun of me because I asked the teacher to call me Hailey and then insisted on being Snow White during the school Halloween party. Mama had to come and get me at school that day, and when Daddy got home, she told him to punish me for lying. He spanked me, and I cried so hard, I thought my stomach was going to come out through my mouth." Hailey's voice cracked, and she gave an apologetic half-smile for becoming emotional. "After that day, I kept my feelings to myself."

"That's why you always tell us to tell you the truth?" Marcus asked, the Game Boy now in his lap.

"One of the reasons." Hailey smiled slightly at her son. "Your mother and I want you to tell the truth for many reasons."

"If only you'd follow your own rules," Gray mumbled, then looked guilty, as if realizing that she'd broken her own agreement.

"I'm trying." The comment was as defeated as Hailey's slumped shoulders. For a moment, her breathing was all anyone heard, and she appeared startled every time her heart beat.

Janis shifted again in her seat, plopping down hard, and letting a whoosh of air release from her mouth. "Fucked if I'm going to listen to this gender drama."

"Do you want to share something, Janis?" Cotton asked, though she knew the question did what Janis wanted: it refocused the attention on her.

"Who'd want to listen?" It wasn't Janis's modus operandi to be cool, calm, and collected.

"I do."

"And so do I," Gray and Hailey responded in unison. They glanced at each other again, eyebrows arched, surprised that the old habit of simultaneously speaking each other's thoughts continued even though the marriage was over.

"Okay. Okay, alright. I really want to say something then." Janis's chest expanded with a deep breath. She lowered herself to the floor and crossed both legs under her yogi-style. "I just don't understand what the f—what the hell's going on..."

"Language ...." Gray warned.

"I'm trying to explain, but it might take a while." Hailey's hand fluttered to her mouth as she choked back sobs.

"Not *that*, Dad. I don't care if you're male, female, or banana. I want to understand why you left us! You just walked out like this problem... this thing... whatever it is, like it's not ours. Like it's just your problem. What about us? What happens to *us*? Just because you want to be a woman doesn't mean we just disappear, you know! Crap! How the hell do I explain this to my friends? I don't even have anyone over to the house anymore because people ask too many questions. Shit, Dad. What were you thinking?"

Janis bounded out of the chair and headed for the door. Cotton stood, blocking Janis, longing to place her hands gently on Janis's arms, but she learned not to physically touch anyone without permission, no matter how much they were crying out for some comfort.

"Give her a chance to answer your questions, Janis, okay?" Cotton said. "Give her a chance. There's lots of talking to do." She scanned everyone in the room. "And it's time your family communicates. Either that or all the pain every one of you feels is going to stay inside." Cotton pounded on her own chest a little, as if making her point was a case of life and death. Then she pointed to each of them individually, engaging them, warning them. Against all her therapeutic experience. "Maybe if you talk, we can share some of that pain with someone else. Maybe you'd all feel better. If you keep it inside, someone, or all of you, is going to wind up getting sick."

This type of warning worked once and only once. Cotton had flashed the therapist's proverbial ace up her sleeve. She wouldn't get another chance.

Head down, arms across her chest, Janis slouched back toward her place against the wall, sinking into her haunches. This time, she appeared broken rather than defiant. Everyone watched her in silence, and as Cotton studied each face, she wondered whether Gray was taking care of her kids. She needed to take care of these children. Cotton stifled a momentary wave of panic.

"So, if you become a woman, does this mean we don't have a dad anymore?" Cherylynn's question for Hailey surprised Cotton and sounds small and sad.

"Of course not." Hailey set her pocketbook aside and slid next to her younger daughter. There was a softness around her eyes and a quiver to her lip that she tried desperately to control. "I'll always be your father; I just won't be a man. I don't know how to reassure you, tell you how much I love you, Cheri. I love all my kids—you, too, Janis and

Marc. That's never changed. That never *will* change. I don't think there's anything I could ever do for the rest of my life that would be as important as being a part of your lives. I'm so very, very proud of you. Do you know that?" Hailey cupped Cherylynn's face in her hands and kissed her forehead gently. Tears ran down both their faces.

"You just don't look like Dad anymore." Cherylynn sobbed into Hailey's chest, then pushed away. "You have breasts."

"I know, Sweetie. But I'm me. I'll always be me in here." Hailey tapped her head, then her heart.

"Gimme a freakin' break," Janis muttered as she stood once again. Her eyes closed into slits, and she balled her hands against her sides. "This isn't some happily-ever-after movie. For chrissakes, Dad! This is too weird."

"Janis!" Gray snapped, but other than calling her daughter's name, she couldn't summon any other stinging reprimand.

It was enough. Janis slid back down the wall and studied her chipped, black fingernails.

"So, sweetie, if I was horribly burned and unrecognizable, you wouldn't want to know me?" Hailey quietly asked, her question directed toward Cherylynn but meant for everyone, Cotton was sure.

For a moment, no one moved, and a light winter rain fell against the office windows, the sound like silver needles against a mirror. The family created a tableau of contradictions: Gray, in the chair closest to the windows, her hand up near her mouth, a resolute expression in her eyes. Cherylynn and Hailey huddled on the floor, Hailey's arm around her daughter's shaking shoulders. On the other side of the room, Marcus perched on the end of his seat cushion, the Game Boy beside him, forgotten. Tears filled both his blackened eye and the normal one. With her pale face pale averted to the windows, Janis was the only one who wasn't connecting with the others. From her perspective, Cotton watched Janis's Goth makeup make its muddy way down her cheekbones.

"There are only fifteen minutes left in the session." Cotton announced. "You've made progress, but there's lots to do before I'm going to let you all walk out the door. Though you've released some pent-up emotions, I'm sure there's much more to come. I'll clear more time on my schedule for your family's visits, as well as individual. We might need to double up on some visits for a while."

She did not expect an answer and didn't waste time waiting for one. "I think that y'all have to spend some more time together. It appears to me that each of you has been pulling away from the other members of the family in one way or another, perhaps because it hurts too much to deal with the fact that the family structure is changing. You're all going through major changes. You're having growing pains. All of you. But that doesn't mean that you can't still be a family. It'll just be different. And that's okay. Every single one of you will handle that differently, but you'll get through it, and if you want to be, the Prescotts can be stronger than ever."

Cotton paused a moment, allowing space for everyone to say something, but no one took the opportunity. "If there's one thing I think I've figured out since I've come to know you all, it's that you love each other. No matter what. And that's a good thing. Love is important. Gray and Hailey, both of you have told me at one point or another that you appreciate the other's parenting skills. That's important for everyone in the family to know. You're the parents, and you are partners in that role. As you go forward, you'll need to remember that, because you will both retain those parenting roles for the rest of your lives. And, Marcus, you and your dad have a special relationship. You share not only a father-son relationship, but you also respect each other's game-playing skills. I know you don't want to lose your partner in the guild, right, Marc?"

He nodded and shyly looked at Hailey, who nodded back and reached out a hand.

"Janis, it seems to me that you take care of this family in a lot of ways and that it angers you that nothing's working the way you want it to be. Am I right?"

"Yeah, right," she snarled, still looking out the window.

"It's okay to be angry about what has happened. It's okay to think that this is going to be the toughest thing you've all had to deal with as a family, because maybe it is, but you are a family, and we can talk about whatever is going on within this group of Prescotts." She held her arms out to the sides as if encompassing the room. "If you do your part and talk and listen..."

Gray cleared her throat. "I don't know how that's going to happen, Dr. Barnes, but as long as I'm alive, I'll make sure these children are taken care of. Obviously, I will not have help doing that anymore." The venom in Gray's voice surprised Cotton, especially since she felt they'd made a bit of progress. But no, Gray's distanced herself from the whole family situation in more ways than one, from the third-person pronouns she used when writing about herself to the ways she ignored the kids' need to see their father.

"Don't discount me, Gray," Hailey said. "I have every intention of helping to raise these kids, just like I always have, just like Dr. B said a minute ago."

"Well, bless your heart, Hayden Prescott, but I haven't seen you in our home for almost three months, so I do not know what you mean." Gray's tone matched the sarcastic bob of her head. She looked like an older, more conservative version of her downcast oldest child. "Do you intend to take care of 'these kids,' as you call them, long distance? You really think it's going to be healthy for them to be with someone who doesn't even know what sex he is?"

"Gender," Hailey corrected gently. "I know what gender I am. It's not what's between your legs that counts. It's how you see yourself in your mind and what you feel in your heart. And in my mind, I've always been female. That doesn't change anything else about me. I'm still the person who was up with you all night when Cherylynn had tonsillitis. I'm still the person who has more patience helping Marcus with his math homework. I'm still the one who taught Janis how to swim. And I'm still the one who listened to you complain about the people at work. I'm still a writer. I'm still a Prescott. Just because my name and my body changes, doesn't mean that my personality and that my...uh...my *self* changes." She tucked in her chin, as if suddenly realizing a basic truth. "Yes, my 'self.' My 'me' has never changed. Capital M in Me. I'm just more of the Me I've always felt. In fact, the Me I am right now is the truest one, the honest one. That should make it better for everyone. Don't you think?" Her last words rushed out, as if she'd been running and was out of breath. She looked at Cotton for verification. *Am I done?* the glance asked silently. *Have I covered all the bases? Will they understand? Will they ever understand?*

"Everyone—everyone in this room, everyone in the world—is on a journey to find their identity from the time they are born," Cotton started, not quite knowing where she was going to end up but thinking that something needed to be said to underline the importance of Hailey's comments. "We're always wondering how other people feel about us and about what our future will be like. I'm sure you're wondering what you're going to be when you grow up, right, Marc?"

He glanced sideways at Cotton, thinking. He shook his head. Silent, withdrawing. *Godammit, I'm losing him.*

Family therapy sessions reminded Cotton of beach balls floating on waves. You think they're nearby, then they hop over the top of a wave and they're down the beach. Gone. Each one of the Prescotts does a beach ball runaway at least once during the session. She let the Marcus ball disappear for a minute and turned to Janis, standing almost behind Cotton's chair by that point.

"And, Janis, I'm sure you're worried about what your friends think about you, right?"

She refused to look at Cotton, but that was all right. Cotton had expected an argument, which she wasn't getting. *Twelve, thirteen, fourteen... no, I'm not counting.*

"You're thinking about your friends and your family, too—right, Cherylynn?"

Cherylynn shrugged; her cheeks squished as she leaned her face into her hands. Apparently unsure of her stance, that uneasiness had taken the smile off her happy pre-teen's world. She no longer had an identity in the family. At least not one she could readily access. But Cotton remembered the day on the soccer field when the players surrounded her, looked up to her. Cherylynn couldn't find herself at home, so she was defining herself on the ball field.

"Even when we become adults, we're still struggling to find ourselves," Cotton continued. "We still worry about what everyone says. But the most important thing in our lives is what we think about ourselves. Us. Not someone else. We must find our own happiness. We need to be proud of the person we are with our family and our friends. When we act in a way we can be proud of, we're automatically happy, and we can explain that happiness to those who love us."

Hopefully.

Cotton paused. Was she painting too bright a picture? One of her jobs was to color in the reality of life and all its difficulties. She couldn't lead people to believe that becoming emotionally healthy was easy. It took a lot of work. And being emotionally healthy looked different for everyone. It wasn't one size fits all.

"Unfortunately, sometimes even when we discover who we really are, we realize that the person we are might not be the one someone else needs us to be. If that happens, all we can do is to let go and love them from where we are." She paused. *Too much talking. Must listen.* "Does that make sense?"

Another silence. She wondered if she'd said enough or too much.

"That's fine, picture pretty and tied up with a bow," Gray said, "but this man ...." She pointed to Hailey. "This *person*... I personally don't think he deserves as much as an extra sheet of toilet paper."

The comment drove a sword into the room's tension, splintering it, destroying any bit of safety anyone had felt up to that moment. Janis pressed her face into the blinds, twining her hair between her fingers tightly, while Cherylynn stared at her mother, then her father, mouth open, and Marcus silently cried into his Game Boy. Cotton vainly searched for words to respond. She came up empty and hated herself for her inability to assuage the situation. Then she hated herself twice as much for judging herself so harshly.

"You have a right to be angry about that." Hailey finally broke the silence. "I've always regretted the way I handled that. But what can I say besides I'm sorry?"

"You're sorry? You leave your family, show up like...like...this ...." Gray dismissively waved her hand at Hailey, as if she wishes she had a magic wand to make it all disappear. "And you expect us all to be okay? Well, we're not, Hayden. Hailey. Whatever the damn fuck your name is. None of us are okay, and it's your fault, damnit."

No one in the room had dry cheeks except Cotton, who glanced at the clock, desperately wishing she didn't have an appointment with Dr. Carbinetti for her own therapy session in fifteen minutes. The Prescotts needed more time.

"I'm sorry, but we're just about out of time," Cotton said, rising from her chair. "I really regret it, but I have another client booked for the next time slot. However, I have a homework assignment for everyone. Will you all promise to do it for me?"

Shrugs and nods. That vague acquiescence was enough. A start.

"I want everyone to make a list of what they can offer to this family and what they want from the family. The only rule is that the list must be even. If you have five things you want the family to give you, then you must list five things you can give back. Understand?"

Everyone nodded again.

When they left, Cotton leaned against the doorjamb, her forehead against the cool paint, and took a deep breath. The hard work had just begun, and she never even brought up the subject of Christmas.

Shit, what would Freud say about that one?

On her desk chair sat a manila envelope. She opened it. More of Hailey's journal. She shoved it back into the envelope, threw it into her briefcase with her yellow pad and her laptop, grabbed her jacket, locked the office up, and left.

~ Book Twenty-five ~

Cotton Barnes

Keep silent for the most part, and speak only when you must, and then briefly.
—Epictetus

When Cotton got home, the house was quiet. She liked it that way. No sounds. No unnecessary small talk. No television going non-stop with the crisis du jour.

Peace.

Thomas was off to another meeting in Europe, scheduled to return on Christmas Eve, which left her to do the shopping and the cooking, which put a lot of extra work on her plate, though she didn't mind. She'd buy an extra bottle of wine to drink while she cooked. By the time he came home, she'd be missing him. Right now, she enjoyed her alone time.

She heated some microwaveable vegetarian lasagna, poured a glass of Rombauer chardonnay, letting it roll over her tongue and to the back of her throat. When she inhaled, the aroma of vanilla and apricots filled her sinuses. It always reminded her of pumpkin pie when she drank this wine. It was perfect for nights like tonight, and as she swallowed, she remembered what Gray Prescott said about that chardonnay she drank in Venice.

Cotton appreciated that Thomas had learned about wine in his twenties and always said he'd been fearless because of his college days as a coffee barista at Starbuck's. He shared his knowledge with her for the past ten years with a weekend in Napa or Sonoma and an occasional trip to Italy or France. Nothing like buying wine from the people who tenderly cared for the grapevines throughout generations. She loved those vacations.

Taking another sip, Cotton wondered if Gray had appreciated a glass of wine since she left Venice. She'd hinted that she'd been drinking too much lately, and when Cotton saw the kids, she listened hard for signs of alcohol abuse. So far, the shifting of duties within the Prescott household had made everyone uncomfortable, but no one was being abused. That she could see. She won't mention it or ask leading questions, but she'd listen during their conversations.

And that was one of the many reasons the adults in the Prescott family had to catch up with their kids. Janis, Cheryl, and Marcus might have forced her to dig deep as a therapist, but at least they talked. Hailey and Gray still shoveled 50-100 pages Cotton's way after each session. *How did they find time to write so much?*

But that was a question for another time when there weren't ten other issues that were far more pressing. For now, she relished the notes of pear and maybe a little lemon that the wine left in her sinuses and the back of her throat.

The fire she built crackled and popped and burned brightly, cozying the living room. Through the sliding glass doors overlooking the deck, a full moon lit up the tree ridge. The sky slowly filled with brilliant stars that cast vague haloes into the chilly Carolina night. Even if she hadn't just come in, she'd know by glancing out the window that the night air was razor sharp. *Snow tonight.*

Polishing off the last bite of lasagna with the rest of the wine in her glass, she reached for her laptop to catch up on today's session notes. She tapped her index finger against her upper lip and counted to ten. Three times. "Priming the pump," Dr. Carbinetti, her therapist, called it. She followed the same routine every time she wrote notes. The tap against the lip, counting to ten, three times. It worked to employ that part of the brain that holds memories of her sessions so she can jot her notes.

Cotton remembered everything she saw and heard in brilliant, sensual detail, as if she was experiencing the event again in real time. Always had. If she worked hard at it, she could make herself see and hear things she had only been told about. It used to drive Thomas nuts that she could repeat every word he'd said to her three days before. Now, he just shrugs when she repeats his words back to him. The skill isn't a good one for marital communications, she realized, but it was perfect for writing notes hours after a session.

Dr. Carbinetti asked about Cotton's memory at their therapy session a few hours ago. *How many times have you counted today*, he asked. *Have you had any more nightmares recently? When was the last time you thought about Brighton, Cotton? Now, please tell me the truth. You know I can tell when you're lying to me.*

He had to ask tough questions. He was the one who decided whether she was fit to see patients. She had to pass his mark. So, she did. She told him what he needed to hear. *I'm the one they need right now. Let me do my job.*

She flexed her fingers, grabbed her notepad, and wrote: *Development of Family History.*

~ Book Twenty-six ~

Hailey Prescott

To me, gender is not physical at all, but is altogether insubstantial. It is soul, perhaps it is talent, it is taste, it is environment, it is how one feels, it is light and shade, it is inner music.
   —Jan Morris

Hailey had no problem talking about her family during their sessions. She loved her parents, and talking about them seemed to comfort her.

"My kids never met my parents, since they both passed before Gray and I got married," she'd told Cotton in a wistful, soft voice. "I've always felt bad that my kids didn't enjoy the unconditional love and support that generation can give. My Nanny and Papa were people I loved more than breath itself. I wish my kids could experience that feeling."

"It feels like there's a 'but' in that statement," Cotton said. "Tell me about your parents."

"Ok. Mama and Daddy. Married in the early '70s (1972, I think). A little after Woodstock, a little before disco." Hailey laughed, giving Cotton the feeling she'd used that line before.

Casual and warm, recanting family stories, Cotton wrote in her notes.

"They graduated from high school, met each other, chemistry sizzled, and pants fell," Hailey said. "I arrived right after they got married. (The joke always was that they conceived me on their wedding night, but that would have made me a five-month preemie. I'd say that I was the reason they married in the first place, but it doesn't really matter.) Fact: Mama and Daddy never really had time to grow up before the three of us kids came into their lives."

"Three kids," Cotton said. "I didn't know you had siblings. Tell me about them."

"Well, Cameron's two years younger than me. The science whiz of the family. He'd gone off to college, went to Silicon Valley, and never came back. Got a family somewhere out west and is always promising to visit. Never has. Chloe, my sister, six years younger than me, is the baby of the family, and we haven't spoken for eight years. She got into drugs in college, and after Mama and Daddy were killed in the accident, she disappeared. Last time I talked to her, she asked me for money for meth."

"How did you feel about that?" Cotton asked. Sometimes she hated that question, but it always worked to get more from the client.

Early childhood trauma. Parental deaths.

"I hung up on her, and to this day, the only time I hear about her is if I run into one of her friends. From what they've told me, she spends most of her time on the street and in shelters. In a way, it's good our parents never saw her as sorry as she has gotten these days. They'd have had a kitten." Hailey threw her head back and laughed. She pushed her hair back over her ears and fiddled with one of her small gold hoop earrings as if memorizing it with her fingers. "Between me and Chloe, Mama and Daddy had a lot on their hands." For a moment, she seemed lost, looking out the window.

"Funny, because when I think of Mama and Daddy, I always picture a somewhat off-kilter couple, a little weird, not quite normal—hippies with Carolina accents," she continued. "It's as though I was older than they were from the moment I was born. I had to be protective of them because no one understood them. They were never quite 'in' but always had loving friends and people recognized them wherever they went. Probably because they laughed all the time. Mama had the cutest laugh, a real high, woodpecker-type of twitter that always ended with a snort.

She'd get embarrassed every time and turn red, which would make everyone else laugh even more."

"You have a tendency to laugh, too," Cotton said.

"Runs in the family, I guess." Hailey's eyes crinkled at the edges. She'd used some brown eyeliner, and it had smudged. "Anyway, I don't remember them ever fussing with each other or anyone else. They were 'nice,' and you know what that means. People used to talk about my parents behind their backs, then follow their comments with 'Bless their little hearts.'"

She glanced up at Cotton, sharing the unspoken understanding that in Carolina blessing someone's heart is the universal way of excusing whatever sins they may have committed. Or showing that the person they're blessing is a bit out of touch with reality. *Poor soul.*

Hailey could have continued talking about family, but Cotton asked: "Do you remember the first time you thought about gender?"

Hailey folded her hands in her lap and gazed down at her fingers. She'd shown off her first manicure last week and has been admiring her own hands ever since. "I always loved my father, but I never realized that I should be like him until I was about five. That's the first time I realized I wasn't like him. Daddy took me to the State Fair. I have no idea why we went alone. Maybe Mama was feeling exceptionally down after her twin sister died in a car crash. She had days when she wouldn't come out of the bedroom at all, and if Chloe and I stood really still at the door, we could hear a muffled sobbing. Broke our hearts. But being with my daddy alone was just the most special thing I had ever experienced. 'You can sit up front,' he whispered to me when we got into the car. 'Mama won't know, since it's just us boys.'"

Hailey flexed her fingers, made fists.

"I couldn't even see over the dash, but it didn't matter to me," she said. "To this day, I remember the fluorescent green dials on the radio, the worn spots near the glove compartment lock, the square shape of my father's fingers as he held the wheel, the car's jerkiness when he shifted the Mustang from first to second gear. The tight feel of the seatbelt against my hips."

Cotton saw all of Hailey's talents in that description. She had gone from being a client to a writer at that moment. She spoke from a place deep in her head, a place of imagination informed by reality, and by reliving the story she'd told herself about that day at the Fair. Cotton let her continue.

"In the dimness, my father's profile caught stripes of sunlight as we drove through the streets of Raleigh. He wore a faded Durham Bulls baseball cap and a gray t-shirt and jeans. Simple but clean. Mama ironed every stitch of clothing we wore, so it didn't matter how old Daddy's jeans were. Mama made sure they were creased. Every so often, Daddy'd take a puff of the cigarette he held in his right hand. A Lucky Strike, I think. He turned to me and winked conspiratorially, as though we were doing something dangerous and wonderful. My heart felt like it would pop out of my chest with excitement.

"'Let's have some music,' Dad said, and he flipped the channels until he found a rock 'n roll station. It was the first time I remember singing with my father, but by the time we arrived at the field where we would park, I knew the Rolling Stones' *I Can't Get No Satisfaction*. Every time I've heard that song since, I flash back to that moment."

Hailey sang a few notes, giving the words an appropriate growl. She and Cotton shared a laugh.

"We arrived just as the sun was setting, and the sky filled with stripes of hot pink, persimmon, and lavender like a garden of Dutch tulips. I was convinced that the sky had created this incredible sunset just for Daddy and me. He lifted me to his shoulders, grabbed my hands, and laughed at my chortling: 'You okay up there, buddy? Ready to go?' and I think I said something like, 'Go Daddy, go!' because he wasn't the only one who laughed. When I looked around at the people below me, all of them had their faces turned up to me, and I swear, every single one of them was smiling.

"We headed across the street and strode through the field toward the flashing orange and yellow neon lights on the enormous Ferris wheel that towered so far above me I could only see shadows at the very top of the wheel. The sounds of the Fair reached us: the dull roar thousands of people make, the screams of children on the sparkling roller coaster, the calliope music from the merry-go-round, the barkers' calls to 'buy your cotton candy here and 'throw one more ball for your girl. Get the BIG prize!' The smells. Good Lord, those smells! Sweet and sour. Fried and barbequed. Exotic and familiar."

Hailey took a good, long inhale. "I love those damn fried turkey legs. What about you, Doc? What's your favorite fair food?"

They talked about fried Milky Ways and cinnamon-flavored sweet potatoes, giant fruit drinks, and greasy pepperoni pizza. Then the small talk died out, and Hailey began again, always at the same point where she stopped. That's what made her a storyteller worth listening to.

"On Daddy's shoulders, I loomed above the crowd, thrilled by the bobbing heads of the surrounding throngs, the spin of the wheel as someone won a giant pink panda bear, and the garishly colored signs that made my mouth water for French fries, giant drumsticks, and cotton candy.

"With every step we took, I held onto Daddy's hands more tightly. With him, I felt safe and free to enjoy every moment of the raucous fair. If my mother had been there, I would have been on the ground, unable to see what was going on, and she probably would have been nervous about losing me. But with Daddy, I got the whole impact without the fear my mother generated just through the touch of her quivering hand. Anyone who thought my mother the hippie was also a feminist was dead wrong. She relied on my dad completely, and he reveled in keeping her safe, playing the caveman.

"We rode every ride at the Fair that night—the giant Ferris Wheel, the biggest horses on the carousel, the flying kites, the bumper cars, that terrifying roller coaster—and we visited all the prize-winning farm animals, marveling at the three-legged sheep and laughing at a cow that wouldn't stop licking my face. We ate deep-fried drumsticks, bright pink cotton candy that melted on my tongue like a sugar snowflake, fried Snickers (Yuck. Tastes as bad as it sounds.) and drank at least three sodas. By the time we started home, my stomach swelled like a pumpkin, my head swam, and each bump in the road felt like a mountain. Oh, man, it was awful. I threw up all over the back seat of my father's vintage Mustang. It took him weeks to get the smell out, but he never complained. And I never forgot a moment of that trip, especially since it was one of the few times we were alone together that I wasn't being forced to throw a ball or to play some sort of game that required me to act like a boy."

That was the moment Hailey stopped. Cold. Cotton thought she was done, but then Hailey looked up. Her face had softened, her eyes swam with unshed tears, and her lips quivered. Then she caught herself and straightened her shoulders.

"At the Fair, Daddy allowed me to be a kid. It didn't matter what gender I was; I was just a kid, but it was at that moment that I knew I wasn't the kid Daddy thought I was. I was a girl, not a boy."

Hailey finished, her eyes shining. She looked at Cotton as if she wanted approval, and Cotton didn't include in the report that she reached over and squeezed Hailey's knee without asking for permission. She wanted Hailey to know how moving her story had been, but she couldn't get the words past the tightness in her throat. Grabbing a client's body part was never okay, but she'd done it.

A flash in the glass, probably a reflection of the fire or something flying by, caught Cotton's attention. It was dark outside, the moon invisible. The clouds had moved in. She checked the clock. She saw the hand tick to the 10, and she needed to wrap it up, but she couldn't help asking one more question. "Do you think your parents knew?"

The question stopped Hailey, and she seemed shocked by her own realization that she'd never thought about it.

"I spent so much time hiding, I am not sure if they ever figured that out." She wiped away a tear. "I wish I had that answer."

Now, with the fire dying in the hearth and her microwaved dinner eaten (though she had no idea what it was), Cotton wrote in her notes *I wish I knew, too.*

~ Book Twenty-seven ~

Cotton Barnes

A therapist is like the weather. They provide the climate for change.
   —Milton Erickson

"Penny for your thoughts."

Thomas's voice brought Cotton out of her deep reverie, and with a guilty laugh, she realized why he asked. She'd had several nightmares during the week when she slept. Thomas was trying to figure out what was going on with her, because Cotton hadn't shared that she'd spent the entire week listening to the Prescotts sharing memories of earlier years, and several of the conversations reverberated long after the last sentence. The different versions of each memory made her revisit her own childhood and wonder what her memories were versus the ones her sister shared. She'd been careful to steer the Prescotts to their ordinary memories rather than personal traumas since those memories were stored differently

"Thinking of home," Cotton answered. "The old days when I was a kid and had no problems."

He laughed warmly, and she looked at him for what she thought might be the first time today. He wore his brown knitted sweater, the one she called his grandfather cardigan. No matter how much she teased him, she secretly loved the sweater, and thought it made him look like an English professor about to light his pipe. With his hair tousled and his glasses halfway down his nose, he was adorable. She never used that word except with this very look of his, but she adored Thomas at this very moment. She wrapped her arms around his throat and kissed him, hard.

"What brought that up?" he said when she let him up for air.

"A lot of stuff. My week. The clients." She wanted to say: *The trans patient I have has been writing about her childhood. Really emotional stuff. And her wife told me about hers the other day. Practically bucolic. Grew up on a farm with horses and cows and a big family. They all worked together, supported each other, went to church, and made for the great American family. I think that big, safe, happy family did less to prepare her for the trauma she's experiencing now than if she'd been exposed to a few bumps and bruises earlier in her life.* But she finished with, "It's like putting a crack in the most perfect glass vase. The vase is still pretty, but now it's flawed. Know what I mean?"

"Sure. Sure. Sounds like you could use some fresh air to work some of it out. Good time to put your jacket on and go for a walk with me and Fred." Their Labrador's head popped up at the mention of his name.

"But I have work ...."

"And it will be here when you get back. Come on." Thomas reached out his hand and walked her to the hallway, where they shrugged into flannel jackets and hiking boots.

In the chilly early winter air, Cotton breathed deeply, relishing the way it instantly cleared the stress. Her husband was right. Fresh air cleared her brain. She took Thomas's hand and scuffed through the leaves along the dirt road that led to the Falls River. Fred dashed on ahead with the lopsided joy only a Labrador feels when titillated by thousands of smells generated by vegetation and other animals. Cotton threw her head back, watching the lacy pattern of the treetops against the hard blue sky.

Images of the Prescotts filtered around the edges of her mind as she and Thomas walked. She was figuring out the roles the Prescott family members played. Who was closer to each other? Which of the family members sparred with each other? Was anyone uncomfortable with change? She thought she had some answers, but the trick was getting them to tell her how they felt. She held the proverbial therapeutic mirror up for them to recognize themselves, but sometimes, even if they saw themselves, clients weren't happy to share their truth with their therapist. Any therapist. Then there were other times when clients talked nonstop, filling every one of their therapy hours with news about work or whether the electric bill was high or low. Sometimes it took months to tease out one clue to what they felt. It was frustrating.

"Tell me about your favorite childhood moment," she asked Thomas, all the while thinking of her own childhood and her dog Spencer, about the time she lost him walking along a river much like this one. She hunted for hours, well past dark, and when she realized it was so dark she wouldn't be able to see him, even if he ran up to her, she went home in tears. And there he was, waiting on the porch steps with her parents and her sister. Everyone had a bottle of Coca Cola in their hands as if they were at a BBQ. Spencer ran to her, tail wagging as if wondering where she'd been. *When you're certain all is lost, a miracle happens.*

"Where the hell did that come from?" Thomas was used to her questions and probably had answered this exact question at least a dozen times, but he usually played along. He walked ahead of her without looking back, his feet keeping an odd time with the walking stick he carried. "My grandfather and I used to sit on a rock in his backyard and talk about cars. He loved his old Buick." He navigated a bundle of roots, laughing at Fred as he skipped ahead. "Big, fat car. Grey body with a white roof. White leather interior. Red dashboard and red door walls. Sharp."

"How old were you?"

"I dunno. Eight, nine. Maybe ten. It didn't matter what we talked about. I loved sitting on that rock and having Grampa all to myself."

She didn't expect that kind of a memory, but she wasn't surprised. This was what she loved about Thomas. He surprised her.

"What about you?" He stopped on the path and turned toward her. The sun behind his head framed him in a halo. She couldn't see his eyes.

"I have lots. Dog moments. Dad. Mom. A time by myself when I climbed to the very top of the tree on our property." She lifted her face and imagined the way the sun felt then. "I felt like I was a bird that day, up in the sky, over everyone else's head. But my mother almost had a heart attack. She started screaming so loud she almost knocked me out of the damn tree."

Thomas threw his head back and laughed. "You never told me that one."

"We both have years and years of memories stored up in our brains. It would take us a lifetime to share them, and we're making more every day." She squeezed his hand.

"Isn't it funny how many of them are anchored in our childhood days?"

"They're the most memorable. The memories that stick with us longest. Alzheimer's patients have no trouble remembering their childhood memories, but don't ask about anything that happened five minutes ago."

"I still miss my grandad. I always thought I could run over to his house anytime and get away from my parents and my siblings. That was a safe place. The house enthralled me. All the cubbyholes, the place where he stored his tools, the cookie jar my grandma kept on the kitchen counter just for us. Molasses cookies. Paper thin and crispy." He paused, then kept walking. "Makes me kinda sorry for people who don't have a good childhood. There have been many times when I thought the world was going to get me, then I thought of Grampa and Grammie, and they would always give me someplace to run away to. Even if it was just the memory of them."

"Many people don't have that," Cotton said, and Thomas nodded solemnly. Nothing else needed to be said.

Fred bounded through the undergrowth, leaves and branches sticking to his tail and around his mouth. He was a goofy dog, able to make her laugh whenever she's down. Absurd, uncoordinated, and dumb, but he was their dog. They'd raised him from puppyhood, adopting him from a friend who had made it her life's purpose to rescue dogs. He'd paid them back with love ever since, as most animals do.

"Do you ever wonder what he thinks about us?" Thomas said, pointing to the dog, who gazed back as lovingly as one could when your tongue was eight inches long. "Does he think we're his pack or his parents?"

"Pack, probably. We don't need to give him any more human traits than he already has. We're his pack. Not his parents."

"Well, he might be the closest I get to having a son." He reached down to give the dog an affectionate pat. "Could do a lot worse, huh?"

When Thomas moved forward down the path, he no longer reached for Cotton's hand.

For a moment, a very shadowy moment, Cotton heard another child's voice. *When will I know who I am, Dr. Barnes?* And she shivered.

Two hours later, Cotton held her own journal and scribbled by the light of a little bulb thing she got free from a book club, because Thomas was sleeping, and she didn't want to wake him. She also didn't want him to see what she was writing.

Tonight was a disaster, in more ways than one.

Thomas would be angry because she took time away from their date night, but it did not prepare her for the eruption she had to face when she got home.

"You spend way too much time on this family, your patients," he said. "I rarely say this, and it's not a bad thing, normally. But you're consumed. You don't think of anything else, damnit! There's not a night that you're not doing some sort of research or reading whatever they give you or taking emergency phone calls from them. I'm not sure you were ready to go back to work, Cotton. I think you could have used more time off."

She couldn't answer him, couldn't find the words.

Then he said, "What you're doing is avoiding what's really hurting us. We need to talk about starting a family. A serious conversation. Because if we're not, well, Jesus, Cotton, you're thirty-five. And I'm thirty-eight, and I've got to admit I'm feeling like I'd really want to play with my kids without shattering a hip. We need a plan. One way or the other."

She told him she knew. She understood, but she didn't have the answer that would satisfy them both.

What she didn't tell Thomas was that she couldn't even think about her own life right now, especially when she watched the Prescotts struggling and felt so frustrated trying to convince them they needed to work together to get through the confusion they were all feeling.

Her chest burned. She knew her argument with her husband was normal. Hundreds of people argued daily about kids. But she worried about what the families she treated went through and what Thomas and she might face if they had a family. She doesn't want to face anything like this in the future. No tragedies, please. She couldn't admit that out loud, even in therapy, and she wasn't sure why. All she knew was that in the darkest part of the night, an icy fear took over her, and her OCD world quickly turned into paranoia. She shivered, thinking about the possibility of losing reality. Nothing drove her to her knees more than that fear.

One in four Londoners has paranoid thoughts. 1.6 percent of the American population has BPD. Borderline Personality Disorder. Almost 15 percent of the general population has occasional paranoia.

This family was nowhere near done.

This was the second stage of Hailey's emergence. The first was discovery and disclosure, and though Hailey hadn't disclosed her transition to many people outside the family, the kids were accepting the realization that Hailey's transition wasn't going to stop. Each of them experienced the turmoil of this stage in ways indicative of their place in the family.

Next, they'd deal with negotiation, a time when everyone will realize they have to adjust to the reality of this situation. And, hopefully, they would eventually reach the last stage: finding balance as individuals and as a family.

It was Cotton's job to help them heal; she knew that, and that was why she was often awake at 3 AM, churning over strategies in her head—therapeutic healing. If she couldn't help them find a path, she would have failed. She can't take another failure. Cotton's stomach twisted when she dared to think of what might happen if.

She'd asked her colleagues—Dr. Carbinetti, her supervisor and personal therapist, and Dr. Logan, the therapist Hailey sees occasionally—to help her locate support groups for the Prescott kids, as well as for Gray. Hailey had already connected with a group of her own, but that only helped *her,* not the rest of the family. She often neglected the damage left in the wake of her emergence and how substantial and widespread it's been. That was typical of most patients who left the family home. No one seemed to realize their actions affected many people. Without additional help, one or more of the Prescott family might not have the skills they need to move forward.

I can't let that happen.

"Are you freaking listening to me, Cotton?"

She turned to respond, but Thomas had already turned his back and left the room.

~ Book Twenty-eight ~

Gray Prescott

If I am what I have and I lose what I have, then who am I?
—Erich Fromm

"I quit work. I'm going to step down as CEO and let someone else take the stress for a while," Gray announced as soon as Cotton posed her usual "how's-your-week-been-going," question. "I can't concentrate with people staring at me all the time, so I'm doing everything online. Besides, we still sell Hayden's books. Yes, Hayden's. And I have to walk by the new release table every day where his book is front and center. Don't tell me I'm not trying to deal." The last statement is a challenge. Dark circles framed Gray's eyes. She wore another of her shapeless sweaters and her hair was piled in a haphazard bun on top of her head. During their last visit, Gray had seemed perkier, and Cotton thought she was improving, but today's Gray appeared deep in depression.

Her response derailed Cotton's plan to talk about where each member of the family was in their grieving process. Hayden was no longer part of the family, and they all had to go through whatever they felt about not having him in their lives any longer. Cherylynn immediately reconnected with her father, especially when Hailey told her daughter, "I might not look the same, but I'm still your father. I'm not a mother wannabe. I'm your dad. Always will be."

Gray often fell silent during their sessions now, so Cotton asked whether Gray had written anything this week. Gray fumbled in her bag and produced a scant two pages.

Two pages. Last week it was ten or twelve. Usually, she produced that many or more.

"Didn't have much happen this week, huh?" Normally, patients who struggle to communicate face-to-face would find another way to release their emotions. Gray's had been her third-person narrative. It was a muffled voice, but at least it was her voice. A voice that could be silenced completely if she didn't work on her depression.

"I don't have any friends or family members who've gone through this." Gray's voice was so muted, Cotton could barely hear her. Even the scratch of her pen on the yellow pad was louder than Gray. "Friends, family, colleagues who are gay. Yes, I know them and love them, but I am not familiar with anyone who's transgender. Most of my friends, they don't even get what that means, and if they do, it's because they know some celebrity who 'did it.'" She provided air quotes and a smirk.

Cotton couldn't read the look. It was either a smirk that said her friends were truly clueless or a smirk that said she'd rather not even talk about this. Gray's body language said a lot more than her words. Through the reticence to speak, the spitting insults when Hailey was in the session, and the caved-in shoulders and lack of body care, Cotton discovered Gray has a lot of anger. She doesn't fight cleanly, though, and seems like she doesn't want to learn. Those jabs! Those passive-aggressive jabs. Her psychosis was part of the reason this family was dysfunctional, yet she would never take responsibility.

"So, you're home with the kids now during the holidays?" The change of topic was more for Cotton's benefit than Gray's. She needed to change the subject, because what she wanted to do was to take Gray to a group therapy session for people who are transitioning. Maybe listening to their stories and meeting people she wasn't related to would show her the very human struggle she appeared unable to understand.

But I can't force her.

Gray's face crumpled. She reached for the tissue box and a torrent of tears began. "It's never been harder to shop for Christmas presents than ever. Not only do I have to worry about Marcus with the schoolyard bullies and about Janis and Cherylynn going through therapy, and about my husband who's now decided she wants to be like me, but now I also need to worry about money. I don't know how the hell I'm going to make it." Her shoulders knifed together, and she looked like a broken sparrow. Small, brown, nervous. Yet there's something about her demeanor that was raising Cotton's antennae. *Where was the woman's compassion?*

"Let's talk about it," Cotton said. "See if we can put together a plan of some sort. And if we can't figure something out, we'll get you some help from a financial advisor."

"What's a financial advisor going to do? Give me money? That's what I need. Advice isn't what I need. I need money. Hailey's giving money to the kids, but she's not giving enough to me! What about me?" Her hands shook as she described struggling to decide whether to use one of the credit cards to buy Marcus a computer game or take out some of her savings to get that argyle cashmere sweater for Cherylynn.

"There were years when we didn't have a ten-dollar bill between us," she said, "but we had a great time trying to find bargains— shopping on Black Friday at 4 o'clock in the morning with the kids' wish lists, groaning about our poor feet, giggling about the fights people have over the toys on sale, and sighing afterward at McDonald's as they shared a breakfast bought with the change from the bottom of my purse. As much as I hate to admit it, I miss that. I miss Hayden. Or the person I thought was Hayden." The tears started again.

Cotton asked a question or two about Gray's inability to use Hailey's chosen pronouns. A simple, "think about why you use the incorrect pronoun," was often all that was necessary to teach the client to adapt their language. *How many times do I have to remind her?*

Through her tears, she told Cotton that the kids didn't realize that their Santa lists had to be smaller this year, and in response, they made it very clear they want to share the holiday with their father—despite Hailey's "aberrant" behavior.

"When I told them last week that we'd be spending Christmas at home and that Dad wasn't invited, Janis stormed into her room, slamming the door, calling me a bitch. Can you believe that? Then Cherylynn cried like her heart was going to break, and Marcus disappeared. I found him two hours later on the computer, playing that online game of his. Probably playing with his dad. None of them would talk to me. Why am I the bad guy? Why are they angry at me?"

Gray drew her sweater tighter around her and the movement made her appear even more fragile. Her voice strengthened, but it was still fairly flat and disaffected. The anger simmered, which was often more dangerous than if it would erupt. If someone was in-your-face-angry, you could see it. They were there, right in front of you. Their eyes were open, tunnels to the emotions that were impossible to ignore. Anger was a pane of glass behind which you could not hide.

"When I'm not depressed about Christmas presents or about being alone with three kids who hate me for reasons that have nothing whatsoever to do with anything that I have done, I think about what my future looks like," Gray continued. She looked out the window as she spoke, little pulses at the corner of her eye, a heightened color on her cheekbones. "I'll have to learn how to fix everything in the house that breaks (if I can afford to keep it); I'll have to work years longer than I expected and I really have no retirement started; I'll have to support the kids throughout their years in college; and I'll never again be able to date without wondering whether the guy is really jealous of my lacy underwear or longing to borrow my stiletto heels." Her voice changed. She was using sarcasm as a shield now.

Cotton rarely got a word in throughout the rest of the session, which was fine. She wanted Gray to talk, and with the help of the rest of the Kleenex box, she did.

The crux of it was that Gray hated her life. She couldn't understand anything that's going on. She didn't enjoy going to therapy once or twice a week. And she felt a failure as a mother. But the worst thing about her life was the realization that her husband was becoming a woman. Does that mean Gray was not feminine herself? "I look in the mirror now and don't recognize the faded woman looking back. Nor do I like her. The only thing that's a positive is that I've lost fifteen pounds, but even that's negative. I can't afford new clothes."

For the first time in half an hour, she stopped crying and took little sips of air like a child who'd sobbed her heart out.

Gray pulled herself together and sniffled. The heat came on in a whoosh, and Cotton glanced outside at the gray winter sky. The weathercaster said there might be snow in the forecast. Maybe it would take away some of the gloom that's hung over the Raleigh area for days and help cheer up some people who suffer with seasonal affected disorder.

Gray sniffled again and sighed, exhausted. "I want to run away."

"I feel like that sometimes," Cotton said. "A nice island. Pink sand beach. Warm sun. It's a fantasy we all have occasionally."

"Maybe I can go somewhere they have cabana boys," Gray responded with a tired laugh.

"If you're going to fantasize, go big or go home." Cotton watched Gray's face lift into a smile.

"Wouldn't it be nice to go somewhere where no one knows you and let loose for a few days?" Gray settled back into the chair, her body language open and relaxed for the first time. "Yes, it would. Why don't you do that? Plan a vacation for yourself. Get your sister to take care of the kids for a few days."

"I have no money. And I just took a major pay cut." She laughs, a tad maniacally. "The papers have gone to the lawyer."

One of the 'deals' Gray and Hailey had made was to keep any discussion of the divorce proceedings out of their family therapy sessions with Cotton. Though it often caused tense moments when someone would venture into forbidden 'divorce talk,' it was much easier to focus on what the family could do learning how to deal with their new reality rather than dwelling on something that they can't change and fighting about it.

That was Cotton's biggest challenge: getting Gray to stop replaying the trauma of the past couple of months.

Maybe going away for a week or so might not be a bad idea. I could use a vacation myself.

"Don't you have a friend who lives down on the beach?"

"I'm surprised you remember that." Gray sat up straighter. It was obvious she was considering the possibility.

"I hear everything you say." Cotton nodded, underlining the truth of what she'd just said.

They wrapped up the session on a positive note, talking about what the beach was like during the winter, and as Gray left, Cotton jotted a note in red at the top of her chart: Check with Dr. Logan re: Gray's prescription.

Maybe a simple dose of sunshine might be the best medicine for Gray Prescott. Maybe better than Prozac.

~ Book Twenty-nine ~

Cherylynn Prescott

Sibling relationships - and 80 percent of Americans have at least one - outlast marriages, survive the death of parents, resurface after quarrels that would sink any friendship.

They flourish in a thousand incarnations of closeness and distance, warmth, loyalty, and distrust.

—Erica E. Goode

December 23, 8:12 PM

Cherylynn Prescott: can u get me appt w Dad Want 2 C him bf Xmas

Cotton Barnes: You can call him. I'm sure he'd be glad to hear from you.

Cherylynn Prescott: no new phone #

Cotton Barnes: You don't have his number?

Cherylynn Prescott: mom sez no

Cotton Barnes: You have appt w/me tmw. Why don't we talk then?

Cherylynn Prescott: want 2 tlk 2 dad now

Cotton Barnes: Can you email him?

Cherylynn Prescott: tried

Cotton Barnes: Doesn't Marcus have his phone no.?

Cherylynn Prescott: dunno ill ask

Cherylynn Prescott: he dosnt have ill tweet dad c u tmw

Gray dropped Cherylynn off for her appointment on Christmas Eve, made sure she had what she needed, then left as if the Hounds of Hell were at her heels. Years ago, Cotton heard horror stories from her colleagues about parents who dropped off children for therapy appointments and never returned, which caused a massive headache for the therapist and was traumatic for everyone involved in the abandonment, especially the child. Cotton wondered every time Gray walked about the door and left her kids whether she'd be back, but she put the fear aside and saw the kids alone, without the specter of their mother on the other side of the door. It helped the younger Prescotts talk more freely.

Cotton knew it was imperative to control her own emotions, and to articulate them if she needed to with a client, but she could not ignore the frustration Gray aroused. If only Gray would let go of the fact that she's unable to understand her husband and admit that she should start paying attention to her kids. Maybe then this family would recover. Maybe if she recognized the parenting Hailey's been doing all along and how important she is to this family's axis ... maybe if Gray could see Hailey as an ally instead of an enemy, she could help her kids heal, too.

A mother should be able to see how severely depressed Janis and Marcus were, how hard Hailey struggled with her limited contact with the kids, how Cherylynn's reaction to everything might seem the healthiest right now, her bubbly exterior sending the message that she's looking on the bright side, yet her frequent texts to Cotton revealed that all that glitters was not gold.

Both Cherylynn and Cotton breathed an audible sigh of relief as they settled into their chairs. Cherylynn, smiling and relaxed, shrugged out of her hot pink parka and kicked off her shearling boots, then plunked onto the wingback.

Cotton asked, "Did you get hold of your father last night?"

"Yeah, Hailey texted me back, and we talked for a while, but I still haven't seen her." From the first discussion about pronouns, Cherylynn had been consistently using them correctly, which surprised Cotton because of Cherylynn's severe dyslexia. Now she pulled a piece of her hair into her mouth and swung her legs back and forth as she chewed. Then her eyes brightened, and she said, "Hey, do you think it's okay for me to still call her Dad, even though she's gonna be a woman after the operation and all that?"

"That's a question you'll have to ask her. I'm sure you guys can have a conversation about that. Your dad's pretty open about talking to you, don't you think? Hailey's made it clear she's still your father, not your mother."

"I guess ..." Cherylynn continued chewing on her hair, which concerned Cotton a bit. When someone chewed on their own body or picked at themselves, it indicated the person suffered from nervous anxiety. There was no doubt Cherylynn's habit of chewing her hair was directly related to the family's stresses.

Cotton made a mental note to watch it and to slide a mention of it to either Hailey or Gray, sneakily dropping it into conversation, to see whether it was a new habit or something Cherylynn had always done.

"I'd love to continue to talk about what we talked about the last time we were here." Cotton put her forearms against her knees and leaned forward a little.

"About my dad?"

"Yes, about your dad and about transgender people, in general."

Cherylynn arched her feet up and down, then dropped her hair. "Well, I guess how you explained it was pretty cool. I mean, if a guy's not okay with being a man and if he thinks being a woman is going to make him happier, I guess that's okay."

"How do you feel about that?"

"About a guy becoming a girl?"

"Yes. How do you feel about him becoming a woman?"

"I dunno. I mean, when I think about Dad, guess I really don't think someone can have two moms. I mean, who'd want to?" She laughed, delighted with her accidental joke.

"Do you think Hailey wants to be your mother, or do you think she'll want to stay your dad?"

"She won't be a man anymore, right? So how could she be my dad? That's silly! We should call her something else, like 'Mad' or 'Dom.'" She laughed again, a completely uninhibited and delightful sound that flits up and down the musical scale. "But she keeps saying she'll always be our dad, so I guess she is, huh?" Squeezing her eyes halfway closed, she seemed in deep thought.

"Like she said the other day, she's changing on the outside," Cotton said. "Inside, she's still the person who's loved you throughout your whole life, still the same person who spent all those years with you."

"Yeah, doesn't that mean that inside she's still my dad?"

"I would think that's exactly what she meant, but maybe you should ask her that directly and see what she says."

Cherylynn considered that for a moment and "mmm's" her assent. It surprised Cotton that they haven't discussed this, especially since Cherylynn was talking to Hailey more than the other two kids.

"Why don't you tell me a little about the way you and your dad talk to each other? Tell me what you like most about him. What you miss about him?" Cotton tucked her feet under her hips.

"My mom doesn't really want me to talk to him," Cherylynn started, then she seemed to think twice about what she wanted to say and stopped. She cocked her head a little, pulled her chin in, and glanced at Cotton, a look that said, *you know what I mean.*

"And how does that make you feel?"

"Scared." Her eyes rounded and she sank a little in her seat, a response too automatic to be faked.

"Scared of what?"

"I'd rather not ...."

"I know how you must feel, but remember what I told you in the very beginning? What we talk about here is just between the two of us.

For me to help you, I need to learn how you feel. That's why we therapists promise not to share anything."

Judging Cotton, Cherylynn paused a moment as if she had been reassured, then she plunged in. For the next half hour, she talked of nothing but her father. Cotton didn't have to prod her or ask any questions at all. Cherylynn volunteered it all. She talked of her childhood memories and how Hailey picked her up at school every day, took her to ballet lessons, shot hoops with her in the driveway, spent summers with the family at the beach where her father taught her how to swim.

No wonder Gray had such a problem dealing with the kids. Hailey was there for them all the time. Every day. Gray was the secondary parent, the major wage-earner, and now she'd quit her job. *Forces Hailey to cough up some of the household expenses.*

Cherylynn's stories drew a road map to the truth: she missed her father tremendously, and though it wasn't clear whether Marcus did as well, Cherylynn was the only one of the three children who really wanted Hailey back in the house and who would accept her the way she was. "I mean, we have another bedroom. She could stay in there, right? That way, she'd be there for our games and stuff."

It dawned on Cotton that the traumatic narrative had caused Cherylynn to build her own family story, and in that story, Dad would always be the lovable human being she had known all her life, and it didn't matter whether Dad was male or female, green or purple, a writer or a mad scientist. Just as long as Dad still loved her. The hard part was that Cherylynn's narrative wouldn't have the ending she wanted: Dad back in the house and everyone happy again. Hailey had already made it clear she was on her own for the duration.

When she finally wound down, Cherylynn leaned back in the chair, a beatific smile on her face. "Do you think I could live with Daddy? Mama probably wouldn't like that very much, but it would probably be fun being in an apartment with Dad."

"I don't know, Cherylynn. Don't you think that would be up to your parents?"

She shrugged. "Maybe, but I think I have something to say about that, too. I'm almost a teenager, and Janis always tells me teenagers have rights, too!"

For a split second, the pre-teen looked five years old again, and Cotton restrained herself from wrapping her in a big hug. Then Cherylynn's face changed as quickly as the smile appeared. "My friends'll probably make fun of me if they hear about my dad. That's the reason I haven't said anything to anyone."

"Does that change the way you feel about your dad?"

"Nooo, but ..."

"Does what everyone says change your dad at all?"

She thought a little longer about this question. "Nooo... not really."

"Do you think if you lived somewhere else or if you had a different set of friends, that it would change the way you feel about your father?"

"No, I don't think so." She screwed up her nose, probably thinking more deeply than she ever had in her young life, and suddenly she looked uncomfortable.

With a start, Cotton realized she was doing exactly what her husband had accused her of the other night. Obsessing. She gave herself a mental slap. As a therapist, she shouldn't be falling into the trap of labeling people instead of treating them as individual human beings with unique and personal histories. But even therapists get drawn into the cultural discourse. With the constant media drillings, it was easy to place labels on people, even if it's simple ones like "teens" and "adults."

Cotton had spent her academic life trying to understand the dominant discourses that marginalized people and had struggled not to be one of society's judges, not to be the one who sat on the sidelines of life, determining what social constructs exist within the world. Working with families like the Prescotts reminded her just how impressively the large-scale narratives shape how we deal with the social community and within the nuclear family group. It always amazed her that children—even twins—had individual personalities even though they came from the same gene pool, the same two parents, and that those children could be independent since they were most strongly impacted by the force of the family, their peers, their school culture, the culture in which they live, and all the other social groups that swirled around them.

Makes me freaking dizzy.

Yet here Cherylynn sat, a composed, still loving and understanding, pre-teen. Yes, she could be sarcastic, and it was often difficult to tell whether she was kidding or serious, but that was normal for her age. When they first met, Cotton thought Cherylynn was going to be the one who would be the most difficult to work with, and she suspected the pre-teen might never spin a narrative, but Cherylynn had surprised Cotton. Maybe it was because Cotton regularly saw Cheryl in a natural setting with friends. (She'd gotten into the habit of watching soccer games, always out of sight of Cherylynn and Gray, and whoever else was there).

Within the family structure, Cherylynn was the middle child, and she really had assumed the typical behavior of one: more relaxed about life in general but more likely to compete for a parent's attention. Perhaps that longing to live with her father was a natural move for her. The other two children were pushing Hailey away—or keeping her at arm's distance: Marcus doesn't know how to take Hayden's change into Hailey and only seems capable of dealing with his father in the online game format, and Janis had withdrawn from everyone while she took care of them all, though she had been asking for attention by dressing and acting rebelliously. That left plenty of room for Cherylynn to move into that empty "love space."

Though nothing was ever empty, according to the law of physics.

Cotton forced herself out of her thoughts and back to the office. "Cherylynn, if you could tell me the story of what your life might be like ten years from now, what would you say?"

"Ten years? I would be twenty-two, right? Isn't that when people can drink?" She giggled.

"Twenty-one is the drinking age."

"Yeah, right. Twenty-two years old." She looked up at the ceiling and tapped her index finger against her upper lip with a smile she could have copied from a leprechaun. "Well, I'll be rich and beautiful, of course." She giggled again. "I'll live on a big boat somewhere. It's nice and warm, and Janis will probably live with me, too, but Marcus won't. He'll still be in school. He's not very smart, y'know. He thinks he is, but that's just because he's real good at WarCraft, not because he's smart in books. He'll definitely still be in school, probably still a junior." She giggled again, tickling herself with the idea that she could put her brother in his place by imagining him as less successful than herself. "And maybe Mama will come visit every once in a while, but Dad'll be captain of the boat. She'd like that. She'll drive us around anywhere we want to go, and she'll have all the time he wants to write."

"Will Dad be a man or a woman?"

"Oh yeah, I didn't think of that. Well, whatever she wants to be! If she still wants to be a woman, then he'll be a woman. If she wants to be a man, she'll be a man, but whatever she is, she'll be a rich and famous writer just like she's always wanted. And I'll be a dancer or an actress or maybe—ooh, ooh, maybe I'll design clothes for celebrities like Taylor Swift or Sia, if they're still alive!" This last statement brought a full laugh, delighted and bubbly.

They played with this narrative for a while, and when it was quarter to the hour and she heard the outside door to the lobby close, it surprised Cotton that the therapy hour had passed.

"We need to finish now," Cotton said. "Is there anything else you would like to talk about before we say goodbye for today?"

Cherylynn thought for a moment and remembered. "Merry Christmas! It's tomorrow!" A cloud came over her features. She settled back down into the seat. "It's going to be different this year without Dad there, huh? We usually open at least one gift on Christmas Eve, but I don't know where Mama is hiding the presents. Dad likes to pile them under the tree as we get them, but there's nothing there right now." She looked at Cotton with watery eyes. "Y'know, I'd really like you to help us get Daddy back home."

"If she doesn't come home, what would that change for you?"

"Lots. It's just not the same. Everyone's so sad. And Mama doesn't even know how to help me with my homework. I just want Daddy home s'all."

"I think that's going to be up to all of you Prescotts." Cotton reluctantly rose from her chair and moved to the door. *Why was it that the best moments are always at the end of sessions?* "That's it for today. You've done good work. You should be proud of yourself."

Cherylynn beamed and moved into Cotton's open arms. A hug has become the natural way to close their sessions, but always with the door open and Gray in sight. This time, they hugged for a moment, then Cotton patted Cherylynn's full hair lightly and smiled down into her face, before opening the door. Gray was sitting right outside, her cell in her hand.

"She's ready for you, Mom," Cotton said, "but I'd like to speak to you for a moment about the next appointment before you leave. You don't mind if I steal your mother for a minute, do you, Cherylynn?"

"Nope. S'long as we're home in time for 'Naruto Shippuden'." In a flash of pink, she flitted out into the lobby, plopped down in a chair, and dug out her iPad.

~ Book Thirty ~

Gray Prescott

In the last decade or so, science has discovered a tremendous amount about the role emotions play in our lives. Researchers have found that even more than IQ, your emotional awareness and abilities to handle feelings will determine your success and happiness in all walks of life, including family relationships.
—John Gottman

"This'll just take a minute, right? I wasn't planning on an appointment today. I made plans ..." Gray entered the office. She perched on the arm of the chair, still in her business clothes: a simple black skirt suit and a white blouse. She must have had a meeting. Or an interview. Her pale lips and shadowed eyes show she's still not sleeping well, but at least she'd taken a shower and washed her hair.

"You look a little tired," Cotton said. "I hope you're going to take some time for yourself over the holidays."

"It's been a long day. Long *week*." Gray laughed a little ruefully and completely ignored the reference to the holiday. "Shit, who am I kidding? It's been a long couple of months!"

"How are you handling it?"

"About as well as can be expected." Gray fidgeted, shaking her keys a bit, and resembled Janis at that moment, as she often does. Rebellious and cantankerous. She pushed herself up from the chair with straight arms, then stood like a soldier, feet spread, arms crossed over her chest.

"Let me make it quick, then. You probably want to go home, eat dinner, and relax for the night, especially since it's Christmas Eve. So, I'll come right out with it."

Cotton paused a beat and within that brief amount of time, she felt the struggle Gray went through every moment of every day, and she wanted to lift that struggle for her client, the way she always does when people are floundering and going down for the third time. One of the most frustrating parts of her job was watching people walk away at the very moment of a breakthrough. What was worse was when they left her office and took their own life within twenty-four hours. *That doesn't happen all the time, but when it does, it's... it can break you.*

She involuntarily shivered and saw Brighton's face in her mind's eye, the way she squeezed her eyes to a slit and screwed her mouth up to the side when she answered questions, the cloudbursts of tears and heartrending sobs when she remembered her father, that brief but megawatt smile as she walked out the door. The silence afterwards.

Cotton tightened her jaw and dismissed the memory, focusing on Gray. "What I wanted to ask you is whether you've considered letting Hailey see the kids. Remember, we talked about the Family Acceptance Project? We need to make sure everyone knows their lives are important, that the family needs to accept each other 'as is.'"

"Oh no, that's not about to happen." Gray waggled her finger back and forth and cocked her head. "You're not really asking me this again, are you? You can't be serious. Hailey's in no shape to take care of my children or to answer any of the zillion questions they've been asking. Hell, no! He's not in tune with the universe enough to take care of himself! No. Absolutely not. Besides, he talks to them now. He... she gets to talk to them now. That's enough." Gray paced, three short and jerky steps, then turned and repeated.

"Have you talked to them about your decision? The kids, I mean."

"I told them they wouldn't be seeing him until we have all this—this mess—straightened out. They're all dealing with it." Gray ducked her head.

That's not true. None of the Prescotts are "dealing with" anything.

Cotton squirmed in her chair, caught within a small web of guilt about whether to give Gray a hint that the kids have all told her at one point or another that they miss having their father around. But she couldn't do that, because she knew Gray would return to the house and interrogate each one of them, and it might end up becoming a punishment of sorts for the kids. Cotton backed off, tucked the thought away, and concentrated on responding to Gray.

"Do you think letting Hailey take some of the responsibility for the kids might make life a little easier for you?"

"I'm supposed to give up the kids *to him*? I'm sorry—to her. It. That weirdo? No, damn way!" Gray raised her voice, then immediately lowered it, as if realizing the kids were right in the next room. Her eyes brimmed with an anger that was closer to the surface than any she'd displayed to Cotton previously.

Christ. You can take a horse to water... what do I need to do to help her understand? If Gray continued stirring the pot, the whole family would keep spinning in this unhealthy spiral. No one was getting any better.

"Okay, can I make a suggestion? There are a few books that are superb for understanding what the transgender person goes through. Some of these authors are trans. Others are family members or therapists. Maybe they'd offer something to help you negotiate this difficult period." Cotton had suggested doing some research before, but that was early in the family's therapy, and she hadn't offered a list of books. Now, she kept her voice even and opened her upper body, placing her hands on the arms of the chair, ensuring that her body language was warm and inviting. If Gray perceived the discussion to be a threat of any kind, she'll shut down again. *And we'd be back to square one.*

Pointing to a small pile of books on the table next to her, Cotton said, "Would you like to borrow them, or should I write down the titles for you?" She'd gotten them together that morning, flipping through several of them as if they'd provide the magic elixir for Gray, and she planned on giving them to Gray at their next meeting. But this moment seemed the perfect time.

Gray immediately shook her head and twisted her lips. "Not really. I don't want them. I don't have to understand this. I know what I know: he left his family to become a woman. He didn't even have the balls to tell me this—this truth of his, his... narrative, as you call it Dr. Barnes— he didn't even tell me to my face. Ha!" She laughs, a bit hysterically for a minute, then shakes her shoulders. "He hasn't come to the house since he left, and he hasn't sent me one dime to pay for his kids' meals or the heat or the mortgage and the car payment. All those bills he helped make. All the KIDS he helped make. And I'm supposed to understand *him*?"

Though she longed to correct Gray's pronoun usage, Cotton instead said, "I understand that. You're angry now. But, later, if you are curious, the books I'm suggesting are written by people who have gone through the same thing you have, families of transgender people trying to understand the loved one who is going through a transition. Some of them have experienced the same confusion and anger you're feeling. It's sort of like families of alcoholics who get together to give each other support and understanding. Nothing works better than sharing with someone who might empathize with what you're going through, right? People find comfort in building groups. So, what I'm saying is that it helps to see that there are others going through the same thing you are. Would that help?"

The look on Gray's face says she wasn't convinced but may be willing—maybe, just maybe—she might think about it. *But that was all she was going to do, and you'd better not push your luck.* "Listen, I have to go..."

"Okay, but think about what I said. I'll be in the office the day after Christmas for a little while. Call me if you want the list, okay? Or if you want to schedule some visits with Hailey." Cotton paused a moment, offering Gray the opportunity to make an appointment. What she didn't say was that Hailey could probably go to court and get visitation rights, but she'd told Cotton that she wouldn't do that. She wouldn't put the kids through anymore trauma. Instead, she'd sit back and wait for Gray to "come to her senses."

Abruptly, Gray nodded, then hurried out the door, gathering Cherylynn, and leaving without looking back.

As soon as the door closed, Cotton realized she held the book list in her hand. She stared at it, regretting that she pushed Gray to where she felt compelled to leave without setting up another appointment for Cherylynn, or herself, for that matter. Folding it carefully, Cotton planned to use the list as an excuse to call Gray and get her in again. If Gray didn't come, the whole family would be affected, and Cotton had worked too hard to lose them now.

Must fix the Prescotts. No choice.

Her hands started shaking. She counted the pens in the cup on her desk—five. Two blue, one black, one purple. She counted the rings holding up the curtains on the window, and at thirty-two, her breathing returned to normal. She took a breath and turned to the window. *Dr. Barnes, when will it be okay again? When will I feel better?* A small voice. A quick flash of that Brighton smile. Cotton's heart skittered in her chest so rapidly that she raised a hand to her breastplate and stood like a statue until it calmed down. *Fuck, do I need to take an Ativan?*

She counted the keys on her keyboard, added up the numbers two by two, added up the keys with words, the ones with numbers, the ones with letters, and finally, the thrumming in her chest melted into a regular rhythm again.

Returning to her notes, she called and set up a consultation with Nancy Wentworth, one of her fellow therapists, a specialist in family therapy. She needed to meet with her colleagues, and the perfect time to do it was between the holidays, when the most dedicated were office-bound and happy to have a drink after a day of listening to depressed men who coped with the holidays by drinking too much and anxious mothers who were determined to do the best imitation of Martha Stewart by putting together the perfect holiday dinner. Give everything, be everyone to everybody, all the time.

On any given Thursday night between the middle of November and the middle of January, The Poet's Corner, the oldest bar in Wake Forest, was host to at least three local therapists who gathered to raise a glass of wine and offer each other some support. By the end of the night, they'd empty at least two bottles between them. When they left, wobbly and worldly wise, they had solved each other's cases more effectively than they diagnosed their own.

Yes, it was time to admit treating the Prescotts overwhelmed her. Cotton Barnes needed help. *Poet's Corner, here I come.*

~ Book Thirty-one ~

The Prescotts

The passion for setting people right is in itself an afflictive disease.
—Marianne Moore

Cotton still owned every piece of technology she'd ever bought. She often joked about being a Luddite. She still used her first flip phone; the CD player she bought for her first car, a 2000 Honda Civic; the DVD player where she watched her collection of Star Wars/Star Trek/Indiana Jones movies. She only bought new electronics when the old ones no longer worked. *Why contribute to the pile of dead motherboards?* Her home phone still had a cord attached to the wall, and she still used the answering machine she's had since high school. It echoed downstairs in the kitchen as she worked from her office upstairs. She liked it that way: the old-fashioned answering machines with their flashing numbers to warn how many messages warrant her attention. *Eleven, twelve, twenty-two, fifty-six.* If she needed to answer the call, she knew immediately by the emotion resonating in the person's voice on the machine. If not, she continued doing what she's doing. And somewhere in the bowels of the answering machine's memory was a message she doesn't want to delete. *Or two or three.*

Having a private practice allowed her the freedom to work at home, as she was now. Her home office was a redesigned walk-in closet between the master and guest bedrooms. Small, but convenient, she thought, yet it would never work as an office where she could bring clients. For that, she needed what she called her "official space," the place she shares with several other therapists—individual practices, like hers. HIPAA regulated. Each of the therapists has a separate space, but they share the waiting room, and their shared appointment calendar ensures they don't bump into each other.

"Dr. Barnes? It's Hailey. I can't get Gray, and I really need to find out where Marc is... oh, God. Omigod. Please answer. Please pick up the phone. Please." Her voice was high-pitched, the words frantically tumbling over each other.

Normally, Cotton let the therapist-on-call take her after-hours emergencies, but despite it being against best practices, the Prescotts had all her numbers—office, home, text, email—and she'd made each of them promise to call whenever they needed her. Because the Prescotts haven't abused that privilege, she picked up the phone.

Hailey talked so quickly that Cotton couldn't separate one word from the other. "Whoa, whoa, whoa. Slow down. I can't understand a word you're saying."

"I'm sorry, I'm sorry. Sorry for calling you at home, too, but I had to. I just had to." Hailey was out of breath. "See, I was on WarCraft tonight. Marc and I were playing together in the same guild, as we usually are, then suddenly, he started unloading all of his loot... his character did, I mean. It took me a minute to understand what was going on. He was doing the Hari Kari thing, Dr. Barnes!" Hailey's voice cracked like an adolescent boy's. "He did it right in front of everyone. He never would do that unless something is really wrong. I need to get him, I need to talk to him, but no one is answering the phone...you've got to help me!"

"Of course, I'll help," Cotton said, not thinking about the implications until the words were out of her mouth. She couldn't fix every problem these people have. She knew that. *But I'm damn sure going to try.*

Hailey paused for a moment, took a couple of quivering breaths. "What if he's really thinking of killing himself? He's too deep in this game. Christ, I shouldn't have gotten him into this. He's addicted... Damn War Crack!"

"Okay, slow down, slow down. Why do you think there's something else wrong if he just died in the game? Can't he do that as part of... the game... or his personality? His avatar? I thought he had many unique characters."

"No, if someone dies, either they're saying they're out of the game completely or there's something else wrong. Like last year, this Chinese kid killed himself for real and the kid's family sued the company that made the game. It became a sign of honor with some teens. I don't want my kid to be that kind of statistic... Doc, you have to help me get hold of Gray, or else I'm going over there myself! In fact, I think I am ..."

"Hailey? Hailey?"

Nothing.

Cotton held the phone against her cheek for a moment, shocked into silence.

Thomas walked in from the hallway, book in his hand, his reading glasses atop his head. "What's wrong, hon?"

"A patient," Cotton answered as she pulled a Duke sweatshirt she's had since her undergrad years over her head. Her mind splintered in twelve directions. "Potential suicide. I'll be back in a while." She ducked Thomas's eyes, knowing perfectly well that they have a movie date tonight, and that Thomas would be angry that she would miss it. But this was life or death, and she couldn't tell him that. *I'd lose my license. Therapist-client privilege.*

He stalked out of the room and though she was sorry to break another date with him, *I'm not going to turn my back on the Prescotts.* She tamped down a feeling of guilt and simultaneously felt annoyed that Thomas didn't understand. But how could he? She couldn't tell him anything. *The best way to take care of the client is to rely on the therapist, but what if that therapist has no clue whether what they're doing is right?*

It was the movie or a dead patient. She knew which one won the lottery for most important, and once Thomas thought it over, he'd agree with her.

In the car, she dialed the Prescotts' home phone number (Hailey had installed a landline, and the family still used it), and when there was no answer, she hit redial. Still no answer. She hit redial again at the next stoplight. No answering machine, no busy signal. No answer of any kind. Strange. No wonder Hailey was concerned. *Next phone call is to Hailey.*

When Cotton arrived at the Prescott house, every light was on, which made it more suspect that the phone wasn't answered. She quickly assessed the contemporary split-level that appeared much happier (*how can a house seem happy*) and more normal than the people who lived inside. Neat boxwood bushes lined the front driveway and stressed the house's squareness. Everything was tidy. The house's brick base was framed by formal black shutters and trim, and the body of the house painted a sunny yellow. A home for a happy family, it would seem.

Someone stood in the arched doorway between the front room and the back of the house. The kitchen, she suspected. Purple hair. Janis. She was talking to someone in the kitchen, her back to the front of the house, maybe the dining room. Cotton couldn't tell. She put the car into park and shut off the lights. Janis gesticulated and seemed to laugh, then reached forward. Cherylynn drew under her arm, and they had a moment, profiles to each other. Janis ruffled her sister's hair, then drew their heads close, squeezing, kissing Cheryl's forehead, before letting her go, pushing her toward what Cotton thought would be the hallway to the second floor. She could almost read Janis's lips: *Go do your homework.*

What was going on? The scene appeared perfectly normal. Cotton was determining her next step when Hailey pulled into the driveway, and without even bothering to get out of her car, she spotted Cotton and yelled, "We need to go to the hospital! I'll meet you at Wake Med." She left rubber as she backed out of the driveway.

Cotton cast one last glance back at the house, but the kids had disappeared, and she had to hurry to follow Hailey's Jeep.

The hospital's emergency room buzzed with people: a heavyset man with a red beard and gaping gunshot wound moaned on a nearby stretcher; a quiet Hispanic family with a crying, sick baby huddled in the corner; and an elderly couple with their heads together tried to figure out their paperwork. Hailey was already at the admissions desk asking for her son, but the clerk's head shook back and forth. *Not good news.*

"Not here," Hailey said when she spotted Cotton, though Cotton wasn't exactly sure what that meant. Hailey shoved her dark glasses aside and adjusted the turban on her head. She wore a black cardigan and a pair of skinny jeans with black ballet flats. Somehow, she pulled off a skinny Audrey-Hepburn-meets-Adam Levine look even though she appeared taller than the 5'10" she listed on her intake sheet. "I'm sure this is the only place they'd take Marcus," Hailey said, taking Cotton's hand and pulling her down the hallway. "There's no other hospital closer."

"Unless they aren't at the ER," Cotton pointed out. "Maybe they're already in a room or at one of the other intake points? Or maybe they're not here at all."

"Where else would they be at this time of night? No one's home. And Marc's... he wouldn't do that. It's just not something he would do. God, I hope he wouldn't do anything stupid. Nothing makes sense anymore. Nothing."

Hailey referred to Marc's actions in the online game, and her fear that Marc was thinking of suicide, but Cotton felt torn about how to respond. *Not Marcus. Not the youngest.* "Why don't you try their cell phones again? Both Gray's and Janis's."

Cotton leaned against the door, watching the hubbub of the ER, while Hailey tried to find a quiet spot to call her kids. In the long hallway, she tucked into an alcove, and all Cotton could see was a shadow.

After a moment, Hailey pulled her head back, nodded, and hurried back over to Cotton. "I got Janis. They're out looking for Marc," she said with a small sigh of relief. "He disappeared earlier tonight. He must've been playing the game on someone else's computer. I don't know where to go now. I just don't know." Hailey found a chair and slumped into it, throwing one slim-panted leg over the other, and studying the large turquoise rings on her fingers. "I did this. I did all of this. I've made such a mess of it. The little bullies at school just made it worse." She cradled her head in her hands, massaging her temples.

"Tell me what happened." Cotton scooted over and sat down, hoping that they were not too late, and that between them, they could figure out what happened to Marcus.

"I was making dinner tonight, and as always, I was listening to the chitter-chatter from the Guild." At Cotton's raised eyebrows, Hailey added: "When WarCraft first came out, we used to talk to each other like we do when we instant message, but now we all have headsets, so I just hooked into my stereo, and I can listen to the chatter all the time. I know, I know, I'm 'addicted,' and I'm afraid Marc is, too. I used to think I could protect him. I was the one who'd say, 'Okay, it's time to walk away now.' God, I hate myself for getting Marc into this. I hate hate hate it." She pounded her fists against her upper thighs and swore under her breath. In the hospital hallway, a disembodied voice asked for Dr. English to call extension twenty-four.

"Anyway, it was around 8:30ish when I sat down to eat," Hailey said, "and I turned the laptop on and watched some streamers that I like, then I looked at the game. I noticed Marc was on—he's got a couple of different avatars, but his newest favorite is Nyphon. And Nyphon's pretty spectacular. Marc's gotten really good at battles and gaining loot-Nyphon's loaded." She glanced at Cotton with a smile, proud of her son's creation.

"I just sat and watched and listened for a while until I finished eating, then I was going to play for a while before I went to bed. Before I started, though, I heard Marc's voice, and he sounded pretty upset.

The others in the guild were trying to calm him down, y'know, talking to him, asking questions, but it took a couple of minutes before I realized what he was doing. Little by little, Nyphon flamed up. Then Marc made sure each piece of gear was disenchanted. One piece at a time. Each time a piece of loot disappeared, Marc gave this little shriek, as if he was hysterical, crying and laughing at the same time. It was horrible. Scary. I feel like I've gotten my son into drugs."

"Did you talk to him?" Cotton asked.

"I couldn't. He didn't answer me." Hailey took a deep breath, and the same empty look appeared in her eyes that Cotton had seen on heroin addicts' faces. A helplessness that seemed hand-in-hand with that soul-stealing need for a drug. Cotton jotted a note to research the latest treatments for online addictions. Though she'd heard her colleagues discuss how difficult it is to treat, she'd never had a client experience the full throes of this type of dependence. Maybe she should handle game addictions differently.

With a shudder that moved from her face through her shoulders and down to her hands, Hailey said, "I'm responsible for this. I'm responsible for whatever has happened to him."

Cotton sat beside her and gently squeezed Hailey's arm. "We'll find him. I'm here with you, and we'll find him."

As Hailey quivered with soft sobs, Cotton stared down the hallway and hoped she was right.

She picked up her phone, prepared to call the cops, when it buzzed with an incoming text.

Janis Prescott: Dr. B, Hailey with you?
Cotton: Yes
Janis: Tell her to answer her phone. And Marc's back. He's fine.

In a flurry of phone calls and relieved sighs, Hailey spoke to Janis who repeated what she'd texted to Cotton, and with only a goodbye wave, Hailey bustled out the door, hoping that she could get to the

Prescott house before Gray got home. "I have to give my kids a hug," Hailey said. "I just have to."

When Cotton was in her car heading to her own home, she realized with a start that she had missed the movie completely, but there was still time to make Thomas' business holiday party.

~ Book Thirty-two ~

Cotton Barnes

The ability to be in the present moment is a major component of mental wellness.
—Abraham Maslow

"She's a social deviant." Lisa Phillips leans back, her perfectly penciled crimson-red lips tight, and her perfectly even eyebrows arched. She was the new partner at a Raleigh law firm no one's heard of, and she thought because she'd spent a couple of years as a public defender working with indigents who are often psychologically impaired, she had the right to diagnose anyone who might be even slightly psychotic. "No one wanted anything to do with her," Lisa finished, satisfied with herself that she'd brought Cotton that message.

They were at Thomas's company Christmas party. It was Christmas Eve, almost midnight, and she had wanted to leave since 9:35 when David Mitte leaned over to give her a holiday hug, and his scotch-tainted breath almost knocked her over.

Thomas had been by Cotton's side listening to Lisa rant and glanced away, bringing a hand to his mouth to cover a smirk. He always understood what Cotton was thinking, and right now, Cotton was thinking *Lisa Phillips is an idiot.* If she could, she'd punch the smug look off Lisa's face, then school her on why a lawyer had no right to deliver psychiatric diagnoses without the appropriate degree. *Not a very*

Christian way to act on Christmas. Thomas said that Cotton wore her emotions on her sleeve and that she'd be amazed if she saw a video of herself reacting to what people say, but he was wrong. Her patients would have stopped coming to her long ago if they could guess what she was thinking. *Embarrassing.*

But there was more to why Cotton couldn't stand Lisa Phillips. When she was a public defender, she'd put a man back on the street, even after Cotton testified he was psychotic, off his meds, and violent. He'd sexually abused at least six girls that they knew of, and Cotton had treated three of them. When Phillips questioned Cotton's diagnosis for one girl, saying that she was already in therapy before she accused the man, that she had a history of lying to teachers and other adults. That poor child had been brutally raped and still couldn't leave the house. That girl, ripped and beaten, would never have the satisfaction of knowing any justice, and Phillips had done that by establishing a reasonable doubt about the victim, one that the jury bought and caused enough doubt that they couldn't convict.

Enraged by the results of the trial, Cotton worked for a year with the girl's attorney and they finally brought the man back to court. Though he eventually ended up behind bars, Phillips considered the first trial a win, and whenever she ran into Cotton at public functions, she flaunted her newfound "knowledge" of psychiatry.

When the party's five-piece blues band started playing "When a Man loves a Woman." Thomas stretched out a hand to her, which Cotton took gratefully. The best thing for her to do now was to stay away from the lawyer from hell. Besides, Cotton had been working long hours and being in her husband's arms was what she needed.

He encircled her waist and drew her close. They swayed to the music, and she leaned in to the musky and familiar sweetness of his shoulder. Years ago, they found Hermes Eau de Narcisse Bleu, a cologne that they both now use, yet she'd always sworn it smells better on Thomas than it does on her. She breathed it in now and felt her shoulders relax.

"Why do you always talk me into coming to these things?" she whispered in his ear.

"Best place to pick up new clients, right?" He laughed, the little lines around his eyes crinkling, and squeezed her waist, sliding his hand down to her backside, which he knew always embarrassed her.

"Shhh..." She glanced around, afraid someone had heard. Or seen.

"It's only once a year," he continued. "Besides, how often do I get to see my wife in a slinky silver dress and sexy red heels? Can I tell you how much you're turning me on right now?" He nibbled her neck and pushed his hips against her.

"You don't have to tell me." She giggled. "It's painfully obvious."

Tilting his head back, he grinned. "Gotta tell you. You have this Southern Harry-met-Sally thing going on tonight .... some guys even asked me who the hot babe was."

Her giggle turned into a full laugh at that comment.

"What? You don't believe me? Look at yourself in the mirror. You're a hot mama, Dr. Barnes."

The music slowed, and the lights lowered a bit more. A few couples joined them on the floor, but this was the band's last song. Most partygoers left a long time ago. And she must admit she couldn't wait to leave herself.

Thomas hummed in her ear a little, massaged her lower back, and they swayed together, hip to hip.

"Get a room," a male voice next to them slurred

She turned her head. David Mitte's face was less than an inch from hers. She drew away.

"David, you're a little impaired, pal," Thomas said.

"What makesh you think dat?" David asked, bobbing his head and smiling crookedly. He held a redhead in his arms, who appeared just as lit as he was.

"You're drunk," Thomas said. "Give me your keys, bud."

The music ended. The bandleader thanked the crowd and removed the mouthpiece from his sax. The rest of the band began packing their instruments.

Thomas arched his brows apologetically at Cotton, then turned to David again. "Give me your keys, bud. We'll give you a ride home."

"I'm fine, I'm fine, totally fine," David insisted, wobbling a little.

Cotton felt she had no choice but to back her husband, and before she knew it, David and his redheaded friend were in their backseat, and Thomas was getting their addresses so they could take David and his friend home.

By the time they pulled into their own driveway two hours later, Thomas was yawning, and she couldn't wait to peel off the silver dress and to kick off the red high heels that made her feel like Cinderella's stepsister trying to fit her oversized foot into a tiny glass slipper.

The bathroom was still steamy from their showers when they crawled into bed, and the sky outside was brightening.

"Do me a favor, baby?" she murmured as her husband pulled her close.

"Anything." Thomas yawned again, his body warm and muscular against hers.

"Let's skip the company Christmas party next year. Deal? I can't stand it when Lisa Phillips thinks she knows my business better than I do," Cotton spoke into his chest hairs, her breath making the hairs tickle her nose. "I should diagnose *her*. Friggin' narcissistic bitch."

"I'm surprised you didn't give her hell."

"If you hadn't been there, I probably would have."

"What does that mean?" His chin pressed against the top of her head. She could feel every word he said.

"I didn't want to embarrass you. You don't like it when I call people out."

"True." Thomas drew the word out slowly, as if he knew Cotton needed to rant, but he wasn't sure where she was going with this.

"It's people like her who enforce stereotypes. That woman she called a social deviant is quite successful. The only reason Phillips doesn't like her is because she's transgender." Cotton lifted herself up on her elbow.

Thomas groaned a little. "Do we have to talk about this right now?" He cupped his hand on the back of her head and tried to draw her back down to his chest. "How about we forget about everything else? I'd like to make love to my wife, the hot blond in the sexy red heels tonight."

In the pit of her stomach, Cotton felt a tightening, a warning that she was getting angry. She fought it and pulled her head away from his grip. "Why don't you want to listen to me right now?"

"Because I'd rather make love..."

Even in the dark, she could tell his arousal was weakening. She knew he could sense she wasn't in the mood. "People like Lisa Phillips are the reason people like the Prescotts suffer." Her throat constricted.

Silence. She turned over, snaked her arm over him. Because *if we don't resolve this discussion, it'll hang over us for days.*

"I can't understand why you don't get that," she continued.

"I get it, babe, believe me, but I've watched you do this before, and I don't want to see you...you know... go down the rabbit hole."

"What are you insinuating?"

"I'm not. I'm just worried about you."

"Because I'm concerned about my patients?"

"No. You are right that Lisa's a bitch. You're right that people like her perpetuate stereotypes. You're right." As always, his voice was calm and even. "What I'm worried about is that you get so involved with your patients that you... well..."

"What?"

"You become a bit obsessed."

"A bit?"

"Too much. You know what Dr. Carbinetti said."

Cotton didn't need to be reminded that Carbinetti told her after Brighton's suicide that Cotton needed to maintain her professional distance with other patients. She especially doesn't need Thomas to remind her. If he, of all people, couldn't support her and listen to her, who would?

"You just overstepped." This time, she turned over and away from him, punching her pillow and settling into it.

Behind her, Thomas shifted in the bed. "Guess there'll be no sex tonight, huh?"

"I don't think so," she replied and blinked back the tears that unexpectedly filled her eyes, thankful he couldn't see.

Christmas day, the morning after, Cotton followed Thomas up the stairs to the Barnes house, and even though they had polite talk over coffee, the distance between them was palpable.

Thomas's parents' stately Southern mansion, perched on a hilltop in Wake Forest, was beautiful and elaborately decorated for the holidays, white lights snaking around every column, individually decorated trees in every room, and giant nutcrackers guarding the front door. Cotton had always found all of it ostentatious. Everything about visiting his family during the holidays made her uncomfortable. And, today, the last thing she wanted to do was to act festive and jolly. What she wanted was to drive by the Prescott house and to see them all gathered around the tree in front of their picture window. What she wanted was to see them happy. But she couldn't sneak out this morning without Thomas asking a lot of questions, so she did the family thing, all the while planning on sneaking out later.

At the top of the stairs stood Hilde Barnes, Cotton's mother-in-law, dressed in an off-white Chanel skirt suit, her white hair naturally curling around her face. She smiled at them coming toward her and opened her arms, squeezing both of them together like a mama bear. She smelled like lilacs.

"Ice blue," Hilde pointed out as she took Cotton's hand in her cold, yet elegantly manicured one, and gestured with the other toward the hallway. Hilde had decorated all four ceiling-high house trees in the foyer in blue ribbons and bells, and the inside of the house was awash in ice blue lights. The silver and blue accents throughout the house were elegant and simple.

"Not that sickening Carolina blue or Duke royal blue. Ice blue. Like the color of deep snowdrifts." Hilde was a Radcliffe grad, and she didn't hesitate to remind her UNC and Duke friends she considered herself a step above them.

The whole family arrived early, bustling into the house on the heels of Thomas and Cotton. Thirteen grandchildren, ten nieces and nephews, nine uncles, eleven aunts (three of them are great-aunts), two grandparents (one from each side of the family), and four sisters- and brothers-in-law. Forty-nine people, plus Thomas and Cotton and his parents, for a grand total of fifty-three souls in this grand house—and the house still didn't feel full. It's a crowd and a half, and Hilde just "loves it to death," as she'd tell anyone who'd listen. Cotton felt swallowed up by the crowd and often ended up with the children, only because they were easier to talk to and they had more fun.

The chef and staff served the traditional Christmas dinner (fried goose, oyster stuffing, turnip casserole, and sweet potato pie) around 1 PM, around a table loud with conversations Cotton listened to half-heartedly, sending an occasional glance at Thomas, who was on the other side of the table. Even though she smiled at him after dinner, when small groups congregated around the house and outside to play games, have coffee and tea (or brandy in crystal snifters), he wandered away with one of his cousins. That left her with the matriarchs, which was exactly what she wanted to avoid.

"So, how's your work, sweetheart?" Great Aunt Isabelle perched on a stool in the large family kitchen where all the women gathered to help prepare the dinner that Hilde already had under control, barking orders like a Southern drum major. Isabelle was 86 and dressed in Chanel white wool pants and cashmere sweater, with a matching white, chin-length bob.

"My client base has grown," Cotton told her. *Growing from zero to 5 isn't hard.* "And I've had several articles published in academic journals in the past couple of months."

Isabelle nodded enthusiastically and patted Cotton's hand as if she knew how important this was in a therapist's career and that she was proud of her great nephew's wife.

"I'm hoping to expand my practice to a small office in Cary a couple of days a week by spring of next year," Cotton continued, again lying and wondering why.

But that's not what Isabelle wanted to hear. She traced her painted eyebrows with her pinky finger. "You sound mighty busy! When are you going to have time for that family Thomas wants to start?"

Inwardly, Cotton groaned. It's ironic that she was a professional who counseled people all the time about how to handle family members, but she couldn't deal with them appropriately herself. Her favorite way to get out of questions like these was to slip out the side door and join the group of teenaged cousins throwing a football on the front lawn or take a walk through the gardens, but this time, Isabelle's stool blocked her way.

Instead, Cotton smiled as she opened the refrigerator, sticking her head inside and giving Isabelle a muffled answer that made no sense. Isabelle wouldn't be able to hear it anyway, so it didn't matter.

Unfortunately, the questions didn't stop there.

Throughout dinner, Isabelle popped in one comment after another about happy families and beautiful babies. She cornered Thomas and asked him whether he knew about how hard his wife had been working. And if that wasn't enough, Hilde and Marylee joined the action after dinner, and everyone had gathered in the parlor for coffee and pumpkin pie.

By the time they'd redirected the conversation Cotton's way several more times, she felt her face burning, but it wasn't until they asked her whether she was going to take a break when she and Thomas had children that she finally lost it.

"I don't think that whether Thomas and I intend to have children anytime soon is a matter of concern for the whole family." Cotton's tone sounded snappy, but she couldn't help it, nor did she want to. *Enough is enough.* "It's almost as if you're asking me how many times we've had sex in the past couple of months, and personally, I find that invasive. I will no longer answer those questions, so if you have any curiosity, you're probably best to keep it to yourselves."

Isabelle gasped. Hilde's cup clinked to her saucer. Marylee turned her head, purposefully sidestepping the conversation.

It wasn't bad enough that Thomas and Cotton disagreed on the topic but to get quizzed by his family made her furious. She rose from the couch and smoothed her pants. It was time for them to go, and it wouldn't be easy to find her husband without everyone in the family knowing what's happening.

Without another word, she left the living room. She passed the Christmas tree in the formal living room, its base loaded with the presents that all the children were dying to open. It was usually her favorite part of the day, but right now, all she could think of was finding her coat and her husband and going home.

He was outside with the men on the wraparound porch, as she suspected, nursing a beer, and leaning against the railing. As soon as he saw her, he said, "You okay?" and encircled an arm around her protectively.

"No. I'm tired of the questions and comments today. I need to leave. Let's go."

"What about —"

"I want to go now."

He knew better than to argue, so within three minutes, they had their coats and were maneuvering the BMW down the long driveway. "My mother wanted to know what was wrong," he said, and from the sound of his voice, he did, too.

"I'm sure she does, but she heard the questions your aunts were asking me all day. Enough is enough. I don't need to report on my fertility to your whole family."

"Christ." He wiped a hand across his forehead. "I'm sorry."

"Not your fault. Let's just go home."

For the first time in their married life, they spend Christmas night together, alone, quietly watching television and drinking brandy. Her stomach didn't settle down until almost eleven o'clock that night. She took a couple of aspirins before going to bed.

Thomas didn't say anything when they climbed beneath the sheets except, "Goodnight, babe. Love you."

She responded with a grunt.

~ Book Thirty-three ~

Janis Prescott

Perhaps a child who is fussed over gets a feeling of destiny; he thinks he is in the world for something important, and it gives him drive and confidence.
  —Benjamin Spock

Janis was ten minutes late. Cotton paced her office, straightened the pillows on the couch—*three shakes each, two pats, then a karate chop to the top of each pillow.* She warmed up her cup of Earl Grey, peeked out the blinds, straightened her white button-down and the gray wool sweater she kept in the office because the heat ranged from comfortable to freezing in the span of seconds, and tried to quell the anxiety attack she'd been fighting for days.

She hadn't admitted to Thomas, or to Dr. Carbinetti, or even to Deb that the attacks had returned. Full-fledged. Meditation, long walks, sleeping pills, and hot baths had kept them at bay for a while, but *they're baaack.* One yesterday at 6:05 PM. Lasted until 6:17. Another this morning at 9:01. She'd counted to 60 ten times before the tightening in her chest subsided. Then, an hour and a half of yoga and deep breathing. *Inhale to the count of 8, exhale to the count of 10.*

She was determined to handle it without medication. *No meds this time. No hospitalization. No extended sessions with Dr. Carbinetti,* who'd probably suspend her privileges indefinitely if he knew what she was doing. She'd been by the Prescott house at least half a dozen times since Christmas Eve. No one knew that.

Finally, a bright orange Mustang peeled into the small parking lot, dropped Janis off, then screeched rubber down the driveway before disappearing into the late afternoon sun. Janis stood and watched the car leave for a good ten seconds, shielding the afternoon sun with her hand, before heading into the office.

The door slammed, and Janis stomped into the office wearing Doc Marten wannabes, an old Army jacket, and huge sweatpants, plopped into the wingback before Cotton even said hello. Today her hair spiked along her head in a crest, dyed crimson red, like a rooster's comb. Her clothing appears à propos to her mood: dark and angry. A couple of weeks ago, Cotton would have steeled herself for battle with this teenager. That was before she'd discovered Janis's secret. She had a soft and caring side, and she fiercely guarded her sibs.

"Some days I hate my life," Janis said. "some days I feel like everything in the whole damn world sucks. Then there are days when I wish I could paint myself into someone else, you know? I realize it's freaking impossible. But I always ask myself why I am who I am and why I end up doing things I do and sometimes even I can't figure out myself."

"Sounds like you're having a bad day," Cotton responded. It was obvious Janis needed to talk, and this was the right space for it. *Go, Janis, go.*

Janis nodded and slid her fingers up one spike of hair, tapping it a little to see if it would stand. "All I can say is that people fucking suck. School sucks. Life sucks. But no matter what happens, you only get to live once. I hate I was born human. Why wasn't I born a duck or a black fox or something cool, like a Rothschild's giraffe, the ones that look like they're wearing knee socks? Anything would be better than suffering human emotions like sadness and compassion and empathy. That one will kill you: empathy. I could spend 24/7 wallowing in empathy for every soul who's ever roamed the earth—including the scumbags. I hate that. I wish I could hate all of them—the losers, the poor people, the crazies, the angry murderers. Instead, I think about the sad lives they must live and how painful it must be, and I get all engrossed in that feeling and pretty soon I'm as messed up as all the people I was busy feeling sorry for. It sucks being human." She paused and rubbed her fists against her eyes. Her black makeup smudged, creating raccoon circles.

It was an illusion that Janis was strong, and she had even fooled her mother into believing that. She hadn't fooled Cotton, though. "Maybe I should ask how you feel about being here today?"

"Fine." She looks out the window, black leather boot beating against the floor.

"The eye roll tells me differently, Janis." Cotton laughed as though it didn't bother her, though it did. She didn't want Janis to think she was trying to be her parent or a teacher. "It's okay if you don't want to be here. We can talk about that. I won't be offended."

"Right." Janis curled her lip as if she didn't believe Cotton, though deep down she knew the therapist was only doing her job. Janis scrunched deeper into the chair. "Sometimes I wanna crawl under a fucking rock. I'm not a baby anymore, but I'm also not ready to be the only parent in the house! I keep thinking about this girl who killed herself in ninth grade, and I wonder whether that's how Marcus felt before we found him that night. It's how I feel right now."

Cotton's head snapped up. *Janis can't possibly be talking about Brighton. Did they go to the same school? Christ.*

"Do you believe Marc would do that? Would you? Or Cherylynn?" There was a pause, a short one, but enough of a silence that Cotton's heart thumped a couple of hard beats. "And if you don't want to talk, that's okay, too."

Janis coughed. "Can you find out how to fix my dad and get everything back to normal? Or at least just make things better. I don't care if Hailey is around. I just want my family... not fucked up. What kind of therapist are you if you don't even know how to fix anything?"

"What would you have me do?"

"Fix it."

"Fix what?"

"Make Dad come home again."

"Would that make you feel differently?"

"Not really, but it would fix my family, I guess. Everyone's so fucked up that I just can't believe it anymore. Marc's into the games and never even looks up or speaks to anyone anymore. Cherylynn's in her own little world, acting like nothing's happened. And Mama can't even cook dinner without crying into the food. It's gross!"

So Gray still can't cope at home. When a parent can't move on, the kids are stuck as well.

Folding her arms across her chest, Janis drew her mouth into a straight line. "I don't even want to eat at home anymore. And I have to do everything!"

"Like what?"

"The wash, the cleaning, answering the phone." Ticking the items off on her black-manicured fingertips. "Shit. I'm surprised she hasn't handed over the checkbook and told me to pay the damn bills! She's useless."

"How does that make you feel?"

"Really, Doc? What do you think? It makes me feel crappy. I'm not a house cleaner! But if I don't do it, no one does. It may not look like it, but I really like everything neat and clean. Like Dad. And I like it when the kids are happy, and they don't cry themselves to sleep." She whispered the last phrase as though she was ashamed of feeling that way.

"Does it make you feel better when everything's neat and clean?"

"Shit, yeah! I hate it when I go to my friends' houses and their rooms are a disaster area. How the fuck do you find anything? I like my stuff. I want to see it!"

Janis-the-rebel wanted/needed some structure, something to push against. What surprised Cotton though, was that Janis identified with her father, the caretaker. That told Cotton volumes about the role Hailey played in this family before she left. If she was the one all the children went to with their problems, and if she was the one who taught them, who played with them, and who monitored the way the household ran, then Gray was now expected to fill that role. And it was a role she hadn't filled up to this point, one that she couldn't (or won't), so she relied on Janis to step up to the plate.

"You can't change what happened or what your parents choose to do," Cotton said, "but you can change your understanding of it through the lens of your own experiences. Think about what you already know about your father."

"Yeah, he's clean. I mean 'she.' Point is, I don't need to clean up after everyone else." Janis stuck her index finger in her mouth and chewed on it.

"Tell me about your stuff. What do you have?" Cotton asked, thinking that following Janis's line of conversation might be less stressful than trying to show the teen that she could control her own perceptions. "What do you treasure?"

Janis paused, looked at the ceiling. "All kinds of stuff. You know...room stuff."

"I'm curious. I'd like to get a visual of what your room looks like. Can you describe it to me?"

"Why?"

"I'm just curious. It would give me a better idea of who you are if I knew what the place you live in looks like."

When Cotton drove by the house, she'd tried to figure out whose room was whose, and she spotted Janis through the window one night. But she'd never admit to it. She was embarrassed to even think about it, that drive she made after dinner. The visceral pleasure of seeing the Prescotts at home. Part of her wishing they'd close their blinds, but thrilled that they didn't. Sneaking back into her house afterwards and finding Thomas in the bathroom, wondering where she was.

"Always wanted my own room," Janis said, shuffling her feet, "and when we moved to this house, I got it. It's in the back of the house, so I have a perfect view of the full moon when it rises." Janis stared straight at Cotton and laughed a bit like a mischievous Peter Pan. "All my friends who are into wiccan stuff think that I chose the room just for that reason, but it's not. I just like the fact that it looks out over the trees, and I can't see any other houses. It's private. Quiet. Everyone else is at the front of the house. Plus, I have my own bathroom, and there's nothing cooler than that!"

"Sounds like a tree house. I always wanted a tree house when I was growing up, but we had no trees."

"Yeah, it's just like a tree house. We don't have anyone behind us cuz there's a big gully out behind the trees. When I was little, I used to go down there and catch frogs. Mama used to freak out when I brought them in the house, but Dad and I would go online and look them up to see what kind they were. He even knew how to tell whether they were boys or girls." Smiling, she shifted her eyes and gazed out the window thoughtfully. Wistfully.

"Really? How can you tell?"

"Well, the males are the ones that croak at night, and they usually have a dark patch on their throat. You ever notice that?"

Cotton shook her head. "Interesting. Tell me more about the room."

Leaning back, Janis twirled a bit of hair around her black fingernails. "Well, I have posters on the walls, of course, and they change depending on which new movie posters I like. I have a couple of good ones: the last Michael Jackson movie. The one he was working on when he died?"

"Wow, that one's going to be worth some money someday."

Enthusiastically, she nodded. It was the first time Cotton had seen her this excited. "I know. That's what I collect: movie posters. I have an entire closet full. I also have 'Where the Wild Things Are' and 'New Moon.' That one's cool. They're really old movies, y'know? Then I have a bunch of old ones that I don't usually take down, like the 'Transformers' movies, and even one that's from a long, long time ago. And when we go to the movies, I usually ask if I can have one after the movie's finished. I just saw 'Dangerous Butterfly.' You know that one?"

"Yes, I do, as a matter of fact. You have that one?"

"Yup."

"I'm impressed."

She smiled and prayer'd her hands together, proud of herself.

"Let me guess, you have chosen your own furniture and probably painted your own walls, too."

"How'd you guess?"

Often Cotton felt surprised at her own curiosity about this family. As they talked more about Janis's room, an unbidden memory of hot summer days in a cement playground came back to Cotton, and with it, the longing for the type of space Janis described. A childhood escape.

Suddenly, Cotton was Janis's age again, and the room she shared with her sisters felt smaller than when she was growing up. She understood why Janis lit up when she talked about her room. It was her space, her private place, and there was nothing more precious for kids than space. Personal space.

Beneath Janis's heavy makeup, there was a child who just wanted to be a kid for a little longer, yet she was on the precipice that most adolescents balance on precariously right before they make the move into young adulthood. *The hardest time of anyone's life.* Cotton knows very few people who want to relive it. It's filled with angst and self-doubt, questions about one's identity and trying to find a surety that no one understands. Teenagers were always the most challenging of her patients, and without fail, she wanted nothing more than to hug them and to assure them that this, too, would pass, and that one day, they would look back on this horrible time and be glad it didn't last.

For the rest of the next half hour, Janis told Cotton about the antique furniture she chose with her mother's help and about what she'd like to do when she gets an apartment of her own. By the time they came to the end of their session, Cotton knew more about what made Janis Prescott happy than if she had answered a 100-question survey. The lines of communication had opened fully. When Cotton announced their time was up, Janis appeared disappointed.

"I feel like we got to know each other a little better. Do you?" Cotton asked.

"Yeah, I think you're not that bad, y'know. I'm sorry if I made you feel that way before."

"No worries. You didn't. Wonder if I could ask you to think about something before we meet again?"

Janis nodded, though she pulled back a little, as if worried that before she left, Cotton was going to give her homework, but she listened.

"Can you think about how you feel when you do something you really don't want to, then kind of keep mental track of how often you tell people how you feel about that?"

Janis seemed surprised. The question wasn't what she'd expected, but she paused thoughtfully, giving it some weight. "Yeah, I'll do that. See you next week."

Cotton wanted Janis to see that she didn't have to keep her resentment inside, that it might not be too bad an idea to tell others how she felt. It was okay to do so, and it might relieve some of the pent-up frustration Janis felt. When they started talking today, Cotton would have laid bets she could not control the anger Janis was suppressing. Now, she felt like they'd had a breakthrough.

As Janis left, Cotton felt a warm rush of emotion that she imagined was akin to what a mother felt for a child.

She shivered. *Need to be careful.*

~ Book Thirty-four ~

Gray Prescott

Like all sciences and all valuations, the psychology of women has hitherto been considered only from the point of view of men.
—Karen Horney

After Janis sped off in the same orange Mustang that dropped her off, Cotton turned on her laptop, tuned in to NPR, and listened to the news while reading Janis's latest posts on UrPlace. Two complaints about homework and tests, three about her mother's nagging, and four long chats about someone named Journee that Janis has never mentioned. Then a story about the ban on transgender people in the military sidetracked her. *How does Hailey feel about that?* she wondered. *On the other hand, why would anyone choose to be part of an organization of any kind that doesn't want them—especially one where everyone is heavily armed?*

She pushed the laptop away and walked the five steps to the couch, lay down, and closed her eyes. For the past week, she hadn't slept a whole night, waking at 2 or 3 every morning. Lying in the dark, she counted Thomas's breaths until she reached a hundred, then started again. It was the only thing that calmed her, took her mind off the Prescotts, but Thomas wasn't there, and Gray Prescott wasn't due for her appointment for another hour. Perfect time for a nap.

She closed her eyes, fighting the urge to punch the pillow five times. *Inhale. One, two, three, four, five, six.* "Shit." She punched the pillow—*one, two, three*—looked at the clock: forty-six minutes and Gray Prescott would walk in—*four, five.* Couldn't close her eyes. Counted her breaths. *One, two, three, four, five.* Checked the alarm on her phone. Closed her eyes again. *One, two, three, four, five, six.* Shifted her legs, settled her ankles atop each other, thought about Gray and Janis's power play. Then her mind took off in twelve different directions, and she gave up, swinging her legs off the couch and letting her feet hit the floor. She felt the tightness in her chest heralding another anxiety attack.

"Damn." She spoke aloud, and without counting her steps to the desk, reached inside the top drawer for the bottle always there in the back corner and popped a little yellow pill into her mouth, swallowing it dry.

Like her daughter who just left two hours ago, Gray was ten minutes late today, so Cotton calmly *maybe a little too calmly* reminded her she was losing part of her hour before it even began.

Gray's eyes filled up, and she made a pretense of finding something in her pocketbook to hide it. Getting caught up in that unexpected moment of emotion made Cotton forget to tape the session, and they lost even more time.

"How's Marcus doing?" Cotton finally asked when the dust settled. "I haven't seen him since he was in the hospital."

Gray shook her head slowly from side to side. "He won't say much. I feel like I'm losing him, Dr. Barnes. He comes home and goes straight to his room, and he won't come out no matter what. I knock on the door. I texted him on his cell. I scream like a banshee... I cry. I just don't know what to do anymore. He blames this on me, and it's not...it's not...my fault. You know?" She cried, digging in her purse for tissues.

Cotton passed the box that was always on the table. "What makes you think he blames you? Have you talked to him about it?"

"He ignores me. I don't want to be a terrible mother, y'know? I don't want the kids to think I'm a meanie. The disciplinarian. But someone must do something. Lord knows, I have no help anymore. No one...no one's there at the...end...of the day." Each sob almost choked her.

"Tell me how that feels, Gray. What emotions does that bring up for you?"

"What do you think?" She glared, mirroring how Janis looked at Cotton earlier today. "It makes me feel like crap. That's how!"

"What does crap feel like emotionally? See if you can name the *emotion* for me."

"Crap isn't an emotion? I feel crappy! Full of crap. Crapiola. It's painful. Sad. Hopeless. Is that what you want?"

"Hmmm. You're saying painful, sad, and hopeless, but your voice sounds angry. Is that one of your emotions, too? Are you angry?"

"I'm not mad at the children. They're confused."

"Who are you angry with Gray?"

"It would be simple to say Hayden," she answered, wiping her eyes with the tissues. "Hailey. God, it's hard to stop a habit that you've had for over twenty years." She studied Cotton's face for a long moment, but Cotton kept her features flat and unaffected. Undeterred, Gray searched Cotton's eyes for clues to her opinion. Apparently seeing none, she continued. "Yes, I'm angry at him. I'm madder than a wet hen at him!"

"What are you mad about? Pretend she's here right now in that seat," Cotton pointed to the chair next to Gray. "Tell her what you're angry about."

"I can't do that."

"Why not?"

"He's not here. I'm sorry, again. She." Gray rolled her eyes.

"This is just to get out the anger. A person doesn't have to be in the same room with us, Gray, in order for us to voice how we feel about them at this moment. You might feel better if you can get some of this out. C'mon, let's explore this feeling you're having." Cotton patted the seat next to her. "Hailey's sitting right here. You can say whatever you want to her."

"I'm mad about her leaving me and the kids."

"Don't tell me," Cotton said. "Look at Hailey in this seat next to you and tell her. Go ahead. Tell her exactly how you feel."

Clearing her throat, Gray looked a little uncomfortable, but that's not unusual. Most people had trouble role-playing at first, but once they warmed up to it, they found it incredibly empowering. She stared at the empty chair, as though trying to balance her memory of her husband with the reality of Hailey. Her eyes flickered, she swiped away a tear, and lifted her chin a little.

"Hayden—Hailey—I don't think I'll ever be able to forgive you for not being there when I got home that day, but worse than that, I can't forgive you for letting us go for that first couple of months with no contact." Pausing, she glanced at Cotton for reassurance, who nodded at the seat, urging Gray to continue. "Yes, I heard you talked to Marcus on that WarCraft game, but it's not the same as being there at night when they go to bed or helping with their homework or even just giving them the benefit of being able to ask you questions. All of that came down on top of me. Me. Alone. You left the kids. I can't forgive you for that."

She stopped, squirmed, glanced again at Cotton as if asking whether that was enough. Cotton nodded encouragingly, again wordlessly urging Gray to continue.

"If you hadn't taught Marc how to play, he wouldn't have gotten into the fight or disappeared that night." Though her voice had risen a little, it's obvious that Gray's still aware that Hailey's not in that seat. This is all pretend, and she wasn't comfortable acting out. "He could've been killed, Hailey! Or could have done something stupid to himself. Do you understand that? I never would have forgiven you for that. Never!"

"Would it help if I pretend to be Hailey?" Cotton suggested, feeling the intensity of Gray's words. "Some clients simply can't place the face of their loved one on a pillow."

"I guess."

"Okay, let's do this. I'll sit here, and you can start telling me what you would like from me right now. I'll try to respond so we can continue a dialogue. Okay?"

She nodded.

"You're mad at me, Gray?" Cotton began, keeping her voice non-threatening, as she imagined Hailey's would be if she were saying the same thing.

"Yes, I am. I'm furious with you." Gray's eyes were a little out of focus. It looked like she was remembering how she felt when the numbness wore off, how the sizzling red rage she felt toward her husband replaced that numbness. The pain of realizing her life hadn't been one what she had believed it was. Her fingernails dig into the chair's arms.

"Why are you mad?"

"I just told you why."

"Do you think I really wanted to leave you all?"

"If you didn't want to leave, why did you go?"

Cotton could have predicted that question. Mentally, she listed the Stages of Gray's grief:

Fear

Feeling of being powerless

Hurt

Physical pain

She's not progressing.

Cotton hoped that the next stages would include Gray's ability to trust herself again, to love herself unconditionally, but something told her that Gray wasn't finished. Her complete distaste for transgender people, coupled with questioning her marriage, had resulted in a complete loss of identity. Why would she be the wife in this narrative? Why did it happen to her? That made sense, Cotton figured, yet she had a nagging sense that there was another reason. She just didn't know what to ask that might trigger an answer. When she realized a heartbeat later that she'd probably lose another night's sleep trying to figure it out, both of her fists instinctively closed.

Gray was still talking. "Maybe for you that decision makes sense." Her voice rose. Strong. Empowered rather than an out-of-control rage. "But it's not good for me. You're the one who's a mess, but I'm the one who must be the bad guy with the kids. They hate me! They want you back!"

"What does being the bad guy feel like?"

"I don't know what I feel anymore." Her voice squeaked a little, and she paused.

Cotton sat still for a moment, as Gray caught up with her feelings. Watching her struggle, Cotton longed to say something comforting, to reach deep into her bag of therapy tools and bring out something that would help Gray face the anger and discomfort she felt, but as a therapist, she knew Gray needed to find her own tools. The silence sat between them. Someone in the neighborhood was burning wood. The smell made Cotton's nose twitch.

"How did that feel, Gray?" Cotton moved back to her original chair so Gray could understand the role-playing was over.

"I don't feel like I said everything I wanted to." Gray's face was sheepish, as if embarrassed she didn't fulfill the assignment appropriately.

"If you had it to do over, what would you add?"

Letting out a whoosh, she leaned her face against her pale hand. "There's so much I want to say, but... y'know, I think I want to say some of it to myself. Is that weird?"

"What would you like to say to yourself?" Cotton smiled slightly, pleased with where the session was going.

"I want to give myself a good talking-to about the way I've been with the kids lately. I don't mean to ..." A fresh wave of tears welled up. Gray reached for the box of tissues. "I just don't have patience with them. I've been neglecting them, kind of letting them take care of themselves. Shoot. Janis even makes sure they're all ready for school in the morning since I have to leave before they do, but that's the way it must be. It's all Hayden's fault. If he were still there. if he ...."

She rocked her head, then she looked at Cotton. A wave of fatigue suddenly washed over her. "I'm overwhelmed," she said with a sigh. "I have so much stuff to take care of, so much to think about—not just why this happened but how I'm going to pay bills, when I'm going to find the time to do things with the kids, how I'm going to keep my family from knowing what's going on."

"You've talked to your sister, haven't you?"

"I told her Hayden—Hailey—left, but she still doesn't know why. No one does except the kids. And maybe one of the guidance counselors."

"Is there a reason you haven't shared that with your sister?"

"She wouldn't understand. She'd think he's a freak. Just like I do."

"Remember I told you about those books, Gray?"

"Yeah, but I haven't picked them up. Don't want to."

"Why not? What's that bringing up for you?"

Gray hit the arm of the chair with her palm. "Why do I have to do all the understanding? Why do I have to be the one to read a book about his—her... affliction? That doesn't seem fair!" She dissolved into another bout of sobs, and this one heaved her body back and forth.

"That's good. Let it come." Cotton made soothing sounds and let Gray cry, loudly and fiercely. Cotton's grandmother's words rang in her ears every time a client went on a crying jag: *Let it out, honey. Tears wash away the pain. You'll feel a lot better if you let it go.*

Occasionally, she handed Gray a tissue and assured her once again that it was okay, but other than that, they didn't speak for a full five minutes. Finally, the sobs abated, and Gray struggled to get back to steady breathing again. Her face was flushed, her nose red, and her eyes swollen, but she could focus. She had sobbed like this quite a few times in the past several months, and this wouldn't be the last time she'd cry as she continued to heal.

"I'm sorry," she said. "I didn't realize I'd be so overwhelmed."

"That's why we're here." Cotton laughed quietly and patted Gray on the arm. Gray leaned into Cotton's hand, as if hungry for the human touch. At least that was an improvement compared to their first visits when Gray almost rolled her whole body into a fetal position if Cotton leaned in her direction. But the black circles under Gray's eyes and the rumpled clothes she wears for days speak of a deep and debilitating depression.

"I'll check on your prescriptions," Cotton said. "Maybe adjusting one of them will help you sleep. And it's healthy to cry it out. You should do it completely and fully. Grieving the end of a relationship as you know it is as much of a process as dealing with someone's death."

"That's it. He's dead to me."

"Is that how you feel?"

"Right now. Yes. I just need to make sure I can help my children get past it."

"Get past what?"

"What he did. What he's doing."

"How would you feel if they couldn't get past it? Or how would you feel if they accept it completely?"

Gray took in a breath and let it out. "I don't know."

Before Cotton said a word, Gray continued: "I'm going to the lawyer's tomorrow, and I'm going to get a restraining order against Hayden. Hailey. I want to get her parental rights taken away. She's not a fit parent for my children."

WTF. Cotton's mouth fell open, and her head whipped as if she'd been rear-ended. *Was I totally blind? This session had helped Gray turn the corner. Didn't it?* She flipped her mouth shut immediately, knowing such a reaction wasn't professional. She wasn't here to pass judgement, yet it was hard not to when clients dropped bombshells like this. "Why not? What makes a fit parent?"

"You've got to be kidding me! Do you really think he is? 'Scuse me, you think *she* is?" Gray snorted a little. Looking down her nose, amazed at Cotton's response. A totally different person from the one who'd just broken down in tears. Not one tear left on her cheeks.

"I'm asking you for your definition of what makes one fit. I'm not passing judgment on her or anyone else, for that matter." Cotton withdrew her hands, tucking them underneath her, an automatic response when she sensed someone trying to trap her.

They had done a lot of work in this session, but Cotton still wanted Gray to recognize how she truly felt about Hailey. Instead, her anger had spiked, transforming into a resentment that made her want to cut Hailey off from her children. In this power struggle, the adage is true: the children would be the ones to suffer, unless Cotton stepped in. Gray had admitted not being there for the children herself, and it didn't seem that was going to change overnight. In Cotton's professional opinion, Gray wasn't the best parent in the family, but few courts would give custody to Hailey. That conservative behavior was not something Cotton liked about North Carolina, but it's a fact of life. Because her home state was not LGBTQ-friendly, the likelihood of Hailey attaining legal custody was practically nil. Cotton's struggle was to ensure that the Prescott children wouldn't lose the part of their family identity that they attributed to their dad. All of them have shared more positive stories from them about his parental role than they have about Gray's.

Though Gray was being unreasonable, she was not a horrible mother, but right now, she wasn't in the best shape to care for the three children who are struggling to make sense of their new lives. What she needed to do was let them talk, encourage them, but she punished them if they did.

And what about Gray's own identity? For her to move forward, she needed to find herself, the Gray she had always been down deep inside, rather than to identify herself as Hailey's wife or the kids' mother. As the mother, she was the nucleus of the family, yet everyone else in the family was turning away from her, finding their own identity. Now every time someone in her orbit veered off to discover something about themselves, she felt like she'd lost her center of gravity. She was an extension of each of them, reliant on them to help her stay grounded, but she needed to have her own core. Her own place where she stood on her own two feet. Strong.

In the past, Cotton knew families of transgender individuals who held together despite all their questions and their fears. Wives stayed with husbands, husbands with wives, kids with families, all realizing that the person they loved was still that person, and if that person had changed in another manner—if that person had been disfigured by a horrible accident or had lost a limb or had been torn apart by psychological issues—the family would still support him/her/them. So why not support their family members during the most dramatic decisions in their lives?

Cotton looked at Gray now, sitting across from her, a determined look in her eyes. It would be a long time before she was past those four stages of dealing with the emergence of her transgendered husband. All a therapist could do now is to help her face whatever she is feeling now. *And right now, Gray is fragile.*

"Have you talked to the children about this idea, about taking away Hailey's right to parent?" Cotton asked.

"No, it's my decision. I'm the adult."

"How do you think they would feel? When you're making a decision that will affect others, you usually think about how they'd handle the change, right?"

"I think it's the right thing to do." She nodded definitively and took a deep breath, her lips firmly together.

"Is it something you just thought of, or have you been considering it for a while?"

"Both." She sat rigidly in the chair now, almost defying Cotton to question her decision. Suddenly, she was the scrappy junkyard dog defending her pups.

"I know this is difficult for you, Gray."

She nodded her head affirmatively.

"I just want you and the kids to be okay with whatever decision you make."

"We will be," she assured Cotton.

"Let me just give you the name and information of that support group for families of trans people. I gave it to you before, right?"

Gray shrugged, as if saying she'd take it again but probably wouldn't use it. Again.

"Maybe talking to them will help you," Cotton continued. "Sometimes someone who's going through the same thing you are actually can be better than talking to someone like me." Cotton half expected Gray to argue, but she didn't. Cotton jotted down some contacts, checked with Gray that she was taking the antidepressants and asked, "Are they working for you? Do you notice any side effects? Dry mouth? Weight gain?" then watched her walk out the door, clutching the paper in her hand.

After she left, Cotton pulled Gray's paper file folder out of the desk drawer. She kept paper folders for active clients, but when a client left, she digitally copied everything and archived all the hard copies. She kept telling herself she'd go digital completely one day, but deep down, she loved seeing the pages of prescriptions, hospital reports, and copies of other therapists' notes all in one place, easy to flip through. Those pages created a story.

Somewhere in this file, there had to be a hint, something that would provide the answer to the question about what made Gray despise trans people so deeply.

~ Book Thirty-five ~

Hailey Prescott

If you look at alcoholism and Internet addiction, it's the exact same pattern of behavior.
—Kimberly Young

At 7:55 PM on December 31, Cotton stepped out of the shower to pick up her ringing cell. She'd been thinking about how she could get out of another lame New Year's Eve party, and ironically, had cooked up a sick stomach. A real one. She didn't need to fake an excuse.

Hailey said, "hello," but didn't wait for a response. "I was researching facelifts online and half listening to my WarCraft Guild on Ventrilo when my cell phone rang around 7:45 PM. Before I even say hello, I can hear sounds like screech owls on the other end of the line. I had to raise my voice and repeat, 'hello?' several times before Janis finally answered." She gasped for breath and sobbed.

"She says, 'Dad? You need to come home right now!' In the background, Cherylynn's crying, and Gray's screaming at Marcus (he's online. I just heard him introducing his new avatar to the Guild). You know, normally, I wouldn't bother you with this kind of stuff, Dr. B., but the kids haven't been allowed to call me when Gray is home, and I've had very little interaction with Janis in the past couple of months, so both the call and what's happening on the other end of the phone made a shiver go down my legs. But I tell myself that's just the writer in me, my imagination's running amok, and I need to calm down." Hailey's words slammed into each other like cars on a freight train.

"I asked her what's the matter and was she okay, and she screamed, 'No! Mama's going berserk! You need to come home right now. She's called a lawyer, and she wants to make sure we don't see you—'"

"Okay, okay. Breathe a bit." Cotton wrapped a towel around herself, as her blonde curls flopped over her forehead. Putting the phone on speaker, she set it on the bathroom counter. *Had a feeling the Prescotts would meltdown during the holidays.* She rubbed a smaller towel roughly over her wet hair and slid into the terrycloth robe hanging on the back of the door.

"Then the phone goes dead," Hailey continued, his voice echoing into the still steamy bathroom. "This is my worst fear: Gray will take my kids away from me, and I'll never see them again."

The fear was valid, Cotton knows, but "there are lawyers for that," she said.

"Gray's got a temper and when she screams, she's reached the end of her rope and is no longer thinking rationally. When she is at that point, anything can happen. She's reached out to hit the kids when she's angry, and sometimes (if I hadn't been there), she probably would have connected. Hard."

"Have the kids told you that lately?"

"Not directly, but Cherylynn's been sneaking calls to me, and Marcus and I have always had a tight bond, so we talk when we play WarCraft. But for Janis to call... someone's in jeopardy. Otherwise, she'd take care of things herself. She's just that type of kid: overbearing sometimes, but like a mother bear with her siblings."

"Let's not get worried, yet" Cotton said, but in her mind, she was already in the car, heading for the Prescotts'. "Why don't you keep trying to call Janis back, okay?"

Hailey sighed. "That's all I can do, at this point. If I showed up there right now, I'd only make it worse."

"You're right. Wise answer," Cotton said. *Damned if we do, damned if we don't.* "Keep me informed, okay?"

"I will," Hailey answered, the strength back in her voice.

Cotton disconnected. *Maybe I won't go to the party with Thomas.* She turned for another towel and bumped into Thomas.

"How long have you been here?" She hadn't heard the door open.

"Long enough to know you have an issue going on." Thomas's eyes darkened to a smoky gray. The lines beside his mouth deepened, a telltale sign he was clamping his back teeth together. "New Year's Eve is our night, Cotton. Right?"

He didn't need to say more. They'd made the deal on their first New Year's Eve together almost fifteen years ago. The night would always be a memory of their first NYE together, the night Thomas told her he loved her, that he'd never imagined an emotion as sweet, and that if he died tomorrow, his life would have been perfect for having spent NYE in her arms.

"As long as I'm alive, New Year's Eve will be ours and only ours," she'd said. She had meant it.

"It's still ours," she said now, wrapping her arms around him.

They hugged tightly, but briefly, before Thomas stepped into the shower and conversation died. Cotton turned the sound down on her cell, thinking it wouldn't be breaking her promise to Thomas if she checked her phone during ladies' room breaks.

~ Book Thirty-six ~

Cherylynn Prescott

Adolescence represents an inner emotional upheaval, a struggle between the eternal human wish to cling to the past and the equally powerful wish to get on with the future.
—Louise J. Kaplan

8:12 PM

Cherylynn Prescott: Dr. B r u there???
Cotton Barnes: yes what's up?
Cherylynn Prescott: can u tlk 2 me
Cotton Barnes: does your mom know you're txtng me?
Cherylynn Prescott: not here
Cotton Barnes: she isn't?
Cherylynn Prescott: nope gone
Cotton Barnes: is Janis there?
Cherylynn Prescott: yes
Cotton Barnes: does she know you're txtng me?
Cherylynn Prescott: no need u 2 call her scared
Cotton Barnes: you're scared? Why?
Cherylynn Prescott: bad fight mom sent us away
Cotton Barnes: you're scared mom is gone or about the fight?
Cherylynn Prescott: both we tryed 2 call dad

Cotton Barnes: did u get him?

Cherylynn Prescott: mom hung up

Cotton Barnes: can Janis call again?

Cherylynn Prescott: mebbe

Cotton Barnes: ask her

Cherylynn Prescott: k

Cherylynn Prescott: gonna call dad thnx

~ Book Thirty-seven ~

Cotton Barnes

Considered together with information from animals, then our study supports the hypothesis that gender identity alterations may develop as a result of an altered interaction between the development of the brain and sex hormones.
—Zhou, Hofman, Gooren, and Swaab

A little past 8:30 PM. Thomas was getting ready in the bedroom, and Cotton was putting on makeup in the bathroom, her cell buzzed. She closed the door quietly and answered. *Sucks to hide.*

Cherylynn whispered, "Mom left. I have no clue where she went. Can you come over?"

"Where's Janis?" Cotton asked the question because Janis was perfectly capable of keeping an eye on them. If Gray was taking a break from the stress of being home alone with the kids for a little while tonight, maybe it would be best. Best to get out of the house rather than taking her anger out on them.

"I called her, and she said she's at the store."

"Where's Marcus?"

"Here. Can you come?"

Cotton's mind raced, torn between calling a social worker and getting the kids to a safe place (*because being at home obviously isn't these days*), or simply going over there herself. There was a third option:

calling Hailey and risking Gray's anger. Or fourth, call Gray and really put herself in the middle of Prescott family drama.

"Don't get mad at me for calling." Cherylynn's voice sounded small and vulnerable, nowhere near the leader she embodied on the playing field.

"I'm not, honey." Cotton needed to get off the phone and get someone—probably herself—over to the house. Now. But she didn't want to hang up on Cherylynn.

She was about to text Janis when she heard Cherylynn yelling "Up here," to someone in the background. Someone must have come home.

"Is your mother home?"

"No, it's Janis. She's coming upstairs. Do you want to talk to her?" Cherylynn sounded relieved.

"Sure." Outside the bathroom, Thomas shuffled his feet. *Probably putting on his shoes.* He always sat in the chair at the foot of the bed. It was the last thing he did before shrugging on a suit jacket. That gave her two more minutes on the phone before he started looking for her. No use starting off the evening with him nagging her about taking a patient call.

"Hey, Dr. B. What's up?" Janis sounded a little breathless from coming up the stairs.

"Just checking with you all to see how things are going. Are you home for the night now?"

"Yup. I got some pizzas and Perrier so we can all celebrate."

"Is your mother there?"

"Nope. Right now, I'm mad at Mama. Cherylynn called me. I'm sure she called you, too. I get the phone calls, and Mama gets to escape whenever she wants to." Janis sounded strung as tightly as dental floss. Cotton imagined Janis's eyes flitting back and forth, and her toe bouncing against the floor.

"Did she leave a note? Say what time she was going to be home?"

"Just said she was going out for a while. I have no idea what time she'll be home or whether she'll even be here tonight. She doesn't give a shit anymore, so neither do I."

"I'm sure she cares deeply about you, Janis, and I know you care, too. Listen, go eat your pizza with Marc and Cherylynn while it's still hot. I'm going to call you back in about fifteen minutes to see if your mother's there yet, okay?" Cotton did a mental calculation. By the time they got out of the house and drove the three minutes to the venue, it'd be exactly thirteen minutes. She'd duck into the bathroom to make the call. *Perfectly natural to go to the ladies' room for a touch-up upon arriving.*

Janis paused, but Cotton heard her walking back and forth and breathing hard. "I don't want a damn pizza," Janis said. "I want my life back."

~ Book Thirty-eight ~

Hailey Prescott

The chief symptom of adolescence is a state of expectation, a tendency towards creative work, and a need for the strengthening of self-confidence. Suddenly, the child becomes very sensitive to the rudeness and humiliations which he had previously suffered with patient indifference.
— Maria Montessori

Cotton felt the buzz of a new text as she reached to shake Ken Martini's hand. He served on the Board at Duke University Hospital, a great contact for her, Dr. Carbinetti had reminded her frequently. Now, she forced herself to make small talk and smile at his inane reference to his plaid bow tie and new round glasses: "I look like an academic instead of a real estate developer." She wondered exactly what a real estate developer looked like as Thomas grabbed her elbow, forcing her to remain in place. Another buzz and another. She mumbled an excuse and headed for the ladies.

Four mirrors, six stalls, one handicapped, two hand driers, four sinks, four soap pumpers.

She sat on the toilet seat without lifting her dress and scrolled through Hailey's texts. Before leaving the house, she'd texted Hailey that she'd been trying to reach Gray and had Hailey heard anything. She'd been right that the text would make Hailey contact the kids.

Hailey wrote: "Forgive this long message. I purposely got online tonight to see if I could engage with Marcus, and I've also texted Cherylynn, but she is giving me one-word answers. Marc hasn't been communicating well lately either, but as soon as I opened WarCraft, Marcus disappeared like he didn't want to talk to me. I'm trying to curtail my writer's imagination and not worry, but it's strange, and I'm trying to pay attention whenever I have gut reactions as strong as this one. Trying to trust myself. Marc said something about his mother earlier, then when I asked Cheryl if she was okay, she said her mother was being 'biatchy.' And I just found out from Janis that their mother isn't home. Something's not right with Gray. I'm worrying for my kids."

Someone rattled the stall door.

"I'll be right out," Cotton said, imagining Marcus sitting in his dark room, slumped at his desk, wearing a headset, his computer screen flickering with scenes from WarCraft's Wrath of the Lich King. A shimmering green field and a purple and blue mountain range in the distance. A large feudal castle rested at the base of the range. One by one, the Guild's avatars filled the field. Each of the players announced their entrance, and they greeted each other like long-lost friends, though most had just played together less than a couple of hours before.

She imagined him placing headphones over his ears, so he couldn't hear his mother yelling at his sisters, felt him sink into an imaginary world where he was safe, where he was strong, where he could express his anger, where he might be happy, and she knew she needed to try harder with him, teach him the tools he needed to comfort himself. *Protect him.*

Protect all the Prescotts.

Her phone vibrated again as she considered a reply to Hailey's concern. *Put nothing in writing that'll incriminate you.*

She answered: "What do you want to do, Hailey? Marcus is home."

"None of my kids are answering my calls or texts now," Hailey wrote. "I've cried, I've become resolute, I've returned to crying, and now I'm getting pissed off. My emotions are all over the board in a matter of sixty seconds. Damn hormones! I'm feeling like I'm losing my mind! Why aren't they answering me? It's got to be Gray. She confiscated their cell phones. Wouldn't surprise me."

"Keep trying. You'll get them," Cotton answered, though unsure of it herself. *The kids are probably in no real danger, right?* Janis was old enough to babysit. The kids knew how to take care of themselves. But, and it was a big 'but,' they had no clue where their mother was. It was New Year's Eve, and they were not answering their father's calls or texts.

How much longer should I wait for their mother to come home? Should I tell Hailey I think she should go over there? Goddamn, what the fuck should I do?

Cotton considered talking to Thomas. He was always the one she'd confide in, always her sounding board, always the voice of reason. But if she told him she'd been in touch with almost the whole family tonight, he'd flip. *He'd lose his shit.* And she would break the therapist's code of ethics to keep client information private. Could she sacrifice her relationship with her husband in order to rescue the Prescotts? Just this once?

She had to trust her intuition. She had to. Even if every text mirrored the ones she received from Brighton during the worst parts of her recovery. *Dr. B, I need you.* Brighton would text at midnight, 2:15AM, 3:45AM. And she expected Cotton to answer. *I always did. Always.*

The Prescotts were different. These kids weren't Brighton. They were working it out. Little by little. *Right? They're improving, starting to see the light. Am I right?*

During their last session, Marcus had talked about home and school and family, and in some ways, seemed more serious than his own mother, when he'd said, "It got kinda hard, after Dad left, when the kids started calling him 'the lipstick undead.' The teachers knew I threw the first punch, because I was the one who ended up in the hospital, y'know? But I wasn't sorry about it. I'd do it again. Those guys, enema bags, think they're cool. They don't know nothin' about my family." He smiled lopsidedly. "My family takes care of each other. Dad always says the Prescott clan is the stick-with-us clan. We do this together. Even when we don't."

Cotton rose from the toilet seat, straightened her dress, and checked the time. She'd only been in here five minutes, though it felt longer. Thomas wouldn't suspect anything. A makeup do-over could sometimes take longer, especially if she needed a break from small talk. Another buzz stopped her from leaving the stall.

"Cherylynn finally answered my texts," Hailey texted. "One short sentence: 'Mom's still not home, Marc won't open his door, & Janis is a PIA.'"

Typical Cherylynn. She always says Janis is a pain in the ass.

"But why the hell isn't Gray home with three adolescents on New Year's Eve?" Hailey continued. "Where could she have gone? Screw it. I'm going over there. I'm kicking into parent mode."

"Maybe you want to text them before you do," Cotton suggested. *This might not go well.*

It took a while for Hailey to answer, and when she did, Cotton realized why. *It's a goddamn mini essay.*

Her chest tightened. *1,032 characters.* Thomas was waiting for her, but she read Hailey's text as she moved toward the door.

"They might be a bit put off by my appearance, but I'm going, anyway. Even though I wasn't going out, I'm all dressed up for New Year's to celebrate me. Yup, I'm celebrating myself. I planned this weeks ago and bought myself a gold lamé gown and the prettiest shoes I've ever seen-gold kitten heels with tiny bows at the back of the ankle. My hairdresser streaked my hair. Now it's light brown with silvery blonde highlights, and it's grown to shoulder length. I look very festive if I say so myself. So, the hell with it. I'm going out this way. The kids and Gray must get used to me this way, so I will not change before I leave. Besides, it would take too much time to change. By the way, I'm dictating this and am already on my way. Gotta stop at the store first."

"Good. Go," Cotton texted, and she opened the stall door, her silver halter dress reflecting the bathroom lights in the mirror like aluminum foil. What would she say if Thomas wondered why she'd been gone so long, but when she saw the back of his head, she put an imaginary hand on her anxiety to hold it in place, forced a smile on her face, and returned to the party.

~ Book Thirty-nine ~

Cotton Barnes

No one who, like me, conjures up the most evil of those half-tamed demons that inhabit the human breast, and seeks to wrestle with them, can expect to come through the struggle unscathed.
~Sigmund Freud

December 31
11:50 PM
Thomas released Cotton's hand and gave her a wink, then slid his black satin mask back into place. He wore a black tux with satin lapels and the jacket hugged his shoulders and tapered his waist, defining his body in a way no exercise video could. He was super-star handsome tonight, and he looked like he knew it as he cut through the crowd, head up, a slight strut in his step, nodding to people as he passed them like he was a politician running for office and the people in the crowd were his paeons. Thomas had promised Cotton a glass of champagne, and she hoped he'd get it to her before the crystal ball in the middle of the room dropped.

The Black and White Masquerade Ball at the Silver Fox Bistro celebrated New Year's Eve with Raleigh's finest young entrepreneurs, those people that Thomas insisted he needed to rub elbows with in order to take the next step in his career and move into management. The crowd was full of partygoers in glittering masks that hid their identities and allowed them to say outrageous things and act in inappropriate ways. *Overachievers always party harder than people who are satisfied with their lives.* A group like this one could provide enough data on narcissism to fill a manual on the topic. If you weren't narcissistic yourself, you were dating one, married to one, or had spawned one (or two).

Sidling over to a doorway, Cotton leaned against the jamb, surreptitiously slipping her foot out of her way-too-high heel. *Who the hell invented these damn things, anyway?* She rubbed her toes against her other calf, then switched and did the same with the other foot. People gathered in the center of the banquet room, most holding champagne glasses and laughing. Though Thomas's entire team was somewhere in this room, Cotton would be hard-pressed to identify anyone since they all wore masks like hers. After midnight, the masks would come off, and everyone could breathe. *Only seven more minutes.*

The last text was a few minutes ago. Again, she'd ducked into the bathroom, already planning to escape as soon as everyone sang Auld Lang Syne and exchanged drunk, sloppy kisses. She could make apologies, use the excuse that she's drunk too much, encourage Thomas to stay, and head for the Prescotts. He'd be none the wiser.

She spotted a head that looked like Thomas's, but it disappeared. Then, for one moment, the crowd shifted, and Cotton spotted his profile as he lifted his mask, smiling. He didn't have any champagne glasses in his hands. *Where's our champagne?* Even in her thoughts, she heard the yearning in her voice.

The crowd shifted again, and she lost sight, but she headed in his general direction. It was too close to midnight to be without the requisite champagne. Maybe she could help him find a glass or two. Or snatch a couple of glasses from the wait-staff roaming around with trays.

More people headed to the center of the room, leaving the hallways a little emptier. Her view improved again, and there he was, halfway down the hall, less than twenty feet away, nestled into a corner. His mask was up, and he was reaching out his hand, a smile on his face.

Someone's head was in the way, a tall white-haired man with an enormous belly. Cotton moved to the side a little. Then she stopped.

Thomas's outstretched hand caressed the cheek of a lithe blonde woman, her softly curling hair cascading over her bare shoulders. She smiled up at him, an intimate smile, the smile you give to someone who's not your colleague, not even a friend, the smile you give to a lover. He focused totally on her, engaged in every word she said, smiling that intimate smile that made his eyes crinkle shut *after sex*. He leaned in a little further and brushed his mouth against hers, *the kind of kiss that promises more later.*

Cotton's belly constricted, and her throat muscles cut off her breath. Her hand unconsciously rose to flatten against her diaphragm as a thousand prickles danced down her spine, through her stomach. Her skin moistened.

Cotton wasn't a jealous person. She trusted Thomas and had never checked his phone or his mail or his credit card bill. But she wasn't blind. She could not deny what was happening right in front of her. She was seeing something she shouldn't. *In full view of everyone*. He was so bewitched he wasn't even ducking into a bathroom or closet.

Thomas lowered his mask back into place, glanced up and down the hall as if suddenly aware someone might have seen them, though he didn't spot Cotton, then he touched the woman's hand, squeezed it, raised it to his lips and kissed her fingertips, before he turned to walk away. One last glance over his shoulder, and he blew her a kiss. *Can't believe what I'm seeing.* And the woman returned that airborne pucker with her own fire-engine-red lips.

A rush of searing blood awakened every nerve in Cotton's body, throwing her off, so she had to reach out to steady herself against the hallway wall. A man bumped into her, asked if she was okay, laughed at something someone else said, and moved on. Cotton felt the rest of the blood drain from her cheeks.

She didn't want to believe.

Unable to move, she stood still. The mask hid the tears blinding her. She needed a restroom, but the countdown had begun. *One minute before midnight*. And Thomas was now heading in her direction, a smile on his lips, two glasses miraculously in his hands.

"Bet you thought I would never return," he said as he pressed a champagne flute into her fingers *like he hadn't just kissed another woman*. "You wouldn't believe the line at each of the bars. I had to go to three of them before I could get a glass."

Cotton nodded, forced a smile, and tipped the glass to her lips, downing half of it before he laughed and said, "You're supposed to drink that for the toast!"

"Sorry. Thirsty." She turned to the front of the room, unable to look at him.

The crowd was counting down. "Ten... nine... eight." And all she could think of during those interminable seconds to midnight was how different her life would be in the year to come. That's how sure she was of the demise of her marriage. But she turned her face up to her husband's anyway and let him kiss her lips as tiny bits of silver and gold and white and black confetti fell from the ceiling, but she did not remove her mask.

The ladies' overflowed with inebriated women, masks finally removed, fixing their hair and faces, as if the best part of the evening had just begun. Cotton waited in line, still wearing her mask. Hiding behind it. Her face would need far more than a dash of lip gloss.

In the stall, she collapsed onto the toilet seat and leaned her head into her hands.

One, two, three, four, five.

Like a repeating meme, she saw Thomas lean in for the kiss, then retreat, glancing around guiltily. Leaned in, kissed, retreated, glanced guiltily. *Leaned, kissed, retreated, glanced.* She shook her head, squeezed her eyes shut, and thought, *I know how Gray Prescott feels. Betrayed. Blind to the obvious. How could I have missed that?*

But she knew how. Cotton deserted her husband for the Prescotts. She asked for this.

She sucked in a gulp of air, tapped her fingers on the side of her head: *one, two, three, four. One, two, three, four.* The last two women left their stalls and met at the sinks. They knew each other, shared some hellos and Happy New Year's wishes, then one said to the other: "Horrible about those killings on Christmas Eve."

Cotton's eyesight shifted. She could see the hems of their gowns. One: white chiffon; the other: black satin. The shuffling, shining heels.

"I know! And I heard they haven't caught the ones who did it yet."

"I mean, I don't totally understand how you suddenly decide to switch genders, but, Jesus, they're not hurting anyone. They don't need to be murdered."

The hand dryer powers on, stealing some words, but Cotton heard, "not exactly... trans people aren't who everybody sees... the right gender ...." The dryer roared again.

"... whatever the case." The dresses shuffled toward the door. "I hope it stops. How many have been killed now? Eight? Nine?"

The voices drifted away as the doors closed, and Cotton exited the stall, car keys in hand, hoping she could get to the parking lot and find her car before Thomas realized she was gone.

She'd deal with her marriage later. Hailey just sent another text, and she was ready for a showdown with Gray.

Ethical or not, Cotton headed for the Prescott home.

~ Book Forty ~

Cotton Barnes and Hailey Prescott

Depression has been called the world's number one public health problem.

In fact, depression is so widespread it is considered the common cold of psychiatric disturbances. But there is a grim difference between depression and a cold.

Depression can kill you.
—David D. Burns

It was the worst night of the year to be driving, compounded because Cotton had a few too many glasses of champagne, and two powerful emotions fueled her: fear and anger Her nails left half-moon impressions in the leather steering wheel, but it was her foot on the accelerator that would get her into trouble. Doing 45 in a 30mph zone on New Year's Eve wasn't the smartest move she's ever made. Social media would implode if she, a psychotherapist, was caught speeding and drunk on the way to a client's house to intercede in a family drama.

She backed off the gas, watching her speed drop. *41, 38, 36, 28.* And then her gas gauge fell below the red line.

"Shit. Where the hell am I going to get gas at 12:30 on New Year's Eve?" Her breath left a white cloud in the air. She shivered, turned on the seat heaters to high. Pumping gas in this weather wouldn't be fun in a sleeveless dress with no coat. Another "shit." She'd left her grandmother's cashmere shawl in the coatroom. Funny, she hadn't been cold at all when she dashed out to find the car. Now, it felt like the temperature had dropped twenty degrees, but the car was warming and would be even warmer when she got back in after pumping the gas.

She left another "shit, shit, shit," in her wake as she dashed to the pump, shakily inserting her credit card, and cursing the gasoline smell as she stood, sleeveless and shivering in the darkness. The pumps were lit by a single, dim bulb, but the small, 24-hour store beamed with fluorescent signs, painfully bright interior lights, and a few, sad-looking Christmas lights looped haphazardly above the counter where the clerk checked out her customers.

In a futile effort to warm up, Cotton stamped her heels, flapped her arms, but a frigid breeze whipped up a pile of oak leaves nearby. "Fuck it." She released the gas handle. *Got enough to get me where I need to go.* Right now, all she wanted was to get back in the warm car and head to the Prescotts'.

Her hand was on the door handle when a commotion near the store's large, pane-glass windows literally made her jump. A screaming, tall woman in a gold gown, her back to Cotton, fended off what appeared to be a couple of teenagers in jeans and sweatshirts, the hoods flipped over their heads. They appeared to be jabbing at the woman. One would charge forward, yell something, then skip back. The second one would do the same, then the third. *A strangely choreographed bullying attack.* Inside the store, the clerk watched, laughing soundlessly as she twirled a long black braid hanging over her shoulder with her right hand while she held a cell phone up to the window with her left.

"Couldn't find any high heels to fit, laaaaaadddeeeee?" One teen yelled as they prance-walked behind the woman. "Nobody teach you how to dress at tranny school?"

The woman stumbled and turned around to face the other two, drawing closer to the streetlight where Cotton stood. The light cast stripes on her cheekbones, spotlighted dark blue eyes.

Hailey. God, no.

The kids flanked her now. One clapped their hands. A female whose long curly hair escaped her hoodie laughed and shouted another insult. *Familiar.* The other was taller. Maybe 6 feet. A boy, holding something in his hand. *Something shiny.* Laughing loudly, his head thrown back like a jackal.

Were these the people who'd been terrorizing Raleigh? Cotton reached for her pocket, her phone, then realized she didn't have any pockets. And everything was in the car. She'd never felt so unsafe. She shivered, wishing she'd worn a coat to get gas. *Funny what you think of when you're terrified.*

"Lookit the tranny manny! Mannnny Trannnnyyy," the boy hollered as he advanced toward Hailey, swaggering a bit, lifting a leg, and throwing it out to the side as if walking a runway.

In one small flicker of her eyelashes, Hailey went from shock to recognition to understanding. She reached out her hand to Cotton though they were still ten feet apart, ignoring the teenagers, and said, "What are you doing out here without a coat on, girl?" Beads of sweat popped out on Hailey's upper lip.

"Don't worry about me."

"What are you doing here? Period." Hailey cast a sidelong glance at the kid who continued to prance, laughing at himself, and encouraging his friends to do the same. "You shouldn't be here. Get in your car, Dr. B. Go home."

Ignoring Hailey, Cotton turned to the teens and yelled, "Why not just leave us alone? We're not doing anything to you." Her voice sounded much more confident than she felt. She raised her hand and pointed to the cashier in the window. "She's got you on video. Why don't you just go home? No one will get in trouble."

The boy stepped between Cotton and the store window. The streetlight revealed a twitching eye and the gun jerking to the side as to keep time with the twitch. *What was he on?* "Move over there," he told Cotton, pointing toward the trash bin. "You, too, bitch." He pointed the gun at Hailey.

In the few brief steps, Cotton glanced at the other two still waving their own guns and laughing, and she realized why the girl was familiar. Her picture was all over Facebook because she disappeared a couple of months ago. They'd cast a net far and wide to find her, even sent teams to the local hospitals and mental health clinics. *Off her meds*, they'd told Cotton and the rest of the therapists who shared her building. *Diagnosed psychotic.* Childhood trauma: mother murdered by father in front of the four-year-old child and baby brother. They'd been left alone for days. *So, this is what she's been doing. Killing members of the LGBT family.*

Behind them, the other person with the frizzy hair pulled the hood further down over their face. The gas station light reflected on what the person held in their hand. *Another gun.*

They were surrounded.

Hailey held both of her arms up in surrender and nodded to Cotton to do the same. "I'm so sorry, Dr. Barnes. You shouldn't be caught up in this."

"Shut the fuck up!" Suddenly, the boy held his gun to Hailey's head and pushed the barrel until Hailey's head snapped back. Then he laughed, a wild, wolflike howl. "If I had my way, you'd be dead by now, but we got this minor complication here." He leaned in Cotton's direction and the reek of alcohol made her recoil.

The kid was about 19, greasy blonde hair, a nose covered in blackheads, and absolutely no chin. Rubbing his hand on his stomach, he pulled aside his leather jacket long enough to reveal a pornographic holiday sweater.

"Pearlie Girl here," he pointed his chin at the girl Cotton recognized from Facebook, *Beth Pearl, yes, that was it.* "She's the one who gets first choice. This here's her game, not mine. I'm just along for the ride, right, Pearlie Girl?"

The girl pulled back into the shadows with the other person, the glint on their weapons almost mesmerizing.

Cotton shivered, thinking about the pepper spray she had on her key chain in the car that she had kept running and warm. She glanced at the BMW, mentally measuring how long it would take to get to the door. Only about ten feet away. *Couple of seconds?* But then she caught a glint of that steel barrel to her left and realized there was no way she and Hailey could overcome these armed teenagers.

The girl—Beth Pearl—stepped closer, held her gun sideways with one hand, her thumb hooked in her jeans' belt loops as if she'd been practicing this stance for a while, as if this was the moment she felt all-powerful. Invincible.

Yes, psychotic.

Cotton glanced at Hailey. What the hell were they going to do? Both of them were in gowns and heels. Even if they kicked them off, no way they could get very far. Was this the way they were going to die?

"Hey, you two! You think this is a joke?" Beth Pearl lifted her handgun, pointed it at Cotton's head.

Keep calm. Soft. No eye contact. Cotton lifted her hands, palms up. "It's not a joke. I can tell you're very serious. But you know if you do anything here tonight, you're going to jail, right? There's more than one video now." A trio of people stood with the cashier in the store, all with their phones out.

What was that third person doing coming around behind them? Why weren't the people in the store doing something other than taking pictures?

"Bet your sweet ass we're serious. Who's your friend here? This little Suzy Q?" Beth Pearl flipped her gun over at Cotton, who involuntarily gasped. "How do you know each other? Are you one of these fuck buckets, too?" She stood back, still pointing the gun, flipping from one to the other.

"I'm a therapist," Cotton said and immediately regretted it.

"Even worse than a fucking tranny," Beth Pearl hissed into Cotton's ear, circling slowly around, close enough that Cotton smelled the beer on the girl's breath. The gun barrel smashed into Cotton's cheekbone. Her knees buckled. The lights went out for a second.

"Listen, guys," Hailey deepened her voice. The sound startled the teens, then they exploded in cackles. "Listen, don't hurt her. She's not... she's not like me."

"Step back!" the third person lifted their hand. Two glints. A diamond ring and a gun. A female. *How many teenagers wear rings like that?* The voice was oddly familiar. Was this person on Facebook, too? "This one's mine, Cat. Jerry, get out of the fucking way!"

Hailey moved in front of Cotton and threw her arms out wide. A crack and Hailey rocked on her heels. *A gunshot.* She fell backward, her weight knocking Cotton out of the way. Her gold gown glimmered, ripped at the shoulder, revealed a gash. *Blood.* And a sweet smell. Perfume. Chanel No. 5.

Something warm trickled down Cotton's forehead. A fierce and deep pain burned its way into her arm. Another shot. And another something ripped into her abdomen. *Christ, it's hot.*

Her cheek grabbed at the gravel. A deep well of darkness pulled her in. *Fight,* she told herself. The word sounded like it came from far away. *Fight.*

Facebook offers 54 custom identities to help users identify themselves, she whispered against Hailey's heaviness. *Hundreds of nonbinary pronouns.* In the distance, she heard their murderers running away. *90% of the participants in the National Transgender Discrimination Survey reported being harassed or discriminated against in the workplace.* Blue lights flashed everywhere. *Twenty-six percent of transgender people report attempting suicide.* Sirens.

"Dr. B.." Hailey's voice. A whisper. Raspy. "Don't blame Gray. She didn't know. Take care of my kids. Please."

Cotton wanted to answer, worked her lips, but nothing.

~ Book Forty-one ~

Cotton Barnes

Carl Jung calls secrets "psychic poison." That phrase repeated itself like a ticking clock, again and again and again, as Cotton struggled to reach the surface.

Psychic poison. Psychic poison. Psychic poison.

Occasionally, she broke through the denseness that weighed her down like a coat of cement. She saw Thomas once or twice. They might have had a conversation, but she doesn't remember what they said.

Disjointed images of Brighton. They talked about her family, how they didn't accept her, how she'd gone to school administrators to change her pronouns. *Please keep it a secret, Dr. Barnes. I don't want them to know. Please don't tell anyone.*

Secrets, though. Plenty of secrets. Hers. His. Every one of the Prescotts. Poisonous secrets. *Psychic poison. Psychic poison. Psychic poison.*

She drifted. Once she imagined a woman in a white lab coat talking to someone who looked like Gray Prescott. Gray twisted her wedding band. Gold with one diamond in the middle. *Was Hailey dead?* Another time, the room was dark. Something was beeping. Someone in the shadows said her name.

She remembered gun shots. Loud cracks. The suffocating weight held her to the ground. *Hailey.* She remembered the smell of roses, the heat of something sliding down her thigh. Finally, she rose to the surface, found a moment in the fuzziness where everything was clear. *Where am I. What day is it?* And suddenly, the room was full. Thomas, at her side, Gray Prescott and Janis, several nurses, a woman holding a tablet. *The doctor?*

She couldn't breathe. The machine beeped. The nurses cleared the room. Only Thomas remained. He clenched her hands as tears ran down his cheeks.

Why's he crying? Does he know she saw him in the hallway? Does he think she forgot how the night began?

She tried to ask him when it started, whether the affair had been going on for a while, whether it was her fault. She'd thought about that kiss for what felt like centuries, though it must only be hours. Minutes.

"God, Cotton, I thought—we thought—you were going to die." Thomas kissed her fingertips and nuzzled her hair back from her forehead. "I don't know what I would have done."

Cotton swallowed, trying to summon up some moisture to speak, motioned to him she needed some water. Her throat felt like someone has taken a razor blade to it. She sips what he gives her. Lukewarm. Perfect. *One sip. Two. Three sips. Four.*

"You would have lived," she said. "Go on without me. You already are."

He backed away, shocked, as if ready to argue, but she shook her head and gave him a weak smile.

"You don't have to be here," she whispered and took another sip.

"What do you mean?" He seemed confused, looked over his shoulder, as if he thought someone else should be witness to their interaction.

"I know."

"What?"

"I saw you on New Year's Eve. That woman. Kiss."

Thomas stopped breathing. If he'd been hooked up to one of her machines, the alarms would go off. His eyes appeared to be downloading all that psychic poison.

She turned her head from him and pretended to study the bags of plasma and the screens measuring her breathing and her heartbeat and her brain function. *Be damned if he'll see me cry.*

"You've been having a rough time of it lately. That's not an excuse, but you must admit you haven't been... right... for a while." Thomas found his voice and he was trying to be rational. Had he always sounded like this? So condescending? "After that girl took her own life, you went into a dark hole, and I was there for you, Cotton. I was there. Remember those nights?"

"Brighton. Her name is Brighton."

"You had us all worried after that. I've never seen you so broken."

"If you were so worried, why wouldn't you talk to me about her? No one talked to me." *People purposely didn't talk to me. People blamed me. I blamed myself.*

"Because you were talking crazy, honey. You were talking like it was all your fault, like that girl would have been better off without you, like you didn't protect her the way you promised. You made little sense, and you wouldn't listen to anyone."

"It *was* my fault. Brighton called me four times that day. You know that. You were with me. You told me to turn the phone off. You made me shut my damn phone off." She reached for her glass of water, gulping past the tennis ball in her throat. "I shouldn't have listened to you. She couldn't get hold of me. If I'd been there..."

Thomas gazed out the window, his mouth set.

"You remember I shut my phone that day for you? I did it because you and I had that big fight about it, remember? What was that fight about? Jesus, I can't even remember." She took another swig of water and felt tingles go down her arms. *Where's my pocketbook? My pills?*

Thomas twisted further away from her, stretching the shoulders of his blue wool sweater. She'd bought it for him last Christmas, pairing it with a gray checked button-down, telling him the professor needed to look more academic and that she'd get him the tweed jacket with elbow pads for his birthday. They'd gone upstairs after opening their gifts and cuddled naked in the middle of their down comforter, warm with good food and love and plans for the future. It felt like such a long time ago.

She suddenly felt bone-weary. "I was the last person she called. She was calling me for help, and I wasn't there." She drained the water glass and reached it out to Thomas for a refill. An unspoken request that he immediately fulfilled. The water bubbled from the pitcher and for the short time to refill her glass, neither of them spoke, and it felt normal like a married couple visiting each other in a hospital room.

"You were just as obsessed with her as you are with the damn family you're working with now. Do you think I don't know where you go at night? Do you think I'm blind to the piles of papers you bring home every night? The endless hours you're spending researching... whatever they need. And don't you think I know you haven't been taking your meds? Don't look at me like that. I've known for months. I can tell you need them because you are counting everything. I watch you put the key in the door three times, turning it halfway each time, before you unlock it. You give Fred exactly three ounces of food every day. Weighing it out three times before finally putting it in his bowl. Christ, even when we make love, I can tell you're counting your own orgasm pulses. You need your meds, Cotton. And you need more therapy than your clients do." He rose out of the chair, pushed it away from the bed.

"We're over, aren't we?" *Why do I feel completely calm?*

Thomas tapped his glasses up his nose. "I can't leave you like this. I'm a better human being than... this." He held his hands out, showing he'd be a complete ass if he left her in a hospital bed hooked up to a dozen machines.

"What is... this?" She realized she hadn't asked, and since a rumbling train was splitting open her head, she needed answers. "What happened to me?" And, with a jolt. "Hailey?"

As if on cue, the doctor, a short, young, Black guy wearing a bowtie and round glasses, knocked and came in, tapping the screen he held in his hand. "I'm Dr. Allipow. You're looking a sight better than you did yesterday."

She didn't recognize him, but he had apparently known her for days and rattled on about the two surgeries she'd already had. "The first bullet went through your upper arm... repaired muscular damage..." *It's too much.* "... and the second ... the damage to your kidney. Luckily, we salvaged enough to keep it active. You'll be fine, but it'll be a while before you're out of here."

Her eyes fluttered. She fought against a wave of paralysis, but before she succumbed, she asked one more time. "Hailey?"

From the back of the room, "She's down the hall," Thomas answered from the back of the room. "But maybe you ought to be asking where the people who shot you are."

~ Book Forty-two ~

Hailey Prescott

Growth takes place in a person by working at a deep inner level in a sustained atmosphere of silence.
— Ira Progoff

The wheelchair pushed against Cotton's door again and again before it angled just the right way. With her foot in a full cast, Hailey shoved her way into the room, announcing, "Ta daaaa," as if she'd made her appearance as a Rockette for the Radio City Music Hall. Cotton laughed, fully, for the first time in what felt like a very long time.

"Well, Doc, we're both a bit more holy these days, huh?" Hailey pulled up against the bed and reached for Cotton's hand. "You doing okay? I'm going to be here a while longer. What about you?"

"Last operation was two days ago," Cotton said, parsing her words out because it still hurt to talk. "They say I'll recover fine. Lots of physical therapy, but I'll be okay. You?"

"Surprisingly, the shots I took got me in the limbs. My leg,"—she pointed to its autographed cast—"and my arm." Another autographed cast. "I don't know when I'll be writing again soon."

"Lucky we're here, huh?" Cotton squeezed Hailey's hand and fought the tears gathering in her eyelids. "How are the kids? Gray?"

"Kids are good. They visited me last night. Brought me a vintage Scrabble game. You play?"

Cotton nodded.

"And Gray..." Hailey paused. "They left it up to me to tell you."

"They who? Tell me what?"

"The cops. That night, when you were being loaded into the ambulance, I saw her. Gray. Her wedding band. I gave that to her. How could she think I wouldn't recognize it?"

"I'm sorry. I don't understand." Cotton struggled with her pillow, wanted to sit up straight so she'd be alert and able to comprehend whatever Hailey was trying to tell her..

"That was her that night. The third person. Remember, she said nothing until..."

"Right before the gunshots." Cotton laid back. "I thought I recognized her voice. God, Hailey. Did she shoot us?"

Hailey nodded, and the purple and pink striped turban she wore bobbed up and down. "She was... broken, Dr. B. I broke her. A psychotic break is what they're calling it. She's in a psychiatric ward until her court date." Hailey swiped at a tear running down her face. "I'm not sure what's going to happen to her or to the kids. That's why I need your help. I need you to help me prove I'm fit to take custody of the kids."

Head swirling, Cotton stared at the pin-pricked tiles that graced the ceiling of almost every hospital room in the world. She'd misjudged once again. She'd seen the warning signs, and she'd ignored them. Gray was the Prescott she had needed to worry about. Hailey was fine. The kids would work together to heal. But Gray might never come back from this, especially if she spent any time in jail.

"Maybe it's just as well it was us," Cotton told Hailey. "If it wasn't us on New Year's Eve, it would have been someone else and then someone else and someone else. Now, at least she's going to get the help I couldn't give her. I'm so sorry, Hailey. I should have."

"It's not your fault, Dr. B. You were only trying to protect all of us Prescotts. And you did. You really did."

With a groan, Hailey reached her arm over for half a hug, and they clung together for a long while.

~ Book Forty-three ~

Cotton Barnes

Grief is so human, and it hits everyone at one point or another, at least, in their lives.

If you love, you will grieve, and that's just given.

—Kay Redfield Jamison

Cotton cradled a hot cup of hyacinth tea in her hands and inhaled the spicy floral odor, her eyes half closed. She was waiting for the Prescotts to come for their family therapy session. They were due in an hour, plenty of time for her to enjoy her cup of tea and reflect on the past couple of months.

Today would be the first time she'd seen the Prescotts since Gray's arrest. Though the daily news no longer covered the shootings, Cotton was certain that would change once the court proceedings began. She told someone the other day that she might just turn her TV off for the next couple of months. It would be easier than suffering through the endless videos and talk/chatter about the case and about Hailey and herself. Depending upon which station you watch, she was a well-known writer who was transitioning or a full-blown psychologically depraved weirdo. No media outlet ever got the entire story right. And, depending on what media resource you listened to, Cotton was Hailey's lover, or her mentor, or her transgender friend, or her therapist.

After they released her from the hospital, Cotton spent a couple of days wandering around the house, alone and confused about what she was feeling. Whenever she thought she understood everything that had happened and her role in all of it—everything, throughout the past year—something else would come up to make her doubt herself. At one point, she'd concluded that the psychological stressors the Prescott family experienced had impacted her and, as a result, her marriage. But she had to admit there'd been fissures in her relationship with Thomas before the Prescotts came along and before Brighton, too.

The combination of all those stressors was the perfect storm to awaken the OCD beast that had haunted Cotton for years. She'd told no one—not even Dr. Carbinetti—how guilty she felt about not answering Brighton's calls and how much she hated herself for listening to Thomas. Her own supervisory team would spot her transference. They'd be able to diagnose her instantly because they'd been trained in what to look for, because they could recognize her, and all those secrets would be practically transparent to them. They were professionals, after all. So, instead of sharing her fears, she covered them, and no one knew the difference. *Or did they?*

Before she left the hospital, she'd realized that she could never go without her medication again. It would be easy enough to continue the prescription, since she was the only person who had any idea she hadn't been taking it. No one could ever tell the difference because she'd never let it happen again.

She felt comforted putting the blame for losing her marriage on working too much, though she knew that was only part of the reason. When she thought about her life with Thomas, she realized there were many moments when she shut down. She remembered a time at the grocery store when Thomas saw a baby in a grocery cart and did his utmost to make that infant smile. He felt an almost-Superman power when he made that child grin. She'd never understood it. And she knows now that it's not the Prescotts or work that has damaged her marriage. It's the way she and her husband envisioned their future together. Their goals are nowhere near aligned.

They talked in one-word statements now. (*Coffee? Made. Dinner? Ate. Leaving. Okay. Divorce? Agreed. When? Soon.*)

Then Thomas moved out, and Cotton felt her lungs expand to take in a complete breath. It was the first time in a while that she slept all night. Fred sensed the change in the house and took up residence at the end of the bed, his head on her feet.

Thinking about it now, she inhaled deeply and checked her watch. A car door slammed. It was time.

~ Book Forty-four ~

The Prescotts

There is, of course, always the personal satisfaction of writing down one's own experiences so they may be saved, caught and pinned under glass, hoarded against the winter of forgetfulness. Time has been cheated a little, at least, in one's own life, and a personal, trivial immortality of an old self-assured.
—Anne Morrow Lindbergh

The Prescotts quietly came in the door, respectful of each other, each of them still fragile and shell-shocked. They settled into the chairs like delicate birds, each fluttering feathers and making little sounds. Hailey, the mourning dove in a gray sweater set and matching pencil skirt, to Cotton's left in the wingback. Janis, the jittery crow, in her standard black turtleneck, jeans and Doc Martens, on the floor, leaning against the couch where Marcus (the sparrow—brown hair hiding his eyes) slouched lazily holding his Game Boy but not playing, and Cherylynn, the bright bluebird still in her soccer uniform, perched at the other end of the couch, legs tucked under her like Cotton's. The other wingback was noticeably empty.

They all simultaneously looked at her, and at no other time in her life had Cotton felt more vulnerable.

"I'm so sorry," she started, but all the words she'd planned to say simply disintegrated into fragments like the ashes of a cigarette left ignored. She couldn't get a full gulp of air and reaching for it made it worse. She gagged. *That was attractive.*

Marcus and Janis were immediately at her side, holding her shoulders, hugging her. "It wasn't your fault, Dr. B.," Marcus whispered in her ear.

"It's okay, it's okay," Janis chanted. "Take a breath."

Cotton gathered herself, wondering who Janis was trying to convince. "I'm sorry. That's not how I wanted this session to start." She drew her shirtsleeve across her face. "I wanted to ask you how you all are doing."

No one replied, then Marcus turned his head. She was close enough to count the hairs that created the downy foam of hair along his brow, and she could smell the strawberry jam gum he'd been chewing. *But I won't count. I don't need to count.*

"I want to know something, Dr. B.," he said.

"What is that?"

"Did my dad Hailey tell you her story? The one about how she was made?"

Cotton paused for a second, then realized Marcus equated his father's transition to characters being made online. Aware of Hailey's glance from across the room, she kept her focus on Marc. "Yes, as a matter of fact, we've talked about it a lot."

"Can you tell us the story?"

Everyone in the room nodded. *Of course, they want to hear stories. They want the missing pieces of the family narrative so they can figure out the best way to understand and to move forward. Healthily.* "Well, Hailey gave me her journal at one point. Maybe you'd like to hear it? Is it okay, Hailey?"

They nodded again, three expectant children and one adult. They looked both unsure of what to expect and expecting the magic that happens when someone reads to you. The power of the story. Personal story.

Cotton pulled the leather-bound journal from a locked file and handed it directly to Hailey. "They should hear your story from you, not me."

And, finally, together they heard Hayden's story become Hailey's. They listened intently to the beginning of her story, her "re-birth" as she called it. They heard her feelings about being female, the happiness she felt when she could finally emerge as herself. And their tears fell as freely as hers did while she was writing.

When Hailey finished reading, she took a sip of tea, her voice raw from the full forty-five minutes of narrating the tale, and she smiled at Cotton, who knew at that moment that she'd done the right thing. No matter what happened after they left, the Prescotts now had one more tool in their self-comfort bag of tricks.

Hailey was the first to speak. "Thank you," she said shakily as she rose from her chair to cross the room and wrap her arms around Cotton. Then Janis joined them, and Marcus slid over. Finally, Cherylynn hugged Hailey's back, pushing her nose into Hailey's hair. Everyone was crying, a pure funereal wail of a cry, a primal sob that felt like it could tear skin from bones. A cleansing dirge. A mere few moments later, they were all laughing and talking, apologizing to each other as they found their way back to their chairs.

"We're way over your hour, but that's okay," Cotton said as she handed the tissues box around the circle. "I think that the world decides far too often what is 'acceptable,' and that... that kind of judgment call often breaks up families. When we think we must live our lives according to others' expectations, we're in trouble. I know that's when I'm in trouble!" She laughed and wiped at her tears. "Remember that scene in 'Fiddler on the Roof' when the youngest daughter wants to marry someone who's not Jewish or from the village where the family lives and Tevye, the father, decides the girl is dead to him? He's splitting with the pain of losing his daughter, but his commitment to his religion and to his societal values gets in between his love for his beautiful, strong daughter and the belief—expectation, really—that he needs to feel a certain way and to act a certain way. He loses the child of his heart because he's so sure that he needs to follow the rules."

Cherylynn nudged Janis. "See? Now you get an excuse to break the rules." A sisterly jibe, one that brought a few knowing laughs.

"I'm angry at the world that says it's okay to abandon your children for your religion," Cotton continued. "I'm mad at the neighborhood that goes along with shunning that girl. I'm freakin' sick about people who are never accepted because of their religion or the color of their skin or the person they choose to love. Or who they choose to be. It shouldn't happen. It just shouldn't."

Absentmindedly, Hailey put her hand on Cherylynn's head. The touch, an unconscious and affectionate gesture, spoke volumes about the relationship between the two of them, a bond that Cotton never saw between Gray and her kids. It was a very strong familial bond, maybe even an obsession to be together, a primordial need to fill the roles each of them has shaped for themselves. What's ironic, Cotton thought, *is that they get exactly what they need from each other.*

"Love shouldn't be wrong." Janis agreed, shoving her hair behind her ears. Most of the purple tint had grown out, a royal blue replacing it. "No matter what you are. No matter who loves you. Love shouldn't split families up."

Hailey bowed her head as if overwhelmed by Janis's impassioned speech.

Almost in response, Janis straightened her shoulders. She paused and studied each of her family members individually for a moment, then tossed her head defiantly. "What's right for us is right, not what society feels." Her voice grew stronger, angrier. "Love is most important, and it doesn't matter who we love but that we love. We don't need to choose sides in a family. We need to support each other. If it means we must be in therapy, then that's good for us. But we need to work it out. We need to feel what we do for each other, instead of what society wants us to. What's important is us. Our family. We're the Prescotts. We'll always be the Prescotts. That's the one thing that will never change."

There's nothing to be said after that. No one could speak. Janis was right. No matter what happens to this family, they will still be family. You can't erase blood ties.

They remained quiet for another moment, then everyone stood up and gathered their belongings, knowing that their time was over, apparently relieved and ready to move on. They hustled through the door and Cotton closed it behind them. She sighed and turned around, ready to gather her notes from the session.

She gasped to see Marc standing in the middle of the room. He stepped forward as if he had a mission but remained, his facial features resembling those of a much older boy. At 10 years old, he's more serious than most 40-year-olds. When the kids at school bullied him, he understood the psychological underpinnings of his tormentors' lives. He knew the boys were abused at home, and he understood they struck out at him because they found him weak. His hypersensitivity opens him up to depths of emotion that most never feel, yet he is far too young to experience the various textures of despair, anguish, and grief that life has given him.

"Are you okay, Marc?" she asked.

His eyes, round and solemn, a younger replica of Hailey's, appeared more serious than a moment ago, a deeper blue gray rimmed with a charcoal shadow of pain. The emotion in his eyes shocked her more because it was unexpected. He rarely lifted his eyes from his games, so the visceral connection of his gaze disrupted her train of thought. Even after the first days of learning how to deal with his mother's crimes and then her absence from the house, Marcus hadn't lifted his head. Maybe his sorrow was the reason he hid behind his games. By deflecting the issue, he could deny any sadness existed. Only now he had no other choice. His mother was gone, and it hurt like hell.

Cotton gripped the sides of her chair, wanting more than anything to hug the youngest Prescott child.

"Are you okay, Marc?" She kept her voice low and didn't move.

"Sometimes people hide who they are." He looked up at the ceiling. Thinking. "But eventually, you can't. It kind of comes out, doesn't it?

Sort of like Gragon and Rothkine. Gragon's so mean and angry, but when Rothkine's around, he relaxes and laughs, and you can kinda tell that's who he really is." He reached under the bulky gray hoodie he always wore and pulled out a black-and-white composition notebook.

"This is yours." He handed the journal to Cotton. "Mom kept all her notebooks separate. She kept one for each of us kids and one for HaileyDad. One for each of her stories. Some from when they traveled, and this one. That's about you."

"So, she was still keeping journals," Cotton said, turning the notebook over in her hands and putting her palm flat against it as if it would project some warmth. Comfort. But it was cold.

"Yes. In the attic, way over in a corner near the big old fan up there." He shifted from foot to foot. "I'm going to give the rest of them to Dad, Janis, and Cheryl later, but I thought I'd give you this one now."

"Did you read them all?"

He swallowed hard and the beginnings of an Adam's apple bobbed faintly in his throat. His eyelashes darkened with moisture. He nodded.

"Do you want to talk about it?"

"Not right now. Maybe never. Just wanted you to have that one." He moved to the door, then turned. "My mom, Gray, really liked you, Dr. Barnes." Hand on the doorknob, he stopped. "She really liked you. She's just fucked up."

~ Book Forty-five ~

Four Years Later

I believe that imagination is stronger than knowledge. That myth is more potent than history. That dreams are more powerful than facts. That hope always triumphs over experience.

That laughter is the only cure for grief. And I believe that love is stronger than death.

—Robert Fulghum

"The senator's waiting for you to call him back," Cotton hears Janis's voice down the hall before she's even had time to put her briefcase on the desk.

"About?"

"The hearing about the amendment to the HB law."

Muttering about the inability of politicians to see the bigger picture, Cotton heads down the hall and absent-mindedly raises her eyes to the dual portrait of Hayden/Hailey hanging midway, tapping her fingers three times against the frame as she always does: *once for each of the Prescott kids.*

At nineteen, Janis has become the catalyst behind the idea of the non-profit office where they both now serve the LGBTQ+ community in the Triangle. During the day, she's going to law school at Chapel Hill, but on her days and evenings off, she's at the office. Cotton teases her every day that Janis will be the first black-nail-polish-wearing lawyer in

North Carolina. Janis shrugs and smiles whenever Cotton says it. Secretly, she likes the idea.

Cotton holds therapy groups for families, as well as local concerns, advocating for education and equality for all gendered people. The private joke is that the rest of the world has Cotton pegged as an LGBTQ advocate when what she really means by "gendered people" is everybody. All humans. No need to identify.

Cotton leans on the doorjamb at Janis's office. "Call Hailey last night?"

With a roll of her eyes that reminds Cotton some things never change, Janis sighs like an adolescent. "Yes, and all she could talk about was Cherylynn's cheerleading tryouts."

"And Marc?" Cotton's voice softens. He's never recovered from his mother's violence and her disconnect from reality once they admitted her to the East Coast Carolina Mental Health inpatient clinic. He'd never been comfortable visiting her, especially since she didn't recognize him most of the time. Marcus has spent more time in counseling than the rest of the Prescotts combined.

"He'll be at camp a couple more weeks. Hailey says the new therapist believes taking away all technology will force Marcus out of that deep dark hidey-hole he's so fond of." Janis lifts her ever-present Starbucks cup to her mouth. "What about you? How was the date last night?"

"No laughing. Promise." Cotton leans on the desk. "This one was actually fairly normal."

"Anything's normal after the one with all the shoeboxes full of dead birds."

They both groan. Then Cotton shares a Twitter-length version of the date before retreating with the excuse of seeing her first client. Janis nods knowingly. It's a passion they share, one that has given them both a purpose.

Cotton opens the door to the lobby and calls her first appointment, a teenager with shy brown eyes. She reaches out her hand and says, "Welcome to the Hailey Prescott Clinic. I'm Cotton."

~ end ~

Acknowledgments

This story sprouted from a seed of an idea that I discussed during my interview for the PhD program at The Union Institute and University. Little did I know that it would become the narrative that would not only force me to face my own pre-conceived stereotype but would also become the backbone of research for my dissertation on transgender authors and their voices, pre- and post-transition. Throughout the years I spent writing the dissertation, my peers in the program listened to ideas, offered suggestions, pushed me scholastically, and provided a shoulder when my personal life fell apart. Without them, this novel wouldn't have had a safe birth. So, my first thanks goes to Cohort Two: Drs. Kezia Carpenter, Glenn Kendall, Mary Wilby, Mina Kerr, John Fraire, Bryan Partridge, Jacquie Taylor, and Ginger Rodriguez. The deans, faculty, staff, and visiting instructors all played a role in the shaping of this novel.

Without precious writing time provided by the Weymouth Center for Arts and Humanities in North Carolina, I would have struggled with the many drafts and changes this story demanded. That place encourages creativity like none other I've ever visited.

Thanks also goes to the Vermont College of Fine Arts special novel retreat workshop run by the novelist and memoirist Connie May Fowler. The time I spent on the campus of my alma mater gave me the uninterrupted time I needed to reshape the novel.

My friends and fellow writers have generously given of their time and expertise at various points in time during the creative process of this manuscript. Carolyn Burns Bass, Christine Mojica, Ron Jackson, Mary Kathryn Kimray, Lolita Guerraro, Melissa Seligman, Barbara Younger, and Melissa Rooney have all listened to this story or read the many versions I've created. I cannot state how much I value their time and talent. Their brilliance helps me bring my best to the page.

I offer this story as one of the millions of narratives that can exist when a family is challenged. I offer this story with love to anyone who has struggled to exist between the social mask others expect them to wear and the truth of who they really are.

I offer this story with the understanding that we are all human under it all.

About the Author

Dawn Reno Langley's many books include novels, such as *The Mourning Parade* (Amberjack, 2017), as well as nonfiction books such as *You Are Divine: A Search for the Goddess in All of Us* (Llewellyn, 2022). Her published works include children's books, nonfiction books about art and antiques, hundreds of articles, theater reviews and blogs, dozens of award-winning short stories, essays, and poems in journals such as *Hunger Mountain* and *Superstition Review*. A Fulbright scholar and TedX speaker with an MFA in Fiction from Vermont College and a Ph.D. in Interdisciplinary Studies from the Union Institute and University, she lives in North Carolina with her scientist husband, where she teaches yoga and offers writing retreats.

Note from Dawn Reno Langley

Word-of-mouth is crucial for any author to succeed. If you enjoyed *Analyzing the Prescotts*, please leave a review online—anywhere you are able. Even if it's just a sentence or two. It would make all the difference and would be very much appreciated.

Thanks!
Dawn Reno Langley

We hope you enjoyed reading this title from:

BLACK ROSE
writing™

www.blackrosewriting.com

Subscribe to our mailing list – *The Rosevine* – and receive **FREE** books, daily deals, and stay current with news about upcoming releases and our hottest authors.
Scan the QR code below to sign up.

Already a subscriber? Please accept a sincere thank you for being a fan of Black Rose Writing authors.

View other Black Rose Writing titles at www.blackrosewriting.com/books and use promo code **PRINT** to receive a **20% discount** when purchasing.

www.ingramcontent.com/pod-product-compliance
Lightning Source LLC
Chambersburg PA
CBHW060655190726
48289CB00002B/422